THE WINTER BRIDE

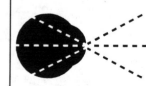

This Large Print Book carries the
Seal of Approval of N.A.V.H.

A CHANCE SISTERS ROMANCE

THE WINTER BRIDE

ANNE GRACIE

THORNDIKE PRESS
A part of Gale, Cengage Learning

GALE
CENGAGE Learning·

Farmington Hills, Mich • San Francisco • New York • Waterville, Maine
Meriden, Conn • Mason, Ohio • Chicago

GALE
CENGAGE Learning®

Copyright © Anne Gracie.
A Chance Sisters Romance Series #2.
Thorndike Press, a part of Gale, Cengage Learning.

Thorndike Press® Large Print Romance.
The text of this Large Print edition is unabridged.
Other aspects of the book may vary from the original edition.
Set in 16 pt. Plantin.

LIBRARY OF CONGRESS CATALOGING-IN-PUBLICATION DATA

Gracie, Anne.
    The winter bride / by Anne Gracie. — Large print edition.
      pages ; cm. — (Thorndike Press large print romance) (A Chance sisters romance series ; #2)
    ISBN 978-1-4104-7160-4 (hardcover) — ISBN 1-4104-7160-8 (hardcover)
    1. Marriage—Fiction. 2. Sisters—Fiction 3. Large type books. I. Title.
PR9619.4.G727W56 2014
823'.92—dc23
                                                  2014016328

Published in 2014 by arrangement with The Berkley Publishing Group, a member of Penguin Group (USA), a Penguin Random House Company

Printed in Mexico
1 2 3 4 5 6 7 18 17 16 15 14

With thanks to my friend Julia Byrne for her encouragement and feedback.

Also thanks, as always, to the Maytoners for support, friendship and laughs.

*And to my readers —
a heartfelt thank-you.*

CHAPTER ONE

"The world is pretty much divided between the weak of mind and the strong — between those who can act and those who cannot, and it is the bounden duty of the capable to let no opportunity of being useful escape them."

— JANE AUSTEN,
SANDITON AND OTHER STORIES

Devon, England, 1816

"I want you to look after Aunt Bea and the girls while Abby and I are on our honeymoon," Max, Lord Davenham, told his friend, the Honorable Frederick Monkton-Coombes.

Freddy almost choked on his wine. *"Me?"* he spluttered after the coughing fit had passed. "Why me?"

"You're my oldest friend."

Hard to wriggle out of that one, Freddy thought. But damn, it was a hell of a thing to spring on a fellow the night before a wedding. As if being best man weren't trauma enough. He rose and jabbed at the fire with a poker, sending sparks twirling up the chimney. The two men were ensconced in a snug private sitting room in the local inn, a mile or two from Davenham Hall in Devon.

Max's idea, doing the honorable thing, sleeping under a separate roof from his bride the night before the wedding. Bad luck to see the bride and all that. And naturally his best man must come too. Not that Freddy minded.

The less he had to do with the bride's sisters the better, as far as he was concerned. Pretty, unmarried, respectable girls were not Freddy's female of choice. Good girls? No, he much preferred the company of bad girls — the badder the better. Good girls, especially good pretty girls, were . . . dangerous. And one Chance sister in particular was, to Freddy's mind, more dangerous than most. She . . . disturbed him. In ways he preferred not to examine too closely.

And now Max must come up with this. And playing the "oldest friend" card, dammit.

"You mean *all* of them? All the girls?"

"Yes, of course all of them," Max said impatiently. "There are only three. They're not exactly a horde."

That was a matter of opinion. "What does *look after* entail?" Freddy asked cautiously.

Max shrugged. "Nothing very arduous, just the kind of thing I'd do if I were there. My aunt is well up to snuff, of course, but she's still somewhat of an invalid and would appreciate having a man to rely on if needed."

Having a man to order about, more like it, Freddy thought.

Max continued, "And Abby's been fretting a little about leaving her sisters — you can understand that after all they've been through recently. Knowing you'll be on hand to protect them if necessary will ease her mind."

"Isn't there anyone else you could ask?" Freddy said desperately. "I mean, you know my problem with unmarried females."

"Your problem is with the kind of unmarried female you call a muffin. You told me Abby and her sisters were most definitely not muffins."

"They're not, but —"

"Then there's no problem."

The noose was tightening. Freddy ran a finger around his suddenly tight collar. "Am I really the sort of fellow you want associating with Abby's sisters? I don't have the best reputation around women; you know that," he said hopefully.

"I have complete faith in you."

Damn. "What about Flynn? Didn't you say he'd be arriving any day now?" Flynn was the head of the company in which Freddy and Max were major partners. "Couldn't you ask him?"

Max frowned. "Yes, I expected Flynn to be here by now. Shame he'll miss the wedding."

"You don't think anything bad has happened to him?"

Max gave a wry half smile. "Sea travel is uncertain at the best of times, but Flynn has a knack of turning disaster into success, so I'm not worrying yet. If he turns up, the two of you can share the responsibility if it makes you feel better. But Flynn doesn't know Aunt Bea and the girls like you do. Nor does he know anything about London society. In fact, I'm hoping you'll show him the ropes."

"Oh," Freddy said. More responsibilities. Delightful.

Max's grin widened. "He'll need your fashion advice too. He's planning to cut a swath through London society, and currently he's a little . . . unorthodox in appearance."

"Oh. Joy." Just what he wanted, to play guard dog to respectable females and social and sartorial adviser to a rough Irish diamond.

Max laughed. "Don't look so glum. Flynn is a good fellow. You'll like him. But you don't need to worry about Flynn — he can look after himself. It's my aunt and the girls I'm most concerned about."

Freddy sipped his claret thoughtfully, trying to work out a way to wriggle out of what, on the surface, seemed quite a reasonable request.

Max, misunderstanding his silence, added, "Look, it won't be hard. Just drop around to Berkeley Square every few days, make sure they're all right, see to anything if there's a problem, protect the girls from unwanted attentions, take them for the occasional drive in the park, pop in to their literary society —"

"Not the literary society. The horror stories those girls read are enough to make a fellow's hair stand on end."

Max frowned. "Horror stories? They don't read horror stories, only entertaining tales of the kind ladies seem to enjoy, about girls and gossip and families —"

"Horror stories, every last one of them," Freddy said firmly. "You asked me to sit in on their literary society last month, when you went up to Manchester, remember? The story they were reading then . . ." He gave an eloquent shudder. "Horror from the very first line: *It is a truth universally acknowledged, that a single man in possession of a good fortune must be in want of a wife.* Must he, indeed? What about the poor fellow's wants, eh? Do they matter? No. Every female in the blasted story was plotting to hook some man for herself or her daughter or niece. If you don't call that horror, I don't know what is!"

Max chuckled.

"You can laugh, bound as you are for parson's noose in the morning," Freddy said bitterly, "but every single man in that story ended up *married* by the end of the book! Every last one." He numbered them off on his fingers. "The main fellow, his best friend, the parson, even the soldier fellow ended up married to the silly light-skirt sister — not one single man in that story escaped unwed." He shuddered again. "Enough to give a man nightmares. So no literary society for me, thank you."

"I need you there," Max said simply.

"Why? Your aunt holds her literary society in her own home — you can't get much safer than that."

"It's not so much their safety I'm worried about," Max admitted, looking a little sheepish. "It's my aunt."

"What about her? She's in her element there — all her cronies about her, dozens of *tonnish* ladies, even a handful of men."

"Exactly. And therein lies the problem."

Freddy shook his head. "I don't understand."

"I don't trust her."

"You don't trust your own aunt? Your only relative?"

Max sighed. "You know she almost died while I was away."

Freddy nodded.

"The girls nursed her back to health and it's given her a renewed lease on life — which of course I'm delighted about, don't get me wrong. The trouble is, it's made her think she's invincible."

"She *is* invincible," Freddy muttered. "Always was. I remember her from when I was a schoolboy. A force of nature even then."

Max nodded. "My uncle kept her more or less reined in. Now she's a law unto herself."

Freddy frowned. "Hasn't broken any laws that I know of."

"Not laws, as such," Max admitted. "But think about it — she already has more than

13

half the *ton* believing that the girls' mother was her wholly imaginary half sister Griselda — Griselda, I ask you! — and their father was an Italian marchese called Chancealotto."

"I heard he was Venetian," Freddy said.

Max threw up his hands. "You see? Venetian. The whole of the *ton* knows it."

Freddy shrugged. "Nothing people love more than a hushed-up scandal."

"But it *wasn't* a hushed-up scandal," Max said, exasperated. "It wasn't *any* kind of scandal at all! Her mother *never* ran off with an Austrian nobleman *or* gave birth to another daughter who grew up to marry any blasted Venetian marchese — she died! It's all a ridiculous tale my aunt invented."

There was a long silence. Freddy sipped his wine. Max stared into the fire, brooding, no doubt on his father-in-law, the late and imaginary marchese di Chancealotto. Must be hard for an honorable fellow like Max, having to accept — at least in public — imaginary in-laws. And he was getting married in the morning. That was a worse fate than having to listen to a few horror stories.

"All right, I'll attend the literary society," Freddy said in a soothing tone. "But I warn you, I'm not going to read any of those dratted books."

"No, that's all right, it's not the kind of literary society where people read — they have the stories read to them. So I'd be grateful if you'd just keep an eye on Aunt Bea." He glanced at Freddy. "And stop her if she starts telling any more outrageous tales."

Freddy choked on his wine again. "*Me?* You think *I* could stop her from spreading outrageous stories? You couldn't, so what makes you think I could? She still treats me like a schoolboy!"

"I know, but I'd feel better if you were there, at least. And you could always *try* to stop her."

Yes, and Freddy could always *try* to fly. But he didn't say so. Max was his oldest and best friend. Max was also the reason Freddy was now independently wealthy. If it hadn't been for Max and his trading company, Freddy would still be eking out a living on the inheritance he'd received from his aunt — or worse, dependent on his father — and that didn't bear thinking about.

Max had never really asked him for anything.

Freddy drained his glass, his sixth for the night, and in a moment of vainglory said, "Very well, I'll *try*. *And* I'll attend the blasted literary society *and* keep an eye on the girls for you and Abby, *and* I'll look out for Flynn, if he ever arrives." Flynn was the other reason Freddy was now a rich man. He probably owed Flynn a few favors too.

"Good man," Max said. "I'm probably worrying about nothing. I'm sure you'll have a delightful time with Aunt Bea and the girls. There's no one I'd rather trust them to."

"You're the only person in the world who'd trust me with a bunch of unmarried girls."

"I know you better than most people. Now, don't look so glum. Abby and I will only be gone for a month or so, and they'll be no trouble, I'm sure."

China, eight months earlier
She breasted the hill and stopped, catching her breath at the sight of the line of brilliant blue that shimmered along the horizon. The sea. She took a deep breath, breathing in the clean, fresh salt tang of it, the taste of freedom. . . .

Then her heart started to thump as she saw in a dip between the hills three slender vertical lines silhouetted against the blue. Tall masts. Which meant a European ship.

Pray it was English. It should not matter,

16

as long as it took her away from this place where she would always be foreign, unwelcome, no matter that she'd lived all her life here and knew no other place. But she was English, and an English captain would understand and, pray God, an English ship would take her home. To what, she did not know — she had no living relatives that she knew of — but first things first.

She started to run, then stumbled to a ragged halt. She was hot, filthy, dusty and sweaty from the endless walk. She'd lost track of how many days she'd been walking, hiding from others, sleeping under bushes and foraging for whatever food she could find along the way. She could not approach the captain of a European ship looking like a filthy beggar.

She scanned her surrounds and spied a ragged line of green meandering across the dusty brown landscape. A stream. Just what she needed.

In the stream she washed, head to toe, immersing her body, fully clothed, in the water, then stripping to the bare minimum for modesty; it would not do to be caught naked in the open. She scrubbed as best she could without soap, using sand on her skin and beating her wet clothing on the rocks, as the women back home did.

No, not home; the mission would never be home again. England was home, no matter that she had no memory of it. It was where she'd been born.

She rinsed, scrubbed and rerinsed until her skin and scalp tingled and she felt clean again. She combed out her hair in the sun, using her fingers to ease out any tangles. She braided it neatly and wound it around her crown in a damp coronet, tucking the ends in and fastening them with her last two pins. The heat of the sun ensured her clothing dried quickly, wrinkled, but clean looking, at least.

She wished she had a proper English dress, but she'd worn her simple black Chinese peasant tunic and pants to the market so she wouldn't stand out as foreign, and everything else had been destroyed when the mission was burned. She had no other clothes, no other possessions at all, only her mother's locket on its thin gold chain. She never took it off.

She did a quick check that she was as neat as possible, put on her hat and set out toward the three black masts silhouetted against the strip of shimmering blue.

Pray that the ship was English.

A small port, with a straggle of buildings scattered around it. In her faded black tunic and pants and her conical straw hat she drew no notice from the coolies busily loading bundles and boxes and rolls of fabric onto smaller boats and ferrying them out to the big ship that floated serenely at anchor a few hundred yards from shore.

She squinted against the glare of the sun on sea to read the name. *Liverpool Lass.* English. Thank God. Tears of relief pricked at her eyelids. She blinked them back.

She searched among the swarming coolies for an English face and found a tall young seaman with ginger hair supervising the loading of a boat, checking items off on a list and rapping out orders in a mix of pidgin English and bad Chinese.

She approached him quietly and, when he had a moment, said in English, "Excuse me, sir, could I speak to the captain, please?"

"He's bus—" The young seaman stopped and looked up. "*What* did you say?"

She repeated the request.

His jaw dropped. He stared at her in disbelief for a moment, taking in her faded coolie clothes and hat. "You can't be *English*!" He pulled off her hat. "And what the hell — you're a *girl*?"

She couldn't move. The weight pressed her down, crushing the breath from her lungs.

The heat, the sweat, the stench sickened her. She struggled to resist, to block out the words echoing insidiously in her ear —

Damaris jerked upright, gasping for breath, fighting desperately to get free . . . and encountered nothing but cold air and tangled bedclothes. She closed her eyes briefly, trying to catch her breath — she was panting as if she'd run a mile — and waiting for her pounding heart to slow to normal. Her body was slicked with sweat. It chilled slowly in the cold predawn air.

The dream again. The third time in as many days. It was getting worse.

She sat in her bed with her arms wrapped around her knees, hugging them to her chest and rocking slightly. The weight of the dream hung over her. The weight of memory.

She was not that girl, she told herself. Not anymore. She'd left Damaris Tait behind; she was Damaris Chance now.

It was supposed to be a fresh chance, Abby had said; a chance for a new life for them all. And it was true. Mostly.

But the dreams, the memories stayed with her, returning in the night, vivid, intense and horribly real. Even now, the acid bile of panic — and shame — scalded her throat.

She took a sip of water from the glass by

the bed. Nothing would wash away those memories; the dreams would keep them fresh.

She rocked gently in the chill gray dawn, contemplating her options. There weren't many. She knew what was stirring up the dreams.

She couldn't go on. She had to stop it now, before it went any further. The sooner the better.

She broke it to Jane after luncheon when they were getting ready for a drive in the park.

"Not make your come-out?" Jane dropped the pelisse she was about to put on and stared at her in shock. "But why? It's what we always dreamed of."

"You dreamed, Jane, not me." Damaris picked up the pelisse and handed it to Jane. "Now get dressed, Mr. Monkton-Coombes will be here any minute."

Jane didn't move. "But why would you not want to make your come-out, Damaris? It'll be such fun — new dresses and dances and balls and routs and —"

Damaris shook her head. "I can't do it, Jane. I just can't."

"Can't what?" asked Daisy as she entered the bedchamber. She was carrying a half-finished pelisse. "Try this on before you go out, will you, Damaris? I want to make sure the sleeves are right before I finish it off."

Damaris removed her warm winter pelisse and slipped on the almost completed garment. Made in Daisy's distinctive mix of old and new fabrics, it was light, intended for spring or summer wear.

"Oh, it's lovely, Daisy," Damaris exclaimed. She touched the contrasting brocade collar and cuffs, currently only pinned on. "These are from one of Lady Beatrice's old gowns, aren't they? I remember the embroidered birds, so pretty and still looking so fresh — the colors are so clear and bright. And the contrast of the different fabrics — I would never have thought to put these together but it's perfect. You have such an eye." She stood before the mirror, admiring the elegant fall of the pelisse, while Daisy frowned in concentration and re-pinned one of the cuffs.

"It's beautiful, all right," Jane said, "and you're very clever, Daisy. But it's going to be wasted on Damaris."

"Hmmph?" Daisy looked up, frowning, her mouth full of pins.

"She says she's not going to make her come-out."

"Hmm-mmph?" Daisy didn't take the pins from her mouth but let her eyebrows do the talking.

"I'm sorry," Damaris said. "I just can't bear the thought of it."

"Bear the thought of what?" Jane asked. "A come-out is fun."

Daisy gave Damaris a long, considering look, then shrugged and returned to her pinning.

"I'm sorry to have disappointed you both." Damaris *hated* letting people down. It was just . . . she couldn't do it. The dread had been growing, day by day, and this morning, when she woke with the familiar feeling of sick apprehension, she knew she had to say something. It was better to let everyone know now, several months before the season started. Surely.

"But why? I still don't understand," Jane persisted. "Is it because of the brothel? Because you were only there a few days longer than me, not quite a week, and —"

"It's not the brothel," Damaris said. She hadn't told anyone what had happened before the brothel, not even her sisters. And she never would.

"I should say not," Jane said. "It wasn't our fault, and I refuse to let my life be less because of what that evil man tried to do to us. And so should you."

"It's *not* because of the brothel." The pinning complete, Damaris carefully eased off the pelisse and handed it to Daisy, then shrugged herself into her winter one again.

"The false name then?" Jane persisted. "I know your parents were missionaries —"

"My father was. And no, it's not the false name — though heaven knows how Lady Beatrice is going to explain —"

"Explain what?" The old lady stood in the doorway. "Are you gels ready? Featherby tells me Freddy Monkton-Coombes is downstairs awaiting our pleasure, and while I approve of making a gentleman wait, who knows what the weather will do? Come along now." She flapped a pair of lilac kid gloves at them. "You can explain on the way. Daisy dear, give me your arm, would you? These dratted stairs."

Daisy hurried to take the old lady's arm. Lady Beatrice was still a little weak and unsteady on her feet after months, if not years, of being ill, bedridden and neglected. Since Abby had discovered her, and the four girls had moved in to become Lady Beatrice's "nieces," the old lady had made a gallant recovery, but stairs were still her bugbear. She could walk down them with assistance, but climbing them required the strong arms of William, their footman.

"Now, what were you gels saying?"

"It's Damaris," Jane told her. "She says she doesn't want to make her come-out."

"What's that? Doesn't want her season, you say?" She swiveled around on the stairs and gave Damaris a sharp glance. "Is that right?"

"Yes, Lady Beatrice, and I'm sorry, but I won't change my m—"

"It's because of the brothel, I know," Jane said. "Only —"

"It's *not* because of the brothel," Damaris said in a low voice, glancing downstairs. "And keep your voice down, please. I don't want . . . anyone to hear." Below them in the hall, the Honorable Frederick Monkton-Coombes paced restlessly, long, loose-limbed strides in gleaming high boots. Dressed in a many-caped coat of superfine merino, and holding a curly brimmed beaver hat in his long fingers, he was the epitome of masculine elegance.

He looked up and met Damaris's gaze. She forced herself to look away.

"Then why —"

"Hush, Jane! Damaris is right — this is not something to be discussed on the stairs," Lady Beatrice instructed. "Freddy, my dear boy, how very punctual you are."

"Punctual?" He glanced at the clock in the hall. "But it's —"

"We won't be long. The girls and I need a moment's privacy." She gave him an enigmatic look. "A female thing, you understand. Featherby, fetch a pot of coffee and some muffins for Mr. Monkton-Coombes."

"No, really, I —"

"Nonsense, I know how much you love your muffins and Cook has made a fresh batch especially. We won't be long," Lady Beatrice declared and swept the girls into a small sitting room farther down the hall. As the door closed behind her she said, "The dear boy is looking after us quite splendidly while Max and Abby are on their honeymoon, isn't he? Normally he avoids respectable gels like the plague."

Daisy snorted. Jane giggled and after a moment Damaris joined in.

"What has cast you gels into whoops, now?" Lady Beatrice demanded.

"Respectable girls?" Jane spluttered. "Two escapees from a brothel — three if you count Daisy —"

" 'Course you count me. I grew up in one, din't I?"

"And we're all living under a false name, pretending to be your nieces," Damaris added.

"Stop that nonsense at once!" the old lady snapped. "I don't want to hear any more about that dratted brothel! You *are* respectable gels — no matter what happened in the past. You're my nieces and if I say you're respectable, you are!"

"And if you say we're your nieces, we are," Jane added mischievously.

"Exactly." Lady Beatrice didn't believe in irony. "And when your sister married my nephew that made everything legal, so that's the end of it."

It was nothing of the sort, not when Damaris and Daisy were no relation to Abby and Jane, but none of them wanted to argue.

The old lady raised her lorgnette and turned it on Damaris. "Now, m'gel, what's all this about you not making your come-out with Jane in the spring?"

Damaris bit her lip. "It's true. I . . . I don't want to do it."

Jane said, "But Daisy's already designed a whole coming-out wardrobe —"

"Leave me out of this," Daisy said bluntly. "I won't ask Damaris to do nuffin' she doesn't want to."

"Anything," Lady Beatrice, Jane and Damaris corrected automatically.

Damaris gave Daisy a grateful smile.

"But we've had it all planned out for ages," Jane said unhappily.

"Only a month or two," Damaris said.

"Before that we never even had a chance of a season. The height of our ambition then was for you and Abby to attend a public ball in Bath." Jane still looked unhappy, so she added, "And the start of the season is still months away, so there's plenty of time to adjust our plans."

There was a short silence. Damaris was uncomfortably aware of the old lady's shrewd gaze on her. "Think of the money you'll save, with only one of us." A London season was fearfully expensive, she knew.

Lady Beatrice snorted. "It's my money and I'll spend it how I like." Technically it was her nephew's money, but they all knew Max, Lord Davenham, would deny his aunt nothing.

Jane said sadly, "It won't be half as much fun if we don't have our season together. I won't know anyone."

"Of course you will," said Damaris in a bracing tone. "What about all those people who come to the literary society?"

"Oh, the literary society," Jane said. "They're all old."

Lady Beatrice cleared her throat and leveled her lorgnette at Jane, who blushed and said hurriedly, "I mean, of course, they're all charming and quite delightful, but it's not like having your sister with you, is it?"

Damaris didn't bother pointing out that Jane would have Abby with her, and Abby was a real sister, not a pretend one. Abby was married, currently away on her honeymoon, but she'd be back in time for the season. But Jane had a point; having your married sister there wouldn't be the same as two unmarried girls entering the marriage mart together.

"I could come as your companion."

"A companion?" Lady Beatrice turned her lorgnette on Damaris. "A *companion*?" She spoke the word with loathing. Clearly it was not an option.

"But if you would attend social gatherings as a companion, what's the difference from making your own come-out?" Jane asked.

"Nobody would ask a companion to marry him."

Jane's brow furrowed. "I don't understand."

"I don't want to get married. I have . . ." Damaris swallowed. "I have an abhorrence of marriage."

There was a short, shocked silence.

It was a ludicrous statement in most people's eyes, she knew. Not want to get married? How else could a girl without property or means expect to live?

She would work. She wasn't afraid of hard

work; she'd worked all her life.

Being sponsored into society, being given the chance to marry a man of wealth and position would be most girls' dream of a lifetime. A year ago it might have been Damaris's. Not anymore.

"And what," Lady Beatrice said after a moment, "does getting married have to do with making your come-out?"

All three girls blinked at her in surprise. "But isn't that the whole purpose of a come-out?" Jane said. "To find us husbands? That's why they call it the marriage mart."

"It's *some* people's purpose," Lady Beatrice conceded graciously. "Most people's, perhaps. *We* are not most people."

Jane looked worried. "But I *want* to find a husband."

"I know, Jane dear, and I'm looking forward to seeing all the young fellows making cakes of themselves over you. Don't fret, you'll have your pick of them." The old lady turned to Damaris. "As for you, my dear gel, nobody said you *had* to find a husband."

"But I thought —"

"Oh, the young men will make cakes of themselves over you too, I'm sure, and quite a number of the old ones as well, as we've seen at my literary society. You'll have plenty of eligible offers, take my word for it — and a few ineligible ones. But there's no need to *accept* any of them."

"But . . ." Damaris frowned. "If I don't find a husband, isn't it a terrible waste of money?"

Lady Beatrice's elegantly plucked and dyed eyebrows rose. "Waste of money? Pish-tush, what nonsense is this? There is only one reason for you to make your come-out, Damaris — to have fun."

"Fun?" Damaris echoed, bewildered. Squandering a fortune on her so that she could have *fun*?

"You've had precious little fun in your life, haven't you, my dear?"

Damaris swallowed. "How did you know?"

The old lady snorted. "Daughter of a mis-sionary? Raised in the Wilds of Foreign? One could make a wild guess." She chuckled at Damaris's expression. "Cheer up, my dear, nobody will compel you to marry. It would, however, please me greatly if you made your come-out with Jane, attending balls and routs and parties, dancing till dawn, wearing Daisy's beautiful dresses — and making her the most fashionable man-tua maker of the season —"

"From your mouth to God's ears," Daisy said fervently.

"— having flocks of men falling over

themselves to please you — bringing you champagne and ratafia and delicious morsels from the supper table, sending you bouquets and posies in the morning, writing poems to your eyes — such delightful nonsense." The old lady sighed reminiscently, leaned forward and patted Damaris's hand. "You don't need to take any of it seriously and no one will press you to do anything you don't want to do. Leave the husband hunting to young Jane here. You and I, my dear, we'll just have fun."

There was such kindness and understanding in the shrewd old eyes that Damaris felt a lump forming in her throat. Lady Beatrice hadn't even asked her why marriage was so abhorrent to her. She swallowed. "You don't mind that I don't want . . . that I . . ."

Lady Beatrice squeezed her hand and said softly, "My dear gel, you told me when we first met that you never wanted to get married. Did you think I had forgotten?"

Lady Beatrice had been ill and bedridden at the time. Why would she have remembered what a strange girl had told her? Why would she have cared?

"Why would you do this for me?"

The old lady smiled. "You gels have brought me such happiness at a time of life when I thought it was all over. It would give me enormous pleasure to give you a season of carefree, uncomplicated fun — without any obligation to anyone." She squeezed Damaris's hand again. "So will you do it for me, Damaris? Kick up your heels, just for a season, and live a frivolous, entirely pleasure-filled existence? Not for yourself, but to please an old lady?" She attempted such an unconvincing mock-pathetic expression that Damaris gave a shaky laugh and hugged her.

"Since you put it like that, dear Lady Beatrice, I can hardly refuse. But it's very generous of you." Too generous.

The old lady flapped a dismissive hand. "Pish-tush, what nonsense! Now, come along, gels, Mr. Monkton-Coombes will have finished his muffins, and while all men should be kept waiting a little — it keeps them nicely on edge, I find — it does not do to keep them dangling too long. And when one finally joins them, they must be made to feel that the waiting was worthwhile. So make yourselves beautiful, gels, and when you see Mr. Monkton-Coombes, smile."

Freddy stared gloomily at the plate before him. Lady Bea was convinced that muffins were the Monkton-Coombes food of choice.

That was Max's fault, blast him. He'd told his aunt that Freddy was obsessed with muffins, and of course the old girl thought he meant these blasted bun things. She had him served with them each time he called. And expected him to eat them. With enthusiasm.

He picked up a muffin, hefted it lightly and eyed the fire with a narrowed gaze. It was a good blaze, strong enough to reduce a muffin to ash in a short time.

But would there be an incriminating smell?

He raised the muffin, aimed and was about to toss it in the fire when feminine footsteps sounded in the hall. He dropped the muffin, turned toward the open doorway and saw four smartly dressed females advancing toward him, smiling.

The hairs on the back of his neck rose. Why the devil were they grinning at him like that? What did they know? What did they want?

He had a powerful urge to flee. But he'd made that promise to Max. He rose, brushing crumbs from his fingers. "Ladies," he said warily.

"Freddy, my dear boy, so sorry to keep you waiting." Lady Beatrice eyed him with approval. "Always so elegant." She glanced at the plate of muffins and frowned. "Were the muffins not satisfactory? Featherby, you must have a word with Cook —"

"No, no, they were delicious, as was the coffee," Freddy assured her. "But I wasn't hungry. Late breakfast, you know — large breakfast. Positively enormous," he added when she seemed inclined to argue.

She sniffed. "You need feeding up. Oh, well, come along. I trust the weather is holding?"

"Yes indeed, a fine day. The breeze is a little on the brisk side, but quite refreshing." He ushered the ladies to the front door. The landau and driver were waiting in the street.

CHAPTER TWO

"It is happy for you that you possess the
talent of flattering with delicacy. May I ask
whether these pleasing attentions
proceed from the impulse of the moment,
or are the result of previous study?"
— JANE AUSTEN, *PRIDE AND PREJUDICE*

The landau only fitted four people comfortably. Freddy offered to ride beside the carriage so it wouldn't be such a squash but the old lady wouldn't hear of it. "I prefer you close by, dear boy." At first he'd thought she meant for protection or some such thing but then she'd winked at him. "I want to flaunt you, such a fine, handsome lad you've turned out to be."

The old girl was always trying to put him to the blush. Freddy hid a grin.

With the aid of a muscular footman, he helped the old lady into the landau. She was frail but indomitable. Freddy turned to assist the young ladies, first Miss Jane, who bounced lightly up the steps, then Miss Daisy, then he held out his hand to assist Miss Damaris.

"I'm sorry, I've changed my mind," she said, snatching her hand back before he'd even touched it.

"Damaris?" Lady Beatrice said sharply.

"It's nothing, just a slight headache. If I just lie down for a while I'm sure the headache will pass."

Freddy was sure it would; in fact, he was pretty sure the headache didn't exist. She didn't look the slightest bit pale or heavy eyed; she looked blooming, as usual, possibly even a little flushed. But judging by the looks and surreptitious nudges being exchanged, there were feminine undercurrents swirling around, and Freddy's policy was to affect an unawareness of such things. Safer that way.

"Nonsense. Fresh air and sunshine is the best cure for what ails you," Lady Beatrice decreed. "In you get, my dear. That headache will be gone before you know it."

Damaris didn't argue but obediently climbed into the carriage. Freddy got in after her, signaled to the driver and they were off. As expected, it was a bit of a squash. Freddy's thigh pressed against

Damaris's.

It shouldn't matter — if he'd sat next to Jane or Daisy he wouldn't have thought twice about it, but somehow, because it was Damaris, he couldn't get his mind off it.

She shifted a little closer to Daisy. Freddy moved, pressing himself against the side of the carriage to give her more space, but with three on the seat, there was simply not enough room. He could feel the warmth of her body down the length of his thigh. As she could no doubt feel his. Not that she gave any indication of it.

She gazed serenely out of the carriage, as lively as a damsel encased in glass.

She was always like that, somehow distant, untouchable. It disturbed him in ways he preferred not to think about. Pretty, quietly spoken and perfectly pleasant, she was — she ought to be — no different from any of the multitude of girls on the marriage mart these days. And yet . . .

He found her unsettling. Those big brown eyes of hers seemed to see . . . too much. He'd always had a soft spot for a pair of brown eyes, but whenever he tried to flirt with her — purely for a little bit of harmless fun — ouch! She'd freeze him out.

And yet he kept coming back for more.

"Nasty things, headaches," he commented

and winced inwardly at the inanity. In some circles he was held to be a witty and entertaining conversationalist. But whenever he tried to make pleasant, meaningless chat with Miss Damaris Chance, it always came out lame.

She nodded, gave him a half smile but didn't reply. The headache, no doubt.

If anyone had a headache, Freddy ruminated as the carriage passed out of Grosvenor Square, it should be he. Last night he'd finally crawled into bed — his own bed — around dawn. His current mistress was planning to marry again, to a much older, richer man, so their affair was drawing to a close. Or rather, a climax. She was determined to go out with a bang. Or three. Freddy was exhausted.

He had his own code about women. It wouldn't win him any prizes for morality but it was a code, nevertheless. He never dallied with innocents of any class; he avoided muffins — eligible girls bent on wedlock — like the plague; and he never chased after married women. If they chased after him, if they were neglected by their husbands and were unhappy, that was another matter. Even so, he only accepted the advances of those who had already provided their husbands with an heir, at

least. He was no cuckoo in the nest —
didn't want the complications.

He preferred widows. When he was just
sixteen he'd lost his virginity to a buxom
farmer's widow ten years older than himself.
She'd taken an eager, clumsy boy and
shown him how to please a woman, as well
as himself, teaching him the value of self-
control and patience. It was a lesson he'd
put to good use ever since.

Remarkable how many men — judging by
the women he'd lain with — didn't bother.
Fools. He yawned.

Lady Beatrice poked him with her elegant
ebony stick. "Been out on the tiles again,
young tomcat?"

Freddy gave her a cool, dignified look.

Lady Beatrice grinned. "Thought so. You
have that look about you."

"Look?" he asked, then cursed himself for
taking her bait. He cast around for a change
of subject. "Look," he repeated in a quite
different tone, and pointed to an organ-
grinder. "Monkey dressed in a red jacket.
Quaint little fellow." An excellent distraction. Miss Jane, he knew, was fond of animals.

Lady Beatrice chuckled. "None so prud-
ish in company as a rake. By all means let
us watch the monkey." She leaned back

against the padded leather squabs, not taking her eyes off Freddy.

He had to laugh.

He hadn't relished the thought of playing substitute for Max while his friend was away, but he wasn't finding it too difficult. Getting up before noon was the hardest. His hours and the hours kept by respectable ladies didn't exactly overlap. Still, Max should be back in a few weeks. Freddy could survive sleep deprivation until then. He hoped.

The carriage slowed as they turned into Hyde Park. Lady Beatrice instantly spotted a couple of friends and ordered the driver to stop. Freddy and the girls got down, and Freddy helped two old ladies up into the landau.

While Lady Beatrice and her cronies took a turn around the park in the carriage, Freddy and the girls would promenade in the park. Pretty tame entertainment in Freddy's view, but the ladies seemed to enjoy it.

He was quite enjoying it too. It was rather pleasant strolling along with three pretty girls, none of whom had the slightest design on him. He was well aware of the symptoms of Matrimonial Intent, and the Chance girls displayed none of them. Jane treated him much as she treated her brother-in-law: as a source of treats, society savoir faire and gossip and a convenient escort. Daisy had no interest in matrimony of any kind and in the park all she seemed to talk about were the outfits worn by fashionable ladies — and how they could do better.

As for Damaris, well, Freddy had no idea what she thought about anything, really. She said all that was polite and pleasant, but what she was thinking? That was anyone's guess.

Unfortunately the mild weather and weak winter sunshine had prompted more people than usual to take the air. The fact was borne in on Freddy when he saw a tall, dark-haired female dressed in a severe riding habit and a smaller one drowning in a sea of pink and white ruffles hurrying toward him.

Fluffy and the Whip. Damn! He'd thought they were safely in Durham. He stopped dead, causing Jane and Damaris to look at him in surprise.

"What is it?" Jane asked.

"The Armthwaite muff— er, sisters. Quick, this way," he said, attempting an immediate about-face. It was more difficult than he'd anticipated with a young lady on each arm. Their curiosity about the approaching pair slowed his retreat and he was caught.

Almeria, the taller of the two, arrived first; Almeria never walked when she could stride. "Mr. Monkton-Coombes, so here you are," she said in an accusing tone that never failed to remind him of Nanny McBride in one of her Moods. "I thought you never promenaded in the park." She eyed his companions with a critical eye and tapped her toe, waiting for him to introduce them.

Her sister tripped prettily — and breathlessly — in her wake. "Mutht you walk tho fast, Almeria?" She reproached her sister with a pout Freddy felt sure was the result of hours of practice in front of her looking glass.

She turned with a winsome smile to Freddy, apparently unable to see his companions at all. "Mithter Monkton-Coombth, how very delightful to thee you here on thith beautiful thunny day." The lisp was something she'd acquired only recently, imagining, no doubt, that it deepened the impression of featherbrained femininity. The idea, he supposed, was to disguise the fact that she was just as iron willed as her more blatantly masterful sister.

He said brusquely, "Miss Almeria Armthwaite, Miss Annabelle Armthwaite, may I present the Misses Chance? Miss Damaris Chance, Miss Jane Chance and Miss Daisy Chance."

While the Armthwaites grilled the Chance sisters on their family connections and — hardly more subtly — their intentions toward him, Freddy looked around for an excuse to leave.

As sole heir to his father's title and fortune, not to mention having his own private fortune, he'd been a target for matchmaking mamas and daughters since he'd first appeared in society. From the beginning he'd made it clear he had no interest in marriage, and once he realized respectable mamas and daughters avoided rakes like the plague, he'd done his best to encourage his reputation as a rake to grow.

But in the last year or so his mother had apparently informed the mothers, aunts and grandmothers of every eligible female in the kingdom that he was contemplating marriage — she might as well have put a notice in the *Gazette,* curse her! — and as a result, wherever he went, muffins popped out of the woodwork.

He wasn't contemplating marriage, dammit! Not with anything other than horror.

Lady Beatrice's carriage sailed toward

them at a decorous pace. Salvation! He held up a hand to signal her to stop, but she waved airily back and continued on her way. Blast! It would be another lap at least before he could escape.

"Mr. Monkton-Coombes, oh, Mr. Monkton-Coooooombes," another voice trilled from behind him. Damn! Another blasted muffin.

"Miss Blee." He greeted her with a curt bow. He was never coming to this park again.

"I'm soooo excited about the house party," she said with an arch look.

"Really?" he said in a bored manner. "Which house party is that?" Whichever one it was, he planned not to attend it.

"As if you don't know." She hit him coyly on the arm with the kind of arch, genteel violence some ladies thought was enticing. It wasn't.

He forced himself to reply with the barest scrape of polite disinterest, "I get lots of invitations."

"But surely — oh, but you're teasing me, you wicked, wicked man. Of course you know about it — you're the guest of honor."

Freddy frowned. "When is this —"

"We're attending too," the elder Miss Armthwaite cut in. "I hope you and I will get some hunting in, Freddy." She had a reputation as a bruising rider to hounds. She'd hinted to Freddy more than once she'd be happy to ride him just as bruisingly.

Whenever this horror-filled house party was, Freddy planned to be a hundred miles in the opposite direction.

"Oh, no, the poor little foxeth," the younger Miss Armthwaite wailed prettily. "Tho thweet."

"They're vermin," her sister snapped. "Besides, where do you think your fox fur muff comes from, ninny?"

"Don't you like my muff, Mithter Monkton-Coombth?" Miss Annabelle gave Freddy an appealing look over her fox fur muff and batted her eyes.

Freddy gritted his teeth. A thousand miles in the opposite direction.

"Are you ladies attending?" Miss Blee asked the Chance girls.

"I don't think so," Jane said. "Lady Beatrice hasn't mentioned any house party."

"I'm not surprised." Miss Blee simpered and fluttered her lashes at Freddy. "It is a very select guest list, as I understand it."

He needed to escape. He looked wildly around. "Lady Beatrice is signaling us, ladies," Freddy said, cutting across the feminine jousting. " 'Fraid we have to go. Recovering invalid, you know. Good-bye." Hooking Damaris and Daisy by the arm and herding Jane before them, he marched them back to the roadway. She'd better stop this time. He'd hurl himself in front of her carriage if necessary.

"Are those ladies good friends of yours?" Jane asked curiously.

"No!" Freddy exclaimed, revolted. "But my mother keeps pushing females of that sort at me, so they think they have a claim on me." He was aware of Damaris's gaze on him, quiet and unreadable.

Thankfully the landau drew to a stop without any need for bodily self-sacrifice. Freddy hurried to help Lady Beatrice's friends down. The sooner they were out, the quicker he could leave.

"Ready?" he asked, and when the girls were aboard Freddy signaled to the driver to move on. He was never going walking in the park again. Nor would he ever hunt foxes; he knew how the poor beasts felt.

He glanced at the old lady. Her eyes twinkled back at him, full of . . . mischief? A trickle of unease slipped down his spine. Max's warning came to mind. He frowned.

Lady Beatrice gave an airy shrug, then pulled out a tiny bottle of smelling salts.

Waving it about six inches from her nose, she said faintly, "I'm exhausted. All this fresh air and exercise, so tiring." She sank back against the well-padded cushions and closed her eyes, as innocent as a lamb.

Untrustworthy creatures, lambs, Freddy thought.

The following morning, Daisy and Damaris sat sewing in the upstairs sitting room. They spent a lot of their time there. It was bright, with large windows that let in the light, making it the perfect place to sew. A fire burned cozily in the grate.

Jane had gone shopping with Lady Beatrice to help her choose a pair of evening gloves. Daisy picked up the half-finished pelisse and began to sew the cuffs. Damaris started hemming a chemise.

They sat sewing in silence for a few minutes, the only sound a faint swishing of fabric and the hissing of burning coal in the grate.

Daisy finished the cuff and bit off the thread. "I know you said it's not because of the brothel that you don't want to get married, but if it was —"

"It's not. It's . . . complicated." She'd never told anyone about how and why she'd been sold to the brothel and she didn't intend to start now. Any marriage she made would be doomed to misery — her misery. Like Mama.

Daisy sniffed and knotted a new thread. "But if you ain't going to nab yourself a bloke, how are you goin' to support yourself? It ain't easy on your own, you know."

"I know." In the weeks before they'd met Lady Beatrice, the four girls had been trying to support themselves in London and had almost starved, it had been so dreadfully hard to find work. Damaris had been the luckiest, having found a job painting china in a pottery.

Daisy went on, "When you start your life by bein' dumped in a gutter 'cause nobody wants you, you soon learn you gotta look out for yourself." She glanced up at Damaris. "If you're useful to people, they'll want you around. But the minute you're not, or someone else takes their fancy, or they change their mind — or die — you're on yer own. So it's up to you to save yourself, 'cause there ain't no Prince Bloomin' Charmin' gonna come lookin' for girls like us, Damaris."

Damaris laughed. "I know. And I'm not expecting anyone to save me. I had a lucky escape from that brothel — if you and Jane hadn't let me come with you . . ." It didn't bear thinking of.

"Now, don't go all misery-guts on me, Damaris, that's all water under the bridge. But yeah, you and me, we don't fit here the way Abby and Jane do. You fit better'n me — you're a lady, at least, with all them pretty manners that come natural to you, brought up wiv 'eathens or not. But them two are real sisters, and blood is thicker than promises — that's all I know."

"Don't you trust them?" Damaris was troubled by the thought. It was the one little piece of security in her whole world, that she and the other three had sworn to be as sisters.

"Now don't take this the wrong way, mind, it's not that I don't trust them — or you — but that I don't trust anybody, not deep down, not really. Only meself."

"Oh, Daisy."

She shrugged. "People change, things change." She hesitated and said, "You know Mrs. B, who used to be the madam of the brothel before she handed it over to that black-hearted son of hers?"

Damaris nodded. "Mort, yes."

"Mrs. B found me when I was just eight. I was a right mess, me life was a misery and this had just happened." She gestured to her crippled foot. "She took me away from the place where I was, took me to see a doctor, spent 'er own money on me — a stranger! — and then she took me home and looked after me. Nobody had before. I was that grateful." She finished a seam and bit off the thread. "She never once pressed me to work for her as one o' the girls, neither."

Damaris nodded. Daisy had worked in the brothel as a maid and a seamstress.

Daisy continued, "I loved Mrs. B, thought of her like a mum — well, I used to pretend she was me mum if you want to know the truth. Thought me and her would be together the rest of our days an' I'd look after 'er in 'er old age." She threaded her needle with a different thread. "And then she went off and left me wiv that bastard Mort, din't she? Chucked me away like a pair of old shoes as if I meant nuffin' to her at all."

"It must have hurt you terribly," Damaris said softly.

Daisy shrugged. "Taught me a lesson I needed to learn, din't it? You got nobody in this life to look out for you except yourself." She looked up at Damaris. "And if you ain't goin' to get married, you'd better think of some way to support yourself."

"I know."

They bent over their sewing, deep in

thought.

Daisy's philosophy might be a grim one but it was true for Damaris as well. She loved Abby and Jane and Daisy as sisters and she loved Lady Beatrice with a mixture of fierce protectiveness and a desperate yearning for her mother.

But she didn't want to live on Lady Beatrice's bounty, like a sponge or a charity case, just because she didn't want to marry. If she'd learned anything in her life, it was that she was strong and could work hard.

"You can work with me, if you like, bein' a mantua maker. I don't mean just helping out, like now, but —"

"Thank you, it's very generous of you, Daisy, but —"

"I dunno if there'll be much money in it for a while, though, even if we do succeed. Any money that comes in is goin' to be needed for the business. I'll need to find a place of me own eventually and rent a shop."

"I know. And though I'll help you as much as I can at the moment, I have . . . other plans for the future."

Daisy gave her a shrewd look. "Still hankerin' after that cottage in the country?"

Damaris nodded. It was her dream to live in a little cottage in the country, with chickens and a vegetable garden, somewhere quiet and peaceful. And safe. Above all, safe.

Daisy wrinkled her nose. "Sounds 'orrible to me. I hate the country, all empty except for mud and cows and trees. What would you do all day?"

Damaris smiled. "I'd be busy growing vegetables and keeping hens. I might even keep bees."

"Nuffin' but bees and chickens for company? Won't you be lonely?"

"If I am, I'll get a dog. Or a cat. Or both." She'd been lonely most of her life. She was used to it. And animals didn't judge you; their love was unquestioning. It would be good to have Daisy and the others close by, but it was much more expensive to live in the city where you couldn't even grow your own food.

"Don't you want kids, Damaris?"

Damaris swallowed. She did, of course she did. "I looked after some little girls in China."

"Foundlings?" Daisy was a foundling herself.

Damaris nodded. The unwanted ones. "The babies and toddlers were my special charge. They were so sweet. . . ." Her voice cracked as she remembered how she'd last seen them. She swallowed again and said in what she hoped was a light tone, "But children are a lot of work." And loving them made you so vulnerable. There had been enough grief in her life. . . .

"You didn't want to leave them behind, did you?"

Damaris shook her head. "No," she said softly. "But there was no . . . no choice." She rose and busied herself putting coal on the fire and stirring up the embers. She didn't want to dwell on the past. It was too painful. She had to think about the future.

If she were to get her cottage in the country, she would have to earn money for the rent. And the sooner she started the better. On that thought she said abruptly, "Daisy, I'm sorry but I need to go out. There's something I need to do."

Daisy gave her a thoughtful look, then nodded. "Off you go, then."

"You don't mind?" Damaris gestured to the unfinished sewing.

Daisy grinned. "Nah, go ahead, do what you gotta do. I got me own plans, you got yours." She hadn't asked what Damaris intended or where she was going. Daisy had learned young to mind her own business. "Just be back in time for the literary society. Lady Bea will have a fit if you're not there to read."

"I'll be there."

Chapter Three

"What! would I be turned back from doing a thing that I had determined to do, and that I knew to be right, by the airs and interference of such a person, or of any person I may say?"

— JANE AUSTEN, *PERSUASION*

The dawn of another day. Mist swirled in ghostly shreds, caressing the lampposts and softening the stark outlines of the bare winter trees in the park. The hoofbeats of the nag pulling the cab echoed on the cobblestones. Inside the cab, Freddy lounged against the grimy seat back, tired and faintly blue-deviled. He'd just bidden a final and quite energetic farewell to his mistress but his mood had little to do with that; truth to tell, they'd wearied of each other, and her decision to marry again was both timely and convenient.

The truth was, he was beginning to tire of

this way of life; having to leave a warm, comfortable bed in the dark, making a discreet exit by the back door, braving the cold, predawn streets.

He yawned. For once he'd like to take a woman to his own bed. And stay there as long as they wanted to. Perhaps it was time to employ a mistress, set her up in a house so he wouldn't have to sneak out before dawn. He'd never fancied the idea of paying for it, but . . . these cold morning risings were killing him. Or perhaps he was getting old. He'd be thirty soon.

He gazed sleepily out of the carriage window. London was stirring, men and women trundling their goods along in hand-carts — everything from cabbages to rags and bones — street sweepers, maidservants scurrying along the street, some with baskets heading to the market, others carrying jugs to purchase fresh milk from the herd of cows kept in Green Park.

Freddy shivered and pulled his coat tighter about him. Better them than him. He was a few moments from home and a warm, comfortable bed. Through half-closed eyes he watched a woman walking briskly along the footpath ahead of him. There was something about her . . . the way she walked. . . . She was swathed in a plain gray cloak, but he thought she was slender, and perhaps young. Possibly pretty. She was moving in the opposite direction, away from Mayfair, toward a much less salubrious district.

His cab passed her just as she was walking under a lamp and out of idle curiosity Freddy turned to look, just to see whether she was pretty or not.

"Bloody hell!" he exclaimed and rapped on the ceiling of the cab. "Stop here!"

"Thought you wanted Mayfair, sir," the cabbie grumbled.

"Changed my mind." Freddy tossed him a coin, jumped down and ran after the girl, who'd turned a corner and disappeared down a side street.

At the corner he spotted her, a slender gray shadow swirling through the mist, insubstantial, but walking briskly and with purpose, seeming to know exactly where she was going.

She turned another corner and disappeared. He hurried after her and found himself in a narrow street. The gaslights didn't extend this far. In the dim, predawn light he could make out a few dilapidated houses with boarded-up windows, a couple of warehouses, narrow yards enclosed by high walls topped with shards of glass, and the occasional chimney of a manufactory. What the hell could she want in such a district?

He followed quietly, burning with curiosity, but when she turned into a dark and narrow alley he could hang back no longer. Didn't she realize the danger a lone woman could face in these parts?

He caught up with her, grabbed her by the arm and swung her around to face him — then ducked as she lashed out at him with — good God! — a cosh? He caught her forearm in his hand and forced it down. The cosh, a small leather bag filled with gravel or some such thing, dangled limply from her fingers, attached by a looped string.

"Wh— Mr. Monkton-Coombes?" Damaris Chance gave him a wide-eyed look of amazement, glanced behind him to see if he was alone, then returned her gaze to his face.

For a moment they stood staring at each other, breathing heavily, small visible puffs in the chill, still air. Her skin was milk pale, luminous with mist, her eyes huge and dark in the dim light. They looked almost black; Freddy knew they were a soft brown like the velvet of pansies. That was in the dark. In the sun, they sparkled like topaz.

Under the drab gray cloak she wore an even drabber gray gown, like some dowdy, down-at-heels governess. In some obscure way it offended him. She always dressed with elegance and style. As befitted her beauty.

And she was carrying a *cosh,* a weapon of the wharves and backstreets. That roused him to further anger.

He shook her by the arm. "What the devil are you doing out here, alone, at this hour, in this godforsaken neighborhood?"

"What are you doing here?" Her voice was cool, low and composed, smoky honey in the chill, bleak surrounds. She tried to pull her arm out of his grip.

His fingers tightened. "I asked you first — and what the dev— *deuce* are you doing carrying a *cosh*?" He was not composed at all.

This — *this!* — was why he should have refused Max's request, this feeling he got whenever she looked at him this way, with silky sable brows arching over fathomless dark eyes. He had no idea what she was thinking, dammit. A man could drown in that liquid gaze. And the way she pursed those full, wild-rose lips . . . they scrambled his brain.

"Defending myself from unwanted attentions, of course." She glanced pointedly at the hand that held her. "Let go of my arm, please."

He ignored her. "If you were where you're supposed to be you wouldn't need to defend yourself at all. What are you doing out here?"

"Walking."

"Don't try that flummery with me. What are you doing here?"

She gave him a look that might have been apologetic if she hadn't answered coolly, "That's my business."

"It's my business too."

She put up her brows in a way that was no doubt meant to make him feel abashed. Trying to look governessy, he supposed, in her drab gray garb.

Freddy had never had a governess — that he knew of — and he didn't feel abashed in the slightest. The contrast between her fine, moon-pale beauty and the dreary clothing buttoned tightly, swathing her slenderness in drabness, only made her look . . . enticing. The thought flashed across his mind that it might be quite entertaining to have a governess. . . .

Not that he was allowing himself to be enticed. Or distracted. She was very much out-of-bounds to him; a duty only. "Max made me promise that I'd keep an eye on you girls while he's away — and a blasted nuisance it's turning out to be."

She glanced again at his hand, which was still clamped around her forearm. "I quite agree."

"Well, it's a good thing he did," he said crossly. "What do you think he'd say to you wandering about in such an area at this time of night?"

"It's not night, it's morning," she corrected him. "And I'm not wandering, I know exactly where I'm going. It's nothing for you or anyone else to be concerned about, so I thank you for your interest and bid you good day." She tugged at her arm.

Interest? It wasn't interest he felt, it was . . . dammit, he didn't know what it was. Annoyance, probably. He could be home in bed by now, and instead he was down some filthy alley arguing with a mule-headed chit who seemed to have no idea of the trouble she could be in. "Does Lady Beatrice know you are here? Does Featherby?"

"Featherby is a butler; it is not for him to approve or disapprove of my doings."

He wanted to shake her. "Perhaps not, but I'll lay odds he would have sent that giant footman with you if he had any idea you were going out at this time of the day — and in these streets. And don't think I haven't noticed you failed to answer my question about Lady Beatrice. I can see from your expression she doesn't know, either. Does anyone know?"

She looked away, her jaw clenched, presenting him with a view of her profile. A beautiful profile, he mused, if currently a touch mulish. The sun was almost up, staining the sky pink and lending a faint blush to her milk-white skin.

"Well?" he prompted.

"Daisy knows."

"Oh, well, that's all right then," he said with heavy sarcasm. "Daisy'd be a lot of help if you got into trouble. Do you have *any* idea of what kind of neighborhood you're in?" He gestured to the run-down surroundings.

"I know exactly what sort of place this is," she retorted. "Better than you, I expect."

Better than he? He narrowed his eyes. "Why? How do you know this place?"

"It's none of your —"

"Don't give me that. I promised Max I'd keep an eye on you all and I don't make promises lightly." Not at all, if he could help it.

She glanced down the alleyway to where a

couple of shabby-looking men had come out of a yard and stood watching them with interest.

"Make all the fuss you want," he told her. "You're not taking another step until you give me a satisfactory explanation."

She made a small irritated noise. "If you must know, I have a job here. Now please release me, or I'll be late."

"A *job*?" He didn't believe her. Girls who lived in Mayfair under the care of a doting aunt didn't have jobs. Even if the aunt wasn't a real aunt, the security she provided was real enough.

"What kind of job?"

"I paint china."

"China?" It was the last thing he would have thought of. "What sort of china?"

She rolled her eyes at him. "What sort do you think? Cups, saucers, plates, bowls, jugs." She bared her teeth at him in a falsely sweet smile and added, "Chamber pots."

"But why?"

She pursed her lips and tried to pull free of his loosened grip, but he wasn't having any of that. "For money, of course."

Freddy frowned. Money? A job like that wouldn't pay much. Lady Beatrice made all the girls an allowance. Pin money, but it would be plenty for their needs. Unless . . .

"Have you been gambling?"

"Of course not."

"Then why are you short of money?" What could be so important that she'd taken up a menial job in secret, in a seedy part of town, at this indecent hour?

He waited, still gripping her slender wrist firmly. A clock somewhere chimed, six sonorous chimes. "I'm not short of money and what I do in my own time is none of your business." She twisted against his grip. "Now let me go! You're making me late." She glanced down the alleyway.

Freddy followed her glance. The two men had been joined by a middle-aged woman.

Freddy returned to the point at issue. "If you're sneaking out of the house to work in a job in this part of town it's Max's business, and Lady Beatrice's, since you're living under his roof and under her protection," Freddy pointed out. "And while Max is away it's my business."

"It's nothing for either of them to be concerned about."

"I'll be the judge of that."

She made a frustrated noise. "Very well, I'll tell you, as long as you promise to say nothing about it to anyone."

She waited, but Freddy would make no such promise. "I'll decide that when I know what it is." What if she was involved in something dodgy or dangerous?

She moistened her lips worriedly, considering her options. Freddy stifled a groan, unable to take his gaze off her rosy damp mouth. Dammit, Max had no business asking him to keep an eye on such lusciousness, knowing he could only look and not touch. It was above and beyond . . .

She bit down on the soft, plump flesh, which almost made him groan aloud — he could practically taste it himself — but she seemed to have come to some decision, for she said, "Well, if you must know —"

"This feller botherin' you, Miss D'maris?"

Freddy felt a heavy hand clamp down on his shoulder.

At the same time a meaty fist grabbed Freddy's neck and something cold — a blade? — pressed against his throat and a different voice rasped, "Let 'er go — she ain't for the likes of you."

Freddy released Damaris's wrist and the pressure of the blade lifted. Now she would understand the danger she courted in districts like this. He willed her with his eyes to flee — things were about to get ugly. Freddy might dress like a pink of the *ton,* but he boxed regularly at Jackson's parlor. He could beat off these two, but he didn't want Damaris in the way, not when knives as well as fists were flying around.

He gave her a hard look, willing her again to run, and braced himself for action. Only to hear her say in that soft, smoke-honey voice, "Thank you, Amos, Henry, but it's quite all right. This gentleman was just leaving."

Amos? Henry? She *knew* these ruffians?

The knife disappeared, but the heavy hand remained on Freddy's shoulder. "We'll see the fancy gent off, miss, don't you worry." There was a wealth of meaning in his voice. And a wealth of onions on his breath. Freddy turned his head away.

Damaris laughed softly. "No, really, he's harmless. He was just satisfying himself that I really do work here."

Harmless? Freddy stiffened. *Harmless?*

"Let him go, please," she said in that governessy tone, and to Freddy's amazement — and annoyance — they did.

"Come, let us go to work," she said, and like little lambs the two thugs shambled in her wake down the laneway, casting threatening looks back at him from time to time. They reached the plump little woman, who put an arm around Damaris's waist and cast an indignant glance at Freddy, then all four of them disappeared into the yard.

Tall iron gates closed behind them.

Freddy followed and looked through the high gates just in time to see Damaris ushered through a doorway by the little woman, who appeared clean, dowdy and respectable. Not at all like a procurer of hapless females.

A large brick kiln dominated the yard. Nearby stood an open shed that held racks and racks of china of various shapes and sizes and in various states of glazing. Amos and Henry started moving trolleys containing unglazed pots.

It was indeed a pottery. How very curious.

He watched as a young lad stacked unglazed pots.

"Oi, you!" It was a harsh, female voice. The woman he'd seen earlier was marching across the yard toward him; a small, aggressive barrel of a female, intent, apparently, on conversing with him.

"Madam?" He raised his hat politely.

"Don't you 'madam' me, you randy rake!" snapped the barrel.

Freddy blinked.

"And don't you come sniffin' around Damaris no more, if you know what's good for you."

"I am not sniffing —" he began indignantly, but the woman stormed on.

"She's a respectable girl, is Damaris — a good girl, and she don't want nuffin' to do wiv fancy gents who ain't got a moral to their name!"

"My good woman —" Freddy began.

"And I ain't your good woman, neither!" she retorted, planting her hands on her considerable hips in a belligerent stance that made Freddy quite glad the gates between them were firmly shut. He didn't mind brawling with men, but women were another matter altogether. And this one barely reached his waist.

"I assure you, mad— er, missus — that —"

She swept on. "I dunno what the world's coming to, rakes an' reprobates sniffin' around the skirts of hardworkin' respectable girls in broad daylight! — oh, yes, you can poker up all you like and look down your nose at me like I'm dirt under your boots, but I know all about rakes and what you do to innocent girls! — and our Damaris is not for the likes of you — understand?"

"I am standing in place of her guardian," Freddy said coldly. He'd never corrupted an innocent girl in his life! "And I did *not* look at you as if you were dir—"

The woman made a rude noise. "*Guardian? Pfft!* Is that what they're callin' it these days?" She snorted. "I saw the way you looked at her. I know a lust-sodden lecher when I see one! Now go on, get out o' here, and if I see you hanging around her again, my lads'll give you the thrashing you deserve, gentleman or not!"

There was clearly no reasoning with the woman. Freddy shrugged. "You are mistaken as to my motives, but clearly you have no interest in the truth, so I will bid good day to you, madam." He turned to leave the scene with dignity, ignoring the extremely vulgar noise the woman made to his back.

Then a thought occurred to him. Damaris should not be walking these streets unescorted at any time of the day. He turned back. "What time does Damaris finish work?"

The woman swelled with visible indignation. "The cheek of you! I just told you to stay away from her. Asking for a beating, you are."

"No," Freddy said coolly. "Simply asking what time she finishes work. I shall escort her home."

"Down the Road to Roon is the only place you'd likely escort her," the woman declared. "My lads will walk Damaris home, right to 'er very door. So how d'you like that, Sir Rake?" she said with an air of triumph.

"Damn. That's foiled me," Freddy said with what he hoped was a convincingly frustrated air. Having satisfactorily arranged the matter of Miss Damaris's safe escort home, he took himself off to catch up on some much-needed sleep.

No trouble? Max had a great deal to answer for.

Inside the pottery, Damaris hung up her cloak — Abby's old cloak, really — on the nail on the back of the door, collected her brushes and sat down at her usual bench. On a stand to the left of her, Mrs. Jenkins had laid out all the pieces to be painted. They'd already been fired with a white overglaze. Each piece would be perfect; anything with even the slightest imperfection would be put aside and painted by one of the other girls. Damaris's work fetched the best prices.

The stand on her right would hold the finished pieces, left to dry, then be taken for a final firing. She picked up a brush and frowned. Her hands were shaking. Why? Surely not from that mild little exchange with Mr. Monkton-Coombes.

70

She'd managed to appear calm and undisturbed while talking to him — she was used to keeping calm when men raged, and Mr. Monkton-Coombes could hardly be said to have raged. Papa in a rage had been far more frightening. She hadn't been at all fearful of Mr. Monkton-Coombes. More . . . annoyed.

So why this reaction? It was almost as though she could still feel his leather-gloved fingers holding her wrist. But he hadn't hurt, or even threatened to hurt, her. He hadn't shouted or menaced her in any way. He just wanted to know what she was doing. Because Max had made him responsible.

It was inconvenient, but not outrageous. And he'd been perfectly gentlemanly about it. So why, now she was inside, had her hands started trembling?

Cold, perhaps? Whatever the reason, she couldn't paint with shaking hands. She rose and went to stand beside the small iron stove — the pottery works were always warm from the kiln, but even so, a fire was always kept going in the workroom stove, for mixing glazes, for making tea and, on mornings like this, to thaw out the cold hands of the girls who painted the china. It had been an exceptionally cold summer, and the winter was expected to be even worse.

She was holding out her hands, rubbing them next to the stove, when Mrs. Jenkins bustled in from outside.

"I sent 'im off with a flea in his ear," she said, dusting down her skirt with a satisfied air. She snorted. "Tomcat in gen'leman's clothing, that's what 'e is — a rake through and through."

"Rake? You thought —"

Mrs. Jenkins snorted. "I knew what he was the instant I clapped eyes on him! Dressed like that in his fancy duds at this hour of the mornin'. The cheek of 'im, thinking he could seduce away one o' my girls in broad daylight."

"But he wasn't —"

"Bless you, my dove, you're too young to recognize a Wicked Seducer when you see one, and I grant you that one is an 'andsome devil, and charmin' as an oiled snake, I have no doubt!" She fixed Damaris with a gimlet eye. "But it don't do for a girl like you to catch the eye of a gentleman, take it from me. He'll soften you up with sweet words and little gifts and . . . and *poetry,* and you'll think 'e's *ever* such a nice fellow, then in the twinklin' of an eye, he'll 'ave your skirts over your 'ead, and there you'll be, rooned forever!"

"But Mrs. Jenkins —"

"Rooned forever!" Mrs. Jenkins repeated firmly. "And we don't want that, do we? Now, I've given him a piece of me mind — blistered 'is ear'oles good and proper, I did — and if 'e knows what's good for 'im, he won't be back to bother you again, so let's get to work."

Damaris nodded and resumed her seat at the bench. Her hands had stopped shaking but she had to press her lips together to hide the smile that kept threatening to break out. She could just imagine Mr. Monkton-Coombes's face when he was confronted with Mrs. Jenkins, four foot eight of Righteous Indignation. "Are there any special requests?"

"No, we'll keep going with the blue and white designs — they're flyin' off the shelves, can't make 'em fast enough, so off you go, me dear, as many as you can. Leaving at two again, are you?"

Damaris nodded. If she left at two, she'd just be able to make it home in time to change and be ready for Lady Beatrice's literary society. She picked up the brush. She was lucky to be able to set her own hours. The other girls who worked here had no such option. Damaris's unique skills gave her choices they did not have.

Once again she thanked God for giving Papa the impulse to send her to Master Cheng for lessons. And for Master Cheng, the gentle, elderly scholar and artist who'd treated a mere girl-child — a foreign girl-child at that — with a generosity of spirit that still humbled her.

It had been forbidden for Chinese to teach foreigners their language, on pain of death, but as a child, Damaris had picked up the spoken language quickly. Papa's great dream was to translate the Bible into Chinese, but he had no ear for the language and struggled to be understood in even the most simple transactions. Almost from the start, he'd relied on her to interpret for him. And after her mother died, he sent Damaris to Master Cheng to learn to write the language she spoke so well.

It was risky for Master Cheng too, but the old man had told her knowledge was a gift to be shared, and that he was too old to worry about being beheaded, that such a death would be clean and quick. Still, it was wise to be careful, so painting became the ostensible reason for her lessons, and because he was a man of his word, he incorporated painting with reading and writing lessons; calligraphy was an art, as well as a discipline, he said.

Had it not been for Master Cheng, Damaris would never have discovered she had a gift for painting.

She lined up a dozen bowls in front of her, then closed her eyes for a moment, visualizing exactly what she would paint. A bamboo theme today, she thought; her bamboo designs were always popular.

In her mind's eye she pictured the bamboo grove that Master Cheng cultivated in his small enclosed garden, the long graceful canes of black-stemmed bamboo, the precise angle of the elegant green leaves. She sat quietly, breathing deeply, until she could almost smell the garden. How many times had he made her paint that bamboo, over and over in black ink, until in just a few strokes she could make it come alive.

With a deep breath, she opened her eyes, dipped her brush in the mix that would become a brilliant blue after firing, and started to paint in sure, confident strokes. A slender stem of bamboo sprang to life on the pristine white glaze, the leaves almost quivering from a sudden summer shower.

Damaris smiled. It would be a good day's painting, she could feel it. She loved this work, really loved it. Even if she didn't need the money so desperately, she would still want to paint. This way she could do both.

After half a dozen bowls, with her rhythm established and her brush moving as if of its own accord, her thoughts returned to the confrontation with Mr. Monkton-Coombes.

He was bound to tell Lady Bea. Damaris had always known her secret would come out eventually, but this was too soon; she didn't have nearly enough money yet.

Lady Bea wouldn't be at all happy about her having a job. Perhaps she could talk to Mr. Monkton-Coombes at this afternoon's literary society meeting, convince him to keep quiet. What she was doing was harmless, surely.

Damaris painted on, her mind a whirl of possibilities, her brushstrokes sure and swift.

CHAPTER FOUR

"Books — Oh! no. — I am sure
we never read the same, or not
with the same feelings."
"I am sorry you think so; but if that
be the case, there can at least be
no want of subject. We may compare
our different opinions."
— JANE AUSTEN, *PRIDE AND PREJUDICE*

Lady Beatrice's literary society met three times a week in the afternoon. At this time of year, with the majority of the *ton* in the country, sophisticated London entertainments were few and far between, so those members of the *ton* who remained in town during the hunting season were delighted to be offered something a little different from the general round of morning calls.

Lady Beatrice's was not the usual kind of literary society; it was, as Lady Beatrice herself informed any new members, just for fun, and not for dreary intellectual posing and prosing on about — there were plenty of other literary groups for that kind of thing. Lady Beatrice simply offered a good story, read aloud by her nieces, and accompanied by tea and cakes. The tea served was often sherry or wine.

It was particularly popular with older people whose eyesight was fading and who found the small print in a book difficult to read. And anyone who so much as mentioned alliteration, allegories or anything else Lady Beatrice called "clever-clogs show-offery" wasn't invited back.

Damaris returned from the pottery with barely fifteen minutes to spare. On their mother's instructions Amos and Henry had insisted on escorting her almost all the way. Damaris had convinced them to leave her a short distance from Mayfair by telling them she'd be in trouble if she was seen with them, that her home was just a step away and she'd be perfectly safe now, thank you.

Ridiculous that they were protecting her from the wiles of Freddy Monkton-Coombes. Almost as ridiculous as imagining Mr. Monkton-Coombes was interested in seducing her.

A line of carriages had formed at the front of the house already. She entered through the kitchen door and hurried up the servants' stairway.

She slipped into her bedchamber. Daisy was there to meet her. "Gawd, I thought you weren't never goin' to get here," she said. "Quick now, let's get you presentable." She helped Damaris out of her outer clothes then handed her a washcloth. "No time for a proper wash today, just a lick and a promise."

"Daisy, you're a saint. Thank you." Damaris dipped the washcloth into the waiting warm water and washed herself quickly.

"Jane's already in there. She'll start. Right, let's get this gown on you."

"Has Lady Beatrice said anything?"

Daisy shook her head. "Nah, but you're gonna have to tell 'er soon. Turn 'round and I'll do you up."

"I know." Damaris glanced at Daisy over her shoulder. "Mr. Monkton-Coombes knows."

"He what? How come? You didn't tell 'im, did you?"

"Of course not. It was just by chance — he saw me going to work and followed me. He even talked to Mrs. Jenkins, the owner."

"Bloody 'ell," Daisy muttered. She tugged the dress to straighten it. "Right, that's done. Now we'll just tidy your hair." She undid the simple knot Damaris always wore for work, brushed her hair out, then twisted it into an elegant plaited coil high on her head. "No time for anything fancy today. So, you reckon Mr. Monkton-Coombes will tell on you to Lady Bea?"

"I don't know. I hope not." Damaris glanced at herself in the looking glass. "Daisy, you're a wonder and a marvel. If you ever decided not to be a mantua maker, you could always find work as a lady's maid."

Daisy snorted. "Nah, I been at other women's beck and call all me life — now I want to do something for meself."

Damaris glanced at her, a little dismayed. "I hope you don't think I was treating you like a maid just now, Daisy."

"Nah, 'course not. This" — she waved her hand at Damaris's hair and gown — "this is what sisters do for each other. Now, get movin', or we'll be late. I don't want to miss nothing of this story."

Damaris gave her a swift hug, then the two girls hurried downstairs to the large drawing room. A babble of conversation wafted down the hall toward them. William, the footman, was bringing in some extra chairs; the society was proving more popular each week.

As they entered the room, Lady Beatrice caught their eye and smiled. The room was crowded — there were forty people at least. The old lady gave a signal and Featherby, the butler, rang a little bell. The din started to fade as people ended their conversations and found their seats.

As one by one the audience members were seated, only one man remained standing, a tall, elegant gentleman dressed in a dozen shades of gray: the Honorable Frederick Monkton-Coombes. He stood at the rear of the room, leaning against the mantelpiece, his arms folded, watching her. He made no move to find a chair.

Damaris pretended not to notice him. Threading her way through the crowd, she joined Jane at the front of the room. Now that Abby was on her honeymoon, the reading was left to Jane and Damaris; Daisy had learned to read in the last few months, but she wasn't up to performing in front of strangers.

Jane smiled as Damaris slipped into the waiting seat. "Just in time," she murmured. "I'll go first, shall I? Give you time to gather your thoughts." She lifted the current book they were reading and a hush fell.

Jane began, *"Though now the middle of December, there had yet been no weather to prevent the young ladies from tolerably regular exercise; and on the morrow, Emma had a charitable visit to pay to a poor sick family, who lived a little way out of Highbury. . . ."*

Damaris let the words wash over her, unhearing. Had Mr. Monkton-Coombes told Lady Beatrice about their encounter in the street? What would the old lady say about Damaris working in a menial position? Would she be upset? She glanced at Lady Beatrice, who was listening to the story with her eyes closed. Of course she'd be upset — in Lady Bea's world ladies simply didn't work. The menial nature of the job would appall her, and besides, she wanted Damaris to have a life of carefree fun.

Once she learned, she'd probably forbid Damaris to return to the pottery. She'd probably want to buy Damaris a cottage, but Damaris couldn't accept that, not on top of all Lady Beatrice had already done for her, and was planning to do. A London season just for fun.

As the daughter of a missionary, Damaris knew only too well that while charity was a blessing, it could also be a burden. It always came with some kind of obligation, explicit or implicit. She'd spent her whole life either giving or receiving charity, mostly at the same time; living on other people's charity so that she and her father could help the children at the mission. Her mother's money had run out by the time Damaris turned fifteen.

For once in her life she wanted to be free to make her own choices. To be answerable to no one.

She had to stop Mr. Monkton-Coombes from telling Lady Bea.

Damaris glanced across the room to where he still lounged against the wall, the only person in the room still standing. She had a clear view of him. And he of her. He was frowning, but he wasn't looking at her. She followed his gaze but couldn't work out who or what had disturbed him. Everyone in the audience seemed to be listening attentively to Jane.

Perhaps he was just staring blankly; people often did that when they were listening to a story, lost in the world of the book. Or lost in thought. She hoped he wasn't thinking about whether to tell Lady Beatrice about her.

"'. . . *she could not but flatter herself that it had been the occasion of much present enjoyment to both, and must be leading them forward to the great event.'"* A short silence fell. Jane, having finished the chapter, passed the book to Damaris, and a buzz of conversation rose.

Damaris hesitated. Should she approach Mr. Monkton-Coombes now and speak to him? There would be a short break now for everyone's refreshments to be replenished — people liked to listen while they sipped tea or sherry or nibbled pensively on a cake or an almond wafer — and then it would be Damaris's turn to read.

But what if he argued? It would only draw attention to them, and she didn't wish that. London society was hungry for gossip of even the mildest sort.

He straightened and stepped away from the wall he'd been lounging against. Damaris rose from her seat, clutching the book to her chest. If he tried to approach Lady Beatrice, she would intercept him, distract him somehow. She had no choice.

Freddy was intrigued. Damaris had kept glancing at him on and off throughout the reading session. Clearly she wanted to talk to him. He headed toward her, but he'd taken a mere half dozen steps when — "Mr. Monkton-Coombes, the very man I wanted to talk to." An elderly female claw hooked him from the crowd. "You know my great-niece Hermione, don't you? Hermione Fullerton-Smith?"

Freddy did, much to his regret. One of the Lincolnshire Fullerton-Smiths and a muffin of the highest order. "How d'ye do, Miss Fullerton-Smith?" he muttered, casting a frustrated glance across the room to where Blenkinsop, a fellow he'd been to school with, was oozing flowery compliments over Damaris.

Dammit, Blenkinsop was exactly the sort of fellow Max would expect Freddy to protect the girls from.

She turned her head, caught his eye and gave him an unreadable look.

At his elbow, the dowager tightened her grip.

"What a lovely surprise," Miss Fullerton-Smith murmured with a coy smile. "I didn't expect to see you until the house party. I'm so looking forward to it. And" — she walked her fingers playfully up his arm — "to getting better acquainted with you." It left him cold. Colder than cold.

He stepped back, ostensibly to let a footman bearing a tray through. "I'm afraid I don't know which house party you mean. And I doubt very much if I'll be there."

She gave a tinkling laugh. "Well, of course you do, and you're being very naughty. Mama and I have been assured by your dear mama you'll be there."

Freddy almost snorted. His mother knew nothing of his social engagements. And wherever this house party was, if the Armthwaite muffins, Miss Blee and now the Fullerton-Smiths were attending, he planned to be as far away from it as possible. Somewhere like France. Or Russia.

A silvery bell rang out. Immediately people began to resume their seats. Freddy took his leave of Miss Fullerton-Smith and her great-aunt and retreated to the opposite side of the room.

Damaris raised her book, preparing to read. The room fell silent. Freddy found another wall to lean against and retired to glower at Blenkinsop and listen to Damaris's beautiful voice reading.

The wretched story continued. These girls seemed to have an endless supply of stories about women whose sole aim in life was to find rich husbands. Ghastly stuff. Who'd write a book about muffins?

"Another chilly morning, Miss Chance."

Damaris, who'd just let herself out of the back gate, jumped as the deep voice came out of the swirling fog. "Mr. Monkton-Coombes?" She didn't even try to hide her surprise. It wasn't quite dawn. He was clearly waiting for her. "What on earth are you doing here?" Again.

"Escorting you to work."

"I don't need an escort, thank you. I'm perfectly all right by myself."

"I'm not going to argue. I made a promise to Max I'd look after you girls and I mean to keep it. It's to stop Abby worrying," he added, hoping it would mollify her. He presented his arm, and after a moment's hesitation, she took it.

"You don't need to worry," she said as they turned a corner. "I know this area. I used to work at the pottery before . . . before we came to live with Lady Beatrice."

"You worked here before?" It was the first he'd heard of anything she'd done before she came to live with Lady Beatrice. Her background — all the girls' backgrounds — was shrouded in mystery. He knew there was something shady about them, that they weren't really Lady Beatrice's nieces, but Max had been pretty closemouthed about it all, and as far as most people knew they were the offspring of a Venetian marchese called Chancealotto. Who had been made up by Lady Beatrice.

"Yes, and I'm working here again."

He wondered what had made a gently raised girl seek work in a pottery in the first place but he could see from the set of her chin that she wasn't going to explain.

"You're sure you're not in trouble from gambling or some such thing?"

"No. I told you before, I don't gamble."

"But there must be some urgency," he persisted. "After all, in a few months you'll be having your season and next thing you know, you'll be married and your future will be secure."

He felt her shiver. "Are you cold?"

"No."

He glanced at her gray cloak. It was thin and rather threadbare. "You shivered."

"I'm not cold."

She didn't look cold. Her cheeks were quite rosy.

"And I won't be getting married."

"Nonsense, of course —"

"I should have said, I don't *want* to get married."

"You don't want to get married?" He swung around to stare at her, then shook his head. "Nonsense. All girls want to get married."

"Not all girls." They moved on.

"Every girl I ever met did. And does."

"Some girls marry because they want to, because they've found the man they want to go through life with, but most marry because they have no other choice. A single woman has very few options in this world, so for many women it's a compromise. They marry for security, for wealth or position, and the chance of children — the man is almost immaterial."

Freddy's mouth tightened. Didn't he know it? The muffins his mother kept hurling at him wanted him for exactly those reasons — and the fortune, lands and title that would come to him after his father's death. Freddy himself was immaterial; a means to an end.

She continued, "A few girls are lucky enough to be given the choice, to marry if they want or to remain single: They're the women with money of their own."

They walked on a few blocks in silence. A small boy swept some horse dung out of their way as they crossed the street. Damaris nodded at the child and gave Freddy an expectant look. He fished for a coin and flicked threepence to the urchin, who caught it in a grubby fist, saying, "Fanks, pretty lady," with a gap-toothed grin. She gave him a warm smile.

"Don't you want children?" Freddy asked.

Her smile faded. "One can't have everything in life," she said quietly and picked up her pace.

"You can't possibly prefer a life of drudgery, working in a pottery for a pittance, to marriage to some wealthy member of the *ton.*"

"Can't I?"

"No, it doesn't —"

She turned on him. "Why all the questions? It's none of your business what I do with my life, never mind the hypocrisy."

"Hypocrisy?"

"You're famous for your aversion to marriage and yet you have the cheek to criticize me for mine."

"I wasn't criticizing," he said, stung.

"No?" She gave a huff of disbelief and walked ahead, hugging her cloak more tightly around her. "And before you ask, yes, Lady Beatrice knows I don't want to marry."

"And?"

"She accepts it, but she wants me to have my come-out anyway. For fun, she says."

Very sensible, Freddy thought. The old lady obviously didn't believe her, either. Damaris was still young, nineteen or so — too young to be making such a momentous decision. She'd no doubt change her mind. And even if she didn't . . .

"Even if you don't choose to marry, there's still no need to work at this kind of job. There are other alternatives for you, surely, more genteel positions than working in a noisome back alley."

"I like painting china."

"You could paint china and still be comfortable working as a — as a lady's companion, for example."

She gave a kind of snort through elegantly flared nostrils.

"What's wrong with being a lady's companion? Lady Beatrice would gladly employ y—"

"Lady Beatrice is too kind and generous for her own good, which is why I will not sponge off her indefinitely. Do you think that's what I want? To take and take and give nothing in return?" She rounded on him suddenly. "Why don't *you* want to get married?"

"What? None of your b—"

She smiled. "Exactly. And yet marriage offers you so much: a wife to run your home and do your bidding —"

Freddy snorted. "Do my bidding? You don't know much about wives if that's what you think."

"A companion, children — isn't it your duty to produce an heir to continue the family name? What do they say, 'an heir and a spare'?"

Freddy loathed the expression.

"Or is it women you have an aversion to? I know some men —"

"I do *not* have an aversion to women!"

"Well then, why *don't* you want to marry?"

Nettled, Freddy stared at her in frustrated silence.

She gave a little grin. "See? Not so much fun when you get a taste of your own medicine, is it?" She took a few steps, then seemed to reconsider. "You're going to tell Lady Beatrice about me, aren't you?"

He wasn't, but he wasn't going to tell her that. He shrugged. They walked on a little.

She said abruptly, "Have you ever had nothing, Mr. Monkton-Coombes?"

He frowned. "In what sense?"

"In any sense. Have you ever had nothing, owned nothing, not so much as a penny to your name?"

"Of course not."

"Well, I have — several times in my life — so don't talk to me about 'need.' You look at me and see a girl who's well fed, well dressed, comfortably housed and elegantly shod."

He couldn't help but glance at the boots she was wearing. They were damn ugly and far too heavy for her.

"Not these. I can't very well tread the filthy backstreets of London in dainty slip-

92

pers, can I? Especially not with the weather we've been having," she said impatiently. "I mean in general, I appear to have everything I could ever want."

He nodded.

"And you know from whom all this abundance comes, don't you?"

"Lady Beatrice and Max."

"Exactly — and don't misunderstand, I love Lady Beatrice dearly and am deeply grateful for her generosity and that of her nephew — but what if, for some reason, Lady Beatrice or Lord Davenham turned against me? Where would I be then?"

"They wouldn't. Lady Beatrice adores you girls and Max adores Abby and Abby wouldn't let him."

"Yes, but let's say, for the sake of argument, they did. Or what if they died? People do die, for all sorts of unexpected reasons."

People did, Freddy knew that only too well. They walked on for a few moments in silence. What if she were left on her own? London streets were full of destitute people — it was one reason he insisted on escorting her. Without family, without a home or an income of some sort . . . Damaris living on the streets? It was unthinkable.

"It's happened to me twice in my life — twice! And I won't let it happen again. I have to have money of my own, that I've earned myself and owe to no one. I don't expect you to understand — people like you grow up with an assumption that you'll always have everything you need — not everything you want, but what you need to live —"

"I understand," Freddy said. And he did. But he could see from her expression she didn't believe him. He found himself wanting to share his own sorry tale with this quiet, intense girl as they walked through the fogbound, silent streets. But he restrained himself. He never talked about it with anyone. Especially not a woman.

She gave him a sidelong glance. "You won't tell on me to Lady Beatrice or anyone?"

"No, but I think you should let her know what you're doing."

She shook her head. "I can't. It would upset her too much. She'd be so hurt to discover I didn't . . ."

"Didn't trust her?"

She bit her lip. "I know it looks that way, but it's not like that. I *do* trust her. I know she won't turn on me as I described, I truly know it, it's just . . ." She sighed. "I can't explain it."

"You know your fear is both false and illogical, but you fear it anyway."

She stopped dead and looked at him, her eyes wide with surprise. "You do understand," she breathed, so softly it was almost lost in the fog.

"Our fears are not always reasonable," he said quietly, glad of the gloom that hid his expression. They'd reached the lane-way that led to the pottery yard. "And so we have reached your destination. Good day, Miss Chance." He bowed and walked away into the swirling fog.

Duty was a bitch of a mistress, Freddy Monkton-Coombes reflected.

If he hadn't made that blasted promise to Max, he'd keep himself as far away as possible from Damaris Chance. He wouldn't have this . . . problem.

Instead, he was forced into her company, day after day. Morning after morning, coming straight from his bed to her company.

If only she were a widow.

He much preferred widows.

He particularly liked widows who had no plans to remarry, who had everything they wanted — security, comfort and the freedom to live their lives as they chose. Heady thing, freedom.

Every widow whom Freddy had enjoyed a

discreet liaison with had wanted nothing from Freddy except himself — his body, his bed skills, a little of his company and nothing else. Perhaps a few gifts, but that was only natural.

He found it endlessly refreshing.

It was a little like that with Damaris. She wanted nothing from him — not his wealth, not his prospective title, not even his body, though he was sure he could change her mind about that.

But she was unmarried, and therefore out-of-bounds.

If Damaris were a widow . . . His mind skipped down a trail of endless possibilities, delightful possibilities. But no. He put a firm clamp on his imagination. She was forbidden fruit.

Forbidden fruit was always the tastiest.

No. He was honor bound to protect her innocence — from himself as much as any other villain.

CHAPTER FIVE

"She was stronger alone."
— JANE AUSTEN, *SENSE AND SENSIBILITY*

Damaris let herself into the pottery works and stripped off her cloak, hat and gloves. What on earth did Freddy Monkton-Coombes think he was doing, turning up before dawn to walk her to work? It was ridiculous, taking a promise to "keep an eye on them" rather too far. He was behaving more like a chaperon than a rake.

As for his questioning her about her reasons for working, and her intentions for the future, what business of his was it?

She jammed her cloak on the hook. Hypocrite, urging her to marriage when he had no such intention himself!

He'd surprised her with that last exchange, though, about fears. She hadn't expected a man like him to be so perceptive.

She set out her materials absentmindedly.

Why must everyone harp on so about marriage? Oh, they meant well, she knew that, but why couldn't they just leave it alone, acknowledge that Damaris knew her own mind and the choices open to her.

Did they think she didn't *want* to be loved, didn't want to have someone whose business — no, whose pleasure it would be to take care of her, protect her? And who would let her take care of him and love him in return?

Did they think she didn't watch Abby and Max together and *ache* for what they had, a love that was almost tangible?

She was as human as they; she ached for love, as any woman did. But she knew, knew with a certainty that reached back to her earliest memories, that it would not be like Abby and Max for her.

Abby had been an innocent.

Abby had been born into a loving marriage and, despite being left orphaned and in poverty at a young age, she still treasured her memories of her parents and their love for each other, and for her and Jane.

Abby had come through the hardships of her early upbringing unsullied, untainted.

Some people were lucky.

And some were not.

For the umpteenth time Damaris wondered about Mama and how she'd felt when she married Papa. Had she tried to love him? Had he ever tried to love her?

She had no memory of a single affectionate gesture between them.

Of course, you couldn't tell what people felt by their behavior, and in the privacy of a bedchamber, anything could happen. That she knew only too well.

How long had it been before Papa moved into his spare, monklike bedchamber and Mama moved Damaris into her room? Damaris had no memory of it ever being different.

Had they quarreled? And if so, over what? Was it something Damaris had done? Was that why Papa blamed her? There were times when he seemed to despise them both, though it was hard to tell what he really thought because he was cold and harsh to most people.

All her life she'd striven to please him, but she'd rarely succeeded. Papa believed in duty and obedience, not love. And original sin.

"There's bad blood in you, just like your mother."

Damaris couldn't see anything bad about Mama. But Mama hated China. She hadn't wanted to leave England and had no interest in missionary work, so that would have angered Papa. Why had they married in the first place?

She missed her mother with a fierce longing. There were so many questions she had for her, questions about herself and her father, but also questions about life and choices and . . . men. Questions only a mother could answer.

When she'd died, and they laid her in the hard, cold Chinese earth, Damaris had wept and wept until her father had shaken her by the arm and said her grief was unseemly and an offense to the Lord. She'd choked back the tears and tried to hide the chasm of loneliness that Mama had left. As if the sun had disappeared, taking with it light and warmth and leaving no life, no joy. No love.

Only duty and obedience. And original sin.

She hadn't wept since. Not even when the worst happened.

"Are you all right, Damaris?" Mrs. Jenkins stood, frowning. "Not feeling sick, are you?"

"No, Mrs. Jenkins."

"Daydreamin' about that dratted rake, I'll be bound." She shook her head. "Young girls and their foolishness! I'm tellin' you, me girl, a man like that will only lead you down the Road to Roon."

"Believe me, I'm not dreaming of him, or any other man," Damaris said firmly.

"Good, then get on with your work, girl, and don't waste time hopin' for a knight in shining armor. They don't exist."

"Yes, Mrs. Jenkins." Hoping for a knight in shining armor? Nothing was further from the truth. Damaris put her faith in work, not dreams.

"I thought you liked Mr. Monkton-Coombes," Jane said. Damaris had just finished telling Jane and Daisy about her conversation with Freddy Monkton-Coombes on the way to work that morning.

It was late and the three girls were gathered in Jane's room, toasting crumpets in front of the fire and spreading them with butter and honey. Lady Beatrice was always tired after literary society days and retired to bed early, while the girls enjoyed an informal supper.

Being together like this, their supper on a tray, with soup, boiled eggs, and toast or crumpets and honey, eaten in their bedclothes in front of the fire, evoked their earliest days together, before they'd even met Lady Beatrice, and reminded them all how lucky they were to have found each other.

Tonight three half-grown kittens watched the butter dish with proprietary interest.

"I do like him," Damaris said. "It's just that he seems to have taken it upon himself to —"

"No, I mean *like*. You know."

"Oh. No, not in that way. He's quite attractive, of course." Damaris took a sip of her hot milk, aware her cheeks were warming.

Daisy snorted. " 'Quite attractive'? He's bloody beautiful and you know it."

Damaris smiled but didn't respond. She envied the other girls' ability to say such things aloud. The freedom to admit attraction . . . without shame.

"He watches you sometimes, when you're not looking," Daisy told Damaris as she buttered a toasted crumpet.

"He — no. You're making it up."

"She's not," Jane said. "I've noticed it too."

"And you look at him in the same way, when he's not looking — like he's a sweetmeat on a stick and you're starvin' hungry." Daisy said the last words with relish.

"I don't!" Damaris's hands flew up to cover her hot cheeks.

"You do. And with a bit of encouragement, I reckon he'd —"

"No! Stop it. You know he's not looking
for a wife, and anyway, you both know marriage is the last thing I want."

Daisy shrugged and bit into a crumpet
oozing with honey and melted butter. "Only
sayin' what I see." The three kittens edged
hopefully closer.

"Besides," Damaris went on, attempting
to recover her composure, "most women
look at him like that. You've seen them in
the park, buzzing around him like bees on
borage."

"Yeah, but he's not lookin' at them, he's
lookin' at you, so with a bit of encouragement — oi, get your nose out of that, you
little devil." Daisy pushed Max, the most
impudent kitten, away from the butter dish.
Named after Lord Davenham before they'd
even met him, Max was the most adventur-
ous — and mischievous — of the kittens.

"No," Damaris said, shaking her head.
"Even if it were true, it's out of the question. You know I have an abhorrence of marriage, and so, as it happens, does he."

"Don't have to be married to act on a
fancy for a feller."

"Daisy!" Jane exclaimed, laughing. "That's
shocking."

"Just sayin'."

"Then don't, please." Damaris's cheeks flamed again and, half laughing, half serious, she said, "Spare my blushes, Daisy, I beg of you."

"It's just talk," Jane said gently. "Just girls having fun in private. You mustn't mind us." She cut off a chunk of butter, broke it into three pieces and gave one to each of the kittens. The sound of purring filled the room.

Daisy sniffed. "For a girl what spent a few nights in a brothel, you blush easy, Damaris."

"I know," Damaris said. "It's just that I've never talked like . . ."

"Like what?" Jane said, cutting her crumpet carefully in half. "Never talked about men and — and feelings and things?"

"No." Damaris had never shared her innermost thoughts with anyone, and she still found it difficult. "My mother died when I was still a young girl."

Daisy frowned. "Din't you have no one else to talk to?"

"No, not really."

"No other girls your age?" Jane asked. "At the Pillbury Home, I always had friends to talk to and share my secret thoughts with, even after Abby left."

Damaris shook her head. She covered the

butter dish and set it on a table out of reach of prowling kittens. "The girls at the mission were in my care, and much younger. It was I who listened to them."

Jane licked honey off her fingers, then wiped them with a napkin. "What about your father? Couldn't you talk to him?"

"No." He would have been the last person in the world she'd share such thoughts with. In any case, Papa thought *all* her thoughts were shameful. "There was nobody."

Daisy said, "What, not even the servants or nuffin'? The girls in the brothel used to tell me all sorts o' personal stuff. I thought everyone talked to servants."

Damaris shook her head. "We had no servants. On the mission I was everybody else's servant." She stacked the dirty dishes on the tray.

"Eh? But you're a lady."

Damaris smiled. "Lady or not, Papa said I was a servant of God and it was my privilege to take care of less-fortunate others for the sake of His Glory." How many times had Papa reproved her with those words?

"Blimey, he sounds a right laugh and a half."

Damaris gave a dry laugh. "He wasn't. Still, I loved taking care of the little ones. They were so sweet and affectionate. . . ."

Her voice cracked. There was a short silence.

"What 'appened to them?" Daisy didn't miss much.

Damaris shook her head. It was too painful to talk about.

Jane picked up Snowflake, the fluffiest kitten, saying, "Aren't the kittens growing fast?" in an attempt to change the subject. Snowflake purred loudly and snuggled against her.

Damaris flipped a feather toy around for Max and Marmalade to chase and pounce on.

"So Lady Bea was right, then," Daisy said. "You got a lot of fun to make up!"

"Lady Bea is very kind, and so are you both." Damaris leaned over and gave Daisy a one-armed hug and at the same time squeezed Jane's hand affectionately. "You know, I used to think being sold into that brothel was one of the worst things that had ever happened to me, but now I'm glad of it, for otherwise I'd never have met you two and Abby and Lady Bea, and meeting you all has been the best thing that has ever happened to me."

They watched the kittens cavorting for a few minutes, then Jane said, "You said the brothel was *one* of the worst things that had happened to you. Do you mean there was worse?"

"Oh, yes," Damaris said softly, but when they pressed her further, she changed the subject.

Damaris lay in her bed that night, thinking over the conversation. Did Freddy Monkton-Coombes really watch her, as the girls had claimed?

It was true that she watched him sometimes. So mortifying to think others had noticed.

You look at him like he's a sweetmeat on a stick and you're starvin' hungry.

She squeezed her eyes shut, as if to block out the image, but it was no good.

Because it was true; she had been sneaking looks at him: at his hands, so masculine and strong, at his long, hard legs encased in gleaming high boots. And worst of all, at his backside when he wore those tight-fitting buckskin breeches.

Papa's voice whispered in the darkness, *There's bad blood in you, just like your mother.* Original sin.

CHAPTER SIX

"Vanity and pride are different things, though the words are often used synonymously. A person may be proud without being vain. Pride relates more to our opinion of ourselves, vanity to what we would have others think of us."
— JANE AUSTEN, *PRIDE AND PREJUDICE*

"Forgive the interruption, sir, but there is a . . . a person wishing to speak with you."

Freddy looked up from his breakfast and frowned at his manservant, Tibbins. "What kind of person?"

"An *Irish* person, sir, rather rough looking."

Freddy swallowed a mouthful of ham. He didn't know any Irishmen. And he didn't want to be disturbed at his breakfast. Even if it was one in the afternoon.

"What's his name?"

"I don't know, sir. He wouldn't say."

"Did he say what he wanted?"

"No, sir."

"Did he give you a card?"

"No, sir."

"Then send him away."

"I tried, sir, but he, er, refused to go."

"Then throw the impudent fellow out."

"He tried," said a deep Irish voice from the doorway, making the valet jump. "But he's a puny wee laddie, and I'm a mite stubborn."

Freddy glanced up from his breakfast. A tall, roughly bearded ruffian lounged in his doorway. He gave Freddy a half grin, insolent and knowing, as if daring Freddy to throw him out. A gold earring glinted in a tangle of overlong black hair.

Freddy eyed the man's violently colored waistcoat and green coat thoughtfully. He drained his tankard of ale, wiped his mouth with a napkin and said in a dry voice, "Blackbeard the pirate, I presume. Max warned me to expect you."

The grin widened. "Patrick Flynn, at your service. And you'll be the Honorable Freddy Hyphen-Hyphen, I take it."

"Insolence!" Tibbins gasped and said to Freddy, "Shall I fetch help to eject him, sir?"

"No," Freddy said with a faint smile and rose from the table. "Fetch another jug of this excellent ale and another tankard and plate. And scramble some more eggs. Mr. Flynn will be joining me for breakfast."

Flynn laughed and ambled into the room. The two men shook hands. "Breakfast, is it? And here's me thinking it was nearly dinnertime. But I'll join you and gladly. That ham and those eggs look mighty good to a man who's spent the last few months livin' on salt beef and ship's biscuits."

Tibbins hesitated, still clearly doubtful of the wisdom of admitting the stranger.

"Tibbins," Freddy said, "this exotically dressed gentleman is the founder of Flynn and Company Oriental Trading, a very successful company in which I hold a quarter share. He's also one of Lord Davenham's best friends."

"Twenty-two percent, not a quarter," Flynn corrected him. "And as for 'exotic' — what's wrong with me clothes?" He stroked the dreadful waistcoat with a loving hand.

Freddy glanced at Tibbins. "See? Perfectly harmless. So fetch the ale and eggs, if you please. And some more toast." Tibbins, silent disapproval etched in every movement, set another place for the Irishman and left the room. Freddy gestured to Flynn to sit down.

"So when did you arrive in England?"

Freddy asked, carving generous slices of ham from the joint on the platter in front of him.

"This morning." Flynn snagged a morsel of ham. "Called in on Bartlett at the London office first." The London headquarters of Flynn & Co. Oriental Trading. "Max left instructions with him. Gave me your direction, said I should call on you."

Freddy nodded. "He told me to expect you. He was sorry you missed his wedding. What delayed you?"

Flynn swiped another sliver of ham and popped it in his mouth. "Delicious. Nothing like English ham. Unless it's Irish ham. Or possibly Danish." Freddy handed him a plate piled with ham and Flynn plowed into it with hearty appetite.

"So Max is married, eh?" he said through a mouthful of ham. "That was quick work. The lass tired of waiting, did she?"

"No, it wasn't that girl. It was another."

"Hmmm?" Flynn's brows rose, but he kept munching.

"I suppose you could call her a connection of his aunt."

Flynn nodded. "Plannin' to call on Lady Beatrice later today. Max left her direction with Bartlett too."

"Max married her oldest, er, niece, Abby."

111

Freddy knew perfectly well the girls were no relation of Lady Beatrice's at all — and possibly not even to each other — but Max had been like a clam as far as sharing details even with Freddy, so it was best to say nothing at all.

Tibbins arrived with a dish of scrambled eggs, a mound of toast and some more ale. Freddy watched Flynn attack the food with gusto and recalled that Max had told him the man was planning to enter society. It wasn't only clothing advice he would need, but a little social polish. Or possibly, he reflected as Flynn ate a slice of toast in one giant mouthful, a lot.

Flynn looked up from his plate. "Did Max tell you anything about me? Me intentions in coming to London, I mean."

"You mean about wishing to be married?"

"To a fine, highborn English lady, yes."

Freddy hesitated, wondering how to put it tactfully.

Flynn said, "If you're thinkin' you need to warn me that I've an iceberg's chance in hell, don't worry — Max told me that the English aristocracy has no love for Johnny-come-latelies — what do they call us? Mushrooms or cits or whatever? — let alone Irish-born Catholics, never mind how lapsed. I know all that, but I also know a tidy fortune will help the bitter pill go down. Besides, I've never met a lady yet who's failed to warm to me Irish charm." He grinned. "And I do enjoy a challenge."

"Good, then the first item on the list is to get you properly kitted out. Tibbins," Freddy called to his manservant, "a bath, a shave and a haircut for Mr. Flynn. And then a trip to my tailor."

"Your tailor?" Flynn said as the valet went to arrange a bath. "I have plenty of clothes."

Freddy gave him a flat look. "A fine, high-born English bride, you said?"

Flynn narrowed his eyes. "That's right. Any objection?"

"Not in the least," Freddy said. "If you're mad enough to want to step into parson's mousetrap, it's no business of mine. But if you want me to help you . . ." He waited.

"Go on."

"Very well, then I'll be blunt. Fine English ladies — and their fathers — might be able to overlook your Irishness; some won't mind your being a Catholic —"

"Lapsed."

"— and some will forgive the vulgarity of your being in trade; but *none* — no fine young English lady — will want to be seen in public with a man in a waistcoat like that. Nor a bright, pea green coat."

"I have a very fine purple coat."

"Burn it."

"But it's my favori—"

"Burn it," Freddy told him. "You can dress like a circus banner or you can marry a fine English lady. But not both."

Flynn scowled. "I like bright colors."

"Like them as much as you want; have your underdrawers made in green, purple, pink and orange if you wish; your dressing gown and nightshirt can be as lurid as you want; but, in public, the only colors a gentleman wears —"

"I'm not a gentleman —" Flynn began provocatively.

"If you want to marry a lady you need to *look* like a gentleman," Freddy told him. "And a gentleman wears muted colors — black, white and gray for evening wear, and for daywear, buff, black or brown breeches and a coat of brown, black, dark blue or green — dark green," he clarified, seeing Flynn was about to argue the merits of his emerald coat.

"What about red?" Flynn said hopefully.

"Only on the hunting field, and then it's called pink."

"Pink? A red coat is called pink?"

"On the hunting field. Otherwise a red coat is what soldiers wear."

Flynn pulled a face. "Damned dull if you ask me."

"I didn't ask you," Freddy pointed out. "*You* asked *me.* Now, do you want my assistance or not? I don't mind. I'm just as happy not to bother."

"I'll do it," Flynn said gloomily. "But I'll not burn me purple coat."

"Keep it if you must, but never wear it in public." Freddy rose. "Now, as soon as we have you shorn and shaved, I'll take you to Old Bond Street and introduce you to my tailor. I advise you to put yourself wholly in his hands."

"To dress me up like an undertaker?" Flynn grumbled.

"Nonsense." Freddy was shocked by the man's ignorance. "Undertakers dress quite differently. They wear black netting veils streaming from their hats, for a start. You would look ridiculous in a long black veil."

"It would be best if you waited until you were more suit— er, fashionably dressed before you call on Lady Beatrice and the young ladies," Freddy said, as Flynn stood with surprising patience being measured for a complete gentleman's wardrobe.

Freddy had to hand it to the man; once he made up his mind to cooperate with

Freddy and the tailor, he went all the way, even to bringing his portmanteau with him, so that Freddy and the tailor could select what was to be kept, which was precious little.

Flynn frowned. "I thought I'd call on them today."

Freddy shook his head. "It takes time to make a coat."

Flynn glanced at a rack containing a row of coats on hangers. "What about that lot? Would any of them fit me?" he asked the tailor.

"It wouldn't matter if they did," Freddy told him. "They're already bespoken — each is made to measure for a particular man."

"A particular man who's used to waitin' for his coat? Who's ordered it but hasn't paid for it yet?"

"Exactly."

Flynn pulled a thick roll of banknotes from his pocket and eyed the tailor. "I wonder, now, would any of those coats fit me?" He fingered the banknotes casually.

The tailor eyed the banknotes. "I will enquire, sir." He eyed Flynn's colorful waistcoat with an opprobrious eye. "A waistcoat too, I think, sir." It wasn't a question.

"Dammit, man," Freddy said to Flynn in a low voice as the man went to look through the coats. "It's not gentlemanly to bribe a tailor and steal another fellow's coat."

Flynn was unperturbed. "I'm a businessman, not a gentleman. Max told me once most gentlemen in London take months to get around to paying their tailor's bills, if at all. Can't blame the fellow for preferring a cash payment."

The tailor returned with a smart dark blue coat and a gray brocade waistcoat and helped Flynn into them. They fitted perfectly.

"Shall I dispose of these with the rest, sir?" the tailor murmured, lifting Flynn's own waistcoat and the green coat fastidiously between finger and thumb. Flynn hesitated and the tailor added, "They really aren't appropriate for a gentleman of your stamp, sir, being unfashionable, foreign made and badly cut."

"Unfashionable, foreign made *and* badly cut, eh? Oh, well, in for a penny . . ." Flynn sighed. "Go on, then, man, do what you want with them." The tailor dropped them in the arms of his assistant, who bore the offending garments away.

Flynn glanced in the looking glass and grimaced. "I look like a wet Sunday afternoon. I presume I'm fit now to meet Lady Beatrice and the young ladies?"

It was a remarkable improvement, Freddy thought, from the unshaven, long-haired, garishly attired pirate who'd sauntered into his apartment that morning, to someone who almost looked like a gentleman. Almost.

"Just remove that earring."

Flynn rolled his eyes but obeyed, pocketing the gold earring.

Freddy gave an approving nod. "Excellent. Now you're ready to meet the ladies."

"You say *this* is the famous Captain Flynn Max has spoken of?" Lady Beatrice eyed him critically through her lorgnette. A sharp old bird, Flynn thought, the kind who didn't miss much, even without that eyepiece.

"Just Mr. Flynn, if you please, m'lady. I'm no longer captain of a ship. And I don't know about famous. . . ."

"Pish-tush! Max told us quite a bit about his friend." She swiveled in her chair and said to Freddy, "Are you sure?"

"Sure of what?" he asked.

"That he's Max's Captain Flynn."

Flynn choked back a laugh. Bloody aristocracy, didn't care what they said about the peasants, never mind that he was right here in front of her. "I'm Max's partner, right enough," he assured her.

She sighed.

"Why would you doubt it, Lady Beatrice?" the pretty blonde asked, giving Flynn a flirtatious smile. Jane, Flynn reminded himself. Angelically fair, and lookin' like a fairy-tale princess. Next to her was Damaris, pale with dark hair pulled up in an elegant knot. She hadn't said a word since they were introduced, but those dark eyes missed little, he'd wager. And then there was the little one, Daisy, sitting on a stool, sewing, taking in everything. Also sharp as a tack, he reckoned. All in all, Flynn thought with satisfaction, quite a collection of interesting females.

The old lady sighed. "Max led me to expect somebody more . . . colorful. Flamboyant." It was clear she was disappointed.

"Hah!" Flynn turned an accusing eye on Freddy. "When I arrived on this shore, Lady Beatrice, I assure you I was a great deal more colorful. But since then I've been shaved, shorn, stripped of me finery and dressed with all the liveliness of a wet week in Lent, all in the name of lookin' more like a gentleman."

"Max said you wore earrings."

"Just one, m'lady, but I was convinced to

remove it." Flynn produced the gold earring from his pocket.

"Oh." Lady Beatrice sat up. "Would you put it in, please?"

Flynn inserted the ring in his ear.

"Ohhh, yes." Lady Beatrice smiled. Flynn glanced at the young ladies. Two were smiling. One wasn't.

"I was informed," he said with a withering glance at Hyphen-Hyphen, "that no English gentleman would wear such an item."

Lady Beatrice nodded. "Quite correct, but you're not an English gentleman, are you?" She smiled in a way that took the sting out. "And there's no point disguising the fact, since the moment you open your mouth everyone will know you're Irish." She turned to the three young ladies. "What do you think, gels? Should Mr. Flynn give up his earring, or do we like the hint of pirate air it gives him?" There was no doubt what the old lady preferred.

Jane nodded. "I think it's very dashing."

Damaris inclined her head thoughtfully, then nodded. "If you'd asked me before, I would have thought that an earring would have detracted from a man's masculinity, but now, seeing Mr. Flynn wearing one, it doesn't detract at all, does it? It only adds to it."

Hyphen-Hyphen scowled and crossed his high-booted legs.

"Daisy, what do you think?" Jane asked.

Daisy glanced at Flynn and wrinkled her nose. "I don't like it. It makes 'im look like a common sailor from down the docks, or some bloke wiv an organ and a monkey."

"Nonsense," Lady Beatrice said briskly. "Mr. Flynn carries it off with an air. And no common sailor or organ-grinder could afford clothes like that, even if they are a little on the dull side."

"Dull?" Monkton-Coombes said indignantly. "He couldn't possibly enter society dressed the way he was. Max asked me to ensure Flynn had access to the finest sartorial advice, and dash it, that's what I did. Introduced him to my own tailor."

"And he looks almost as elegant as you, dear boy; you've done a fine job," the old lady assured him, examining Flynn again through her lorgnette. "Only . . . I think Mr. Flynn needs something a little more . . . distinctive."

"Distinctive?" Both men spoke at once.

She nodded. "Something to ensure the *ton* knows you don't give the snap of your fingers for their good opinion."

"But I thought —" Flynn began.

"I would advise you to keep wearing your

earring, Mr. Flynn. It will bring you a little notice, a hint of notoriety." She gave him a sharp look. "Will you mind that?"

"No indeed, ma'am. I'm here to find meself a fine lady to wed, but I'm not ashamed of who I am or what I've done. And while I'm happy to have me manners polished up a bit, and to wear the kind of clothes Hyph— er, Mr. Monkton-Coombes advises, I'll not be pretending I'm other than who I am."

"A fine lady, is it?" The old lady's elegantly plucked brows rose.

"Yes, ma'am," Flynn said coolly. "The finest young lady in London. I've always aimed high in everything I've done, and I see no reason to change."

"You know that being Irish — and, I presume, Catholic — will count against you? And I understand from Max you have no family remaining alive, and what you had was wholly undistinguished."

She called a spade a spade, this old bird, and Flynn liked her the better for it. "Correct, m'lady. Still and all, I reckon I'm a bit of a catch. I'm a self-made man with a fleet of ships at my command. I'm clean, healthy and have all me own teeth. I'm loyal to me friends and I'll be loyal to a wife. I reckon that makes me equal to some of your fine

English gents."

"I suspect it does, Mr. Flynn, and better than many. And being a friend of my nephew, I suppose you expect me to introduce you to the finest young ladies in London, do you?"

He flashed her a grin. "I don't expect anything, m'lady, but that would be grand." He bowed over her hand and kissed it.

She laughed and waved him away. "You left something off your list of attributes, Mr. Flynn."

"And what would that be, m'lady?"

"Cheek. And a measure of raffish charm." Lady Beatrice grinned and clapped her hands. "I'm so pleased Max sent you to me, Mr. Flynn. I adore matchmaking."

Behind him Monkton-Coombes made a hastily muffled choking sound. She heard, and turned on him with a severe look. "And, Freddy Monkton-Coombes, there is *nothing* more gratifying than working with a man who *knows* what he wants."

Monkton-Coombes rose from his seat saying, "Well, since you've all got plans to make, I'll take my leave. Devastated to depart this jolly gathering, Lady Beatrice — matchmaking, what fun indeed, can't imagine anything more delightful — but I have an urgent appointment with, er, my bootmaker. Flynn, all right if I leave you in the ladies' hands?" It was clear he couldn't wait to be gone.

"Very much so, thank you," Flynn said, repressing a grin. "And would you mind sending a note to that tailor of yours to return me old clothes? If Lady Beatrice says I can wear colors —"

"Too late," Monkton-Coombes said with ill-concealed satisfaction. "His apprentice put them on the back step. They'll have been snapped up by the first beggar that came along. You'll just have to put up with looking elegant and fashionable instead. Let that earring give you the distinctiveness you apparently need. Lady Beatrice, Miss Chance, Miss Jane, Miss Daisy, I'll see you all tomorrow." He gave an elegant bow and left.

Flynn spent another half hour talking with Lady Beatrice and the girls, but the old lady soon tired. "Time for my nap, I'm afraid, Mr. Flynn. But come to dinner this evening at eight and we shall talk more. And come to my literary salon tomorrow afternoon, sir — and wear your earring. Let's see how you dazzle the fine young ladies there."

Flynn took his leave and was ushered out by the butler. The little one called Daisy followed him into the hall, her basket on

124

her arm. She waved the butler away and turned to Flynn.

"You're not happy wiv your new clothes, Mr. Flynn?"

Flynn shrugged. "Never figured meself for the role of peahen, that's all."

She frowned. "Peahen? Don't you mean peacock?"

"In this?" He looked down at himself disparagingly. "There's more color in a muddy puddle."

She moved closer and said in a confiding voice, "I could make you a lovely colorful waistcoat if you liked."

Flynn eyed her. Was the lass flirting with him? He gave her a slow smile. "Could you indeed?"

She nodded and produced a piece of gorgeously embroidered fabric from her basket. "I've got some lovely material 'ere. Make a fine gentleman's waistcoat, it would. Give you that bit of distinctiveness Lady Bea was talkin' about. You could become known for your waistcoats. A hint of flamboyance, but nothin' vulgar. A snap of your fingers to the drabness of male fashion."

Flynn examined the fabric. Chinese silk — good heavy quality too — embroidered green dragons and golden firebirds on a crimson background. Exactly the kind of thing he liked. Hyphen-Hyphen and the tailor would probably loathe it. A point in its favor.

She leaned closer and lowered her voice enticingly. "How 'bout I make this into a beautiful waistcoat, just for you?"

Flynn smiled down at her. She was a pretty little thing. Oh, but a man missed flirtin' in those long months at sea. Not to mention other feminine attributes. "And why would you do that for me?" he asked softly.

She gave him an odd look. "For money of course," she said. "Why else?"

He threw back his head and laughed. It wasn't his body she had her sharp little eye on, it was his wallet. "How much?"

She pointed to his new waistcoat. "How much did you pay for that?"

He told her.

"Mine'll cost you double," she said.

"Double?" It was outrageous, even at London prices.

She shrugged. "You'll like it twice as much." She darted him a speculative glance. "Maybe even three times as much."

He laughed again. "All right, make it up, and if I like it half as much as you reckon I will, I'll pay you double. But I warn you, I'm very particular."

She snorted. "So am I. I'll make you the finest waistcoat in London, just see if I don't. You might even set a trend, if" — she gave him an assessing look, which dwelt for a disparaging moment on the earring — "you can carry it off."

"It's not your ordinary literary society," Freddy explained to Flynn as he rang the doorbell of Lady Beatrice's home on Berkeley Square. "You won't be expected to know anything."

Flynn gave him a dry look. "I do read, you know."

"Of course, but — oh, here we are. Featherby." He nodded to the butler.

"Mr. Monkton-Coombes, Mr. Flynn." Featherby greeted them as he took their coats, hats and gloves and passed them to an underling. "You've timed it well, sir. We'll be starting in a few minutes."

"Much of a crowd this afternoon?" Freddy asked.

"Yes, sir, attendance grows daily. Especially of the younger men. Lady Beatrice is delighted."

The younger men, eh? He'd noticed the trend himself. "I see," he said grimly.

As they mounted the stairs, Flynn murmured, "Problem?"

Freddy shook his head, not yet ready to share his concerns with a man who, after all, he'd only just met, even if he was a friend of Max.

They entered the salon and Lady Beatrice immediately waved them over. "Freddy, dear boy; Mr. Flynn, how delightful; let me introduce you to my friends. . . ." A few minutes later a little silver bell tinkled.

Flynn joined him at the back of the room. "Interesting collection of people," he murmured, then a hush fell as Jane began to read.

"Emma and Harriet had been walking together one morning, and, in Emma's opinion, had been talking enough of Mr. Elton for that day. . . ."

Freddy quite agreed. He would be happy if he never heard another thing about Emma, Harriet, Mr. Frank Elton or any of them.

He glanced at Flynn to see how he was taking it. The Irishman was leaning against the wall, arms folded, and appeared to be listening with every evidence of appreciation.

Freddy scanned the audience. There were more young men here. Why? Surely they couldn't all have developed a sudden taste for literature.

And several of them, while not actively hunting for rich brides, were known to be in need of a topping-up of the family coffers. What could have brought them here? These girls hadn't a penny but what the old lady gave them.

He glanced across the room at the old lady. She caught his eye and winked, looking inordinately pleased with herself.

A cold, prickling feeling slid down his spine. Oh, God, what was she up to now?

In the break between chapters, Freddy sent Flynn over to keep an eye on the girls while he did some delicate investigation. He spied Lady Beatrice in the center of a small group of ladies and sidled up behind them, unseen, to eavesdrop.

". . . Of course it's so difficult chaperoning heiresses," she was saying. "Especially with Max away. And when fortune hunters start circling . . ."

A lady leaned forward and asked in a low, excited voice, "So it's true what I heard. Your nieces are heiresses?"

Blast the old lady and her tricks, Freddy thought. "No," he said in a loud, firm voice. "They're not."

"Oh!" Lady Beatrice glanced at him and clapped a hand over her mouth in stage-worthy dismay. "I forgot! I'm not supposed to —" She broke off with an apologetic grimace. "Sorry, dear boy," she whispered quite audibly.

She turned to her companions and recited like a well-rehearsed schoolgirl, "He's quite right. I know *nothing* of any heiresses or fortunes. And I know nothing *at all* about the Chancealotto inheritance."

Freddy ground his teeth.

"The Chancealotto inheritance?" The ladies breathed in unison.

"*Never* heard of it," Lady Beatrice said firmly. "That's right, isn't it, Freddy, dear boy?" Her eyes were dancing with mischief.

Freddy scowled at her, silently cursing the old lady, and Max for saddling him with her. What the devil was he supposed to do now?

CHAPTER SEVEN

"I can hardly tell why, or in what
the deception originated."
— JANE AUSTEN, *SENSE AND SENSIBILITY*

"A word in private, if you please, Lady Beatrice." Freddy had waited behind until the last of the literary society guests had departed.

The old lady smiled and patted his cheek. "Oh, I do love it when a man gets all stern and masterful. Soooo attractive." Sitting herself down on the nearest chair, she waited with a mischievous expression. "Go ahead, dear boy. Are you going to spank me?"

He couldn't help but laugh, and of course it completely ruined the speech he'd been rehearsing in his mind for the last half hour. He sat in the chair opposite her. "Why did you do it?"

"Do what?"

"Spread the rumor that the girls were heir-esses."

"But I didn't, dear boy. You heard me. I told everyone that I'd never heard of the Chancealotto inheritance, and that there was no such thing."

"Yes, but you must have started the rumor in the —"

She gave him an indignant look. "I most certainly did not! I *denied* it from the very beginning — there's a big difference. I promised Max before his wedding that I wouldn't tell any more lies about the girls, and I haven't," she said with a virtuous expression, quite ruined by the glee that sparkled in her eyes.

"Don't give me that. You knew exactly what you were doing," Freddy said severely. "And if Max strangles you when he gets home, at the trial I will testify on his behalf that it was entirely justified."

She gave a gurgle of laughter.

"But why would you do something so . . . so . . ." Words failed him.

"Clever? The gels needed practice."

He frowned. "What sort of practice?"

"On men. Only men of my generation come to my literary society and, while they're perfectly happy to flirt with my pretty nieces, the gels really need to practice on young men, so they're prepared for their come-out. Inexperienced gels can usually handle older men, but they're more apt to get flustered by the attentions of a handsome young devil. So I enticed in a few younger men for them to practice on."

Freddy couldn't believe his ears. "Were the girls party to this — this strategy?" He couldn't imagine Damaris agreeing to such an outrageous thing.

"No, of course not, dear boy. They worry too much, those gels. Max does too, poor boy."

"I can't imagine why."

She laughed. "Pooh, what's the point of life if you don't make it a little interesting?"

"Have you thought about what would happen if one of the girls fell for a fortune hunter? What then?"

She gave him a serene smile. "My gels won't be taken in by men of that ilk. And in the meantime, they can practice on 'em."

He groaned. She was impossible. The sooner Max came home the better.

It was dark, pouring with rain, and freezing cold. He was mad, Freddy thought blearily as he dressed. Wretched, stubborn, prideful girl.

He glanced in the looking glass and ran a

hand over his stubbled chin. He wasn't going to shave for her, not at this hour. Tibbins was already exuding silent disapproval of this change in their routine.

Tibbins was not what anyone would call a joyful morning riser, but he never voiced his displeasure in words, only through a series of sniffs and sighs and lugubrious glances. Freddy was well versed in their meanings.

"Think of it as the end of a long night," Freddy advised him.

Tibbins sighed and handed Freddy his neck cloth. "But it isn't, sir, is it?"

"I often used to return at this hour and it never bothered you then."

"It is not the same, sir," Tibbins said in an austere voice.

"No. Then I was coming home after a night of pleasure and now I'm leaving a warm and cozy bed purely out of duty. Other than that, it's the same thing."

Tibbins sniffed.

Freddy frowned. Bad enough it was a freezing wet morning; he wasn't going to be sniffed at by his valet as well. "It's not that I *want* to get up before the crack of blasted dawn, but I made a promise to Lord Davenham I'd look after his sisters-in-law. I have no choice, blast it — I gave my word."

"Duty, is it, sir?" Tibbins sniffed again. "I

see, sir." The words said one thing, the tone another. He passed Freddy his hat and an umbrella. "Good morning, sir."

Freddy ran down the stairs, paused on the front step and contemplated the dismal scene outside. Filthy blasted weather. He must be mad to go out in it. But she left him no choice.

Of course, any sensible woman would stay in bed on a morning like this. But oh, no, she was a stubborn wench — she'd be out in the freezing cold rain, tramping through the muddy streets, catching her death.

He put up the umbrella and stepped out into the driving rain. Tibbins was a fool. Why else would he be doing this, except out of duty? He'd given his word.

A carriage drove past, splashing his buck-skins with muddy water. He brushed it off irritably. Blasted Max. It was all his fault.

He waited for her in the lane until she emerged from the side entrance. She looked fresh and glowing and gave him a sunny smile, apparently not the slightest bit bothered by the filthy weather. At least she'd availed herself of an umbrella, even if it was a dainty feminine useless thing with a frill that was bound to drip on her. His umbrella was large and black and far more efficient. He held it over her. "Here. No sensible female would go out in weather like this."

"I have a job," she said tranquilly. "People don't stop working simply because the weather is a little wet. And good morning to you too."

He ushered her to the end of the lane, where he had a cab waiting. She stopped. "A cab?"

"Of course a cab," he said crossly. "Do you think I'm going to let you walk through the filthy streets in this filthy weather? You'll get splashed and wet and dirty and then you'll sit inside that wretched pottery all day in wet clothes. Max wouldn't allow it and neither will I. Now, will you stand about arguing all day and drowning us both, or will you get in the blasted cab?"

She got in the blasted cab without a word, an odd little smile on her face.

He gave the cab the direction of the pottery and the cab set off. She still had that little smile.

"What's so amusing?"

"Nothing much, just a small irony."

Freddy scowled. "Irony? What irony?" People should know better than to fling words like *irony* around at this uncivilized hour, let alone in weather like this.

"Just that the cost of this cab is probably more than I'll earn in a day at the pottery."

"Irony? That's not irony — it's plain female stupidity and stubbornness."

Her smile widened. "My, but you are in a charming mood this morning."

He glowered. "Blame Max."

They lapsed into silence for a while. The cab rumbled along, twisting and turning through the streets. "You won't need to worry about that fellow Blenkinsop," he said after a while.

"Oh?"

"I've warned him off."

"Oh." Her expression was perfectly inscrutable.

Blast it, what did *oh* mean? Was it *oh,* meaning good, well done? *Oh,* thank you Mr. Monkton-Coombes for ridding me of a pestilential knave? Or *oh,* but I enjoy the attentions of idiots like Blenkinsop?

"If he bothers you again, let me know."

"Thank you for your concern, but he doesn't bother me. I'm quite able to deal with Mr. Blenkinsop."

So it was *oh,* stay out of my affairs. Freddy folded his arms and glowered out the window. Blasted stubborn independent female.

"Letter just arrived for you, sir." The porter at Freddy's bachelor lodgings indicated the letter on the sideboard. Freddy picked it

137

up, grimaced as he recognized his mother's writing, pocketed it and continued up the stairs. No doubt she was coming to town and wanted his services as an escort. That was the usual reason she wrote: to drag him somewhere to meet some muffin or other.

He entered his rooms, shrugged off his coat and tossed it to Tibbins, his manservant, poured himself a brandy and sat down to read his mother's missive.

My dear Frederick,

The time has come for you to do your duty. Your father is not getting any younger and the future of the estate and the perpetuation of his family name preys greatly on his mind. As the only remaining Monkton-Coombes son, it is incumbent on you to marry and beget heirs. Your father and I have been very patient but it is clear to us that you have no interest in giving up the frivolous life you lead in order to embrace your responsibilities. Nor have you made any serious attempt to find a suitable bride.

To that end, and since the only time you deign to visit us at Breckenridge is in early December, we have arranged a small house party at that time where a selection of suitable young ladies will be assembled for you to choose from. At the end of the house party your father will announce your betrothal. A spring wedding will follow and by this time next year we hope an heir for Breckenridge will be on the way. Your cooperation in this matter will perhaps enable your father to forgive you, and bring about the reconciliation with him that I have so longed for. We look forward to seeing you at Breckenridge on the fifth.

Your loving mother,
Louisa, Viscountess Breckenridge

He stared at the letter. A house party at Breckenridge — in early December. He couldn't believe she'd stoop so low. . . .

She'd trapped him, dammit. Hoist him with his own petard.

The fifth of December was the one day of the year — the only day — he visited the family seat. In sixteen years he'd never missed and his mother knew damned well why — and it wasn't to see her or his father.

Now, to hold a house party on the occasion. It was . . . it was *desecration,* dammit.

He wouldn't stand for it. He wouldn't go.

He *had* to go. He'd never once missed the annual service held in the little family chapel. His annual atonement.

He glanced down at the letter again. Oh, she could twist the knife, could Mama. *As the only remaining Monkton-Coombes son.* And we all know whose fault that is, don't we, Mama?

His mouth twisted and with a muttered curse he crushed the letter into a ball and hurled it into the fire. It smoked, blackened, then burst into flame.

His loving mother. Indeed. Sacrifice himself on the altar of marriage to a muffin on the off chance of a possible reconciliation with his father?

As if he hadn't tried for years. It wasn't Freddy who'd set his mind and heart against his only remaining son.

He shook his head. After sixteen years of bashing his head — and pride — against the brick wall that was his father, he was inured against the hurt.

He rose and paced the room, tight with anger and frustration. He was accustomed to the hints, the tears, the nagging, but this — this was a new low, turning an occasion that *mattered,* dammit, into a house party with a bunch of muffins jockeying for position.

He would *not* dance to their tune. He was a grown man of eight and twenty, and he'd take a bride when he was damned well ready to — if he ever was. And the more they harped on marriage the less inclined toward it he became.

In the grate, blackened shreds of crested, linen-weave paper twisted gently, ghostly writing still faintly visible, taunting him. Freddy flung the brandy glass into the fire. There was faint satisfaction in the sound of smashing glass and the hiss and flare of the brandy hitting the flames, but not enough.

The noise brought his manservant running. "Sir?"

"Fetch my coat," Freddy said curtly. "I'm going out."

"Anywhere special?" asked a voice from the doorway. It was Flynn.

"I was about to announce him, sir," the valet said. Freddy waved him away.

"Bad time, is it?" Flynn asked.

Freddy harnessed his temper. "Not really. I'd just decided I needed a bout or two at Jackson's boxing saloon."

Flynn's brows rose. "Boxing, is it? Mind if I come along?"

Freddy shrugged. "Be my guest. But I warn you, I'm in a mood to give someone a thrashing."

"Fine. I wouldn't mind a bit of exercise meself."

Freddy grabbed his coat and headed for

the door. The landing outside was busy with workmen carrying boxes and trunks and bits of furniture.

"The set of rooms upstairs is being vacated. Poor fool is getting married," Freddy explained as they waited for a large trunk to be wrestled around the bend in the stairs. He glanced at Flynn. "Tibbins says it hasn't been let yet. If you were interested, I could have a word with the landlord."

Flynn shook his head. "Thank you, but no — I've made me arrangements."

"That was quick."

Flynn grinned. "After dinner last night Lady Beatrice invited me to stay as long as I want."

Freddy's brows rose. "Indeed?" Flynn had been invited to stay? Indefinitely? Of course, Lady Beatrice would do anything for Max, but still, the Irishman must have a way about him to receive an invitation like that. Freddy knew for a fact that Max had no plans to house Flynn with his aunt; he'd mentioned to Freddy that Flynn would need to find bachelor quarters.

Flynn shrugged. "She said she'd feel safer in the house with a man living there."

Freddy snorted. "I could have sworn she already had a butler, a giant footman who used to be an ornament of the ring — he

once fought against Jackson, you know —
and two other strong young footmen."

"Ah, but none of them is Irish." Flynn
grinned. "And Lady Bea told me herself,
servants are all very well, but they're just
not the same."

Freddy wasn't going to argue. These new
arrangements suited him perfectly. If Flynn
was staying at Lady Beatrice's, he could take
over some of Freddy's guard dog duties,
starting with escorting the girls to parks
filled with lurking blasted muffins.

The thought sparked the anger in him
again. "Come on, let's go." He needed to
punch someone; he didn't much care who.

CHAPTER EIGHT

"That is what a young man ought to be. Whatever be his pursuits, his eagerness in them should know no moderation, and leave him no sense of fatigue."
— JANE AUSTEN, *SENSE AND SENSIBILITY*

The bell rang, calling the end of the bout. Several gentlemen applauded.

Flynn was panting. He flexed his jaw cautiously. "Damn, but you actually know how to box, Hyphen-Hyphen. Never would have dreamed a fine gentleman like yourself could throw such a punishing left."

Freddy wiped a trickle of sweat from his brow. "You're not so bad yourself, Irishman."

"Shame those gentlemanly tactics would be no use in a real fight."

Freddy stiffened. "I've been in plenty of real fights."

"Sure, with other gents, I bet. But in the

144

back alleys and down on the docks, if you get into trouble, they won't be followin' Broughton's rules or anything like 'em, you know."

Freddy eyed the big Irishman. He glanced over to where Jackson stood watching. "My friend Flynn here has offered me a challenge, abandoning the rules and showing me how they fight in the back alleys and the docks." There were strict rules about how one behaved in Jackson's boxing saloon.

Jackson considered it, then nodded. "I'll referee, then, so it doesn't get out of hand." Several more gentlemen drifted over to watch.

The bell rang to open the round. Before it finished ringing, Flynn lashed out with a kick to the groin. Freddy just managed to avoid it and took the blow on the thigh. There was a murmur of disapproval from the watching gentlemen.

Flynn grinned. "I did warn you. I'm fighting dirty."

"You don't say," Freddy drawled and, without warning, feinted with his left and at the same time tried to kick Flynn's feet out from under him. What followed was dirty, exciting — and educational. When the first bout ended, Flynn showed Freddy a few of the more devious moves that had flattened him. Then the bell went and it was on again.

After three fast and furious bouts, Jackson called the end of the session. Freddy and Flynn staggered apart, sweaty, panting, battered, bruised, bleeding in a couple of places — and grinning.

A spattering of applause burst from those gathered around to watch.

Jackson examined their injuries himself. "Nothing that won't mend." He signaled attendants to bring towels and bowls of water.

Flynn splashed his face and rubbed a towel over his bare chest and arms. He was panting heavily. "That wasn't a half-bad fight."

Freddy nodded, too winded to reply. He wiped a trickle of sweat from his brow that turned out to be blood. He'd have quite a few cuts and bruises to show for the morning's work — but beneath the tiredness and the aches and pains, he felt both relaxed and invigorated. The bout had purged him of the frustration and anger of the morning.

And somehow, in the process of trying to pound each other into the ground, by fair means and foul, he and Flynn had become friends. They washed, dried off and dressed again.

"Drink?" Freddy said. "Something to eat?"

"That'd be grand."

Freddy touched the cut over his eye gingerly. It was still oozing blood. "My lodgings all right? I'd like to get this covered up before we meet any ladies."

Flynn agreed and they strolled up Bond Street, reminiscing about fights they'd seen and some they'd participated in.

"When did you take up the noble art of pugilism?" Flynn asked as they approached Freddy's lodgings.

"I was a scrawny young runt when I was first sent away to school. Some of the bigger fellows made my life hell, so I learned to box."

"You kept it up, obviously."

"I like the exercise." They entered Freddy's lodgings. He rang the bell for his manservant. "Claret, ale or brandy?"

"Tea, if you don't mind."

"Tea?"

"Picked up the habit in the East. I don't mind the other, but it's a little early in the day for me."

"Tea, then, for Mr. Flynn, Tibbins, and some sandwiches. I'll be back in a moment," Freddy said. "I'll just attend to this cut."

A few minutes later he returned, having

cleaned up the cut over his eye, smeared it with ointment and covered it with a plaster so as not to distress feminine sensibilities. At the same moment Tibbins returned with a tray bearing a pot of tea, two cups and a large plate of sandwiches. Outside it started to rain again. Freddy dropped into a chair in front of the fire and stared into the flames while Tibbins poured the tea, then withdrew.

Flynn stirred a lump of sugar into his tea and drank it in silence. He ate a sandwich. He ate another sandwich. He glanced at Freddy's cup, which was untouched, and the plate of sandwiches.

"Not hungry?"

Freddy didn't respond.

Flynn ate another two sandwiches. In the street outside a wagon rolled past, its wheels rattling over the cobblestones. "The boxing didn't help as much as you hoped," Flynn said after a while. "Care to talk about it?"

Freddy gave him a sharp glance.

Flynn shrugged. "Sometimes helps to get it off your chest." He refilled his cup, stirred in some sugar and picked up another sandwich. "I know how to keep a confidence."

There was a long silence, broken only by the sound of the rain beating on the windows, the fire hissing and the chomping of sandwiches.

Freddy picked up the tea, tasted it, grimaced, walked over to the sideboard and poured himself a brandy. Resuming his seat, he sipped and twirled the glass thoughtfully, gazing through the swirling golden liquor to the glowing coals of the fire.

"Woman trouble?" Flynn asked.

Freddy gave a dry laugh. "Not in the way you're thinking. It's my mother."

"Ah." Flynn ate another sandwich and lapsed into a companionable silence. You learned quite a bit about a man when you'd fought him, Freddy reflected. And he was Max's good friend. Why not? It couldn't hurt.

"My brother, George, died when I was twelve," Freddy began. "He was the heir, you understand, the older brother." He swallowed some more brandy.

"We did everything together — we were only two years apart. He was . . . he was the best brother a boy could have. And the best son. He was . . . perfect. Clever, brave, good at whatever he did, a quick student, a gallant rider to hounds, a brilliant cricketer . . . there was nothing he didn't do well. Everybody loved him. I loved him."

He stared into the flames awhile, then said, "I killed him." He drained the glass.

"How — ?" Flynn began, but Freddy held

up his hand.

"It doesn't matter how — that's old history. The thing is, he died on December the fifth, sixteen years ago. And every year since, I go home on December the fifth — there's a memorial service in the family chapel." He looked at Flynn. "It's the only time I ever visit Breckenridge, my childhood home. I stay away the rest of the year — my parents and I . . . well . . ."

He poured another brandy. "But once a year I go down there and attend the service for my brother. I endure —" He broke off. "My parents endure a day of my company, and the next morning I leave, not to return until the following year."

Flynn frowned. "You don't visit your family? Not even for Christmas?"

"I bump into my mother occasionally in town. She sometimes requires me to escort her to the theater or a party or some such thing. They always come to town for the season. And when Parliament is sitting, of course."

"Your father?"

Freddy lifted a shoulder. "Rarely. We belong to different clubs, move in different circles." He attempted a smile. "Mine are generally less respectable."

Flynn ate the last sandwich. "The fifth of

December is, what, about four weeks away?"

Freddy nodded. He leaned forward, seized the poker and stabbed at the coals heaped in the fireplace, stirring them so that sparks danced in mad spirals and vanished into the chimney.

"I'm the heir now. Because George is dead."

Flynn nodded.

"They want me to marry and produce another heir. Another George." He added, "In our family the oldest son is always George, the second always Frederick."

Flynn crossed his booted feet, leaned back and waited. His gold earring glinted in the firelight. He was a good listener, for a pirate.

"For the past few years my mother has been thrusting muffins at me at every opportunity."

Flynn frowned and glanced at the plate where only a few crumbs and a sprig of parsley remained. "Muffins?"

"Not the edible sort — females. Eligible females. Seriously marriage-minded eligible females, usually of the reforming type," he added savagely, "because I'm a frivolous fool who can't be trusted to manage the estate."

"Can't be trusted?" Flynn's brows rose. "Then they don't know — ?"

"No, and I'm not going to tell them. Even if they believed me — which they wouldn't — it's none of their concern."

Flynn nodded slowly. "I see. Well, I suppose you know your own business. So what's the problem? You can't tell me you're worried by your mother's attempts to marry you off to one of these, er, muffins, because I won't believe it. You're no weakling and you cut the apron strings years ago, I'll be bound."

Freddy nodded. "When I was eighteen. And you're right: She can't make me — *they* can't make me do anything I don't want to. I'm financially independent of them, thanks to Great-Aunt Adelaide and her fortune."

"As I understand it, she left you a competence only, a useful sum. It was you who turned it into a fortune."

"Partly with the help of Flynn and Co. Oriental Trading," Freddy acknowledged. "But that's not the point. The point is that my mother has now invited a flock of the most horrendous muffins to attend a house party at Breckenridge."

"Your family home? And, don't tell me, it's coinciding with your visit on the fifth of December."

"The only reason I'm going there is for George, and she's blasted well desecrating the event with muffins."

There was a short silence. Flynn rose and poured himself a brandy. He refilled Freddy's glass too. "It's a pickle," he said after a while.

"It's a bloody disgrace."

"I suppose you've told her you won't stand for the interference."

Freddy gave him a baleful look. Of course he had. A hundred times.

"And there's nobody else you want to marry?"

"I'm never going to get married."

Flynn's brows rose. "And here's me thinkin' you were quite the lady's man."

"That's got nothing to do with marriage."

"Indeed it hasn't." Flynn gave a gusty sigh of reminiscence. "Still, I've made up me mind to buckle down and become a good husband." He glanced at Freddy. "Comes to us all in the end."

"Not to me."

"Not ever?"

"Never."

"Then you'll just have to put up with your mother's muffin shenanigans. It's that or bite the bullet and get engaged to some female you think you could bear to wed, if the worst came to the worst. If you were betrothed, your mother'd stop shovin' muffins at you. And she'd have to cancel that house party."

"What are you talking about? I just told you I don't want to get betrothed. Or married."

"I'm thinkin' of one of those betrothals that go on forever — could even go on for years if neither of you were in a hurry. And hope that the girl eventually gets bored or fed up with you and calls it off — because as I understand it, in England it's only the females who can call off a betrothal."

Freddy stared at him. He swirled his brandy thoughtfully.

Flynn shook his head. "I know, it's a mad idea. What woman would be happy to wait for years, you bein' such a handsome piece of husbandly temptation, rich, and in line for a title."

"You're right," Freddy said. "It's a mad idea." He put down his brandy glass, looked at the empty plate and gave Flynn an indignant look. "You've eaten all the sandwiches." He raised his voice. "Tibbins, more sandwiches. And a fresh pot of tea."

"What happened to you?" It was the first thing she said to him, not even a good morning.

"Nothing. And good morning to you too."

She rolled her eyes. "You have a plaster on your forehead, your jaw is bruised in several places and you have a swollen lip. And you're limping slightly."

"It's nothing. Shall we go?"

"You've been in a fight."

"No, no. Mr. Flynn was simply demonstrating some of the finer points of the art of pugilism as practiced in places he's familiar with. And before you ask, we came out even."

"Mr. Flynn? You two didn't quarrel, did you?"

He grinned. "On the contrary; if anything, it cemented our friendship."

She gave him a long look. "Men are strange."

"Strange, but women seem to like us nevertheless." He presented his arm in a jaunty manner. "Shall we?"

Damaris took it, giving him a sideways glance. "It does seem to have improved your mood." She'd assumed that by now he'd be sick of walking her to work, especially since he'd been so grumpy and cross about the rain the other day. She'd half expected him either to drop it or to assign a footman to accompany her. Or to inform Lady Beatrice, which would effectively put an end to it anyway.

But there he was, as elegantly dressed as always, except for the unshaven chin.

It fascinated her, that chin. She longed to run her fingers over it, to feel the scrape of his dark gold bristles, the shape of the bone underneath.

Papa whispered reprimands in her head. She ignored him. There was nothing whatsoever improper in the way she was behaving. Any thoughts she had were just that — thoughts.

They walked on for a moment in silence, her hand warm in the crook of his arm. It was pleasant, she had to admit, this feeling of being cared for. Even if she could look after herself perfectly well.

Out of the blue he said, "You know some people believe you to be heiresses?"

"I know. Lady Beatrice started the rumor, didn't she?"

"Oh, no, you're quite wrong there," he said with a mix of asperity and wry humor. "She assured me she didn't *start* a rumor, she merely *denied* one." He glanced down at her. "Thus ensuring everyone —"

"Believes it to be true." Damaris laughed, shaking her head. "And I suppose she shows no remorse?"

"Remorse?" He gave her a shocked look. "Whatever for? She's denied the lie to everyone who will listen, which makes her practically a saint."

Damaris chuckled. "Well, it won't make any difference to me. And Daisy's not planning to marry, either, so it's only Jane who'll be affected. And since she's after a man who's —" She broke off, biting her lip. Jane's determination to marry a rich man wasn't hers to share. These morning excursions, with nobody else around, had caused a kind of intimacy to grow between her and Mr. Monkton-Coombes and she'd spoken without thinking.

"A man who's — ?"

"It doesn't matter."

As they waited to let a heavily laden cart pass in front of them, he turned his head to look at her. "So you're still determined never to marry? You're completely sure?"

She stiffened. "If you're going to harp on about that again —"

"No, no, I wasn't going to try to change your mind — quite the contrary. I feel the same." He hesitated, and she felt him tense. "But if you're quite sure about never wanting to marry, I have a . . . a proposition for you."

Damaris withdrew her hand from his arm and stepped back. She couldn't look at him, she was so disappointed. Daisy was right —

he had been watching her with intent. Mrs. Jenkins too — he was a rake after all. "No, I won't be your mistress."

"Mistress? Have you got maggots in your brain?" He sounded indignant. "Do you think I'd propose such a liaison with the unmarried sister-in-law of my oldest friend? Let alone the fact that Lady Beatrice would skin me alive."

"She wouldn't."

"No, she'd have that giant footman of hers do it. Good God, woman, what *were* you thinking?"

She gave him a wary look. "What were *you* thinking?"

"Nothing immoral or improper, for a start." He frowned. "Well, it's not exactly proper, but it's certainly nothing society would condemn you for." His frown deepened. "Well, they might censure you a little if they knew the whole story, but they won't, so it's me they'll blame. You would — you *will*, I hope — come out of it smelling of roses." He gave her a thoughtful look. "Or gardenias — you're more of a gardenia type."

By the end of this tangled speech she wanted to laugh. She'd acquitted him of dark designs on her person but was still no wiser as to the so-called proposition. "Perhaps you'd better explain what it is you want and I'll be the judge of whether it's immoral or not."

"Right." He took her arm again and they resumed walking. "You know, I think, that my parents have been putting pressure on me to get married — well, of course you know — you've met some of the muffins."

"Muffins?"

"My mother's favored candidates for daughter-in-law, the Armthwaite sisters —"

"What, both of them?"

"Don't be flippant. Either would be quite horror enough. And then there's Miss Blee, and Miss — well, you know what I mean. You've seen 'em in action."

Damaris nodded. "None of them pleases you."

"Good God, I should think not — far from it."

"But there must be other girls, nicer girls —"

"That's not the point. The thing is, I don't want to get married at all. Or at least not for years. I like my life the way it is."

"Without responsibilities."

He seemed about to argue but then shrugged. "Without a wife."

"So what do you want me to do?"

He stopped, turned to face her and took a deep breath. "Become betrothed to me."

CHAPTER NINE

"I am excessively fond of a cottage."
— JANE AUSTEN, *SENSE AND SENSIBILITY*

"*Betrothed?* How many times must I tell you I have *no* intention of ever getting marr—" She stepped away from him, looking unaccountably upset.

Freddy cursed himself silently. For a man of address, he was making a complete mull of this. He caught her hands and when she tried to pull away, he held tighter. "I didn't ask you to marry me, I asked you to become *betrothed* to me!"

She stopped tugging and gave him a puzzled look. "It's the same thing."

"It's not. I don't want a real betrothal — in fact I'm counting on it *not* to be real. I want a pretend betrothal."

She paused. "A pretend betrothal?"

"Just for a week or two. Or a month. Or more."

"Why?"

He explained to her about the house party, and when he'd finished she said, "Why don't you just not attend?"

"Because I have to. It's a trap they've set for me."

"The Armthwaites?"

"My parents." And for the second time in a week he found himself explaining about George and the memorial service. And how he never went home any other time. He didn't go into details, didn't explain why his family home wasn't home to him and hadn't been so for years, just that the occasion was important to him. And if the place was swamped by muffins trailing around after him, popping out from behind bushes, trying to force him to propose — or worse, to compromise them . . . He shuddered.

"And at the memorial they'll be dripping with sympathy, competing to outdo each other," he finished. "I couldn't bear it. I'd have to strangle someone." Preferably himself.

"I see what you mean. It's a difficult situation."

"Then you'll do it?"

She shook her head. "I can't. I'm sorry." She started to walk away. "I'm going to be late for work."

He caught her arm. "But you must do it — can't you see, it's a perfect arrangement. Neither of us wants to get married."

"Hire someone."

"I can't. Apart from the fact that I couldn't trust a hireling, I need a lady, someone who's already part of society, someone my mother would accept. She's a friend of Lady Beatrice's; she'd have to accept you. Please, Damaris."

She shook her head. "I can't. Ask Jane."

He grasped her by the shoulders. "I don't want Jane, I want you." He swallowed. He was completely losing it. Somehow he had to make her accept.

She narrowed her eyes. "Surely it doesn't matter which of us you get to be a false fiancée."

"Your sister Jane does want to get married. Even if she agrees to go along with this scheme, she might change her mind once she sees the house, and realizes I will inherit a title one day."

She stiffened. "You don't trust Jane to keep her word?"

"I don't trust any woman —" He broke off, realizing he was getting deeper and deeper into the mire. "Look, it's not personal and it's no reflection on Jane. Ladies are *expected* to change their minds. If a gentleman and a lady enter into a betrothal and the gentleman discovers she's an evil-tempered harpy, *he* can't break the betrothal without disgracing himself. A gentleman's word is his bond, and once he's publicly given it, he's honor bound to keep it. The poor fellow's stuck with the hag for life. But *she* can call it off without any public censure whatsoever. It's horrendously unfair, but there it is."

"It *is* fair. A woman has more to lose in getting married."

He stared down at her. "What? A woman *loses*? What nonsense. She gets a husband and a home, and she's supported for the rest of her life."

"*If* the husband is good and kind. But if he is not, she is wholly at his mercy for the rest of her life. If she has money before marriage, afterward she has only what he deigns to give her. He rules every aspect of her life — who she sees, where they live, how she dresses — even her body is not her own, and when she gives birth, her children belong to him." Her eyes were bright with emotion, and she was breathing deep, ragged breaths. He tried not to notice the rise and fall of her bosom.

He thought about what she'd said. He'd heard a few other women speak of marriage that way before, but they were all widows, never an unmarried girl. She really had no time for the institution at all. Which for his current purpose was perfect.

She took another deep breath, which, again, he didn't watch. "I'm sorry, but you'll have to find someone else for your scheme. And now I really have to go."

She'd taken no more than three steps when Freddy heard himself saying, "I'll pay you." It wasn't what he'd planned, but now he'd said it, why not? It made the whole thing less personal, more businesslike.

She hesitated, then shook her head and kept walking.

He followed. "I'll pay you well. Enough so you won't have to work in this wretched pottery." Suddenly it seemed the most urgent thing in the world to get her to agree. He didn't want his false betrothed to be anyone else. It had to be Damaris.

Again she paused. She was tempted. But: "No," she said and kept on walking.

"Enough money to support you for several years. Or to buy a cottage, if you wanted."

Damaris stopped dead. *Enough to buy a cottage? Buy* a cottage? Not just enough money to rent one. It was the kind of security she hadn't even dared to dream of. She turned slowly. "You would buy me a cottage?"

"Yes."

"It means that much to you to have a false fiancée?"

"Yes, but you'd have to come with me to my family home, Breckenridge House, make it look real."

Make it look real? She swallowed. What would that entail? Still, a cottage . . . "How long for?"

"The visit? No more than a week —"

"And the betrothal?"

He shrugged. "Let's see how it goes down. A few weeks, perhaps. Maybe a month or two."

She considered it. "So we'd break it off at the beginning of the season?"

"To be honest, I haven't really thought that part of it through. Once we get through the visit to my parents and my brother's memorial service, it'll be up to you. It does occur to me, though, that if we remained betrothed during the season, it would take the pressure off both of us."

That was true. There would be no expectations then of her having to endure any kind of courtship. More and more this crazy idea appealed. And at the end of it, she'd get her very own cottage. A dream come true.

"So we pretend to be betrothed?"

"No, we *become* betrothed. Only you and I will know of our agreement."

"You mean I can't tell my sisters or Lady Beatrice?"

"No, they might let something slip." He must have seen her hesitation, for he added, "And I will want your promise on that."

"I don't like deceiving them."

"There will be no deception involved — we will *be* betrothed. I'll give you a ring and send an announcement to the *Morning Post.* We'll behave in every way as betrothed couples usually behave."

She gave him a doubtful look. "And how is that?"

"How would I know?" he said with an impatient gesture. "A little billing and cooing, I suppose, nothing to make us nauseous. You can blush and flutter your eyelashes at me —"

"I never flutter my eyelashes, not at any man," she said crisply. "And I wouldn't know how to bill and coo— I'll leave that to the pigeons."

He gave her a thoughtful look, then nodded. "Quite right. Well-bred dignity, that's the style. You remain your usual self — cool, distant and dignified. Perfect for the future Viscountess Breckenridge."

Cool, distant and dignified? Was that how he saw her? She'd laugh if it didn't make her want to cry. If he only knew.

"So, you'll do it?"

"You really don't want to get married?"

"No. And you? You really don't want it, either?"

"No, not at all."

"Excellent. Then, my dear Miss Damaris" — he took her hand and went partially down on one knee — not, she noted, enough to touch the filthy cobblestones and thus soil his immaculate buckskin breeches, but just enough to make a parody of a proposal — "will you do me the honor of betrothing yourself to me, in public and in private, for as long as it remains convenient to us both?"

She took a deep breath and ruined the parody. "In exchange for you buying me a cottage, sir, I will."

He rose, grinning. "Avaricious chit." He stepped closer, she stepped back and his smile faded. He frowned.

"What is it?" she asked.

"With another man, I usually seal a bargain with a handshake, but with a woman, it's usually a k—"

"A handshake will do very well," she said hurriedly and stuck her hand out. They shook solemnly, but then he lifted her hand

and planted a light kiss on it.

"Bad luck not to seal a betrothal with some kind of kiss, even one through a glove," he told her. "Now, when shall we announce it? I imagine you'll want to tell your sisters and Lady Beatrice first — shall we return to Berkeley Square now?"

"You can announce it when I have the deed to my cottage."

His brows snapped together. "What? But that will take —"

"The deed or a sum deposited in my name in Coutts Bank."

"You're not very trusting of my word, are you?"

"It's not personal. I don't trust any man's word." With good reason.

"Very well, I'll see what I can do. Is there anywhere in particular you'd like this cottage to be?"

She thought for a moment. "Somewhere in the vicinity of Davenham Hall would be nice, so Abby and I could visit each other. And I'd want a little land around it."

His eyes narrowed. "How much land?"

"Enough for a vegetable garden and some chickens."

"Good God," he said faintly. "Very well, Devon it is, and as near to Davenham Hall as practicable. And if nothing suitable is immediately available I'll deposit an equivalent sum in your name. We shall announce the betrothal in a week, then."

"A week?" She felt suddenly breathless.

"My brother's memorial is on December the fifth, which is almost four weeks from now. I must give my mother time to cancel the house party."

"What if she doesn't?"

He shrugged. "Then I'll tell her I won't go. And I'll threaten to call off the betrothal."

"But I thought you said —"

"It's a bluff. But it won't be needed. She'll be so pleased to think I'm finally getting married she won't do anything to upset the apple cart. So we announce it in a week and two weeks later we go down to Breckenridge."

She nodded, still a little dazed at the speed with which it was all moving.

"And you promise not to tell your family it's not a genuine betrothal?"

She nodded.

"And you will quit that noisome pottery."

"It's not noisome, but very well, the minute I receive the deed or the bank deposit, I will quit my job."

"God, but you're a stubborn woman."

She shrugged. "I've learned to look out

for myself, that's all." She'd had to.

He groaned. "I suppose that means another week of early morning assignations."

"They're not assignations. And since I never asked for your escort in the first place you can please yourself whether you come or not," she told him. "It's nothing to do with me." She walked down the lane and turned in at the pottery entrance without so much as a backward glance.

It did not please him to crawl out of bed before dawn, Freddy thought as he tied his neck cloth with great care, then pressed the folds just so into place with the judicious lowering of his chin, his freshly shaven chin. But for once he did not begrudge the inconvenience. This was an occasion, after all.

Tibbins eased him into his coat, his expression as lugubrious as ever. "Cheer up, Tibbins, this is the last time we'll be up at this appalling hour."

"Indeed, sir?" Tibbins said with a noticeable lack of joy. "How delightful."

Tibbins, Freddy was forced to admit, was not a morning valet. Pity. Freddy was in excellent spirits. He almost felt like whistling. Almost. But whistling indoors a half hour before dawn might be the straw that broke the valet's back.

He picked up the deed to a Devonshire cottage, delivered to him the previous evening, and tucked it into his pocket. Bartlett was a miracle worker. Five days it had taken him to find and purchase a suitable cottage on the very edge of Max's estate, just outside the village and within easy walking distance of the big house.

The wench would have no excuse now to drag him out of bed at an uncivilized hour.

He handed two letters to Tibbins. "Post this one, and drop this one at the offices of the *Morning Post.*" The first was a letter to his mother, telling her to cancel the house party, that he was betrothed already. The other was the formal newspaper announcement of his betrothal. He'd always imagined it as a knelling of his doom, and yet, he still felt perfectly lighthearted.

He popped his hat on at a jaunty angle and accepted the gloves his valet handed him. "And Tibbins, take the rest of the day off," he said in a fit of magnanimity. "I won't need you again until this evening."

"Thank you, sir." There was no noticeable lightening of the gloomy countenance.

Freddy marched through the streets with a brisk step. There was mist, but it was the kind of mist that might even burn off later and reveal a bit of sun — the kind of day it ought to be when a fellow's plans all fell into place.

No more freezing dark-of-morning escort duty; Damaris would be free of servitude to that bad-tempered she-troll in the pottery; and Freddy, why, Freddy would be muffin free for the foreseeable future. Muffin. Free. He whistled the rest of the way.

"Good morning, Miss Chance," he said the moment she stepped through the gate.

She gave him a surprised look. "Good morning, Mr. Monkton-Coombes. You look very pleased with yourself this morning." She smiled, and it was a promise of the sunshine to come, he thought.

"I am. Miss Chance, you may congratulate me. And while you're at it, you may congratulate yourself as well. We are" — he produced the deed from his pocket and presented it to her with a flourish and a bow — "betrothed."

"Betrothed?" She took the paper from him and unfolded it and read it in silence. She went pale, then pink, then looked at him with an expression he wasn't quite sure of. "You really did buy me a cottage?" She whispered it, as if she couldn't quite believe it. She clutched the deed tenderly to her breast. "Where?"

"In Devonshire, not far from Davenham Hall, as you asked. It's nothing to get excited about," he added, feeling a little embarrassed at the wonder in her voice. "I'm told it needs some repairs and a good clean-out — it's been empty for a few years."

"I don't mind. I can fix it up and clean —" Her big brown eyes were shining.

"No need. I had Bartlett — man of affairs, you know — put some men on the job. A bit of thatching replaced —"

"Thatching?"

He frowned. "You don't like thatch? I can have it replaced —"

"No, I love the sound of a thatched roof. My mother grew up in a village with thatched cottages. She used to tell me about it when I was a child. They sounded very quaint and pretty." She refolded the deed and tucked it carefully inside her bodice. Lucky deed, sliding into that soft warmth . . .

He forced his mind back onto the subject of thatch. Of the roofing kind. "Bit old-fashioned, in my opinion, but as long as you don't mind. . . . Other than that, there's a bit of plasterwork to refinish, a handful of small repairs, a lick of paint and it'll be ready."

Her eyes widened. "You're having all that done?"

"Well, I'm not going to present you with a hovel, am I? Besides, it's nothing, a few paltry repairs. Now, let's —"

She clasped her hands together eagerly. "When can I see it?"

"I'll take you there after the visit to my parents' home." Her expression clouded, and he added, "It won't be ready before then, so there'd be no point. Now, have you told that fierce little troll at the pottery that you're leaving?"

She shook her head. "If you mean Mrs. Jenkins, I'll tell her when I finish up today. And she's not a troll; she's very kind."

He snorted. "To you, maybe. Me, she treats like a rabid dog. But you cannot mean to spend another day in that wretched place, surely."

She smiled and shook her head. "I have a dinner set to complete, and I'm not going to leave Mrs. Jenkins in the lurch. She's been very good to me. As have you. A cottage, my very own cottage. Oh, thank you, Mr. Monkton-Coombes, you have no idea what this means to me." She clasped his hands and gave him such a warm, glowing look he felt quite peculiar. Probably because he'd forgotten to have breakfast.

"Very well, if you must work, I'll pick you up at — what time? Two?"

"Four," she said. "There's no literary society today."

He nodded. "Make it four, then, and we'll tell your sisters and Lady Beatrice. I've already sent a notice to the *Morning Post.* It will appear tomorrow."

She took a deep breath. "So it's official, then."

"Yes, it's official." He was about to be formally and publicly betrothed. And still he had no sense of the tolling of his doom. Quite the contrary.

Why had he never thought of a false betrothal before? It was the perfect solution.

It was closer to five than four o'clock by the time Damaris had finished the dinner set, packed up her things and made her last good-byes to all the people at the pottery. She was tired, and a little sad; she'd been happy here, but she'd made a bargain. And as a result she had a cottage all of her very own.

She could hardly believe it. From time to time throughout the day she'd touched her chest, listening for the slight crackle of the deed tucked in her bodice. Her future.

"I'm that sorry to see you go, Damaris."

Mrs. Jenkins had offered her more money to stay on. Damaris's designs were selling like hotcakes, apparently. It was nice to know. Perhaps, when she got settled in her cottage, she could paint pottery again. If there were any potteries in Devon. She had no idea. The only trip to Devon she'd made was for Abby and Max's wedding.

"Thank you, Mrs. Jenkins, I'm sad to leave too." She stepped into the yard and held out her hand to shake Mrs. Jenkins's hand. "But it's for the best, I assure you."

But it seemed Mrs. Jenkins was determined to walk her to the gates. She slipped an arm around Damaris's waist and steered her across the yard, saying, "You're a good girl, Damaris. If you change your mind and want to come back, there'll always be a place for you, you know that?"

"Thank you, Mrs. Jenkins, it's very kind of you but I don't expect to be living in London."

"Where are you goin' — no!" Mrs. Jenkins stopped dead. Her arm dropped away from Damaris's waist. She glared at the gates, where tall, elegantly clad Freddy Monkton-Coombes stood waiting, then turned to Damaris with an expression of horror. "You're not goin' off with *'im,* are you?" she exclaimed. "Not with that rake! Tell me it's not true, Damaris."

"He's just escorting me home," Damaris said soothingly, but she felt her cheeks warming.

Mrs. Jenkins gasped. "Oh, Gawd, you 'ave! You've fallen for his Evil Wiles!" She clutched Damaris's arm. "Don't do it, my girl. Don't go with him. He'll lead you down the Road to Roon!"

Damaris gently disengaged herself from the woman's grip. "It's all right, we're betrothed," she said, seeing no other way to reassure her. Her first lie of many more to come, she thought.

"Betrothed? I don't believe it!" Mrs. Jenkins glared through the gates at Mr. Monkton-Coombes, who made her an elegant bow in response. Rather a cheeky elegant bow.

Mrs. Jenkins bristled visibly. She pulled Damaris close and said in her ear, "Don't let 'im touch you until you've stood before a parson — with witnesses — and you've got a proper legal paper with your marriage lines writ on it. *And* he's put a proper gold ring on your finger. Otherwise he'll roon you as soon as look at you — I know 'is type."

Damaris gave her a quick hug. "It'll be all

right, I promise you. Good-bye, Mrs. Jenkins."

The little woman shook her head sorrowfully. "You're headin' down the Road to Roon, my dear, I feel it in my waters."

Damaris let herself out the gate and took Mr. Monkton-Coombes's arm.

Mrs. Jenkins shouted after her, "And watch out if he starts with the poetry. They got no shame, them rakes."

"Poetry?" Freddy Monkton-Coombes said as he led Damaris down the lane toward a waiting cab. "What does she imagine I'm going to do with poetry? I never touch the stuff."

"Seduce me, I think." She added thoughtfully, "I suspect she's not without some experience of rakes herself."

He snorted. "Can't see it myself. What was she whispering in your ear about?"

"Oh, nothing. She's just worried about me, that's all."

"Worried?" He gave her a sharp look. "About what?"

Damaris smiled. "Your intentions toward me."

"Oh, is that all?" He helped her into the cab. "I thought it might be something serious." He rapped on the roof and the cab lurched off. "Now, how would you like to handle telling your sisters and Lady Beatrice? Do you want to do it in private, or would you prefer us to do it together?"

She'd been thinking about it all day, trying to decide. The trouble was, after her statement that the very idea of marriage was abhorrent to her, there were bound to be some uncomfortable and penetrating questions. She sighed. "I hate the idea of lying to them."

He turned abruptly and grasped her by the upper arms. "Get that nonsense out of your head for a start. It's *not* a lie. We *are* betrothed. We have made an agreement, I've written to inform my parents and the formal announcement will appear in the *Morning Post* tomorrow."

"Yes, but it doesn't make it any less dishonest. The truth is, we have no intention of going through with it."

He frowned. "Stop thinking about the future, then. Right now you and I are betrothed, and that's all that counts. People get betrothed all the time and never marry. People change their minds. And at some time in the future, you will change your mind and we won't be betrothed any longer. But at this moment, we are. So it's not a lie."

She considered it. "You think I should just

be in the moment? And not think about the future?"

"Exactly."

"It's quite Chinese."

"What is?"

"Living in the moment. Buddhists advocate that." Papa would have been scandalized that she even knew about what he called arrant heathenism.

"Excellent. Be a Buddhist, then, if it makes things easier for you."

She laughed. "You're not very religious, are you?"

He shrugged. "Do you mind?"

"Not at all." She'd had a surfeit of Papa's brand of religion. It was a relief not to have anyone else's beliefs shoved down her throat.

The cab turned into Berkeley Square. The moment of truth. "Let's do it together," she said. The coward's way out.

CHAPTER TEN

"Human nature is so well disposed towards those who are in interesting situations, that a young person, who either marries or dies, is sure of being kindly spoken of."
— JANE AUSTEN, *EMMA*

Freddy told the cabdriver to pull up on the corner so that Damaris could slip in by the side entrance, as usual. She didn't want to be caught wearing Abby's old clothes. She would slip upstairs by the servants' stairs, change and then come down again.

Freddy rang the bell and was admitted to the house by the butler. "Lady Beatrice is in the green salon with the other young ladies," Featherby informed him. "I will announce you."

Damn, it was later than he'd thought. It was Lady Beatrice's habit to gather before dinner for a glass of sherry with the young ladies and any other dinner guests. He entered and was promptly invited for dinner. He accepted and stood sipping sherry by the fire, making polite conversation with the young ladies as he waited for Damaris to appear. Luckily there were no other guests tonight.

In a surprisingly short time, she hurried in, luminous in a gown of rose pink with her hair twisted in a simple knot, and breathlessly apologizing for her lateness. "I completely lost track of time." She glanced at Freddy and the faint pink of her cheeks deepened.

Lady Beatrice waved her excuses away. She raised her lorgnette, directing it at Freddy. "Now that we're all gathered, is there any particular reason you've graced us with your presence, young Monkton-Coombes, delightful though it is? You've been twitching like a cat at a mouse hole ever since you arrived."

Damaris put down her untouched sherry glass and went to stand beside Freddy. "I asked him here." Her voice trembled a little. "I — we — have an announcement to make." She swallowed convulsively and looked at Freddy.

He drained his glass, set it on the mantelpiece, took a deep breath and said, "I have asked Damaris to marry me and she has accepted." Not bad for a man saying what he'd sworn he'd never say.

There was a short, stunned silence, then a babble of female excitement broke out.

"Damaris, oh, oh, oh! I don't believe it!" Jane squeaked, hugging her and jumping up and down at the same time. "How exciting. You sly thing, you — I never suspected a *thing*!"

"But I thought you weren't never —" Daisy broke off, shaking her head and grinning. "Well, never say never, is that it? I'm very happy for you, lovey." She too hugged Damaris, though with a little less exuberance than Jane. "Told you he had his eye on you, din't I?" she whispered in Damaris's ear and laughed.

Both girls hugged Freddy, much to his surprise. "Oh, but you're going to be our brother now," Jane said happily. "We can't possibly behave formally with a brother. Oh, when's the wedding going to be? Can we be bridesmaids? And where will it be? In London or in the country like Abby and Max's? That little chapel at Davenham was so pretty. You could be married there too! Oh, I do love weddings."

The flurry of questions was appalling. Women and weddings. Freddy had no idea where to begin.

"We haven't decided yet," Damaris said quietly. "We've only just got betrothed. We haven't had time to make plans." Something in her voice seemed to calm the excitement. The girls stopped jumping around and followed her gaze to where an old lady was scrutinizing them both through her lorgnette. There was a sudden hush.

She continued to examine them through that damned glass. Freddy felt like an insect on a pin.

"Lady Beatrice, you haven't said anything," Damaris said at last. "Don't you approve?"

The old lady sniffed. "Seems to me you haven't even bothered to seek my approval." She gave Freddy a withering look. "In my day when a young man wished to propose to a young lady, he would speak first to her father."

Freddy frowned. "But Damaris's father is dead."

"She does, however, have *an aunt.*"

Ah. Freddy glanced at Damaris, who looked thoroughly miserable. Lady Davenham might not be a real aunt, but clearly the old lady's nose was right out of joint and it was up to him to retrieve the situation. "My apologies. Jumped the gun.

Excitement of the moment and all that."
He assumed his most penitent and earnest
expression. "Lady Beatrice, do I have your
permission —"

"I will speak to Damaris first. In private,
if you would all be so good." For a moment
nobody moved. She rapped her stick on the
floor. "Now!"

Two young ladies, a cat and a butler
vanished. Freddy hesitated, not liking to
leave Damaris alone with an annoyed dowager, but she made little waving motions with
her fingers and gave him a nod as if to say
it would be all right.

"I will wait in the hall," he said with
dignity. "If you need me, Damaris, just call."

Lady Beatrice's well-plucked eyebrows
almost disappeared into her vivid red coif-
fure, but she said nothing, just raised her
lorgnette. If he'd been a bug he would have
sizzled.

The door closed behind him. Damaris
turned to Lady Beatrice penitently. "Lady
Beatrice, I'm so sorry, I didn't mean to hurt
your feelings. I —"

"Pish-tush, you didn't at all, foolish gel.
I'm just concerned that that young rattle
might have pushed you into something you
told me — several times — that you didn't

want. Never wanted." She gave Damaris a shrewd look. "Had *an abhorrence* of, in fact."

"Oh." Damaris felt her cheeks heating.

"Yes, oh. You're not in trouble, are you?"

"Oh!" She looked up, startled. "No."

"Because if you are, you know I'll take care of you, don't you? No matter what you've done. You don't have to do anything drastic, like marry, if you don't want to."

Damaris's eyes filled. She embraced the old lady. "Oh, Lady Beatrice, you're so kind, I don't deserve — but it's nothing like that, I promise."

"You're sure you're not in some kind of trouble? No debt or anything?"

"No, there's nothing like that. I'm not in any trouble at all."

"And this marriage isn't being forced on you?"

"No, not in the least."

"So you're happy with the arrangement?"

"Yes, very." Damaris smiled, trying to look like a happy bride-to-be. She hated this charade. It was much harder than she'd imagined. This darling old lady was worrying about her and Damaris just wanted to throw herself into her arms and confess that it was all a hoax. But she'd promised him she wouldn't.

Lady Beatrice pursed her lips. "You don't look very happy."

"Oh, well, it's just . . ." She trailed off. She couldn't explain.

"Mixed feelings?"

Damaris nodded. "It's a big step. I just feel a little . . . overwhelmed."

The old lady eyed her thoughtfully. "If you say so, my dear." She was silent a moment, then gave a brisk nod. "Well, then, send in young Monkton-Coombes, but before you do, ask Featherby to step in for a moment, will you?"

"You'll give your consent?"

"I'll talk to him first. Oh, don't look like that, gel, you know very well I can't stop you if you want to go ahead with this thing. But it's no bad thing to put a young man on the spot."

"I wish you wouldn't —"

"Oh, pish-tush, don't fret, I'm not going to eat him. He's not a bad lad, young Monkton-Coombes. Just . . . mishandled. His mother is a friend of mine but she's always been blind where Freddy is concerned. Lavished all her love and attention on her firstborn and barely even noticed she had a second son, even after she lost George.

"And then, suddenly, she thought she

could badger the boy into marrying, and of course, the more she pushed, the more he resisted." She shook her head. "Some men can be pushed, and others can only be led, and take my word for it, my dear, Freddy Monkton-Coombes is the type you can only lead — if you're careful not to get his back up."

"I don't intend to lead him at all," Damaris told her.

Lady Beatrice chuckled. "Oh, my dear, I'm counting on you to lead him a right merry dance. It's exactly what that boy needs."

Damaris didn't bother to argue. Whatever Freddy Monkton-Coombes needed, it wasn't herself, except as a pretext. "So you will give your consent?"

"Yes, of course. I'm not against the match, but he's lived for years as a fribble and a rake, swearing he'd never get married, and I'm dashed if I'm going to make it easy for him. You're a splendid gel and he'd demned well better prove to me that he deserves you! Now, send the rascal in — after I've spoken to Featherby."

"So, young Monkton-Coombes, what have you got to say for yourself?"

"I apologize for neglecting to ask your

permission, Lady Beatrice, but —"

"Piffle! You don't give a hang for my permission."

So the gloves were off. Fine. He shrugged. "Not really. But I don't want to upset Damaris, so —"

"You telling me you care what the gel thinks?"

"Of course I do," he snapped, annoyed by her obvious disbelief. "I'm going to marry her, aren't I?"

"Are you indeed?"

Freddy looked at her warily. What was that supposed to mean? Had Damaris confessed the ruse? He decided to brazen it out. "I am. Whether you like it or not."

"Why?" The question hung in the air.

"Why?" What the devil did he say to that? "For the obvious reasons, of course."

She pursed her lips. "And they would be . . . ?"

"Private ones."

Her brows rose. "A wedding is a public affair."

"Indeed it is."

Lady Beatrice sipped her Madeira, eyeing Freddy with a beady expression. She wasn't at all happy about this betrothal. Did she think he'd forced Damaris into it? Ridiculous. The girl couldn't be forced to do anything she didn't want — witness his futile attempts to make her give up that job. No, it might be a fine line, but a bribe was not force.

"In some kind of trouble, is she?"

He stiffened. "Not as far as I'm aware. And before you ask, I haven't laid a finger on her."

She sniffed. "Then why the deuce has she been working in that dratted pottery, eh?"

Freddy's jaw dropped. "You know about that?"

She snorted. "Almost from the beginning."

"But you never said — she has no idea you know."

She made a dismissive gesture. "A good butler knows what's going on in his house and Featherby's an excellent butler. He knows when there are comings and goings at unseasonal hours. As soon as he realized Damaris was slipping out before dawn, he sent William to follow her, see where she was going and ensure her safety. When he found out, he came to me, thinking she must be in some kind of financial trouble."

"Why did you not say anything to Damaris?"

"Because despite what I said earlier, that girl's free to make her own decisions. Those gels had a life before they came to me, and it's not my place to trim her wings, only offer her shelter. I just want to ensure she's not in trouble. She's not, is she?"

"No."

"Do you know what she wants the money for?"

"Yes."

There was a short silence. "And you don't intend to tell me what it is. I see." She pondered that a moment, then sat up and said in a brisk voice, "The other reason I didn't speak to Damaris about it was because when Featherby came to me, he also brought the interesting intelligence that you were meeting my gel at the kitchen door and escorting her to the pottery." She raised her lorgnette. "And why would a gentleman of your stamp do that, I wonder?"

His *stamp*? Her tone was damned offensive. "Because I promised Max I'd keep an eye on you and the girls, that's why."

She eyed him for a long moment and then let out a crack of laughter. "The rake playing propriety?"

"Yes, as it happens," he said stiffly. "Because I promised Max."

That apparently amused her even more. She pulled out a wisp of lace and dabbed at her eyes, then grinned. "You know, it's very attractive when you poker up and glare down your nose at me like that. And can I take it that this betrothal will put an end to her employment at the pottery?"

"You can."

"Good. I notice she's wearing no betrothal ring."

A ring! Dammit, he'd forgotten. "I intend to buy one tomorrow," he said, as if it had been in the plan all along.

"Your mother still wears the Monkton-Coombes betrothal ring. Part of an hereditary set, ain't it?"

"Yes, but I wouldn't dream of asking —"

"Asking your mother for it?" She cut him off sharply. "But it's Damaris's right to wear it, is it not? As the betrothed of the heir to Breckenridge?"

Oh, she wasn't pleased with him, not at all. Now he was undervaluing her niece, not giving Damaris her due. And that was plain wrong. He might have forgotten to buy a ring but he was going to do right by the girl, and he wasn't going to make her wear the Monkton-Coombes set.

"What I *was* going to say is that I wouldn't dream of asking Damaris to wear it. Well, you've seen it," he added as her brows rose. "It's a blasted ugly thing. Wouldn't suit Damaris at all."

"It is ugly," she agreed in a milder tone. "Then if you haven't bought a ring yet and you don't intend to wrest the hereditary one off your mother's hand, perhaps I could solve your problem. Ring that bell for me, will you?"

Freddy rang it, and almost instantly Featherby glided in. Without a word, he bowed, handed Lady Beatrice a small box, then glided out.

The old lady cradled the little box in her bony fingers, opened it, glanced at the contents, then shut it with a snap. "I thought I'd lost my rings during the time when Max was away and I was ill, but as it happened, I'd hidden 'em in a secret hollow in my bedpost. Featherby found them when we were moving to this house. I gave Max the emerald for Abby. I always thought this would suit Damaris. What do you think?"

She tossed the little box in his direction. He caught it reflexively and opened the lid. It was a sapphire ring, the stone square-cut and stunning. The setting was old-fashioned but simple. Elegant. And on Damaris's slender finger it would look, Freddy thought, perfect. But it wasn't right.

He shook his head. "I can't ask you to provide the ring. That's my privilege as the groom." Even if he was a false groom.

"You don't have a ring, and it would please me beyond anything to have her wear it. It would please Damaris too, I think."

Freddy hesitated, turning the ring over in his hand. The sentiment associated with the piece made him uncomfortable. A ring purchased tomorrow from Rundell and Bridge would be better, more anonymous, more in keeping with a false betrothal.

But this was lovely. And Damaris would like it, he was sure.

"Shall we ask the bride-to-be what she thinks?" Lady Beatrice asked.

He almost winced. The bride-to-be. The bride-never-to-be. "Very well," he said and went to the door. As expected, Damaris was waiting outside with her sisters. He gestured to her to come in.

"Everything all right?" she murmured as she passed him.

"I've given my consent to the match," Lady Beatrice said. "And the boy has a ring for you."

Freddy gave her a stern look. "It's actually Lady Beatrice's ring," he told Damaris. "I was going to buy you one tomorrow, but she has offered this, and if you would prefer it . . ." He showed her the ring.

She hesitated, glancing at it briefly with a troubled expression. "Lady Beatrice, it's very beautiful," she said in a soft voice, "but I couldn't possibly accept it. It looks far too valuable."

"Nonsense," the old lady snapped. "I've had it for years. Can't wear any rings myself." She lifted her hands. "Well, you can see how swollen these old joints of mine are. So this one might as well be of use to you, my dear. And don't look at me like that — I have a ring for each one of you gels that I'll give at the appropriate time. Decided it long ago, when Featherby first found them. Max and Abby were happy enough to accept the emerald."

Damaris bit her lip, and the old lady sighed and added in a plaintive voice that didn't fool Freddy for a moment, "But if you don't want an old-fashioned piece like that for your betrothal ring, I suppose you can wear it on another hand. Or have it reset."

"I would never have it reset; it's perfect just as it is." Damaris gave Freddy a speaking look. She loved the ring, he could tell, but was torn because she shouldn't be accepting something like this for a false betrothal.

"Then that's settled," he said, making the decision for her. "Thank you, Lady Beatrice." God, but the old lady was a tricky piece. He felt like he'd gone three rounds in a verbal boxing ring.

Damaris hesitated, then gave him back the little box. Lady Beatrice gave him an expectant look, then cleared her throat meaningfully.

Oh, damn, of course. He opened the box and Damaris held out her hand. She was blushing. He took out the ring and slid it onto her finger. It was a perfect fit.

"Well, go on, kiss the gel," the old lady ordered him. "Not like you to hang back, young tomcat."

This was one part of the charade that Freddy wouldn't mind at all. He'd wondered for weeks what she'd taste like. He stepped forward.

"Oh, I must show the others." Damaris broke away and hurried to the door, leaving Freddy standing. Lady Beatrice gave him a narrow look, then watched Damaris showing her sisters the ring. She arched a sardonic brow at him.

The old girl was no fool. She knew something was not quite right. Luckily Featherby, having anticipated the occasion, brought in champagne and glasses and the awkward moment was lost in the excitement.

Freddy toasted his blushing bride-to-be

— she blushed beautifully, he noted with interest. They needed to do a little more planning if they were to pull this thing off successfully. He was only too aware of Lady Beatrice's beady gaze boring into him.

Damaris lay in bed that night, twisting restlessly under the covers, turning the evening's conversations over and over again.

Everybody — from Lady Beatrice, Jane, and Daisy to Featherby and William, the butler and footman whom they'd brought with them to Lady Beatrice's house, right down to the smallest scullery maid — they were all so pleased for her. Too pleased.

Accepting their well-wishes and happy speculations was like . . . like being flayed. The happier they were for her, the worse she felt.

Jane had never understood why Damaris hadn't wanted to get married in the first place; she'd come to her senses, as far as Jane was concerned. Freddy Monkton-Coombes was handsome, rich, wellborn — and *nice*! Naturally Damaris would prefer to marry him rather than live alone and lonely in some moldy old cottage in the country!

Jane imagined Damaris's situation was the same as her own — of course she did; Damaris had never told her anything to make her think otherwise.

Daisy, having had a great deal more life experience than Jane, if no more years, saw things differently. She could see that Damaris wasn't securing herself a prosperous and comfortable future with a wealthy man. What Daisy thought was, to Damaris's mind, much worse.

Daisy thought Damaris was in love with Freddy Monkton-Coombes. And he with her.

Daisy knew no more than Jane, but somehow she'd sensed the darkness in Damaris that Damaris had tried so hard to hide. Daisy had been raised in a brothel — she had an instinctive understanding of such things. She ought to understand why it just wasn't possible.

But Daisy, like all of them except Damaris, was a girl full of hopes and dreams; she thought love could make the darkness go away.

Damaris knew differently; she didn't believe in fairy tales.

Rain spattered against her window in spiteful bursts. She shivered, though she was not really cold. Was it always so in England? She hadn't been here a year yet, but it always seemed to be wet, dark, damp, gray. Cold.

She missed the sun, even missed the burning, relentless heat of it during the Chinese summer, when it sucked the moisture out of everything, shriveling the plants, cracking the soil and leaving only the driest of dust. Even the shadows were crisp and brittle and sharp, making everything clear.

In England the shadows were soft edged, blurry, insubstantial. Deceptive.

CHAPTER ELEVEN

"A young woman in love always
looks 'like Patience on a monument /
Smiling at Grief.' "
— JANE AUSTEN, *NORTHANGER ABBEY*

"I can't bear it. Everyone's so happy for me, and it's just . . . wrong."

"You're not going to crack, are you?" Freddy steered her around a puddle. "You promised."

It was a cold, bleak day, but they were taking a stroll around the square. She'd been so desperate to escape the house, she'd practically dragged Freddy out the moment he'd arrived. And of course everyone smiled understandingly; young love needed to be alone.

"I know, and I'm trying not to, but it's so hard. It's bad enough accepting the congratulations of relative strangers, the people in the literary society or those we meet in the park, but Jane and Daisy and Lady Beatrice — they're the people in the world I most care about, and to go on deceiving them like this makes me feel just dreadful."

"Is it really so bad?"

She gave him a despairing look. "Jane and Daisy are already planning the wedding, the invitations, the decorations, and Daisy has come up with a design for the most beautiful wedding dress. Featherby and William keep giving me fatherly smiles, thinking us Love's Young Dream — well, you saw the way Featherby saw us off just now — even Cook is planning a very special wedding cake, not to mention the wedding feast. Everyone is being so *nice,* and I don't deserve *any* of it."

Seemingly at a loss for what to say he patted her hand and resumed their stroll. After a moment he said, "Had a letter from my mother this morning. She's canceled the house party."

"Oh, good." That was the main reason for their betrothal, after all. For a fleeting second it occurred to her she could call off the betrothal now and have the whole horrid thing over with. But she'd promised to go with him to his parents' home, and there was no way she could reasonably wriggle out of it. Besides, he'd bought her a cottage.

That cottage was the summit of all her dreams — her reasonable dreams. It was her future, her security. And if the deception she had to perpetrate on her loved ones was difficult, well, that was only fair. Cottages had to be earned.

She just hoped her sisters and Lady Beatrice wouldn't be too hurt when they learned the truth.

As for unreasonable dreams . . . She glanced at the tall, elegant man strolling beside her, listening patiently to her complaints and protecting her from muddy puddles. Anyone who allowed herself to dream unreasonable dreams was a fool.

A man was roasting some kind of nuts over a small brazier. Freddy stopped. "Do you like chestnuts?"

The hot nuts smelled delicious, but Damaris was in no mood for food. "I've never eaten them, but I'm not hungry, thank you."

"Nonsense, you don't have to be hungry to eat hot roast chestnuts." He bought some in a twisted cone of paper and offered it to her. "Try one."

They looked a little greasy, but she pulled off her gloves and took one just to be polite. The outside shell was scorched in places and had been cut in a cross. The ends were curled up, ready to peel. She peeled back the shell and nibbled the exposed yellowish nut. It was a little floury and soft, rather than crisp, as she'd expected, but it was very tasty — sweetness with a tang of salt. She smiled at him. "They're good."

"They're better with a bit of butter. Cook used to make them for me when I was a boy." Freddy passed the cone to her again. She took another.

Freddy was pleased, seeing her enjoy the nuts. He hadn't thought much beyond getting his mother and the muffins off his back, ruining George's memorial. He hadn't imagined it would be difficult for her. And now he could see it did, he had no idea what to do to help her.

"Miss Chance! Mr. Monkton-Coombes!" Freddy turned and saw three ladies approaching, two young — sisters, by the look of them, and muffins for sure — and an older one, presumably their mother, with a liveried footman in attendance. "Congratulations on your betrothal, Miss Chance, Mr. Monkton-Coombes — Mama saw the notice in the *Morning Post.* How very exciting."

Damaris murmured her thanks, wiping her hands on a handkerchief before shaking hands with the ladies. Freddy bowed and tried to look interested as he received their congratulations. He had no idea who they were, hadn't caught their names when Damaris had greeted them, but the older one asked to be remembered to his mother in a familiar manner, so he supposed he must know her.

The two muffins chatted animatedly, quizzing Damaris about their plans and punctuating each utterance with girlish giggles and coy glances at Freddy. "All the young ladies in London will be ready to *slay* you, Miss Chance —"

"Yes, so many have been setting their caps at our *dear* Mr. Monkton-Coombes —"

"Who until now seemed *quite* oblivious to feminine charms —"

"When *all* along —"

"He secretly had his eye on *you*!" More girlish giggles all around, though not, he noted, from Damaris. She bore the nonsense with grace and dignity.

"Have you set a date yet?" the older one asked.

"Not yet," Freddy said. "We're going down to Breckenridge first. Delightful to talk, ladies, and thank you for your good wishes, but it's chilly and we must keep moving — don't want to let my bride-to-be get cold feet." This witticism produced even more gales of laughter as Freddy and Damaris departed.

"Now do you see what I mean?" Damaris murmured. "Unbearable."

Freddy didn't know what to say. Of course he'd found the women irritating, but no other female of his acquaintance would complain of receiving such a flattering degree of attention and frank female envy. But then, Damaris was not like any other female of his acquaintance. And he could see it would get wearing.

He'd been on the receiving end of a little teasing, particularly from his male cronies, but he'd expected that after his oft-repeated prejudices against marriage, and in any case, he didn't care what most of them thought.

"How's the old lady taking it?" He tossed the now-cold chestnuts under a tree for the squirrels and brushed off his fingers.

"She's about the only one who's not behaving all midsummer-moony, but in a way it's worse."

"Worse?"

"Yes, she's almost unbearably kind — always asking me if I'm *sure.* And if there *is* anything I want to tell her, it would make *no* difference; she will *always* love me and take care of me." Damaris sighed. "So I feel like a *worm.*"

"I wish I could help, but I don't see that there's anything I can do." Apart from calling off the betrothal, which he was not prepared to do. His head was still reeling from the speed with which his mother had called off the house party.

Damaris stopped dead and turned to look at him with an intense expression. A feeling of foreboding stole over him.

"As a matter of fact, there is something you could do." She clasped her gloved hands to her bosom in an unconscious gesture of appeal.

Freddy took a deep breath and grasped the nettle. "What?"

"Take me away from here."

He blinked. It was the last thing he'd expected. "Take you where?" he asked cautiously.

"To your family home."

His brows shot up. "To Breckenridge? But that's where my parents are."

"You'll have to introduce me at some stage. Besides, wasn't that the whole point?"

It was, yes, but . . . "But that would mean we'd be there for" — he calculated the days — "more than two weeks, assuming we stay for my brother's memorial service."

"Would that be unbearable for you?" She

looked at him and said quietly, "Oh, I see it would. I'm sorry. We'll stick to the original plan, then."

She took his arm and they continued their walk. Now Freddy was the one who felt like a worm.

Two more couples came up and congratulated them. Freddy watched as Damaris handled their felicitations with quiet charm. She probably had to put up with this sort of thing all the time. He only had to endure it when he was with her, at the literary society or in the park. The rest of the time it went pretty much as usual.

And when he was at home, Tibbins didn't beam at him in a sentimental, fatherly fashion. He sniffed. Meaningfully.

Tibbins had said everything that was proper, of course, but it was apparent to Freddy — well, he would've had to have been a block of wood to have missed it — that Tibbins was Not Happy about Freddy's upcoming nuptials. Tibbins did not like Change. In Freddy's bachelor quarters he ruled supreme. In a properly ordered marital home, he would be one of many, a mere valet — significant, but not supreme.

Three more ladies and a gentleman approached them, beaming, to wish them happy — that made eleven blasted well-wishers in a period of about fifteen minutes!

Damaris was everything that was gracious, but Freddy had had enough. They hadn't even made a circuit of Berkeley Square yet. And she'd said it was worse for her at home.

"I see what you mean," he said after the last well-meaning nuisance had wished them joy and taken himself off. "We'll leave tomorrow morning. I'll write to my mother to expect us on Wednesday."

She gave him a glowing look. "Really? Are you sure?"

He nodded gruffly. "It's only a couple of weeks. It won't be that bad. We needn't spend much time with my parents. I'll take you around the estate, show you a few of the local sights. Can you be ready to leave by nine o'clock tomorrow morning?"

"I can be ready to leave in an hour," she said so fervently he laughed.

"Nine o'clock it is. I will make the arrangements and you can break it to Jane."

She tilted her head. "Why Jane in particular?"

"She'll have to do all the reading for the literary society now."

Damaris laughed. "She won't mind. Oh, thank you, Mr. Monkton-Coombes —"

"Freddy, remember?"

"Thank you, Freddy, you can't imagine

what a relief it will be to get away for a little. I really appreciate it. I promise you I'll do everything I can to make this visit to your parents go smoothly. And to make them like me."

"Oh, you don't have to worry whether they like you or not. They'll like any respectable girl who's prepared to marry me."

Her face dimmed, and he added, "Besides, if they like you too much, I'll never hear the end of it when you come to your senses, break the engagement and send me about my business."

She still looked troubled, so he patted her hand. "So you can be as rude to them as you like — I won't mind."

She bit her lip. "I couldn't possibly be rude to them, but perhaps I could be a bit cold and standoffish —"

"For heaven's sake, don't do that!" he interrupted. "Cold and standoffish? They'd adore you! No, don't worry about my parents. Just be yourself."

She nodded, and gave him a determined half smile, but the glow had gone. He hoped it wasn't anything he'd said.

It was a still morning and the mist hung low. The stark, bare trees of Berkeley Square seemed to float in a lake of cloudy gray.

"Perfect weather for traveling," Freddy said when he arrived. "Shouldn't take this fog long to burn off, and once it does it should be clear and dry, all the way."

He'd come with a postilion, four horses and a smart-looking bright yellow chaise. Carriage lamps burned on either side of the chaise, golden orbs of light in the gray morning.

"Hired a yellow bounder, eh?" Lady Beatrice commented when she saw it. She'd come down the front steps, leaning heavily on her canes, to oversee their departure.

Everyone, it seemed, had gathered in the street to wave Damaris off; the servants spilled along the footpath and peered through the railings from the subground kitchen entrance, Featherby supervised as William stowed her luggage safely in the boot, and another footman assisted Polly, the maid who was accompanying Damaris, into a seat at the back of the carriage.

Jane and Daisy stood on either side of Lady Beatrice, veering dizzily between excitement and misery. They'd each hugged her a dozen times, pelting her with advice, wiping away tears, and generally acting as though she were going away for good instead of visiting Somerset for a few weeks.

Damaris felt a bit teary herself.

Behind the chaise stood Freddy's curricle, pulled by two beautiful bays, snorting and prancing restlessly, under the control of a diminutive tiger who held their bridles and crooned endearments and muttered curses at his charges. A groom sat in the curricle, holding the reins.

Damaris wondered why Freddy would take two carriages, but since nobody else had commented on the arrangement, she didn't ask. What did she know about traveling in England anyway?

But he must have noticed her wondering, because he explained. "Need my curricle to show you around the district when we get there. Lord only knows what carriages my parents have, probably some dowdy old-fashioned rigs you wouldn't want to be seen dead in."

She hid a smile. She wasn't the one who cared about being smart.

"I'll write," she called to Lady Beatrice and her sisters as Freddy helped her into the chaise, then climbed nimbly in after her.

"Mind you take good care of my gel, young Monkton-Coombes," Lady Beatrice said almost fiercely.

As Freddy was in the process of tucking a luxurious fur rug around Damaris to protect her from drafts, he gave the old lady a sardonic glance. For a moment Damaris thought he was going to say something rude, but all he said was "I will, m'lady," and shut the door.

The postilion glanced back, Freddy gave him the signal and the carriage moved off.

"Phew, that's done," Freddy said, leaning back as they turned into Mount Street, leaving Berkeley Square behind them. He glanced at her. "Comfortable?"

"Very, thank you." The fur rug was lovely and soft and warm.

They watched the streets of London slip by, the familiar giving way to the unfamiliar, Freddy pointing out various places of interest as they went. Then, sooner than she'd thought possible, they were moving along the turnpike at a smart clip, with the city fallen behind them and the country all around.

Silence fell between them, talk giving way to the sound of the horses' hooves on the road, the carriage creaking and groaning as it bounced and swayed along. It was a little unsettling. She gripped the straps hanging above the window to steady her.

Apart from a trip to Max and Abby's home, where she'd been unwell most of the way, Damaris hadn't seen much of the English countryside. She supposed she must have when she was little, but she had no memory of it. Mama had talked often of England; it was all so beautiful and green, she'd said. It wasn't really all that green at the moment, with silvery drifts of mist lingering in the dips and hollows and meandering along streambeds, and silver rime coating the open ground where the remnants of frost caught glimmers of weak winter sunlight. But it was beautiful, as Mama had said.

It was nothing like China, or at least the part of China she'd lived in. It was a different kind of beauty.

These English fields were like patchwork on a quilt, in squares or strips or rectangles — all neat and straight and lined with hedges, not following the flow of the land, as they'd done in China.

And the villages . . . some a mere straggle of houses along the road, others a neat, sturdy collection built around a pretty village square. There were tiny cottages and larger farmhouses and from time to time an imposing mansion glimpsed between trees.

They'd left the turnpike now. The chaise swayed and bounced over potholes in the road, throwing them against each other. She gripped her strap more tightly.

"Are you all right?" Freddy asked her.

"You've gone very quiet, and you look a little pale."

"No, I'm quite all right, thank you. Just . . . thinking."

She stared determinedly out the window. She liked the small whitewashed cottages best. Were any of them like the cottage he had bought her? Some had what she could tell would be flower gardens at the front in spring. Mama had told her about English gardens. She'd tried to make one in China once, but it had shriveled in the summer, and Papa said they should grow food, not flowers.

Food . . . The chaise turned a sharp corner. Without warning her stomach lurched and she tasted bile and a bitter echo of her breakfast.

Oh, Lord, not again.

"Are you sure you're not feeling ill? We can stop if you want."

"I'm all right, truly," she managed.

She stared out the window of the carriage, breathing deeply, determined not to give in to the waves of nausea that grew increasingly worse.

Without warning, Freddy opened a window and shouted to the postilion.

"What — ?"

"Stubborn wench," Freddy informed her

as the chaise immediately slowed. "You're now a delicate shade of green." The chaise came to a sudden stop and swayed gently to and fro. "Out you get."

"It's nothing, just that the movement of the carriage is making me a trifle" — he opened the door and lifted her down — "nauseous," she finished and, clapping her hand over her mouth, made a rush to the ditch on the side of the road.

After a short, humiliating episode beside the ditch, she wiped her mouth, threw away her soiled handkerchief and made her way unsteadily back to the carriage.

"Better?" Freddy said as he helped her back into the carriage.

She nodded, thoroughly mortified. "I'm sure I will be all right soon. I have the same problem on ships, but it passes eventually." She settled herself back in her corner of the carriage. "I trust I will not inconvenience you again."

"It's no inconvenience at all," he said. "I was often ill as a child. In another few miles we'll stop to change the horses, and we'll get you some hot tea with ginger. That often helps."

They had to stop twice more before they reached the post inn.

Her stomach was completely empty now, Damaris was sure. There would be no more embarrassing requests to stop, no more standing on the side of the road retching miserably. At least she hoped not.

At the posting inn, she rinsed out her mouth, washed her face and hands and tidied her hair. She glanced at herself in the looking glass. Pasty as an uncooked pie. She pinched her cheeks to bring some color to her face and returned to the travelers' sitting room.

He made her drink a cup of weak black tea with some grated ginger infused in it.

The thought of it repelled her, but when she drank it she had to admit it did seem to settle her stomach a little. He wanted her to eat some bread too, but she refused.

"Ready to continue the journey?" he asked when she had finished.

She put the empty cup down and said in as bright a manner as she could manage, "Yes. How much farther is it to Breckenridge House?"

"We'll stop for the night in Basingstoke and if everything goes smoothly we'll reach my parents' place by tomorrow evening."

Two days of travel. The prospect was appalling. It would just have to be endured. Bracing herself for the next stage, she headed outside.

"Not that one." Freddy took her arm and steered her away from the yellow bounder. She knew now how it got its name. "We'll use the curricle. The fresh air will do you good."

Her heart sank. The curricle was light and flimsy; it was probably even bouncier than the chaise. It was quite a climb to reach the seat, and her skirts kept getting in the way. He ended up lifting her bodily so she could place a foot in the stirrup, then held her by the waist as she grabbed the fur rug that someone had dumped on the seat, lifted it out of the way and maneuvered herself awkwardly into position. A more graceless process she could hardly imagine.

The wretched vehicle was designed for men with long legs, wearing boots and buckskins, she thought sourly as he climbed lithely in and wedged himself in beside her. There wasn't much room. They sat thigh by thigh. She couldn't give him any more room without tipping herself over the side of the carriage.

He took the fur rug, then put two fingers in his mouth and emitted an earsplitting whistle. A manservant came running from the inn, carrying an oblong wood and metal box with two handles.

"Lift your feet," Freddy instructed her.

Damaris lifted them.

The man carefully slid the box under her feet and withdrew and she cautiously lowered her feet onto it. It was warm; she could feel the heat right through the soles of her shoes.

"Foot warmer," Freddy said in answer to her silent surprise. "Hot coals inside it. Should last for an hour or two. We'll change coals when we change horses." He tucked the fur rug back around her as he spoke, then picked up the reins. "Ready?"

She was anything but, but she managed a smile and a nod, and they moved off.

The wind was cold on her face, but it was more refreshing than anything, and her feet, resting on that hot coal contraption, were toasty and warm, as was the rest of her, thanks to the rug. And to the feel of his warm body pressed all the way down her right side. She was aware of every inch of him.

He, apparently, was oblivious.

After about fifteen minutes, though, she started to feel queasy again. Freddy gave her a sideways glance. "Feeling better in the fresh air?"

"Much better, thank you," she lied. There was nothing left in her to vomit, and anyway, this was an open carriage and she'd be able to get down much quicker if she needed to.

"Good, then you can drive."

"What?" She looked at him in shock, not quite believing her ears. "But I can't drive. I don't know how."

"I'll teach you."

"I *can't.* I don't know the first thing about horses."

"You'll soon pick it up." Ignoring her protests that she'd never driven any kind of carriage — ever — and she was not in a fit state to learn anything at the moment, he stopped the curricle, passed her the reins, which he called ribbons, and showed her how to hold them, threading them in a particular way between her gloved fingers.

"Don't worry, these horses are complete slugs," he assured her, and she realized they were different from the horses they'd left London with. "My mettlesome lads are back at the posting inn; my tiger will bring them on to Breckenridge at a more leisurely pace. Anyone could drive these two. Now snap the ribbons and say, 'Walk on.' "

She didn't move, just gave him an indignant look. If he thought he was going to force her to —

He leaned over and flicked the reins in her resistless hands and the curricle jerked into movement.

Damaris squeaked and gave him a terrified glance.

He smiled, folded his arms and leaned back, completely relaxed. The swine.

She gripped the reins tighter. The curricle was moving. And she was in sole charge. A curricle was such a light and flimsy thing. She sat bolt upright, fearful of running the curricle off the road or into a ditch or a stone wall. Or flipping it right over.

After a minute or two he said, "Good, now let's speed things up or we'll be three days on the road to Breckenridge instead of two."

"But —"

"The road's nice and straight, and there's no traffic. Relax your hands a little."

She glanced down at her hands and saw she had the reins in a death grip. She forced her fingers to relax — and one of the reins started to slither out of her hold. She grabbed them back and glared at the man beside her, who'd made no effort to help whatsoever.

The horses picked up speed. Scenery flew past in a blur. They were going too fast. She could overturn them any second. She glanced at Freddy and saw he was smiling.

"Is my terror amusing you?" she snapped.

"Vastly." His grin widened. He leaned

back and crossed his long, booted legs.

If she crashed the curricle, it would serve him right.

Oh, God, there was a bridge up ahead. "There's a bridge," she gasped. It was ancient, built of stone and so narrow they couldn't possibly squeeze through.

"So there is," he said, completely un-ruffled, almost uninterested.

"How do I make them stop?" She was going to kill him, if they ever survived this.

"Lift your hands just a little toward your chest."

She did. The horses slowed a little but kept moving toward the bridge at a smart trot.

"Steady as she goes, that's right," came the calm, infuriating voice on her right.

She wanted to close her eyes but didn't dare. She didn't breathe, she didn't even remember to pray, she just hung onto the reins for dear life, too terrified to move, watching the narrow passage and bracing herself for the sound of a curricle crashing into stone. Or worse.

And then they were over the bridge — and alive. And the road had widened again. She started to breathe once more.

"Well, that was fun, wasn't it?" he said.

"Fun? *Fun?* It was terrifying."

He gave her a lazy smile. "You enjoyed it. And you're a natural."

"I did not. Not the slightest little bit." A natural? She was a natural? If she felt just the teeniest bit exhilarated, well, that was relief. She'd just had a narrow escape from death.

He quirked a brow at her. "Are you feeling cold?"

"No."

"Sick?"

"No." And she realized to her surprise that it was true. She didn't feel at all nauseous or queasy.

He grinned at her. "Took your mind off your misery, didn't it? And you learned something useful. And it was fun. Your face when we approached that bridge . . ." He chuckled.

She stared at him, speechless. Furious. Indignant.

He turned his head to meet her gaze. Those impossibly bright blue eyes were dancing with laughter. "Go on, say it."

"Say what?"

"That I'm a swine, a beast, a heartless —"

She hit him, thumped him one-handed on the arm, because she was still holding the reins with the other hand. "You are," she agreed in a heartfelt voice and found herself laughing with him. Because she was alive and not sick anymore, and she was a *natural.* And because it had been fun, now she looked back on it.

"I really was terrified," she told him when they'd both stopped laughing.

"I know. Most people are, the first time. Do you want me to take over now?"

"Not yet."

He smiled and settled back, his long legs crossed in total relaxation. Total trust, she realized. In the next hour she negotiated several bends without mishap, another bridge, a man on horseback, who gave them a wordless greeting as they passed, and a flock of geese. He showed her how to stop the horses for that. It was remarkably simple.

And then, finally a town appeared up ahead.

"Want me to take over?"

She handed the reins over without a word, thankful, but at the same time a little reluctant.

"We'll change horses and stop for a bite to eat."

She was about to protest that she couldn't swallow a thing and realized she was actually hungry. "Just some bread and butter and maybe some more of that ginger tea."

"And then another driving lesson to take your mind off things?"

"Yes, please."

As the curricle threaded through the traffic in the town — it was market day — she said shyly, "Did you mean it when you said I was a natural?"

"I did. You have good light hands and you judged that bridge to a nicety."

"I didn't judge anything," she admitted. "I left it all up to the horses."

"Exactly," he said. "A natural."

CHAPTER TWELVE

"A young woman of inferior birth, of no importance in the world, and wholly unallied to the family!"
— JANE AUSTEN, *PRIDE AND PREJUDICE*

They reached Basingstoke just as it was getting dark, and though the horses must be tired, Freddy gave no sign of stopping. Damaris gave longing looks at several fine-looking inns as the curricle passed them by. She was no longer feeling ill, but she was very tired and every part of her body ached.

"Wednesday is market day; everywhere will be full," Freddy explained. "Not far to go now. Staying at Dean Gate, just out of town a short way. Bespoke bedchambers and a private salon at the inn there. Good food, and it's quieter too. You'll sleep better there."

Damaris made a polite-sounding murmur. She didn't care where she slept or what she ate. The way she felt, she could sleep right through a trumpet rendition of the "Hallelujah" chorus. But he'd clearly gone to a lot of trouble in planning the journey, so she didn't want to sound ungrateful.

She wasn't ungrateful, just tired.

Finally the glimmer of lights showed ahead through the trees, and soon the curricle slowed, turned into an inn yard and stopped. Blessedly. Two grooms appeared and took charge of the horses. Freddy sprang lightly down and turned to assist Damaris.

By contrast she began her descent from the high vehicle awkwardly, aching in every joint and muscle.

"Stiff?" he asked and before she could answer, he took her by the waist and lifted her the rest of the way down.

"A little," she admitted.

"I know just the thing for you," he said, tucking her hand through his arm and leading her into the inn.

So did she: sleep.

"I'll give you fifteen minutes to freshen up, then I'll meet you down here. Rug up well." Before she could say anything, he turned to her maid. "Your mistress will need comfortable walking shoes — boots for preference — and warm clothing."

"*Walking* shoes?" Damaris began. She could barely move as it was. "But —"

He turned to her with a faint smile. "Don't look so horrified. Trust me, it's exactly what you need."

What she needed was a bed, but he'd turned back to the landlord, saying, "Now, about dinner . . ."

Damaris would have argued the point, but a number of interested faces were following the conversation and she had no intention of entertaining them with a quarrel, even a small one. She followed the landlady up the stairs to a small but clean and comfortable-looking bedchamber. A trundle bed had been made up for Polly, which showed he'd considered propriety as well as quiet.

Such efficiency on his part was no doubt praiseworthy, but somehow she found it just a little bit annoying. After their long journey, she was feeling like a piece of jetsam tipped out of a fisherman's net, and yet he'd sprung down from his curricle, as lithe as ever and looking just as smart and elegant as he'd started out. It wasn't fair.

And now he expected her to go for a walk? When there was this wonderful, soft-looking bed waiting for her? She tested it and moaned softly: a deep feather mattress and the sweet scent of freshly laundered sheets.

She had a good mind to send Polly with a message to say she wasn't moving another step.

A servant arrived with their luggage, and a maid appeared bearing a can of hot water.

"You look all done in, miss," Polly commented as she poured hot water into a basin for Damaris to wash in. "Do you want me to tell Mr. Monkton-Coombes you've changed your mind about the walk? He'll understand, I'm sure — he was that nice about you being sick and all today. Gentlemen are usually uncomfortable with ladies being ill, aren't they? But the way he watched over you — and, oh, miss, when he gave you his handkerchief to wipe your poor mouth when you was crouched over that ditch throwin' up, well, I reckon it was just like Sir Walter Raleigh laying down his cloak in that puddle for Good Queen Bess."

It wasn't. It was just a handkerchief. Clearly Polly had developed something of a *tendre* for Mr. Monkton-Coombes.

Damaris dried her face and hands.

He *had* been kind. And he'd looked after her himself when he could easily have left her in the chaise in Polly's care and taken the curricle himself. Most men would have.

"And that chaise, miss, so comfortable and well sprung — nothing like some of the

229

bone-shakers I've ridden in." Polly chuck-led. "I reckon he's spoiled me for travel on the stagecoach."

About to retort that it *had* been a shock-ing bone-shaker, Damaris suddenly bit her lip. What — had she suddenly become the princess and the pea? She'd walked for days across China and now she was quibbling because a man who'd shown her nothing but kindness and consideration all day thought a short walk would do her good?

"The blue kid boots, I think, Polly. And my woolen pelisse."

She joined him downstairs at exactly quarter past six.

"Excellent. I wasn't sure you'd come. Thought you might prefer to box my ears instead." His eyes danced in an invitation she couldn't resist.

She laughed and took his arm. "It was close, I admit. And I warn you, I'm still feel-ing as cross as crabs, so don't provoke me. Walking is the very last thing I feel like do-ing."

"I've ordered dinner for seven o'clock, so I hope a short walk won't exhaust you."

Was that a faint note of challenge in his voice? It stiffened her resolve. "Not in the least." She wanted to tell him she'd walked hundreds of miles in China, but bit her tongue. The past — her past, at least — must stay buried.

"It's a lovely evening," he commented as they stepped out into the night. "Cold as a witch's — er, clear as a bell; there'll be a frost, I suspect, but what I really wanted you to see was this." He pointed.

The moon was rising, full and fat and golden against the dark, velvet sky.

They watched it in silence. There was something about a full moon, Damaris thought. People often said the crescent moon was the one full of hope, but she'd always felt the full moon spoke to her.

They found a quiet lane, well trodden but not too muddy, and followed it through a landscape etched in silver and black and a thousand shades in between. In the distance something screamed.

"What was that?" she asked, startled.

"Nothing. A vixen screaming, that's all. They do that at this time of year." He glanced at her. "Mating."

"Oh." She felt her cheeks warming.

They trudged on. The air was cold and crisp, ripe with the scent of rich, cold earth. She breathed it deep into her lungs and found herself matching her steps to those of the tall man beside her. There was an intimacy in their silence that she was reluc-

231

tant to shatter with words.

In the dark hedgerows, small creatures made scuttling noises as they passed. Far away a dog barked. Slowly the kinks in her body started to loosen, and her aches to fade, and gradually their pace picked up.

He glanced at her. "Feeling better, Miss Crabby?"

She laughed. "Don't get too cocky, just because you were right. I could still box your ears."

"Nonsense," he scoffed. "You couldn't reach that high. Now, after a good dinner and a sound sleep, you'll be as lively as a lamb in the morning."

They walked on. "I want to thank you for today," she said quietly. "You were very kind and considerate —"

"Fiddlesticks. Now, shall we climb over this stile and head along that footpath leading up the hill? No? I quite agree" — she hadn't said a thing — "the view won't be anything special and that path looks suspiciously wet and muddy, and those pretty blue boots of yours will not thank me if I lead them into mud. That's the trouble with kid."

They tramped on, their boots crunching along the path in time. An owl swooped by on silent wings. On the hillside above them, a cottage stood, spilling golden lamplight from its windows. A faint hint of wood smoke drifted down toward them. She thought of the folk inside, all cozy in their little home.

"You said we will reach Breckenridge tomorrow."

"Yes, if we make good time we'll be there before sunset; otherwise your first sight of it will be in the moonlight."

Something in the way he said it, the timbre of his voice perhaps, made her ask, "You love the place?"

For a long moment she thought he was going to ignore the question, then he said lightly, "Never go there if I can help it. Now, I think it's time we turned back. Wouldn't want dinner to get cold — or worse, burned."

It wasn't the first time he'd deflected her questions about Breckenridge, or his parents, and now, walking through a shadowy landscape alive with secrets and hidden creatures and lit only by the moon's reflected light, she wondered what kind of a situation she was going into.

In London, totally taken up with her own situation and the painful deception of the people she loved, her only thought, her only desire, was to escape. Now, for the first time, she considered — really considered — what this visit would mean not just to Freddy but to his parents.

From all she knew — which was little enough — they'd been desperately eager to get their only son married. And up until now, he'd resisted with all his might, stating far and wide he had no intention of ever getting married. So their relief and joy at this betrothal must be . . . terrifying.

And since she, the so-called bride-to-be, was the focus of all that joy and relief, they'd want to know all about her.

Bad enough that the betrothal was false; how much worse would it be if they discovered her name, pedigree and background were also false?

And they were the least of the secrets she was hiding.

What if his parents had investigated her background? People did that, she'd heard, when it looked like an outsider might marry into a fine old family. His father was a viscount. Would they think her an outsider, or would they accept Lady Beatrice's claim of their relationship at face value?

If she were found out it would make little difference to her — she didn't need society. As long as she had her cottage she'd be safe. But Freddy . . .

She glanced at his handsome profile in the moonlight. If society learned he'd betrothed himself to a penniless impostor whose entire existence was a tissue of lies . . . he would be a laughingstock.

How could she have let things come so far without warning him?

She was selfish, that was why, only able to see the benefits to her. The cottage.

The lights of Dean Gate Inn were in sight. She would tell him the truth — or as much of it as he needed to know — over dinner. Then he could make up his mind whether to continue with the charade or cancel his plans and his visit.

Freddy glanced at the moon-bathed siren walking beside him. She looked worried. Or maybe just tired.

He opened his mouth to ask her what the problem was, then shut it again. He was getting a bit . . . possessive about her. Her cold little hand tucked into the crook of his arm — ridiculous how much he liked feeling it there.

Ridiculous too the degree of anxiety that he'd felt that morning when she'd drooped, pale and clammy skinned, but determined not to show it or complain, foolish stubborn wench.

He could see how Max had become so protective of Abby — and her sisters. Being responsible for someone's welfare . . . he supposed that was what did it, caused these . . . *feelings.* That and his promise to Max.

It wasn't anything he was used to and to tell the truth it was rather unsettling. He was used to breezing through life, carefree and untrammeled by . . . fee — responsibilities, going where he wanted, doing what he felt like without reference to anyone else.

Another reason why he didn't ever want to get married.

Amazing good luck that he'd found a woman who'd never wanted to marry, either. She was perfect. And, despite the travel sickness, very good company. He was quite enjoying the whole little adventure, actually. Or he would be if it weren't for these blasted inconvenient f— thoughts.

Perhaps having to act like a fiancé was making him think like one. In which case it would be over in a couple of weeks. And that, he told himself firmly, was a damned good thing. He had to abandon any thought of stringing out the whole affair for months just to free himself from Pursuit by Muffins for the season.

Desirable as that would be, a problem had

arisen with Damaris that he hadn't at all anticipated. *Arisen* being the operative blasted word.

Of course, it was only because he didn't have a mistress at the moment and his body was feeling the lack, but still, it was dashed awkward, being in a constant state of semi-arousal whenever she was close. Or even when she wasn't but looked at him in a certain way — and she wasn't in the least trying to seduce him — he knew that! All it took was that way she bit her lip occasionally. Or sighed. Or smiled. Or gazed at him with those fathomless pansy brown eyes . . .

Even the stubborn set of her jaw when she was about to argue with him appealed to him. Or, rather, to his body. And when she'd laughed, as she had in the curricle . . .

The slightest reaction on her part, in fact, and his body just snapped to attention, like a good little soldier, dammit, ready and eager for action.

It was perfectly understandable, he told himself. She was a beautiful young woman, without a shred of missishness and with a great deal of natural charm. Allure. Any man would find her damn near impossible to resist.

He wasn't accustomed to everyday intimacy with respectable girls, that was the problem. The kind of girls he usually came into close contact with were deliciously bad, without a virtuous bone in their bodies — without even a bone, some of the opera dancers — and they caused him not a moment's worry, or even a second thought.

And absolutely no frustration. Which was how he preferred it.

Dammit, why was she so opposed to marriage? If ever there was a woman born to be — "What? What is it you're looking so anxious about?" he demanded, finally goaded by her anxious expression.

The door of the inn opened, spilling golden light onto the cobbles. "I'll explain over dinner," she said.

He'd ordered good plain English cooking, just the way he liked it, starting with a hearty pea and ham soup and fresh bread and butter. The talk was mostly polite chitchat and mostly between himself and the landlord — neither he nor Damaris wanted to talk while the man was hovering.

The landlord chatted as he bustled in and out bringing dishes. "You been lucky with the weather today, sir. Last week it were weather for old Noah and his ark, to be sure — now, here's the bread, fresh baked this morning by my wife — and I hear it's even wetter farther west. The ground is drenched, and the farmers not happy — well, when are they ever happy? They reckon the rain'll be back tomorrow or the next day, so you'd best make an early start, sir. Now, you'll want wine with that and I have the very thing."

He produced a very tolerable burgundy from his cellar, and Freddy made sure Damaris's glass was filled. "It will help you sleep," he told her. It might help him to sleep too.

She gave a nervous laugh and gulped down a large mouthful. The wine, or possibly the warmth after their brisk walk, lent her complexion a rosy glow.

He would probably sleep hardly at all.

The landlord brought in the next course — steak and kidney pie, a fricassee of chicken, which Freddy had ordered in case Damaris didn't like beef, and a dish of winter vegetables, all served with a cheery grumble about the state of the roads, especially in the wet. He then retired, closing the door behind him.

In the sudden silence the atmosphere immediately heightened. She put down her knife and fork and picked up the wine, gripping the stem of the glass with a white-knuckled hand. She took a sip. Making up her mind to speak, he thought.

"Why don't you wait until we've finished dinner to say whatever you want to say?" Without waiting for her to respond, he added, "May I serve you some of this excellent pie? And some of these stewed leeks? And do you like cauliflower?"

She allowed him to serve her a little of everything, and as they ate, the tension eased.

"It's apple tart for pudding," he said as it arrived, the pastry crisp and golden, accompanied by a bowl of thick, clotted country cream.

It was a thing of glory, but she had no eyes for the tart: She was drawn tight as a viola string. Her gaze fastened on Freddy with a fixed intensity.

"You may leave us alone now," Freddy told the landlord with a meaning look. "Leave everything. You can clear up later."

The minute the man had closed the door behind him, she said in a rush, "My name is not Damaris Chance." Freddy opened his mouth to respond, but she cut him off, saying, "I'm not finished yet. I'm not Lady Beatrice's niece. And Abby and Jane and Daisy are not my real sisters, either." She took another gulp of wine. "And I don't have a penny to my name. There, I've said it." She slumped back in her chair.

"Well, I'm shocked," said Freddy in as shocked a manner as he could conjure up. "Deeply shocked," he repeated. "May I serve you some of this apple tart? It looks and smells delicious, doesn't it?"

"Apple tart?" she repeated blankly. "Didn't you hear what I said?"

"What you said?" He cut a generous slice of tart. "You mean about you not being Miss Chance?" He slid it onto a plate and passed it to her. "And not being related to your sisters or aunt and having no fortune — yes, and I told you I was shocked. *Deeply.* Will you have cream with that?" Without waiting for her answer he lavished her apple tart with clotted cream.

She frowned and gave him an accusing look. "You knew. All the time I was worrying about telling you, and you knew!"

"You're not eating. It's delicious. Of course I knew."

"Then why did you say you were shocked. *Deeply* shocked?"

"You seemed to expect it and I didn't want to disappoint you." He gave her a wicked grin. "I don't like to disappoint ladies, you see."

But she was too anxious for flirtation. "Did you have me investigated?"

He snorted. "My dear girl, Max had already told me about the night Lady Beatrice invented your esteemed papa, the marchese di Chancealotto, at dinner. And I was there when she invented your inheritance — a delightful surprise yet in store for Max. Serve him right."

"But —"

"I knew you weren't related to the old girl. I've known Max and his aunt most of my life. No close relatives at all. And from the start Max didn't believe that you were sisters."

"Jane and Abby are. But not Daisy or me."

"Yes, so I understand. I gather Lady Beatrice knew of your true identities before she took you in?"

"Yes, we didn't want to deceive her in any way." She stared at him, her lips slightly parted in a way that was seriously distracting. "So you knew I wasn't who I claimed to be all along?"

He nodded. "More or less. Your pudding is getting cold."

"And said nothing?"

"Why should I? I don't mind."

"What if your parents have had me investigated?"

He considered that. "It's possible. We'll cross that bridge when we come to it. I ordered that apple tart especially for you, you know."

She gave him an exasperated look and ate a mouthful. "But what if —"

"Nice?"

"What?"

"The tart — is it nice?"

"Yes, thank you, it's delicious. But what if they ask me about my parents — and they're bound to ask —"

He frowned. "What happened to your parents?"

"They're both dead. Mama died when I was twelve and Papa some months ago."

Only months ago? Freddy braced himself for waterworks, but she remained quite calm, calm enough that he found himself asking curiously, "Were you and your father close?"

She hesitated. "No."

That was blunt enough. There was a story there, but not for tonight. "In that case, if the question comes up, leave it all to me. I'll tell 'em you're in mourning. You won't need to explain a thing."

"What will you say?"

He shrugged. "Lady Bea took you in — distant relatives, cousins, perhaps — I'll give it some thought. Don't worry about it."

Her eyes were troubled in the candlelight.

"I can't help but worry."

"Well, don't. It doesn't matter. What's your real name, by the way? Just out of curiosity."

"Tait. Damaris Tait. Abby chose Chance for our surname because it was a fresh chance for all of us. How can you say it doesn't matter?"

"Because it doesn't. So, were you brought up in Italy?"

"No, China."

He blinked. It was not at all what he'd expected. "China?" She didn't sound Chinese. She sounded like a perfectly ordinary English girl.

"Papa was a missionary."

"Good God."

"Exactly."

"Do you know any Chinese, then?"

"Of course. I lived there since I was four."

"Say something in Chinese, then."

She hesitated, then uttered a rapid burst of singsong speech. He closed his eyes and listened. She really did sound Chinese. Not that he knew a word of Chinese, but it sounded very authentic.

"What did you say?" he demanded, but she shook her head, blushing, and refused to translate what she'd said for him. The blush enchanted him. He opened his mouth, about to pursue the matter, then shut it as she stifled a yawn.

Her eyelids were heavy; she was awake only because she'd been so anxious about making her shocking revelations to him, and now he'd allayed those fears, tiredness was taking over. He'd been on the verge of flirtation, and she was hiding yawns.

He drained his glass and rose to his feet. "Time for bed."

Any other woman of his acquaintance, respectable or not, would have responded coyly to that statement, finding an innuendo in it, regardless of his intention. Damaris simply said, "Oh, is it so obvious? I'm sorry. The wine has made me so sleepy." She set her napkin aside and stood. "What time do you want to leave in the morning?"

"Eight, if you can manage it. In case that rain the farmers predict should show up."

"So, breakfast at half past seven?"

He grinned. "That's a confident traveler speaking."

She gave him a sleepy smile. "As long as we travel in the curricle, I have every expectation of keeping my breakfast — oh, dear." She clapped a hand over her mouth. "Was that indelicate? I see it was. Sorry. So many things one shouldn't talk about in England that are perfectly ordinary in

China." She straightened and gave him a sleepy smile. "Still, you would ply me with wine, so you must share the blame."

He led her down the narrow corridor to her bedchamber. He indicated the door opposite. "I'm in here, if you should need me for anything."

Again, she could have perceived innuendo in it, but she simply nodded and stifled another yawn. She looked soft and sleepy and very lovely in the soft candlelight of the wall sconces and without thinking Freddy cupped her face in his hands and bent to kiss her.

Her eyes flew wide and she stepped back against her door with a startled jerk. "What are you doing?"

Good question. What the hell was he thinking? "Sorry," he said ruefully. "Force of habit, I'm afraid."

She scanned his face with troubled eyes, then nodded. "We can blame the wine for that too, I expect. Good night, Mr. Monkton-Coombes." Putting him firmly back in his place.

"Good night, Damaris. Sleep w—" But she was gone and the door was closing. He heard the lock click behind her, and then the murmur of voices as she spoke with her maid.

Freddy let himself into his bedchamber.

He shrugged himself out of his coat and tossed it on a chair. It was not the wine. He ripped off his neck cloth and tossed it aside. It was the woman.

And that was a problem.

She was an innocent, he reminded himself savagely as he hauled off his boots. And she had no desire to marry.

Neither did he, and if he didn't get himself under control both of them would be trapped in a situation neither of them wanted.

He dragged his breeches off and tossed them on the chair, glaring down at where his blasted little soldier was making a tent in his drawers.

He had to find some way of squashing this inconvenient attraction.

CHAPTER THIRTEEN

"There is a stubbornness about me that never can bear to be frightened at the will of others. My courage always rises with every attempt to intimidate me."
— JANE AUSTEN, *PRIDE AND PREJUDICE*

"Those gates up ahead on your left, turn in there."

Damaris saw the big stone pillars and slowed, ready for the turn. In the last two days she'd become quite skilled at negotiating bridges and narrow roads, and she wasn't intimidated by the large wrought-iron gates standing open between the pillars.

She'd been racing against the oncoming storm. For some reason Freddy had insisted on stopping at a village inn only a few miles from his parents' home, so that she could wash and freshen up. With the storm looming, it had been a ridiculous waste of time, she thought.

"Steady as she goes . . . well done." As they passed through the gates, lightning flashed and thunder rumbled all around them. A few fat drops of rain spattered, warning of the downpour to come. A crow cawed his mournful song across the darkening sky. Freddy laughed. "The raven himself is hoarse that croaks my entrance under my father's battlements. . . ."

She shook her head. "Nonsense. And anyway, there aren't any battlements." She could see the house clearly now, a huge, gray, impressive gothic pile, to which it was apparent several wings had been added in the last century. But no battlements.

"What? You don't recognize the quote? Didn't you have Shakespeare in China?"

"Yes, my mother had several volumes of collected works — she preferred his poetry but books in English were rare, so we read everything. I know that's from *Macbeth.* I'm shaking my head at your pessimism. Or is it cynicism?"

He shrugged. "A little of both, perhaps. You'll see. I hope my father can see us approaching."

"Why?" They headed down the drive at a crisp pace. Big fat drops were falling now.

"Nothing will convince him of this match

more than seeing that I let you drive my curricle, even if it's with job horses. I've never let a woman do so before."

"Really?" She was absurdly flattered, even though she knew that teaching her to drive had simply been to prevent her from being ill again.

"When my grays arrive I'll let you drive them too; then my father will truly be appalled."

"Appalled?"

He said in a gruff voice, "Entrustin' good horses to females? Brr-harrumph! Females are for breedin', not for ruinin' the mouths of good horseflesh." He darted her a wry look. "My father is ever so slightly old-fashioned."

She laughed. "I'm sure you're exaggerating." They reached the semicircular drive in front of the house. Grooms ran out, taking charge of the curricle and the chaise. A footman emerged from the house with a large umbrella, which he held to shelter Damaris as Freddy swung her down. The rain began to pelt down in earnest and they ran up the front steps, entering the house laughing and breathless.

When they were inside, he stopped and turned her to face him. He straightened her bonnet and tucked a stray lock of hair back into place in a very possessive, not to say intimate, way.

A little embarrassed, and very aware they were under observation by the servants, she said in a low voice, "What are you doing?"

"A little billing and cooing of the masculine sort."

"I thought we agreed not to —"

"No, you said it was for birds, but a certain amount is necessary if we're to convince people, so I'm taking on that job. We agreed that your role is to be cold and dignified and treat me with utter disdain, though not too much, else my parents will adore you."

"Why on earth would that make them like me?"

He shrugged. "Odd people, my mater and pater. In fact, my whole family is peculiar." He leaned closer and said in a confidential tone, "I wouldn't marry into it, if I were you."

She laughed. "Oh, very well, I won't."

A very dignified-looking butler came forward. "Mr. Freddy, sir. Welcome home."

"Horwood." Freddy nodded. "My dear, I'd like you to meet Horwood, the butler here. Horwood, my betrothed, Miss Chance."

"Delighted to meet you, miss," Horwood

said, bowing. "And may I say on behalf of all the staff here at Breckenridge, how thrilled we all are at the news of Mr. Freddy's engagement." He beamed at her in a paternal fashion and she felt instantly guilty, knowing for whom that earlier pretense was intended.

"Thank you, Horwood." Freddy grinned and said to Damaris, "Horwood's known me since before I was born, did his best to keep me out of trouble as a boy. Shame it didn't work."

"Nothing but harmless boyish mischief," the butler said firmly. "Now, her ladyship told me to bring you both straight in the moment you arrived. They're in the large drawing room."

"Did she indeed? And in the chamber of horrors? Gird your loins, my dear, a treat awaits you." But despite the light words, the warmth had died from his eyes.

Damaris smoothed her gown with nervous fingers as Horwood announced them.

The "large drawing room" was more like a medieval hall in size and atmosphere. It was large and richly furnished, the walls paneled in oak, the floors scattered with oriental rugs in dark reds and browns and blues, the furniture heavy, ornate and old-fashioned. A huge fire blazed in a fireplace big enough to roast an ox in.

Damaris immediately understood Freddy's reference to a chamber of horrors. The walls were lined with the heads of various slaughtered and stuffed animals: heavily antlered stags, wild-horned goats, a snarling bear, a fierce tusked boar. Their glass eyes glinted in the firelight. Rain battered at the windows.

"Ah, Frederick, so here you are." A slender, exquisitely dressed woman rose and presented a delicately rouged cheek for her son to kiss. A beautifully cut dress of heavy blue silk flowed around her; a fine cashmere shawl dangled negligently from thin shoulders. Her hair was silvery white and cut in a severe, extremely modish style. She barely glanced at her son; her pale blue gaze was all for Damaris, taking in everything about her.

Damaris immediately felt rumpled, grubby and travel worn.

"And this is your affianced bride? Welcome to Breckenridge, Miss Chance." She held out a languid hand for Damaris to shake. "We had almost given up hope of him ever marrying. Yet you seem to have brought him, somehow, to the point." The words were accompanied by a cool smile, but Damaris was in no doubt of the barb buried in the apparent compliment.

She gave a cool smile in return. "How do you do, Lady Breckenridge?"

"Bring me to the point?" Freddy interrupted. "Wrong end of the stick completely, Mother. I had the devil of a time getting her to agree. Had to pop the question — how many times was it, Damaris? three? four? — before she'd agree."

Damaris smiled. "Something like that."

"Indeed?" Lady Breckenridge's finely plucked brows rose.

"Harrumph!" came a noise from the window. Damaris turned and saw a tall, lean man, slightly stooped, with iron gray hair and fierce blue eyes, standing there. Freddy's father. The resemblance was unmistakable. He must have watched them arrive.

"Ah, Father —" Freddy began.

"I've got eyes, haven't I?" his father snapped. "So this is the bride-to-be, is it?"

His hard gaze ran over her, taking in every detail. There was no warmth or welcome in the examination.

Damaris straightened. She half expected him to examine her teeth and lift up her fetlocks. She held out her hand to him. "How do you do, Lord Breckenridge? Delightful to meet you." And if he detected any irony in her voice, so much the better.

His brows gnashed together. "Half Italian, are you?"

"Father —"

"Half Venetian," she corrected him.

"Hmph! You don't sound Italian. Or look it."

"That's because I'm not," she said with perfect truth.

The elderly man gave her a narrow look, then turned to his son. "You let her drive your curricle, I see." It was a criticism more than a comment.

Freddy smiled faintly. "I do. She has the makings of a very pretty whip."

"You drove her in your *curricle*?" his mother exclaimed. "In this weather? Honestly, Frederick, have you no idea of the proper way to treat a lady? You should have sent for your father's traveling chaise, or hired one, at the very least."

"Oh, he did, and very comfortable and luxurious it was, too," Damaris interjected coolly, hoping her outrage didn't show. So very rude to dress Freddy down in front of his new fiancée as if he were a naughty schoolboy. Not to mention unfair. "But I preferred to ride in the curricle." She glanced at the window. "We were very lucky with the rain. I see it's coming down rather hard now, but we had fair weather all the way from London."

Again a well-plucked brow arched in haughty surprise. Damaris had a feeling she was going to become rather familiar with it over the period of this visit. Lady Breckenridge did not like to be contradicted, even politely.

Damaris could see now why Freddy had not been precisely eager to spend much time here. He'd received no sort of welcome at all, no warmth, only criticism.

She knew exactly what that felt like. She'd had it all her life from Papa. And she wasn't going to take it from these two strangers.

"Now, if you don't mind," she said sweetly, "it's been a long trip and I would like to wash and tidy up."

Lady Breckenridge stiffened at the implied slur on their hospitality. Lord Breckenridge's brows drew together in a frown.

The atmosphere in the big ugly room had chilled perceptibly, and it was nothing to do with the fire, which was still blazing.

"Of course," Lady Breckenridge said. "Horwood will show you to your rooms. Dinner will be at eight. Frederick, you will collect Miss Chance and escort her to the dining room."

They didn't like even a tiny taste of their

own medicine, Damaris thought. Good. If they didn't have the good manners to allow their son and his betrothed time to freshen up and visit the privy after a long journey, then they should be embarrassed.

When she was rushed in to meet them immediately on arrival, she'd assumed it was because they were eager to see their son and meet his fiancée. She understood now that was far from the case. They'd given no thought to their guests' comfort. She hoped they hadn't intended to put her — and by association, their son — at a disadvantage, but the suspicion lingered.

Freddy must have expected it. His insistence on breaking the journey at the village inn now made sense. If she hadn't used the privy, washed her face and hands and tidied her hair then, if she'd met that cold, elegant woman all blowsy and blown about and in need of the privy, well, what a first impression that would have made.

"Thank you for arranging that stop in the village," she murmured to Freddy as they mounted the stairs in Horwood's wake.

He gave a quick half smile of acknowledgment.

"Your parents are not particularly happy with this betrothal, are they?"

"Don't worry about it. Noses out of joint,

that's all. Would have preferred I chose one of the muff — girls they'd picked out for me. Hope they didn't upset you." He gave her a searching look as they reached the landing.

"Not in the least," Damaris said. "In fact, I quite enjoyed it."

"Enjoyed it?" One mobile brow rose. She knew where that came from now. Odd how on one person it was annoying and on another it could be quite endearing. He was worried about her, she realized.

"After this visit I won't ever see them again," she reminded him. "You did say you'd prefer they didn't much like me."

"Yes, but the way they spoke to you —"

"Was not nearly as rude as how they spoke to you."

He shrugged. "I'm used to it."

"So am I. My father was constantly critical. I doubt he ever had a kind thought or word for me — or anyone — in his life." She squeezed his hand. "Family can hurt you much more than outsiders can."

He snorted. "Doesn't bother me. It was you I was worrying about."

She smiled at him. "Then don't. After a lifetime with Papa, whatever your parents direct at me will be water off a duck's back."

■ ■ ■ ■

At dinner the interrogation continued. Lord and Lady Breckenridge had, it seemed, no interest in discovering what their son had been doing in the last year; it was all about Damaris.

"Did your mother, the marchesa, teach you how to manage a large household?" Lady Breckenridge asked.

"She did." At least, her mother had; and Damaris had managed the mission and controlled the purse strings since she was twelve. Not that there was much money left by then.

Lady Breckenridge sniffed. "I don't suppose Italian houses are the same."

"As Venetian ones? There is some similarity, apart from the canal frontages. Oh, you mean compared with English houses? I know a little about the running of a large London house and have stayed with my sister Abby in her country home, Davenham Hall, but otherwise it's hard to generalize. These parsnips are excellent. You grow them yourself, I presume?"

"Not altogether a bad thing for an ancient family to gain fresh broodstock." Lord Breckenridge entered the fray. "Don't know

259

about Italians, though."

"Venetians," Freddy said.

"Hmmph!" The old man eyed Damaris critically. "Eat up, gel, you're a bit thin for my taste. There's the succession to think of."

Lady Breckenridge cleared her throat meaningfully and eyed her husband.

He grunted. "Take your point, my dear. M'wife here's always been slender as a willow and still managed to throw two healthy sons." He pointed his fork at Damaris. "We breed sons in this family, missy, d'you hear me?"

"Damaris has three sisters," Freddy put in helpfully.

Lord Breckenridge frowned. "What, no boys?"

"None at all," she admitted cheerfully.

"I like girls," Freddy said.

"Young idiot, what do I care what you like? It's the succession that counts!" He turned to Damaris. "You hunt, of course."

"No. I don't even know how to ride," Damaris said serenely. It was wonderfully liberating not to have to please them; and the ruder they were to their son, the freer Damaris felt to say whatever she chose. When his parents had first started firing questions at her, Freddy had bristled in her defense but once he saw she was quite capable of dealing with them — even quite enjoying it — he sat back.

"Not know how to *ride*?" Lord Breckenridge glared at his son. "What sort of an upbringin' is that for a future bride of Breckenridge?"

Freddy shrugged. "I don't suppose there's much call for horses in Venice."

Damaris nodded. "Gondolas yes, horses no. A gondola is a kind of boat," she explained kindly. "The canals, you see."

The old man glowered at her. "I know what a gondola is."

She smiled at him. "Then you understand why I don't ride."

Freddy leaned forward. "I thought I'd teach her to ride while we're here. Give us something to do."

"Harrumph! Not much point at her age," his father growled. "Only time to learn to ride is when you're a child." He gave Damaris a flinty look. "I was ridin' to hounds by the time I was seven."

"Good for you," she responded. "But even if I could ride, I wouldn't hunt foxes." She'd had a taste of how it felt to be hunted and she wouldn't wish that on any creature.

"Not hunt foxes?" His eyes almost popped with the heresy. "Why on earth not? They're

261

vermin! And it's excellent sport."

"All God's creatures have their place."

"A fox's place is to be hunted, dammit, gel!"

"Not by me." She nibbled on a macaroon, then added provocatively, "Besides, foxes are sweet."

"*Sweet?*" he echoed in disgust. "Foxes are *sweet?*" He turned to glare at Freddy. "And *this* is the bride you choose to bring home to Breckenridge?"

"It is," Freddy agreed. "Delightful, isn't she?"

"Harrumph!" His father hunched over his wine and after a moment muttered, "Almeria Armthwaite is English *and* a bruisin' rider to hounds. You could have had her."

Freddy smiled. "Anyone can, I believe, as long as he enjoys the whip."

There was a short, stunned silence, into which Freddy rose. "Excellent dinner, Mother; convey my compliments to Mrs. Bradshaw. It's been a long day and my bride-to-be must be tired, so we'll bid you good night." And before his parents could recover, Freddy and Damaris made their escape.

The moment the door closed behind them, Freddy gave a small whoop, seized Damaris in his arms and swung her around in an exuberant whirl. "That was wonderful!" he exclaimed. She laughed and as he came to a halt and let her slide back to earth, his voice deepened. "You were wonderful."

He gazed down at her for a long moment, his arms loosely locked around her; tall and warm and strong. She stared back, breathlessly aware of the way her body was still pressed against him, the tips of her breasts just touching his chest, her palms resting lightly on his forearms. His hands were warm as they slid slowly down to circle her waist. Her skirts were twined around his legs. Every nerve in her body thrummed with awareness of him.

She moistened her lips. His blue eyes darkened and he bent his head, angling it to —

A discreet cough behind them caused Freddy to release her and step back. A footman carrying a large tray of crockery passed them by, looking embarrassed and muttering an apology.

Damaris's cheeks were burning. What must he think of her, pressing herself against him like that? There for the taking, right outside his parents' dining room. This was a business arrangement, she reminded herself.

Freddy offered her his arm and together they mounted the stairs. "I meant it," he said in a low voice. "You were wonderful at dinner. So composed and unruffled. Are you sure they didn't upset you?"

She strove to make her voice cool and matter-of-fact. "Not at all. But I was very annoyed by their rudeness to you. Are they always like that?"

"Don't let it bother you," he said. "I don't."

It did bother him, she could tell, and now what he'd told her about only coming here once a year, and not even for Christmas, was starting to make sense. But despite his light dismissal, she recognized the underlying message of "keep out, private family business." And since she was a faux fiancée she had to respect that. For now, at least.

They climbed the stairs in silence. Outside, the rain drummed steadily, pouring off the roof and rattling down spouts and gutters.

"Foxes are sweet?" he quizzed her when they reached the landing.

She chuckled. "I couldn't resist. And what about your comment about Miss Armthwaite?"

"Father walked into that one." They'd reached the door of her bedchamber and paused. His hand came up, as if to cup her cheek, and she stiffened and quickly stepped back.

"I think it's best if we don't," she said and, in a moment of inspiration, added, "We had that moment in the hall in front of that footman — surely that should suffice. It's not necessary now, is it? For our pretense, I mean."

"Necessary?" He looked at her as if trying to fathom her thoughts. "No, it's not . . . necessary."

She fought a blush and said in as crisp a voice as she could manage, "Then I'll bid you good night." She hurriedly let herself into her bedchamber, closed the door and leaned against it in relief. What must he think of her? She'd promised she had no interest in him, no interest in marriage. And it was true, so what business did she have in encouraging him to . . . flirt?

"Tired, miss?" Her maid, Polly, came forward. "I've put a warming pan over your sheets, miss, and your nightgown is warming by the fire. There's hot water in the jug, and I can fetch a hot brick for you if you want one."

"Thank you, Polly, that will do very nicely." She quickly washed, changed into her nightclothes and slipped into bed. Polly blew out the candles and slipped into her own bed in the adjoining room.

Damaris snuggled down. She was cozy and warm, almost too warm. Her body was hot with remembered awareness.

Lust, her father whispered in her head. . . . She buried her face in her pillow.

After breakfast the next morning, Lady Breckenridge announced she would show Miss Chance over the house — the more domestic areas, which would, naturally, be of most interest to a future bride.

Minutes into the tour her true purpose soon became apparent: to impress on Damaris her unworthiness for the position.

"I'd arranged a house party to start next week," Lady Breckenridge said. "I had invited the flower of English young womanhood, and their mothers."

"Mmm?" Damaris made a vaguely interested sound. "These linen closets are most impressive."

"Every girl invited I've known since birth; even before that, you might say. Our families have known each other for generations." She fixed Damaris with a look. *"Generations."*

"No surprises there for you, then," Damaris said cheerfully and looked around for something else to comment on. Did the woman think she was going to wither up and creep away?

"Each girl gently born, delicately bred, skilled in all the womanly arts, each one born to step into the position, knowing everyone, and everything . . ."

"But you had to cancel it. What a shame. Do you make your own cheese?"

Lady Breckenridge's pale blue eyes glittered. "Instead, here you are, a girl I've never met before, some connection of Lady Beatrice's but otherwise entirely unknown to English society. And half *Italian.*" As if Damaris were some mongrel puppy. Which, come to think of it, was not far off the mark, Damaris thought. Papa's family was quite undistinguished.

"Yes, and half English too. Interesting, isn't it?"

From the look on Lady Breckenridge's face, it wasn't. "Do you play any musical instruments, Miss Chance? The harp, or perhaps the pianoforte?"

"No, I'm afraid my musical skills are barely adequate, though I do like to sing, and we are learning to dance — my sisters and I."

The well-plucked eyebrows almost disappeared. "You don't dance?"

"My father didn't approve of it."

"Good heavens, how very peculiar. I would have thought dancing was an essential skill for any young woman aspiring to become a lady. But then, I suppose when one has had a foreign upbringing . . ." Lady Breckenridge tailed off on a disparaging note. "You embroider, of course."

"Not very well, though I do stitch a neat hem, if I say so myself."

"Hems," Lady Breckenridge declared, "are for maids to sew."

"It's a skill I've found very useful over the years," Damaris said cheerfully.

Lady Breckenridge sniffed. "Do you have any ladylike accomplishments at all, Miss Chance?"

Damaris smiled. "I'm not sure how ladylike it is, but I do like to draw and paint."

She was rewarded with a thin smile. "Indeed. Watercolors are quite an acceptable medium."

"I paint china," Damaris said brightly and inaccurately. "Cups, bowls, chamber pots, that sort of thing." She'd been trained to paint with watercolors. The china painting was a new skill. But she wasn't aiming to please.

There was a chilly silence, then: "I should hate to see Frederick marry to disoblige his parents."

"I should hate even more for him to marry simply to oblige them," Damaris said, and when Lady Breckenridge's eyebrows flew up on cue, she added, "I think a man, if he's truly a man, ought to marry to please himself, don't you, Lady Breckenridge? So this is where you dry the washing in wet weather. How ingenious. And of course, necessary — I didn't realize it rained so much in England until I came here."

"This has been an unseasonably cold winter," Lady Breckenridge said, adding waspishly, "I suppose the sun shines all the time in Italy."

"I wouldn't know," Damaris said carelessly. "I've never been there."

"What? But —"

"Venice," she said. "And this is the storeroom? So interesting that English people confuse the two countries. Venice was an independent republic for centuries until Napoleon's invasion. Currently it's part of the Kingdom of Lombardy-Venetia, though we have every hope that the Austrians will leave and the republic be reestablished." And how grateful she was for Abby's insistence that they learn something of their supposed country of birth.

She smiled at Lady Breckenridge, who was looking exceedingly sour, and continued, "I would never mix up England and Scotland, or England and Wales. But then, my mother ensured I had an excellent education. Heavens. What a large flour bin. Do you not find that the flour gets stale in such a large container?"

"No," Lady Breckenridge said thinly. "We do not."

The rain had stopped and they proceeded to the kitchen gardens. Having tended gardens most of her life, Damaris was truly interested and asked the head gardener a great many questions.

As they left the high-walled kitchen gardens, Lady Breckenridge commented, "You seem to have a great deal of *practical* knowledge of gardening, Miss Chance. So unexpected in a lady. One could almost imagine you were the gardener's daughter." She tittered at her own joke.

"Mama never approved of my grubbing around in the dirt, either. She held that a lady should have a variety of accomplishments and interests to occupy her; hers were music and sewing — she did truly exquisite embroidery." Her eyes clouded, remembering how the pieces Mama had embroidered for Damaris's bride chest had been burned. "But I preferred to grow things." It was a necessity as well as a pleasure: The garden helped keep them fed.

Lady Breckenridge arched a brow. "I did not realize Venetians could keep gardens. Surely all that water . . ."

Curses! She'd forgotten about the canals. "Not in the house, no — of course we cannot have gardens around the house, as the English do. But we had gardens and orchards in our" — she groped for a solution to her rash statement — "in our country properties."

"Properties?"

"Yes," Damaris said airily, hoping she wouldn't ask for further details. "Does Breckenridge have orchards?"

When they returned to the house an hour later, Lady Breckenridge handed Damaris over to Freddy with an air of relief, saying, "I have shown Miss Chance the domestic parts of the house and the gardens. She is interested in herbs. And orchards. And" — she shuddered eloquently as she glided away — "bees."

Freddy watched her go, then whistled softly. "Round one to Miss Chance. My mother looks almost crushed. What did you do to her?"

"Nothing, I promise you," Damaris said. "On the contrary, she has spent the last two hours squashing my pretensions in the most relentless, elegant fashion."

"Really?" His eyes danced. "Your pretensions look remarkably unsquashed to me. Quite delightfully perky, in fact."

Seeing the direction of his gaze she pulled her shawl across her bosom. "Those," she said with what she hoped was quelling dignity, "are not pretensions."

"No? Really? What are they, then? Please explain."

She couldn't help but laugh at his wicked, mock-schoolboy eagerness. "You, Mr. Monkton-Coombes, are a shocking flirt."

He gave her a wounded look. "Nonsense! I'm a very good flirt, some would even say excellent, though modesty prevents me from saying so."

She laughed. "It will serve you right when I jilt you. Nobody will wonder at it at all."

"They won't, will they?" He heaved a doleful sigh, but Damaris wasn't deceived; his eyes still danced, blue as the sun on the sea.

CHAPTER FOURTEEN

"I do not want people to be very
agreeable, as it saves me the trouble of
liking them a great deal."
— JANE AUSTEN, *JANE AUSTEN'S LETTERS*

There would be just three for luncheon, the butler informed them while they were waiting for Lord Breckenridge to arrive. Lady Breckenridge had retired to her bedchamber with a severe headache and had ordered her luncheon brought up on a tray.

"Oh, dear, I probably gave her that headache," Damaris admitted to Freddy after the butler had left. "I feel terrible now."

"Nonsense. My mother's headaches are legendary. They come on whenever she fails to get her way. If she were truly ill, she wouldn't have ordered any luncheon at all, let alone on a tray."

Lord Breckenridge entered. He gave Damaris a sharp look. "Heard you asked to be shown the gardens, Miss Chance — the *kitchen* gardens."

"Yes, my lord; it was very interesting. I have an interest in growing things."

"Your only job is to grow an heir for Breckenridge," he grumbled as he seated himself. As the butler served luncheon, the older man eyed Damaris thoughtfully. It was quite rude of him to stare, but she refused to be put out of countenance by him.

"Heard you also found the orchards worth looking at."

She broke open a bread roll and buttered it. "I did."

"The beehives too."

"Yes, I have contemplated keeping bees myself." She picked up her spoon and started on her soup.

His hairy gray brows snapped together. "Yourself?"

She looked up from her soup in faint surprise at his tone and said coolly, "I have a fondness for honey." She glanced at the butler. "Please tell the cook this soup is delicious."

Lord Breckenridge addressed himself to his plate for the rest of the meal, but at the end, he fixed her with a hard gaze once more. "Goin' for a drive this afternoon. Be pleased if you'd accompany me, Miss

Chance."

The words were couched as a request, but it was an order, Damaris had no doubt. She turned to Freddy. "Did you have plans for us this afternoon, Freddy?"

"Wasn't asking him. It's you I want to talk to."

"You said you wanted to go into the village," Freddy said at the same time. She'd said no such thing; he was giving her an excuse.

"She can do that anytime, boy," his father snapped. "Make up your mind, gel, which is it to be?"

She forced her fingers to unclench — the man was so rude. She longed to give him a good set-down, but Freddy was looking tense. False betrothal or not, his protective instincts were strong, she'd learned, and she didn't want to be the cause of any further tension between him and his parents. Better for him to think his father's rudeness didn't bother her at all. Water off a duck's back, she'd said.

No doubt Lord Breckenridge was going to attempt the same kind of pretension-squashery as his wife had earlier. If that was the case, Damaris thought, bring it on.

"As your father said, Freddy, we can go into the village anytime. Thank you, Lord

Breckenridge, I'd be happy to go for a drive with you."

"Hah!" The older man shot a triumphant look at Freddy. "Gel knows which side her bread is buttered on."

"Nothing of the sort; it's just that I was taught to show respect to old people," she said sweetly, adding, "no matter how little they may deserve it."

She ran upstairs to fetch her warm pelisse, hat and gloves. When she came downstairs, buttoning her gloves, Freddy and his father were standing chest to chest, glaring at each other.

As she hurried up, Freddy glanced at her and stepped back, saying something to his father she didn't catch.

His father snorted and turned to Damaris. "Ready, Miss Chance?"

She glanced at Freddy. His face was set and unreadable but he made no move to dissuade her. "Perfectly," she said and sailed out the front door.

"Thought I'd show you the estate," Lord Breckenridge said as the carriage moved off. It was a phaeton, she was glad to see, open to the air but with a hood to shelter them if it rained. After her experience with the yellow bounder, she was a little nervous of riding in stuffy closed carriages. The last thing she wanted was to throw up over her supposed future father-in-law. Though there could be compensations, she reflected.

"What were you and Freddy talking about in the hall just now?" she asked him.

He snorted. "Damned impertinence."

"Who, you or him?"

He gave her a narrow look. "That's enough cheek from you, missy. Bad enough my son thinks —" He broke off and glared at her. "I know how to treat a lady, dammit."

Damaris hid a smile. She was perfectly capable of defending herself against any gibes his father might make, but the thought that Freddy had warned his father off made her feel warm inside.

"And don't think I'm going to let you tool these beauties about the country," he said grumpily, indicating the matched bays pulling the phaeton. "I'm not a reckless fool like my son."

"Your son is neither a fool nor reckless. And if you have brought me here to insult him, you may stop the carriage now and I will get down and walk." She waited with chin high, ignoring his scrutiny.

After a moment he grunted, so, taking that as acceptance of her terms, she added, "And beautiful as they may be, I have no desire to drive your horses."

They drove down the main drive and turned left, away from the village, along a narrow lane lined with high hedgerows. They passed a small cottage, where an elderly woman in a mob-cap stood in the front garden, pruning vines. She gazed intently at them and half raised her hand, as if to wave, but Lord Breckenridge took no notice. Damaris smiled at the woman as the phaeton swept past at a fast clip. "Who was that?"

"Eh? Oh, her. Nobody."

"She was clearly somebody."

He gave her an exasperated look. "Old retainer. Nobody you need notice."

"Oh, I notice everyone," she said blithely. She waited for some crushing response, but apart from another grunt, he didn't say anything for some time.

They drove through endless lanes, and from time to time he'd throw out some comment about whatever it was they were passing. "Potatoes," he said as they passed a field of some crop drowning under sheets of water. "All this blasted rain we've been havin'. Looks set to ruin the harvest."

Another time he jerked his head at a field full of sheep. "Sheep," he informed her.

278

She restrained herself from exclaiming in amazement. While he remained civil, so would she. "For meat or wool?"

He gave her a surprised look. "Wool."

They drove through a small hamlet and he said, "Tenants' cottages." Several children ran out, waving. A woman carrying a basket bobbed a curtsy. A couple of laborers trudging along the lane stood back as they passed and tugged their forelocks to Lord Breckenridge. He ignored them all.

Damaris, not quite knowing what to do, smiled at them anyway.

At a crossroads a broad-shouldered man in a worn leather apron straightened from examining a horse and dipped his head in greeting. Lord Breckenridge gave him a curt nod, saying to Damaris as they passed, "Smith. Good man. Knows his trade."

Gradually it dawned on her that, unless he'd changed his mind at the last minute — or since she'd threatened to get out and walk — this wasn't an attempt to squash the unsuitable bride's pretensions. He really was giving her a tour of the estate. Why, she had no idea, but something inside her unknotted, and she began to relax and enjoy herself.

They came to a muddy field dotted with pigs. Before he could say "pigs" to her, she said, "I used to breed pigs."

It was only a slight exaggeration; a farmer had given them a piglet once, and Damaris had raised it. She'd wept when it had to be killed but she'd still eaten the meat. Meat was always very scarce at the mission and it was sinful to waste food simply because you'd known it as a friend. Pigs were affectionate and intelligent creatures.

He turned his head to stare at her. "You bred *pigs*? Good God!" Then, after a pause, he asked, "What kind of pigs?"

"A Chinese breed. They were experimental," she hastily added.

He grunted and gave her another hard-to-read look. "Experimental Chinese pigs, eh? And do they swim, these Chinese pigs?"

She gave him a blank look. "Swim?"

"Yes, well, they'd need to, because of the canals, wouldn't they?"

She managed to keep a straight face. "Er, no, we kept them on an island, where we had the orchards."

"Extraordinary," he murmured to himself. "Experimental Chinese swimming pigs . . ."

"Well, how was he?" Freddy asked her on their return.

"Perfectly civil." She took off her hat and frowned thoughtfully. "Surprisingly so."

"Why? What did you talk about?"

"The estate."

"The estate?"

She nodded. "It wasn't at all what I expected, but he pointed out the crops he was growing and the apple orchards and sheep. And we talked briefly about pigs."

"Pigs?"

She giggled. "The pigs were my fault, to be honest. I told him I'd bred pigs — well, I raised a piglet once in China, which is close. I thought for a minute he'd bubbled me when he asked if they swam in the canals, but he seemed to accept my explanation — I said they were kept on an island where we had orchards. He seemed remarkably impressed."

Freddy groaned. "He would be. It all makes sense now. Blast!"

"What makes sense?" She tilted her head curiously. "Tell me."

He took her arm and led her toward the stairs. "Those muff — girls they had lined up for me, they're all very different, but they have one thing in common: They were all raised on an estate like this and have some knowledge of how to run one."

She nodded, a little puzzled. "Yes, your mother asked me about running a house the first night we arrived, remember?"

"Yes, but you don't understand. My mother is in charge of the house; my father runs the estate — or, rather, tells the estate manager how to run it."

"Yes, I assumed that's how it would be. So what —" She broke off. "Where are we going?" They'd passed the landing of the floor where her bedchamber was.

"Something I want to show you." He tugged her onward. "The thing is, if my father is talking land management — and pigs! — to you, it probably means he's starting to approve of you." He pulled a wry face. "Come to think of it, they probably both do. First you sent my mother upstairs in a sulk —"

"I did no such thing."

"She called it a headache, but believe me it was a sulk. Which means she didn't manage to crush you, which is a point in your favor. The future Lady Breckenridge must be able to hold her own with the finest aristocratic bitches in the land. They like it that you stood up to them."

"Oh." She digested the implications of that as he led her through a maze of corridors and up a series of increasingly narrow stairs.

She paused on a landing to catch her breath. "So when they're nasty to me, would you rather I burst into tears instead?" She wasn't sure she could weep on demand, and it certainly went against the grain to do so, but he was giving her a cottage in exchange for this performance, and he who paid the piper chose the tune.

"Good God, no, I haven't enjoyed myself so much in years. I don't think any young woman has ever managed to get the better of my mother." He shook his head in amazement. "And not only did you manage to keep my father civil —"

"That was you and your warning off."

"How did you —"

"I asked him."

"And he *told* you?" He laughed. "Well, there you are. And then you discussed crops and pigs with him. Wonders will never cease. Turn here."

"Where are we going again?" She peered doubtfully up a steep narrow staircase that seemed to lead into a cupboard.

He gave a faint smile. "Wait and see. There's a key to unlock it — ah, here we are." He produced a key from the ledge over the narrow doorway, reached past her to unlock the door and waved her on. "Ladies first."

She had to bend to get through the small door, but she stepped outside into fresh air and gasped with pleasure at the view in front of her. He'd brought her to the small towerlike structure she'd vaguely noticed on top of the house. Surrounding the tower there was a narrow walkway about four feet wide, with a railed barrier for safety. She could see for miles in every direction.

"Seeing as you've been driving around the estate all day, thought you might enjoy the bird's-eye view. Besides, with any luck we'll get a sunset. You do like sunsets, don't you?"

"I do indeed," she said softly, touched by his thoughtfulness.

He nodded. "Thought so. Women usually like such things."

Unreasonably annoyed at being part of "usual women," she moved to the edge of the walkway and looked out.

She could see the kitchen gardens, the apple orchards and the beehives she'd visited in the morning. On a rise was the copse of winter-bare silver birches she'd noticed on her drive, and surrounding the estate was a patchwork stretch of small farms and cottages. She spotted the cottage where the old woman had smiled at her. "Who lives there?"

"Our old nurse, Nanny McBride. Why?"

"Oh, we passed her today, that's all. She was in her garden, pruning. I thought she looked nice."

"She likes her garden," he said indifferently.

"Can I meet her?"

"Nanny McBride? Whatever for? She's very old."

"She seemed quite vigorous to me, certainly not too old for visitors."

"I've already dropped in on her. Did it while you were off with my father." With one booted foot he stirred a small pile of rubbish in a corner, bits of wood, an old bucket, a length of rotted rope.

"You've visited her? Already?" He must care for his old nanny to have visited her so soon.

"Only out of duty." He sounded uninterested, but she wasn't convinced.

He leaned forward, frowning, then smiled, and from the pile in the corner, produced a small, weathered-looking wooden sword, the handle of which had once been painted red. "So that's where it got to. He must have hidden it." He turned the small sword over in his hands and made a couple of pretend passes with it. "My brother, George, and I used to play up here every chance we could. Pirates and buccaneers, mainly, but sometimes we'd be soldiers trying to take the fort or the castle, depending what it was. That end was always George's and this end was mine."

It was a dangerous place for small boys to play in. His brother had died when he was a boy. That barrier would be easy to climb. Without thinking, she blurted out, "Did your brother fall? Is that how he died?"

"No." He turned abruptly and walked away, disappearing around the other side of the tower.

Damaris bit her lip, silently cursing herself for her tactlessness. She gripped the rail hard and stared out at the horizon. He'd made it clear he didn't want to talk about his brother, and it was, after all, none of her business. It wasn't as if she were really his betrothed. Should she go after him and apologize? Or should she just let it slide?

To the south, not far from the house, lay a lake, wind-whipped and gray, lined on one side with dark pines. Nearby was a small stone chapel, and beside it, a scattering of headstones. The family cemetery. She shivered.

"Are you cold?" he asked, coming up behind her. Close behind her. She could feel the warmth of his body all down her back.

"No, I'm all right, thanks." But she didn't move away and neither did he.

"That's Devon over there. And Davenham Hall is just beyond those hills." He put a hand on her shoulder to turn her in the right direction. His voice was light, untroubled. She wasn't deceived. She'd hit a nerve.

"London is that way." He pointed. "And on a clearer day you can see the sea, over there."

She squinted, trying to glimpse a line of blue on the horizon, but though the rain had stopped where they were, she could see it pouring down in gray veils farther away. The sun was beginning to set, turning the shallow sheets of silvery water to gold.

"It's very wet, isn't it? It isn't even draining away in some places. We saw so many fields that were quite flooded. Your father said the crops were ruined."

He shook his head. "I told him years ago he should have those fields drained, but will he listen? Not to me. What would I know about anything?" He clenched his fist in frustration. "His idea of farming is medieval. He despises the very idea of change and dismisses every innovation of the new science of agriculture as newfangled nonsense."

"You've tried to talk to him?"

He snorted. "I've given up. My interest

now is in the new technology surrounding steam engines and transport, not just shipping."

Damaris knew from Flynn that Freddy was a partner in their shipping line, but she hadn't realized he was also interested in steam. "Max also has an interest in steam power, doesn't he?"

Freddy nodded. "That's how I first got interested. He was mad about steam engines when we were at school together, and while he was abroad, I followed up on it. I invested in a few developments here and there and they've paid off handsomely. Steam power is the future."

"You say you invested in some developments — what does that entail?" She really said it to keep him talking and to make up for her earlier tactlessness, but he took her question seriously and as he explained how investing worked she became interested herself.

Most fascinating to her was how he had been able to build quite a small inheritance from an aunt into an income that supported him. "A bare competence, but it makes me independent."

He might dismiss it as a competence, but from everything she'd seen, he lived a comfortable, not to say luxurious existence.

She'd never had enough money to invest in anything, but nor had she ever considered that money was for anything other than saving and trying to stretch.

"I'd like to learn more about investing," she said.

"It's not difficult," he said. "Just risky."

"What have you two been up to?" Lord Breckenridge asked as they sat down to dinner. "The boy been looking after you?" It was clear from his manner that Freddy's guess had been correct. His parents — his father, at least — seemed to approve of her. Even if she couldn't ride and thought foxes were sweet. His mother, on the other hand, remained distant.

"Indeed he has," Damaris said. "In fact, he was explaining to me earlier how investments work." It was time Lord Breckenridge learned his son knew a great deal more than anyone gave him credit for.

He snorted. "Boy talks a lot of nonsense."

"Not at all," she said coolly. "I found him most informative."

"Informative?" Lord Breckenridge snorted. "All my son understands about 'investments' he's gleaned from his dealin's with the cent-per-cents. Moneylenders," he added, seeing she didn't understand the term. "But don't worry, m'dear, whatever fortune you bring to this marriage will be well protected — we'll have the respective family lawyers draw up a marriage settlement for you that will keep it out of his spendthrift hands."

"Spendthrift?" Surprised at the accusation, she glanced at Freddy, who gave a tiny shake of the head as if to say "don't worry about it."

His father leaned across and patted her hand. "Don't worry your pretty little head about it, m'gel."

"I won't," she said crisply, moving her hand away. "I have complete faith in Freddy's abilities and would happily entrust every penny I own to him."

His father chuckled. "Which is why, m'dear, we don't allow ladies to dabble in matters they don't understand."

Damaris gritted her teeth. Her father had squandered most of Mama's fortune on bribes and expensive gifts to curry favor with the warlord, and by the time Damaris was twelve there was almost nothing left. Once their income had dribbled to a small, regular charitable donation from England, Papa lost interest and left the entire financial management of the mission to her.

It had been Damaris's responsibility to

make their income stretch and feed them all. She did all the marketing, bargaining furiously to get the best prices, and all the worrying about how to make ends meet and keep everyone fed. Such things were beneath Papa's notice.

Afterward, when they were alone, she tackled Freddy about his silence. "Why do you let him speak of you like that? You're not a spendthrift. You're not a fool — far from it — and I don't care what your father says, you do understand investments. You might act the frivolous rattle in society but I know from Mr. Flynn that you have responsibilities in the firm that you carry out reliably and well. And he said once he has great respect for your business acumen, so why —"

"Good heavens, don't spread that around, I beg you! It will quite ruin the reputation I've spent years building."

He said it lightly, as if it were all a joke, but there was enough truth in it for her to ask, "Why not? And don't hand me any flummery about your society reputation — I'm talking about your parents and what they think of you. They show you no respect, and worse than that —"

"They have their reasons." He looked away, his expression momentarily bleak.

"What reasons?"

"They need not bother you. Your reason for being here is, as you have pointed out several times, merely for the purposes of playacting. You don't need to get involved."

It was a definite warning-off.

"Don't look at me like that," he said. "I mean it for your own good." His finger stroked the curve of her ear.

She pulled back. "What are you doing?"

"Just tidying a lock of hair that came loose. Why? Do you mind?"

"No, it just felt . . . odd." Her hair wasn't coming loose at all, she was sure. He was trying to distract her from their discussion.

"Odd, disgusting? Or my-but-that-Freddy-is-a-charmer odd?"

She fought a smile. "I don't think there is such an odd."

"Of course there is. My grandfather invented it. I take after him. He was a famous rake."

She tilted her head to glance at him. "And are you a famous rake?"

"Not yet, but I'm working on it," he said earnestly.

She laughed. She was beginning to recognize a pattern: Every time the subject got too serious or uncomfortable, he flirted his way out of it. It was clear he didn't want to discuss his parents' attitude to him, so she'd let the subject drop. For the moment.

CHAPTER FIFTEEN

"Where the wound had been given, there
must the cure be found, if anywhere."
— JANE AUSTEN, *EMMA*

Rain was sleeting down next morning, and
after breakfast Damaris excused herself, saying she wanted to write some letters. Freddy
took himself gratefully off to spend the
morning in the stables. His grays had arrived and, besides, the unalloyed delight of
his parents' company was getting on his
nerves. What he really wanted was to go for
a good hard ride, but when he went to
saddle up a horse, his father's head groom
said, "In this weather, Mr. Freddy?"

Collins had put Freddy on his first pony
as a child, and he was right; it would be
foolhardy to take a horse out in such atro-
cious weather. Damn. Freddy seized a currycomb and went to work on one of his
grays. Some of the newer stable lads raised

their brows at seeing the son of the house doing such lowly work, but Collins just nodded wisely and waved the others back to work. He understood Freddy's demons.

As a boy Freddy had worked off many a head of steam in the stables under Collins's benevolent — and critical — eye. Son of the house or not, Collins held Freddy to the same standard as anyone else employed to work with the prime cattle under his care, even if the horses belonged to Freddy.

Stripped down to his shirtsleeves, Freddy plied the currycomb with a will. Blasted weather. Not only was it preventing him from riding off his frustrations, it also kept him stuck in the house, and while he was enjoying Damaris's company to an extent that was starting to worry him, his parents' constant cuts at him were bound to distress her, no matter how gamely she tried to parry them. He was so used to it he barely noticed.

Freddy knew how to take his punishment. He should, after sixteen years.

But then, for years he'd spent only one day a year with them. Hardly enough to notice how they were aging, to know who they were now, one adult to another. They still treated him as a boy, and he, well, he did his best not to notice them at all.

But now he was seeing them through Damaris's eyes. And it wasn't pleasant.

He finished the first horse, then moved on to the next. It had barely taken the edge off. What he really needed was a fight. He finished the second horse and looked around for something else to do.

"Still wound tight as a spring, lad?" Collins asked quietly. "Wood to be chopped out back if you fancy it."

He did. He'd removed his coat and waistcoat to groom the horses in his shirtsleeves, but after chopping and splitting the first dozen logs, he'd started to sweat, despite the cold, and stripped off his shirt. As the pile of neatly chopped and split wood mounted, the tension gradually eased out of him.

There was satisfaction and release in the rhythmic swing of the ax and the contained, precise violence of the action. And the growing woodpile was a visible achievement, be it ever so lowly. He could almost hear his father saying, *Chopping wood? A son of Breckenridge? Good God! Beneath your dignity, dammit, boy!*

He grinned to himself and selected another log. He liked doing things that were beneath his dignity.

■ ■ ■ ■

"Boy's late!" Lord Breckenridge paced up and down in the dining room. Luncheon was ready to be served, and Damaris and Lady Breckenridge were seated. They'd only been waiting several minutes, but Lord Breckenridge was already furious.

"Where the devil is he?"

"I think he went to the stables, my lord," Horwood murmured. "Would you like me to send someone to enquire?"

"No, don't worry, I'll go." Damaris sprang up and hurried toward the door, glad to escape the awkwardly stilted conversation.

"To the stables? It's not suitable for a l—" Lady Breckenridge began, but Damaris affected not to hear her as she ran out the door. She didn't care if the stables were an unsuitable place for a lady, it was better than having to make polite conversation with Freddy's parents, when all they wanted to do was criticize him.

She hurried to one of the back entrances and carefully crossed the cobbled courtyard, keeping her pretty kid slippers out of the puddles. The stables building was large and she halted just inside to let her eyes adjust to the relative gloom.

"Miss?" A young stable boy approached her. "Something you wanted, miss?"

"Mr. Monkton-Coombes?"

"He's out yonder, chopping wood." The boy pointed.

Damaris could hear the rhythmic chunk! . . . chunk! of an ax. Freddy was chopping wood? Intrigued, she followed the sound. She paused in an open doorway, and stilled.

Freddy was indeed chopping wood, dressed in nothing but his breeches and boots. His chest and arms were bare. And what a chest and arms. Not slender and wiry, like the men she'd seen in China, not tattooed and brawny, like the sailors on the ship that had brought her home, or meaty, like their captain, but lean and clean and hard muscled and . . . beautiful.

Her mouth dried. She drank in the sculpted planes of his chest, the hard-roped strength of his arms, the fluid movement of his whole body as he swung the ax. She didn't move — couldn't move, for staring at him. Hungrily.

Unaware of her presence he kept chopping. Swing, thunk! Swing, thunk! He could have been a marble statue of some glorious Greek god, except for the smooth flow of the muscles under his skin, like steel under oiled silk. Swing, thunk!

She felt hollow inside. A deep ripple shuddered through her body.

He bent, still unaware of her presence, and tossed some chunks of split wood aside. Who knew male shoulders could be so beautiful? The line of his spine, the way his back tapered from those superb broad shoulders to the narrow hips and firm masculine buttocks . . .

A faint sheen of sweat polished his skin. She wondered what it would taste like, and shivered, but not with cold. She should not stare, should not wonder about such things as tasting a man's skin; it was wrong, and shameful, but she could not help herself.

A tide of damp heat flowed through her. Papa whispered in her mind, *Lust. Original sin.*

Still she could not drag her eyes off Freddy, half-naked as he chopped wood with a muscular grace and economy of movement that was almost a dance. As long as she behaved correctly, it wasn't a sin. You couldn't be punished for thoughts, could you?

"Miss?"

She almost jumped a foot. An elderly groom stood there, looking concerned. She blushed and stepped back.

He glanced in at Freddy and grimaced. "Sorry about that, miss. That stupid boy — he should have gone looking for Mr. Freddy himself, instead of letting you see . . ." He cleared his throat loudly, at the same time interposing himself discreetly between Damaris and Freddy, sheltering her delicate eyes from the shocking sight of all that bare masculine skin. If only he knew.

"Go on, then, lad, give Mr. Freddy his clothes," the groom snapped to the stable boy, who edged past them and handed Freddy his waistcoat and coat.

Freddy had already pulled his shirt on. From the corner of her eye she could see him tucking his shirt into his breeches. She tried not to watch. No, tried not to be seen watching.

She chatted to the groom, bemoaned the weather and accepted his congratulations on the betrothal, and in a moment or two Freddy emerged, fully dressed. His brows were raised in a faint question.

"You're late for luncheon," she explained. "Your parents are waiting. I came to fetch you."

He frowned. "You came? Why not a footman?"

"I wanted to come." And she was so glad she had. She would treasure the memory of him chopping wood for the rest of her chaste and virtuous life.

As they left the stable area she heard the groom berating the stable boy, saying, "Next time you see a lady hereabouts, you fetch me, all right? Ladies don't want to be seeing men without their shirts on, now, do they, you stupid boy?"

Ladies, maybe not. Damaris, definitely.

"Bringin' the stench of the stables in with you, boy?" Lord Breckenridge was in the hallway as they walked in. "Least you could have done is changed before sitting down with ladies."

He couldn't possibly smell his son from there, Damaris thought. She'd come in on Freddy's arm and she could only just smell him, an enticing blend of sandalwood soap, a very faint aroma of horse that was not unpleasing and a hint of fresh male sweat that was, frankly, too pleasing for her own peace of mind.

"I didn't have time to change," Freddy said carelessly.

"No consideration for others," his father muttered.

"None at all," Freddy agreed cheerfully. He glanced at the footman waiting outside his father's study with a covered tray. "Not joining us, Father?"

"Luncheon is a meal for ladies," his father declared and marched off.

"Pork pie, a tankard of ale and whatever pudding is left over from last night on that tray," Freddy murmured. "But he never eats luncheon."

"He did yesterday. And he was ready to today, until you were late."

"And he will tomorrow, but in his case it's not called luncheon, but 'a quick bite.' He only joined us at table yesterday because it was your first day, and also because he'd heard you'd routed my mother and wanted to get to know you better by dragging you off on that tour of the estate afterward."

"I didn't rout her," Damaris said, embarrassed. *Rout* sounded so rude. She'd merely stood up for herself.

He quirked a humorous eyebrow. "Not what I heard. And by now, the whole village will know."

They entered the dining room, where a light luncheon had been laid out. "My apologies for keeping you waiting, Mother. I lost track of the time."

"You have been neglecting your guest, Frederick," Lady Breckenridge said as Freddy pulled out a chair to seat Damaris. "Miss Chance was left with nothing to do while you were gadding about in the stables."

"On the contrary, I was busy writing letters, and perfectly content with my own company," Damaris said. "And seeing as I have little interest in horses and Freddy loves them, we were both well content with the arrangement. Besides," she added, paving the way for the eventual breaking of the betrothal, "I don't think it's healthy for couples to live in one another's pockets, do you?" She glanced at Lord Breckenridge's empty place.

"Horwood, you may serve the soup," Lady Breckenridge said.

The meal was a light one, consisting of soup, bread and butter, and some cold chicken pie.

"Frederick, Miss Chance has an interest in painting."

"Would you like a roll?" Freddy asked, passing Damaris a basket of warm bread rolls.

"Did you hear me, Frederick? Miss Chance likes paintings."

"Yes, Mother, I heard."

"She would enjoy seeing the family portrait gallery. You must take her there this afternoon."

"She wouldn't be interested."

"Oh, that would be lovely," said Damaris at the same time, then looked at him in dismay, realizing she'd inadvertently sided with his mother.

"Then that's settled," his mother said. "Oh, and by the way, Miss Chance, I had Horwood place in your room a set of water-color paints."

"Thank you, Lady Breckenridge, that's very kind of you." Damaris was stunned by the unexpected gift and felt a little guilty for her previous uncharitable thoughts.

Lady Breckenridge lifted a thin shoulder and said in a bored voice, "It's nothing. I acquired them for the convenience of my house party guests. Since it was canceled, you may as well make use of them."

"I'm sorry," Damaris said to Freddy when the meal was over. "If you don't want to show me the portrait gallery . . ."

He shook his head. "Doesn't matter. It's a complete bore, in my opinion, but I suppose it's your duty as a Breckenridge bride-to-be to view it." He seemed a little tense.

"It can't be that bad, surely." She would dearly like to see a portrait of Freddy as a child.

He glanced at her and his expression lightened. "An endless litany of pompous bores and entertaining rakes. I shall expect you to play close attention and identify which were which from their portraits." The cheerful tone was, she was sure, assumed, but she decided to play along.

"Bores or rakes? I have no other choices?"

"No. The Monkton-Coombes family breed either bores or rakes, usually but not always in alternate generations. Care to guess which group my father belongs to?"

The portrait gallery was a long, narrow room that bordered what had once been the great hall, Freddy explained. "We'll start with the oldest ones and work our way up to the present," he said, leading her down to the far end, where the paintings were darker and the poses a little stiffer.

"It's so interesting. They're so different from anything I saw in China."

"Here's the first lot of ancestors to have been immortalized. Sixteenth century. Bores or rakes, remember — which is which?" There were nine portraits in this section; five ladies and four gentlemen. The men all wore small goatee beards and mustaches — obviously the fashion of the time. The first portrait was of a stern-looking man wearing an impressive gold chain and a feather in his hat.

"Not a rake," Damaris decided. There was

no humor or warmth in his face, both qualities she'd come to associate with rakishness.

"Spot-on."

The second was of a younger man, plainly dressed, wearing a corded beret and a thoughtful expression.

"I rather like the look of him," she said. He was handsome, with a long face and a firm chin, which even his little beard failed to disguise.

"You would," Freddy said, feigning disgust. "A rake of the first order. When he died, several women tried to throw themselves into the grave with him. Can't imagine why — the fellow isn't even good-looking."

Damaris gave him a sideways glance. If he couldn't see the resemblance between them, she wasn't going to point it out.

Next was a stiff-looking fellow with an upstanding lace collar, a firmly buttoned gold coat and a velvet hat with an orange feather.

"He looks a little severe," Damaris said. "But he's quite good-looking."

Freddy shook his head. "Righteous swine, by all accounts. Beat his wives — three of them — not all at once, of course — he was, after all, respectable. He died of the pox. Next."

The next portrait was of a man in a gold and black velvet tunic, very ornate, over a pleated shirt with an embroidered collar. He wore a fur hat and an expression that seemed to indicate that he was either dwelling on spiritual thoughts or bored rigid.

"Dressed like that, I suppose he could be a rake," Damaris said thoughtfully, "but I think he looks more of a bore."

"Badly constipated, I've always thought," said Freddy. "As well as pretentious. He left several volumes of the most appalling poetry. Now, come on, there's one more rake."

Damaris looked at him in surprise. There were only four portraits of men. "You don't mean one of the women, do you?"

He winked. "Clever girl. Now go pick her out."

Damaris strolled back and forth along the line of portraits until she'd narrowed it down to two, both beautiful, both young — one was barely out of childhood. She had a sad but sweet expression, but the other . . .

"This one looks discontented with her life," she decided. "As if she thinks she deserves better."

"Wrong. It's the saintly looking child who grew up to take legions of lovers. Not surprising, though — she was married to the bad poet. Would drive anyone to take lovers."

They strolled along the gallery, stopping in front of each portrait while Freddy told scurrilous stories about his ancestors that got more and more outrageous. According to him, they were all either pirates, rakes, sanctimonious bores, cowards, or poets or some combination of them.

"Poetic-looking fellow, don't you think?" he said, pointing to an eighteenth-century ancestor in a brown velvet coat, a lace jabot and powdered hair. He would have been about five and twenty when the portrait was painted. There was a strong family resemblance.

"Looks as though butter wouldn't melt in his mouth," Freddy continued, "but he was a true scholar."

"A scholar? Really?" She looked again at the portrait in surprise. He didn't look like a scholar. The scholars in the other paintings all carried books or scrolls or had been posed resting their hands on weighty-looking tomes. This young man wore roses in his lapel, his coat was unbuttoned and he lounged in his seat.

"He was famous for extolling the educational value of the Grand Tour," Freddy informed her solemnly. His eyes danced, and she waited, knowing there would be an outrageous end to the story.

"According to his journal, which I discovered as a boy and George and I read in secret, he didn't take in a single artistic or cultural sight in the two years he spent traveling through Europe. He did, however, describe in great detail the education he received from a long line of generous-minded European ladies. Left a string of bastards behind him on his Grand Tour — his father kept getting demands for money years afterward. Amazingly, he didn't die of the pox, but quietly in his bed at the age of eighty-one." He frowned. "At least I assume it was his own bed, and quietly, but now I come to think of it, that was most unlikely. Grandfather kept a mistress, right to the end."

Damaris laughed. "You do resemble him."

"Nonsense, he's a handsome fellow, whereas I . . ."

"You said George and you read his journal? Is that George?" She pointed to a portrait of a chubby-faced little boy with golden curls.

"Yes, he would have been about four then." He pointed to another painting of the same child with long golden locks. "In that one he's eight. Mother had it done just before his hair was cut to what Father called a proper manly look." He pointed to a third painting, of a boy of about twelve in a dark pink velvet suit. "That was painted a few months before he died. He hated that one, thought it made him look a sissy."

"Are there any paintings of both of you?" She was eager to see Freddy as a boy, and she was curious about his brother. Freddy hardly ever mentioned George, but when he did, there was . . . something about the way he spoke of George that she couldn't quite put her finger on. A studied carelessness, as if his brother didn't matter, and yet beneath it she sensed an undeniable fondness.

And each year he came down to Breckenridge for his brother's memorial service.

"A painting of both of us? Yes, of course." He led her to a large, gold-framed painting of a young woman she had no difficulty recognizing as Freddy's mother, seated with her arm around a standing boy, the same boy of the pink velvet suit. Behind her Lord Breckenridge stood with his hand resting on the boy's shoulder. On the other side of Lady Breckenridge was a large urn, overflowing with vines and flowers.

"Where are you?" she asked.

"There." He pointed to the urn.

Damaris examined the painting more

closely, wondering if perhaps he'd been portrayed hiding behind the urn — she could imagine him as a lively and mischievous boy playing hide-and-seek. But there was no sign of any small face peering out between the leaves. She turned to him. "I don't understand."

"After George died, my parents had the artist paint me out of the picture. They put the urn in my place. You can just see the toe of my shoe, there." He pointed and sure enough there at the base of the urn was a small shoe.

He said it carelessly, as if the small shoe were an amusing mistake, but *they'd painted their only remaining son out of the family portrait.* Damaris was horrified. "Why would they do such a thing?"

"Because I killed George. Now, there's a rather charming promenade and a fernery on the east side of the house. Would you like to see it?" He took her arm and began to guide her toward the door.

She yanked her arm out of his grasp, refusing to move. "What do you mean, you killed your brother?"

He shrugged. "Perfectly true."

"I don't believe it. How did you — I mean, how did your brother die? Was it an accident?"

"Well, of course I didn't mean to kill him." Again, he shrugged. "Still, my fault he died. Now, the rain seems to have stopped for the moment, so perhaps a quick walk might be possible. Come along."

Again she pulled back. "Freddy, don't change the subject."

"Why not, it's a boring subject," he said, his careless manner belied by the tension in his body. "What's done is done and no amount of talking is going to change the facts."

"But it's important, and I want to understand." She laid her hand on his arm. "Please, won't you explain to me what happened?"

"I never explain," he said with a hard look she'd never seen from him before. "There's no point. Now, are you coming or not? If you want to stay here with the ghosts of Breckenridge past, you can, but I need some fresh air. And a change of subject."

Damaris could see she wasn't going to get anything out of him in this mood, so she allowed herself to be led from the gallery. But as he took her back through the maze of corridors, her mind was spinning with questions.

How could he have killed his brother? And

if it was an accident, how could he be blamed? His parents obviously blamed him — she was horrified by the cold-blooded act of having him painted out of the family portrait, as if whatever he'd done was so unforgivable he couldn't even remain in a painting.

And he seemed to accept it.

But how could whatever he'd done be so unforgivable? He would have been only a boy when it happened. George was the older brother, and in the picture he looked only twelve or thirteen, which meant Freddy would have been about ten. Even if the accident had been a piece of stupid carelessness, or a foolish risky act, or even the result of a moment of temper — well, that was the nature of young boys. They seemed to have no understanding of risk or danger.

And no matter how dreadful the consequences of a child's act, she could not imagine rejecting him as a member of the family. Even now, so many years later, Freddy's parents barely acknowledged him. If they didn't need him to secure the succession, would they even care what he did with his life?

No wonder he only visited Breckenridge once a year. The wonder was that he came at all.

But it wasn't duty that brought him back here each fifth of December. It was guilt.

She followed him along, her heart aching for the unforgiven little boy who'd grown into the man who pretended not to care about anything. She had to find out what had happened.

The following day while Freddy was initiating her into the mysteries of billiards, she broached the matter again. "My mother died when I was twelve."

He looked up from the shot he was about to take. "You must have been very sad."

"Yes, and my father would never talk with me about her." Not quite true; he talked at her, enumerating all of Mama's faults and warning Damaris not to be like her. "It was very difficult for me at the time, but I have since found it helps to talk about it."

He made a decisive shot and straightened, leaning on his cue. "I can see right through you, Miss Chance, and while I'm sympathetic for your loss, if you think I'm going to talk about my brother to appease your curiosity, you're mistaken."

Miss Chance? It was a formal warning, then. "It's not curiosity."

He raised a sardonic brow.

"Well, not only curiosity," she admitted.

"It's hard to lose someone when you're that age, and it must be even harder to know that your parents blame you. But I'm sure —"

"We will not discuss this."

"But if you only —"

He rested the cue on the table, his expression uncharacteristically grim. "This is not your business, Damaris. Your business is to play the affianced bride — nothing more. And in return I will give you a cottage as we agreed. That's it. Nothing else."

"But —"

He rammed his cue into the cue stand. "I can see you're dreaming up some foolish, romantic female scheme to bring about a reconciliation between my parents and me, and I won't have it, you hear?"

"I only want to —"

"Well, don't. There's no point in stirring it all up again. What's done is done, and nothing can change it, so leave it alone. Otherwise I'll send you back to London — in a yellow bounder," he added in an afterthought and stalked from the room.

Damaris contemplated the arrangement of the balls on the baize-covered table. His parting shot had reassured her somewhat; he would never send her away in a yellow bounder, she was sure. But he was deadly serious in his insistence that she let drop the matter of his brother's death.

She might, if he weren't hurting so badly.

He reminded her of a dog she'd found injured and lying in a ditch when she was a child in China. She'd tried to help it and he'd snapped at her, leaving a nasty bite. But she'd persisted and sought help, and in the end the dog had been saved.

She wasn't foolish enough to think she could save Freddy or even divert his parents from their hurtful stance, but she needed to understand why it had happened in the first place.

And why was that, a small voice inside her asked. As he'd said, his past was none of her business. She was little better than a hireling, employed to play a part. She ought to stay out of it, as he'd told her to do.

But she couldn't. There might be nothing she could do to solve the problem, but at the very least she could understand.

The problem was, how to find out? Neither Freddy nor his parents would talk to her about it, she was sure. The servants might know, but she couldn't embarrass him by questioning the servants, and even so, they ought to be loyal enough not to discuss family business with a guest.

There was, however, someone who was no

longer a servant. She'd be bound to know, but whether she'd talk to Damaris or not was another matter. It wouldn't hurt to ask, surely.

The next day she found Nanny McBride's cottage without too much difficulty and knocked.

"You'll be Mr. Freddy's young lady," Nanny McBride said with a stern look. She looked past Damaris and frowned. "And where's himself, then? Did he no' bring you down to meet me?" She spoke with a strong Scottish brogue. She made no move to invite Damaris in.

It wasn't quite the welcome she'd expected. "No, I brought myself. I hope you don't mind, Mrs., er, Miss McBride."

The old woman looked her up and down, assessing her and, to judge from her expression, finding her wanting. "He said you weren't interested in meeting me."

Damaris shrugged. "He told me he only visited you out of duty."

The old woman's eyes narrowed. "He did, did he? Then what's he playing at? Come you in, young lady. I think we need to talk."

She ushered Damaris into a small, cozy cottage, comfortably but plainly furnished. Over the fireplace hung a simply framed pencil drawing of two boys.

"Sit yoursel' down, miss. You'll take a cup of bohea with me?"

"Bohea?" Damaris was very familiar with the Chinese tea, of course, but it was rather expensive for a former servant living on a pension.

Nanny McBride tried hard not to let her pride show. "Master Freddy knows my weaknesses. He sends me a wee something every month along with his regular letter, and not just tea, but all kinds of delicacies to tempt an old woman's fancy. He spoils me, he does." She bustled out to put on the kettle.

Damaris smiled to herself. So he only visited his old nanny out of duty, did he? Her eyes were drawn to the framed drawing and she moved closer to examine it.

It was a vivid sketch of two young boys, laughing and shoving against each other. The mischievous expression of the younger boy was unmistakable. But the joyous innocence in the boy was well and truly gone from the man.

"Freddy and his brother?" she asked as Nanny McBride came back with the tea tray and set it down on the table.

"Aye, clever, isn't it? Lord Breckenridge had an artist fellow down from London to paint the family. I sat with the boys when he was sketching them — the young devils couldn't stand still to save their lives, but the fellow didn't mind. He made a few sketches — I've never seen anything like it — his pencil just flew. A half dozen lines and there were my boys to the life! He gave me two of the sketches afterward and one of the estate carpenters framed them for me."

She gave Damaris a shrewd look. "That's what you've come for, isn't it? To talk about the boys?"

She nodded. "If you please, Mrs., er, Miss McBride? I'm sorry, I don't know how to address you."

"It's Miss. I never married," the old woman said briskly. "Do you mean both boys or just Mr. Freddy?"

Damaris took a deep breath. "Freddy mainly, but I want to ask you about George, as well."

Nanny McBride fixed her with a gimlet look. "You want to know about the accident."

Damaris nodded.

"You ought to ask Mr. Freddy."

"I have, but he won't tell me."

"So you've come sneaking out behind his back to ask his old nurse."

Damaris lifted her chin at the accusation in the old woman's voice. "Yes."

For a moment, Damaris was sure she was going to send her from the cottage with a flea in her ear, but instead she said, "Why do you want to know about something that happened so long ago? It's nothing to do with you, is it?" There was no warmth in her voice.

Damaris had rehearsed in her mind what she wanted to say to his nanny — she'd expected a doting, garrulous old thing, not this shrewd-eyed Scotswoman. She'd intended some platitude about getting to know her betrothed better — but the woman's judgmental response touched a nerve, and the words burst forth. "Because it's eating away at him. Oh, he says it doesn't matter, and he plays the rattle to hide his hurt, and he says he doesn't mind that his parents treat him so disrespectfully — that he deserves it because he killed his brother. But I don't care what he did, he was a young boy at the time, and even if it was deliberate — which I will *not* believe — he needs to be forgiven. And" — her voice grew husky — "to be loved." She bit her lip and looked away for a moment, fighting for control.

"Milk?" Nanny McBride held up a small

jug. She was talking about *tea*? Damaris couldn't believe it.

"No, thank you. Just weak and black." The way she'd drunk tea in China.

Nanny McBride poured out the tea and handed Damaris her cup. "Why do you care about my boy?"

Damaris blinked. "Because I'm his betrothed."

"Only in name." She saw Damaris's surprise. "Och, yes, he told me about your little arrangement. And I have to say, I wasn't prepared to like you, young lady, not one little bit. Now drink your tea. You don't let good bohea get cold."

Damaris drank her tea.

When she'd finished, the old woman nodded toward the picture over the mantel and said, "I've one or two other pictures of the boys. Would you like to see them?"

"Yes, please." She had no idea what was going on, but the tea had refreshed her and she hadn't been thrown out of the cottage yet, so there was still a chance she could find out what had happened.

Nanny McBride produced several other small framed drawings, one of two small boys, barely out of leading strings, drawn in charcoal. "The boys," she said with fond pride. "A gypsy in the marketplace was doing pictures for a tanner and I had him do the boys for me — and this one." It was Freddy, barely out of babyhood, round faced and chubby but still, somehow, recognizable.

Damaris took it and found herself smiling. "He was a beautiful baby, wasn't he?"

"That he was, young woman, that he was." She took the baby picture back and passed Damaris the last picture.

It was a study of a young boy, unmistakably Freddy, and by the hand of the same artist who'd drawn the first sketch and painted the family portrait. In it Freddy was gazing down at something that wasn't in the picture, concentrating with an endearingly earnest expression, chin resting on hand, his young brow furrowed.

"Chess," Nanny McBride explained. "That artist taught the boys how to play — it kept them still, you see."

"It's a lovely portrait." Pity it wasn't in color. She handed it back and watched as Nanny McBride replaced them carefully on her dresser.

Anger swirled up in her again. "So you have four pictures of Freddy, and yet in that great house up there" — she gestured angrily — "with all its *hundreds* of paintings, there is not one — *not one!* — painting of Freddy. Their only living son!" Hot tears prickled at the back of her eyes. "Do you know they had him painted out of the family portrait?" She dashed the tears aside with an angry swipe. "How could *any* parent do such a terrible thing? Especially to a bereaved child."

"Here you are, my dear." Nanny McBride handed her a handkerchief. She poured another cup of tea and added some hot water from the kettle.

Damaris wiped her eyes and drank the tea, a little shocked at her own outburst. "I'm sorry," she muttered. "I don't usually do that."

Nanny McBride smiled, her face crumpling into a hundred wrinkles. "You'll do, lassie, you'll do. I don't know what foolish game you and my Freddy are playing, pretending this betrothal is all a hoax, but you're the one for him, all right, God be praised."

"Oh, but —"

"Whisht, enough of that now. You canna fool Nanny McBride. You love that boy of mine, and no arguing will change my mind."

"I'm sorry, but you're mistaken," Damaris said. "I like Freddy, but it truly is a false betrothal. Neither of us plans to marry."

"Pfft! I know what I know." She fetched a

tin from the sideboard. "Now, a wee slice of Dundee cake and another cup of tea will settle you down, and then I'll tell you all about my boys."

She cut Damaris a thick slice of dark fruitcake, refreshed the tea with more boiling water, stirred the fire and began her story. "As I said, my dear, I never married, so those two boys were the closest thing I had to children of my own. I couldn't have loved them more if they'd been my own flesh and blood. But their parents . . ." She shook her head. "You've heard the expression 'an heir and a spare'?"

Damaris nodded.

"They took it literally. George was their firstborn son, and it was as if the sun shone out of him — well, and that's as it should be. George was a fine little lad. Clever, strong, handsome, brave — you couldn'a fault him. And two years later Freddy came along. Another fine, strong, bonny boy, but it was a difficult birth, and his mother never fully accepted the child afterward." She shook her head sadly.

"And his father?"

Nanny McBride made a rude noise. "His lordship had no interest in Master Freddy, as long as he was healthy and stayed out of the way. He was the spare — literally.

Everything — all his parents' attention — was for George."

Damaris swallowed. "Freddy was jealous?"

Nanny McBride snorted. "Not a bit of it. Freddy adored his big brother — and George loved him too. No two brothers could be closer. Where one led, the other followed; into mischief — that was usually Freddy — and out of it. If one fell the other would pick him up. Och, they fought and wrestled and competed, as boys do, but their squabbles never lasted more than an hour or two, and they were each the other's best friend."

She sighed. "George was everything the son and heir of a great house should be, and George's parents never looked past him to see that they had another son, equally worthy of their love, attention and approval."

She fetched the baby picture back. "Freddy tried, of course — no child could have tried harder to please his parents — but they simply didna seem to notice him. And after a while he stopped trying."

She gazed at the picture. "I used to pretend he was my own wean, my own wee boy. He was the lovingest little lad, and he's grown up . . ." She shook her head. "I've

325

seen the way he is with his parents, and I canna blame him, but it fair breaks my heart to see it. Well, it's still there inside him, no matter what face he shows to the world."

"I know. He's the kindest man I've ever known," Damaris said unwarily.

The old face crumpled into a smile. "Oh, my dear, see, you do love him. I'm so verra, verra glad."

Damaris opened her mouth to deny it, and then shut it, the words unspoken. Because it was true. She loved Freddy Monkton-Coombes.

CHAPTER SIXTEEN

"I can listen no longer in silence. I must
speak to you by such means as are
within my reach."
— JANE AUSTEN, *PERSUASION*

"So what happened the day George died?"
Damaris pushed on, not wanting to face the
revelation that had just come to her with
Nanny McBride's shrewd old eyes watching
her. She was uncannily perceptive.

"They were playing cricket. It was winter,
and of course they had no business to be
playing cricket in the snow, but they were
boys, and they didn't care about a bit of
snow. They started with snowballs — tossing them and smashing them with the
cricket bat, and then one of them — I can't
remember which — ran into the house and
came back with a proper cricket ball, and
they were off and playing, down by the lake.
It was a bitter winter that year and the lake

was iced over." She fell silent, remembering.

"And then?" Damaris prompted after a minute.

"It was all over in a flash. George bowled a ball, Freddy hit it high, George ran back to catch him out, and without realizing it he went onto the ice. Next minute he'd fallen through and disappeared from sight, and by the time anyone could get to him, he was dead. His foot got tangled in the weed and trapped him under the icy water."

For a long moment, Damaris simply stared at the old woman. Finally she said, "Do you mean that was *it*? *That* was the crime his parents punished him for? The reason he was painted out of the family portrait? For playing *cricket*?"

Nanny McBride nodded. "Aye, they blamed him for the accident. They sent him back to school the day after the funeral."

"But what about Christmas?"

Nanny McBride shrugged. "He stayed at school. His mother said she couldn't bear to look at him."

"But why, when it was so obviously just an accident? A tragic one, to be sure, but nobody's fault. And why would Freddy accept the blame?" But a moment's reflection and she could see why — even if she didn't agree with it. He was a young boy, just twelve years old, and he'd just lost his brother, whom he worshipped. The brother his parents doted on. She could imagine their grief would have been shocking, and if they'd never really loved their younger son . . .

Freddy had hit the ball.

Proper, loving parents would have hugged him, comforted him, reassured him that it wasn't his fault, that it was just a terrible accident, that it was nobody's fault.

Freddy's parents had had him painted out of the family portrait.

And even now, sixteen years later, they treated him as an unwelcome guest in his own home.

Her hands clenched into tight angry fists. It was time this nonsense stopped. She wanted to march back up to that great, rambling house and slap some sense, some decency — some heart! — into his parents.

She couldn't, of course. She was just a fiancée, and a false one at that.

But she could talk to Freddy.

She met him in the drive, returning from his ride. He immediately slid off his horse and walked back with her, the horse ambling along behind them.

"An accident? Playing cricket? And for this you let your parents treat you like, like —"

"Leave it, Damaris. It doesn't matter."

"It does matter."

"No, it's only for one day a year."

"Exactly. You've been shut out of your home and your family and you only come home one day a year. And when you do, the way your family treats you —"

"They're not my family," he said gently. "They're just my parents. I'm a grown man. I don't need parents."

Everyone needed a family, she thought. Even if it wasn't the usual kind. What would she have done without her sisters and Lady Beatrice? "But you blame yourself for an accident that wasn't your fault and that happened years ago, when you were a child."

"I don't. Not anymore. But they still need to blame me. It gives them comfort, a reason for George's death, someone to blame."

"Resentment and blame and willful blindness to the truth can never bring comfort." She knew what she was talking about. "My father resented my mother all my life. I never found out why, and in the end, it didn't matter. Even after she died, he clung to the resentment and transferred a lot of

the blame to me. It poisoned his entire life."
And hers, until he died.

There were parallels here, she realized, even though their lives had followed very different paths. It was a discomforting thought. It was so much easier to look at someone else's situation and see what should be done than to apply the same principles to your own problems.

Was that arrogance? Or cowardice?

"You're making too much of it," he said.

"No, you hide your true self, not just from your parents, but from just about everyone."

He snorted. "Nonsense."

"You're a chameleon, Freddy Monkton-Coombes. To most of London society, you're nothing but an entertaining rattle, a frivolous fellow with not a serious thought in your head."

"I assure you, there's always at least one thought in my head." He waggled his brows at her in a lascivious fashion.

She ignored it. "To Max you're a friend to rely on; to Flynn, a partner with a business brain as sharp as his own; to Nanny McBride you're her darling boy who spoils her with little treats — long after her usefulness has passed, and very few servants in this world command that kind of loyalty; to me you're —" She broke off, suddenly flustered by what she'd been about to say.

"Yes? What am I to you, Miss Chance?" It was his deepest rake-on-the-prowl voice.

She collected herself and replied, "To me, you're very kind."

"Kind?" He sounded quite disgusted.

She smiled sweetly. "*Very* kind."

"Pah! You make me sound like some old uncle."

"You'd make a lovely uncle, I should think," she said demurely.

His eyes took on that twinkle that was such an invitation to sin. "Uncle, eh? Then, come here, little girl, and give your dear old uncle Freddy a kiss."

She laughed and stepped out of danger. "I'm wise to your tactics, Freddy Monkton-Coombes."

"Tactics?" He slapped his palm over his heart with a wounded look.

"Yes, tactics," she said as they reached the house. "Whenever a conversation leads into areas you find awkward or uncomfortable, you change the subject, usually by flirting shamelessly."

"You think I was flirting shamelessly?" He was injured innocence personified. "You couldn't be more wrong." He slid his arm around her waist. "Let me show you what shameless flirting really is."

"Ah, Frederick." It was his mother, coming from the garden with a basket of greenery.

He turned, and in that instant it was as if a mask had dropped over his face. All the liveliness and warmth, all the wicked, seductive joy in him was gone, smoothed into an expression of perfect, polite indifference. Damaris ached, seeing it.

His mother wore the same look. Damaris longed to smash it.

"The vicar and his wife, the Reverend and Mrs. Tyrrell, will be joining us for dinner this evening, so please don't be late." Lady Breckenridge gave Damaris a cool smile. "Good afternoon, Miss Chance." She glided off into the house, strands of ivy trailing from her basket.

"I suppose I'd better go inside," Damaris said after a moment.

"Yes, I need to see to my horse. Shall I collect you before dinner?"

"Yes, please." Damaris entered the house on her own, feeling deflated. It would be several hours to dinner. She should probably read a book. Or write more letters. Or play patience. All were activities she enjoyed, but today none of them appealed. She knew the reason; she wanted to expand her experience of shameless flirtation.

Which was foolish in the extreme.

When she entered her bedchamber, her gaze lit on the box of paints that Lady Breckenridge had given her and her mood lifted. Of course. Painting always soothed her.

Dinner was a quiet event. The vicar was a cheerful man, interested in most things, and his wife worked in deft partnership with him in keeping the conversational ball rolling — and defusing any tension.

Almost.

In his youth, the Reverend Tyrrell had made a most thorough Grand Tour and was delighted when Lord Breckenridge informed him that Damaris was half Venetian. The vicar adored Venice and asked several awkward questions, which Damaris managed to parry quite successfully by answering a question with a question wherever possible.

Luckily he was the kind of man who enjoyed describing his own impressions, and he waxed lyrical about the various sights he had seen, the people he'd met — alas, he'd never met the marchese di Chancealotto — and the grand events he'd attended.

Lord Breckenridge, getting bored with the travelogue, cut across a reminiscence of a masquerade ball, saying, "D'you know, Vicar, that Miss Chance used to breed experimental Chinese swimming pigs."

It brought the conversation to a sudden stop. Everybody looked at Damaris with varying degrees of astonishment.

"Good God, why?" Freddy asked.

"Stupid boy," said his father. "Answer's plain as the nose on your face." Everybody looked at Lord Breckenridge, who rolled his eyes at their inability to see the obvious. "Can't have valuable livestock drowning in those dratted canals!"

"Ahh, I see. Most interesting." The vicar nodded wisely. "And, Miss Chance, in what way were these pigs experimental? The swimming, one assumes, but if you brought them from China, perhaps they had other, more exotic qualities." He smiled at her with interest and waited for her response.

Damaris had no idea what to say. She'd never said anything to Lord Breckenridge about swimming pigs — he'd been the one who'd raised it, and she'd said no. But it would be rude to point that out now, with everybody waiting. Could pigs swim? She didn't see why not. Most animals could.

A large warm hand closed over hers, making her jump. "Oh, pigs." Freddy sighed dramatically. "I'm bored with pigs, Chinese experimental swimming ones or otherwise."

His father snorted. "You would be. No vision, that's your problem."

"Can we not talk of something more of interest to the ladies?" Freddy smiled at the vicar's wife and squeezed Damaris's hand. "I'll be taking Miss Chance to Venice on our honeymoon. She can show me all the sights then." He gave Damaris a soulful look. "And if you want to show me your flying pigs then —"

"Swimming pigs!" his father corrected him. "Experimental Chinese swimming pigs."

"— then I'll try to be interested. Tell me, do they tow boats?"

Damaris managed to keep a straight face. "No."

"Sing?"

She gave him a quelling look. "No."

"Count?" he asked irrepressibly. "I once heard tell of a learned pig that could count. I don't think it was Chinese, though. Clever people, the Chinese. I imagine their pigs might be, too."

"No," she said firmly. "Nothing like that. And I thought we'd agreed pigs were not a good subject for the dinner table."

"Unless they're roasted," he said. "Or hams."

Luckily for Damaris's composure the vicar's wife then asked a series of questions about the wedding plans, which Lady Breckenridge seized on, and since no arrangements had yet been made, Damaris was happy to discuss possibilities for her imaginary wedding.

It was better than imaginary pigs.

That night, Damaris lay wakeful and restless long after she'd blown out her bedside candle. The fire, stoked against the long, cold night, glowed dully through the cast-iron grille. She stared at it, willing herself to sleep.

Mrs. Tyrrell and Lady Breckenridge had thrown themselves into the discussion of her wedding. Which church? The village church — the family chapel was too small — or some big London one? St. George's, Hanover Square — it was the only possibility, declared Lady Breckenridge. All the *ton* would be invited. It would be the wedding of the season.

The dress? Mrs. Tyrrell liked the fashion of white for a bride. No, declared Lady Breckenridge, white would make her look sallow. She would take Damaris to her own modiste. She knew exactly what Damaris should wear.

Her certainty that she knew best got Damaris's back up — white did *not* make her look sallow! — and even though the wedding was pure fantasy and the arrangements wholly theoretical, Damaris found herself having to insist that her sister Daisy would make her dress, as she would make the dresses of her attendants — Abby, Jane and Daisy herself.

Homemade dresses? Lady Breckenridge was appalled.

Mrs. Tyrrell thought it charmingly sentimental and congratulated Lord and Lady Breckenridge on acquiring a frugal daughter-in-law. Damaris could see they were not at all thrilled by the prospect.

She immediately told them she would knit stockings for them all. Freddy had choked when she'd announced that one. She told him kindly that once they were married she would knit all his stockings. From the very scratchiest wool, she added in an undertone when he had laughed out loud.

But though she'd tried to make fun of the whole idea of the wedding, though she reminded herself over and over that she never wanted to marry, that it was a sure road to misery for someone like her, right now, with the wind whistling in the eaves outside, and the fire glowing, the prospect of a solitary life in a sweet little cottage no longer seemed the happy solution she'd once thought it.

Nonsense, she told herself. It would be peaceful, which was more than most people had. Happy? She would just have to make it so. One made one's own happiness — she'd known that all her life. So why would that change, simply because she was living in England now?

But she kept reliving that moment at dinner when Freddy had placed his hand over hers and spoken of taking her to Venice on their honeymoon. The longing for that to be true had swamped her at the time, shocking her with its intensity. Now, as she pressed her hot cheek against the cool linen cover of the pillow, she tried not to dream of how that might be.

She and Freddy in Venice, floating romantically along in a gondola . . .

Yes, pulled by Chinese swimming pigs, she told herself tartly, and punched the pillow into shape.

She probably wasn't in love with him anyway. No doubt it was just some foolish schoolgirl crush, because he was handsome. And because he was kind. And funny.

And because of the way he looked at her sometimes. Making something inside her swell with warmth and . . . and . . . No. She thumped the pillow into shape again. It wasn't love. It couldn't be. She couldn't afford it to be. Because that way lay misery.

It was self-deception on her part. A side effect of loneliness.

He had a great deal of personal charm, that was all, and she was unused to charming men. He was a self-acknowledged rake, and a flirt. And he'd employed her to act the part of his betrothed. It wasn't real — none of it was real. Even the nonsense he called the billing and cooing — which made her weak at the knees and all bubbly inside — it was just an act. Part of the plan to deceive his parents.

If he had any idea that she was taking the least little bit of it seriously he would probably pity her. And that she couldn't bear. She'd agreed to this charade, and she would get a cottage — undreamed-of security — from it.

And if she emerged with her heart a little bruised, well, it was a small price to pay.

Lady Breckenridge planned to spend the day visiting neighbors and had invited Damaris to accompany her, but Damaris had pleaded a headache and begged to be excused. The fewer people who met her, the less embarrassment for Freddy when she eventually broke their engagement. Lady Breckenridge could tell everyone she'd had her doubts from the start, that she'd never liked the girl, and that there was *something* about her. And nobody would blame Freddy. Damaris hoped.

Lord Breckenridge was also absent for the day, gone off shooting somewhere, so they had the house more or less to themselves. Damaris spent a quiet morning painting while Freddy went for a long ride. It was wonderfully peaceful.

Damaris added the final touches to her painting and stepped back. She examined it from several angles and nodded to herself, pleased with the final result. The clock in the hall chimed and she jumped. Lunchtime already? The morning had run away with her. She glanced at the painting. Time well spent.

She hurriedly washed and tidied herself and went quickly downstairs. She saw Horwood on the landing and called out to him before she could change her mind.

"Miss Chance?" the butler said politely.

"When I was visiting Miss McBride the other day she showed me several framed drawings."

He inclined his head politely. "Yes?"

"She told me one of the estate carpenters had framed them for her."

He nodded. "Yes, Jem Biggins, a good craftsman."

Damaris moistened her lips. It was cheek, given what she was going to do, but she had to ask. "I — I've just finished a painting — it's upstairs in my room — and I was wondering whether . . . whether I could get it framed while I was here, instead of taking it back to London with me. I'd pay him, of course."

"Of course, miss. Would you like me to ask Jem to step up to the house and discuss it with you, or —"

"No." She could just see that, the curiosity and fuss it would cause. "I just want it quietly organized." She waited. She didn't have much experience with butlers. Featherby, Lady Beatrice's butler, could organize anything without turning a hair but Horwood was a country butler, an old family retainer, and she was a relative stranger.

Horwood, however, did not disappoint. "Of course, miss. Would you like me to arrange it for you? It is to be a surprise, I collect."

"You could say that, yes." Probably not a very welcome surprise, but she didn't care.

"If you like, miss, I could collect it from

your room myself and have it discreetly conveyed to Jem Biggins with your instructions." He might look impassive, Damaris thought, but he must be curious to see it for himself, else he'd send a maid or footman to fetch it.

"Instructions?" She'd never had anything framed before. She would have no idea what to say. "Just tell him, whatever he thinks is appropriate."

"Very good, miss."

She gave him a warm smile. "Thank you, Horwood. I appreciate your assistance." The clock chimed the quarter hour. Later than ever. Thank goodness Freddy's parents were from home. She hurried down to lunch.

"Headache gone?" Freddy said when she entered the room.

"Yes, thank you."

"Mine too."

She turned her head in surprise. "I didn't realize you had a headache."

He nodded. "I call it Mother and Father. The moment they were off the estate I felt so much better. You too, I bet."

She laughed. "You knew I was fibbing?"

He ran a finger lightly down her cheek. "For all the web of deceit we're weaving at the moment, and for all that you seem to step so lightly through it, you, my dear, are not a very good liar."

She allowed him to seat her, a little disturbed by the lighthearted touch. "I'm not?"

"No, you can't tell anyone a direct lie without blushing or looking away. Evasions you're not bad at, and misleading statements you're very good at, like transforming your own piglet into a Chinese swimming pig — experimental, of course. But ordinary, everyday, in-your-face lies? Nope." He took his own seat.

"Do you think your mother knew, then?"

"Probably, but since it's her own favorite tactic for getting out of anything she doesn't want to do, she could hardly take offense. May I carve you some ham? You will need your strength."

"Why?"

"Because after luncheon I intend to take you for a walk around the lake, and I don't want you fainting for lack of energy halfway around."

She was about to retort that she'd walked for days on end across China with barely any food and without fainting once, but she bit her tongue in time. She'd never told anyone how she'd left China, and she wasn't going to start.

The trouble was, she'd become so comfortable in his company, she'd almost forgotten to keep her guard up. It was a timely reminder.

If anyone knew how she'd left China, she'd be ruined.

An hour later Freddy was wishing he'd never suggested the walk, wishing he were a stronger man, more able to resist the appeal of a pair of big brown eyes, wishing he'd been able to think more quickly when she'd pointed and asked at the start of their walk, "What's that over there? I noticed it from the roof that time."

Like a fool, he'd answered, "My brother's grave."

So of course she'd wanted to see it.

They stood in front of his brother's grave. The breeze sharpened, fresh and invigorating, but it was dry, which was a pleasant change. The world around them was etched in shades of gray: gray sky, gray clouds, gray headstones, bare winter trees; the only variation, the row of dark green pines that edged the small family cemetery. Damaris was the one bright spot in the drab and gloomy landscape.

She wore a crimson wool pelisse, edged with black fur, trimmed in military fashion with black and silver braid and fastened down the front with a double row of silver buttons. Her bonnet was gray, edged with fur and tied with crimson ribbons.

Her skin was pale and silky looking, her cheeks rosy with cold, her lips — he swallowed, looking at them, and his body tightened. Her lips were full, wine dark and satiny. Wine sweet? He forced his gaze off them and met her gaze, dark and a little troubled.

"Each year I come here and I think about everything George missed out on." He turned again to his brother's headstone, silently rereading the words that were engraved on his heart and on his conscience as well as on the cold white marble slab: *Cut off in the flower of his youth.*

"He was two years older than me and every time I come here I try to imagine him another year older, and think about what he might have done, but each year it gets harder. I can't imagine George as a man; I can only see him as a boy, a fourteen-year-old boy." Running for the ball, onto the ice . . .

Each year he stood here, flaying himself yet again for that one stupid, reckless act that had forever denied him his brother. And his family.

"You need to forgive yourself," said a soft voice at his elbow. "You need to let him go."

"I can't. He's with me — not all the time, of course, and not when I'm in London — well, you know I'm not a gloomy fellow there. But when I'm here at Breckenridge he's . . . here. And I catch myself thinking, 'George would like this,' or 'I must tell George that,' and then . . ." He shook his head. "It's like you're walking on solid ground and suddenly" — he made a sharp, emphatic gesture — "you're falling through a black hole." Like in the ice.

She said nothing, offered no platitudes, no words of empty comfort, just laid a hand quietly on his arm. A warm, accepting presence. Someone who didn't know George, didn't blame him for George's death.

He couldn't look at her. It was years since he'd talked to anyone about his brother. As though George were some dirty little secret — but no, the dirty little secret was his own, known only to him, his parents and a few loyal — and discreet — family retainers.

He'd never told anyone how he felt. Not really.

He'd shoved it away, pretended it had never happened, pretended he was someone else — Christ! — all these years. One day of the year he faced it, his annual act of penance; to come home and let the crows peck at him again.

This year was the first time it had been . . . different.

"Sometimes I stand here and I think of everything I've done over the years, all the things George never got to do. Christ, he'd never even been kissed." He glanced at Damaris, standing quietly at his side. And caught a fleeting expression, a flicker of something in her eyes. He gave her a searching look, and she glanced away.

"Damaris?"

A faint flush rose in her cheeks that had nothing whatsoever to do with the fresh wind. She refused to meet his gaze.

"Damaris, no," he murmured. "Really?" He took her chin in his hand and gently tilted her face up. "You've never been kissed?" This lovely creature? It was a crime against nature.

She said nothing, just swallowed and made an awkward little shrug, half-careless, half-embarrassed.

He slid his arm around her waist. "Well, then, as your betrothed, I think we need to remedy that."

"False betrothed," she said quickly and tried to pull away, looking embarrassed and troubled. And very, very kissable.

"Then will you do it for George?"

"George?" Her brows pleated in puzzlement.

"A kiss for George, right here, right now." And just as he was sure she was going to refuse, he added, deepening his voice, "His first kiss. And yours. It seems fitting, somehow."

She hesitated, so long that he thought for a moment she was going to break from his loose hold and flee like a startled doe into the forest.

She swallowed again. "All right," she said. "For George."

Freddy's pulse leaped, but he kept his expression light. He drew her closer then cupped her face gently in his hands. Cool, silky soft skin. A nerve in the soft underside of her jaw was beating frantically. She was almost quivering, strung as tight as a bowstring. Lord, all this, just for a kiss?

His own hands, oddly, were trembling a little. The cold, of course; he'd removed his gloves.

He looked down at her, smoothing his thumbs along her jawline. Lord, but she was a lovely creature. She gazed up at him through eyes wide and dark enough to drown in, like deep forest pools, clear, and tannin dark. Slowly he stroked his thumb over her full lower lip, warm and satin soft. Her breath hitched and her lips parted slightly.

As he bent to kiss her, her eyes fluttered shut and he felt her brace herself. Slowly, enjoying the unfamiliar sensation of leashed desire, he brushed his mouth lightly over hers.

She hesitated, sighed and slowly relaxed. Her eyes opened. "Thank y—"

He smiled at her innocence. "We're not finished yet." She gave him a doubtful look, and he continued, "Did you think that was a kiss?"

She did, he could see it in her eyes.

"No," his voice roughened. "That was just the preliminary."

"Oh." He wasn't sure if she said it or breathed it. She moistened her mouth with her tongue and waited, looking so deliciously expectant, he wanted to devour her.

She held herself stiff in his arms, but he could feel — or did he just imagine? — her wanting to soften against him. Slowly he lowered his mouth to hers, teasing, tasting, nibbling gently on her lips, her glorious, soft, responsive mouth.

Her lips parted and, oh, Lord, the taste of her. Sweet, intoxicating.

And then she softened against him and

suddenly she was kissing him back, learning from him, her tongue first shyly touching his, then copying every movement he made . . . and, oh, Lord . . .

He'd never kissed an innocent before, and this — God, this was the last thing he'd expected. Her kiss was untutored, yet somehow . . . knowing. Licks of fire sizzled and snapped along his nerves, the heat sweeping through his body, pooling in his groin, swelling . . .

He hadn't been aroused as instantly, as easily — as embarrassingly — since he was a green youth.

That must be it — the lure of her innocence.

He tore his mouth from hers and, with an effort, released her and stepped back.

What had just happened? He'd intended the kiss as a little bit of playful sport, a pleasant distraction from the discomfort and emotion of their graveside conversation. He'd always used dalliance as a distraction. It had never failed him before. . . .

She swayed slightly, her eyes still closed, her face blank with . . . rapture? Arousal? God. He clenched his fists, then thrust them into the pockets of his greatcoat so he couldn't snatch her back into his arms.

Her mouth was red, a little swollen, maybe

351

even bruised, her pale, satiny skin roughened by whisker burn. Her first kiss and he'd all but ravaged her mouth like a . . . like a satyr, dammit.

What the hell had gotten into him? She was an innocent and this was a sham betrothal. He'd only proposed it because he'd thought she didn't want to have anything to do with men. And because he'd sworn never to marry.

Fool that he was.

She hadn't moved yet. Then her long, long lashes lifted and she looked at him with an expression he couldn't read — dark and a little dazed.

She took a deep breath. "So that's what it's like." She sounded perfectly collected, quite unruffled. She turned to the headstone. "Thank you, George. Our first kiss. I don't believe I'll ever forget it."

Illogically, Freddy felt a surge of jealousy. He wanted to swing her around to face him, snarl that he — not George — had kissed her. Which was perfectly ridiculous. It was just a kiss, for God's sake. Nothing to get so . . . unsettled over. And besides, he never snarled. He was famous for his light touch with women.

And where the hell had that gone?

"Well, it won't be your last kiss, I can

guarantee that."

She turned to him with a little half smile and a raised brow. "Oh?" she said. It was almost flirtatious.

"You were born for it," he told her.

She reacted as if he'd slapped her, a perceptible, instantly controlled recoil. She turned away, but not before Freddy saw that the color had drained from her face, leaving her chalk white.

"What is it? What did I say?" He held out his hands to her.

She stepped back quickly. "Nothing," she said. Did her voice sound strained? He wasn't sure.

"Nothing," she repeated and shivered, wrapping her arms around herself. "It's cold. I think I'd like to go now." She half turned but didn't meet his gaze. Her lips were compressed, her nose pinched.

"But what is it? What did I say?"

"Nothing at all. Thank you for the kiss and for telling me about your brother." Her tone was light, inconsequential. Her face was a mask showing all the right, polite expressions, but her eyes were flat, shuttered.

He stepped forward, reaching toward her, but she stepped quickly back, her palms raised as if to fend him off. "No. I'll walk back by myself, if you don't mind. I'll see you at dinner."

She turned and walked quickly away. And then started running.

Freddy stood stock-still, watching her flee — *flee* from him, dammit. He wanted to go after her, but he knew it would probably only make things worse. What the hell had just happened?

It wasn't the kiss, he was sure of that. She could have stopped it anytime, could have stopped it before he'd even started. And when he'd stepped back and released her she'd looked like a woman ought to look when she'd been thoroughly kissed — dazed, aroused and adorable.

Adorable? Where did that come from? He turned the unfamiliar word around in his mind and dismissed it. *Kissable,* that was what he'd meant.

She'd surprised him, he had to admit. He'd never kissed a woman and felt such connection, such an upwelling of . . . joy? No, passion. His body still ached with it. He could still taste her in his mouth, the sweet, wild, dark-rose-honey taste of her.

She'd looked at him with the sweetest, shyest, most wondering expression, and his pulse had leaped because he saw then — dammit, he'd bet his life on it — that she'd

354

enjoyed kissing him as much as he'd enjoyed kissing her.

And then suddenly the joy, the delight, the wonder had drained from her, leaving her white and wounded. Wounded? He examined the thought.

Why wounded? All he'd said was that she was born to be kissed, and dammit, that was a compliment. Any woman would think so. So what the hell was she so upset about?

She was a missionary's daughter. Had he shocked her, putting his tongue in her mouth? It had been a very carnal kiss. Best kiss of his life, come to think of it — and he prided himself on his kissing skills.

He would have sworn she wasn't shocked when he'd done it. She'd welcomed him so naturally, so warmly . . . Delayed reaction, maybe?

He sighed. "Did you understand what happened there, George? Because I sure as hell didn't." The wind soughed through the pines. A crow cawed a mocking counterpoint.

No, of course George didn't understand women. He'd died a boy of fourteen.

Cruelly snatched from life in the flower of his youth. The eternal reprimand.

Freddy tugged the collar of his greatcoat

higher and headed toward the house. He needed a drink.

CHAPTER SEVENTEEN

"Elinor was then at liberty to think
and be wretched."
— JANE AUSTEN, *SENSE AND SENSIBILITY*

Damaris ran until a painful stitch formed under her ribs and she was forced to stop. She stood by the lake, gasping for breath, silently castigating herself for the unnecessary dramatics of running away.

You were born for it. She tried to thrust the hateful words from her mind.

She ran shaking hands over her face. She couldn't return to the house yet; she was a positive stew of conflicting emotions. She sat down on a nearby rock. She needed to calm herself. And to gain some reasonable perspective on what had just happened. And some control.

The kiss had moved her. Moved — such a plain, blunt word for the complex threads of feelings tangled inside her. Physical feelings of sharp arousal and desire but underlying it all, a piercing sweetness. She'd never felt such tenderness, such *connectedness* with another person. It had left her aching, yearning.

She was confused, because it threatened to undermine all her resolve. And she was annoyed with herself for overreacting to a simple kiss.

Her first kiss. There was grief in her too, for the innocent girl she'd once been, the girl for whom that kiss would be the summit of all her dreams. A kiss to treasure.

She was so far from being an innocent now that it made a mockery of her reaction, a mockery of the innocence implied by a first kiss.

And yet it *was* her first.

It had shaken her to the core with its unexpected tenderness and promise.

False promise, she reminded herself; as false as their betrothal. A playful kiss from a rake, for a dead boy to a girl who in some ways had died also; certainly the girl she had been no longer existed. Damaris could never be that girl again, no matter how hard she might wish it.

How had he known she'd never been kissed? It shouldn't be possible. But somehow, he'd known that — and more —

because afterward he'd told her, *You were born for it.*

The very words the captain had said as he'd handed her, bound and tied, to the brothel owner.

Pain sliced into her. You couldn't undo what life had done to you. You could only live with the consequences. And live she would — on her own terms, no one else's.

She'd earned her cottage and she would make a good life for herself. Her parents' marriage had been a lesson she'd learned well and she would not put herself in the same position as Mama, living under constant reproach, endless condemnation, having been judged and found wanting. The life, the joy had been sapped from her mother, her life corroded by Papa's bitterness.

It didn't matter now. The past was done, immutable. Only the future was hers to shape, if she could. As long as the past didn't return to bite her.

She knew what she had done, and though she was shamed by it, she would not apologize or beg forgiveness.

Others — if they knew — would judge her harshly, but they did not know, *could* not know from their cozy, safe lives, how it had been.

Given the same situation, she would make the same choice again.

Knowing that, she would have to live with it.

But she would not be condemned for it as Mama had been. Mama was good and kind and loving. Whatever she'd done, she hadn't deserved a lifelong penance.

Better a life of solitude and self-acceptance than to live crushed under a yoke of guilt and regret.

Calmer now, she rose and began the walk back to the house. This charade would be over soon and she need not justify herself to anyone. As for the kiss, it would be a thing to treasure, a memory to bring out on cold, lonely nights. A kiss to dream on.

Her first kiss — forget the rest of it — it was a blessing.

But it could not go any further. It was hard enough to resist Freddy Monkton-Coombes when he was simply flirting, but that kiss had taken things to a new level. Being a rake, he no doubt took kisses lightly; he'd probably think nothing of stealing a few more. And he was so deliciously persuasive she'd probably weaken and let him. Again.

But she couldn't risk it. It was playing with fire, and she'd be the one left burned.

Gravel crunched under her shoes as she trod the pathway that led back toward the house. She had to end this farce of a betrothal soon.

As Damaris approached the house, an elderly gardener greeted her by name, bobbing his head and giving her a gap-toothed smile. Damaris smiled back.

She entered the house by a side door. The motherly-looking housekeeper, Mrs. Brown, was supervising a young maid. They both stopped what they were doing to smile at her, and as Damaris passed, Mrs. Brown touched her on the arm and said, "Thank you, miss."

Puzzled, Damaris gave them a smile and continued on her way. If the servants were starting to greet her as if she belonged here, it was definitely time to draw this thing to an end.

But first there was Freddy Monkton-Coombes to confront and her retrieval of the thing that the Chinese called "face." She peeped into the sitting room he usually favored, the one without all the mounted heads, and found him perusing a newspaper in a bored sort of fashion.

Best to broach it at once. "I'm sorry about before. I overreacted a little." She gave a shaky little laugh. "A girl's prerogative, I believe, after her first kiss." Lord, she was more unsettled than she'd thought.

Freddy lowered his paper and eyed her thoughtfully over it. He'd been turning the moment over and over in his mind, unable to forget the draining of color from her face and her subsequent flight.

"It wasn't the kiss that overset you," he said slowly. "It was something I said afterward." Though what it was, he had no idea.

"Nonsense." She tossed her head. "As I recall, you were quite complimentary."

He wasn't convinced. "Whatever I said to upset you, I'm sorry."

"You didn't upset me at all." She still hadn't met his gaze. "Now, do you want to keep reading that paper? Because if you have the time, I'd quite like you to continue my education in the art of playing billiards."

He folded the paper and set it aside. "It would be my pleasure to further your education."

If she wanted to play games, he'd play along. He'd get to the bottom of the mystery eventually.

"Miss Damaris, Mr. Horwood, the butler, is waiting outside to speak to you," Polly, her

362

maid, said in some awe when Damaris was dressing the following morning. "He's got something for you, but he says he wants to give it to you himself."

The painting couldn't be framed already. It had been less than a day since she'd finished it. Curious, Damaris quickly finished dressing, then opened the door.

It wasn't just Horwood waiting for her, it was the housekeeper, Mrs. Brown, as well. Horwood carried a large, square object, wrapped in brown paper and tied up with string. "Jem Biggins went to work on it right away, miss."

"Oh, then I must give you some money to pay him. How much is it?" She turned to find her purse.

"No, no, no, miss, you don't owe him a thing," Horwood said, shocked. He set the parcel on the dressing table and pulled from his pocket a small knife, with which he cut the string. "The estate would pay, but even so, Jem wouldn't take a penny for a job like this. As soon as he saw what it was, he put everything aside to frame it. Very fond of Master Freddy is Jem."

"As are we all, miss," Mrs. Brown said. "And such a portrait of the young master it is, it fair made me weep." She pulled out a handkerchief and dabbed it to her welling eyes.

"I took the liberty of showing it to the staff yesterday," Horwood admitted.

"It's Master Freddy to the life, miss," the housekeeper said. "And anyone can see you care for him. I'm that happy he's found a young lady like you. Perhaps now he'll come home to Breckenridge more often."

"Oh, but . . ." Damaris was dismayed at their interpretation of the facts. It was just a simple painting. But at that moment Horwood finished unwrapping the painting and she gasped.

She'd expected a plain wooden frame, much like the ones made for Nanny McBride, but this was more like the ones in the portrait gallery — carved quite ornately and then covered in gold leaf. It made her ordinary watercolor into something quite special.

She knew immediately what she wanted to do with it.

"Horwood," she said, "are Lord and Lady Breckenridge downstairs yet? In the breakfast parlor, I mean."

Horwood and Mrs. Brown exchanged a conspiratorial glance. "No, miss, they're still in their bedchambers."

"Good." She bundled the paper back

around the painting.

Horwood cleared his throat. "Do I apprehend, miss, that you intend to place this painting in the breakfast parlor?"

She nodded. "Over the mantel, yes. Beside the painting of George." She added defiantly, "There are numerous paintings of George in this house, but none at all of Freddy."

Horwood smiled. "We know, miss. And if you would allow me, I'd be honored to take the painting downstairs for you and put it in place."

Mrs. Brown nodded eagerly. "So we can all — all of the servants — see it up there before his lordship sees it."

Before his lordship had it removed, she meant. There was a lump in Damaris's throat. Such loyalty, such love. Did Freddy have any idea? she wondered. She nodded. "I'd be honored if you would, Mr. Horwood."

"What the devil —,?"

Damaris let out her breath. She'd been on edge all through breakfast, waiting for someone to notice the painting. Amazingly nobody had, even though to her it was as obvious as a slap in the face. Guilty conscience.

Horwood, misunderstanding her intentions, had slightly exceeded his brief, and instead of placing the painting on the mantelpiece as she'd planned, he'd hung it where George's painting usually hung, and moved George's painting to another wall.

Finally, just as he was getting up to leave the table, Lord Breckenridge had noticed it. He stared at the painting over the mantel. His eyes bulged. "What is the meaning of this?" he roared.

Damaris took a deep breath. "It's a painting of your son and heir." She was surprised to hear she sounded quite composed. Inside she was shaking like a leaf.

"It damned well is not! Horwood!" He bellowed for the absent butler. "Where's the proper painting? The one of George?"

"It's over there." She pointed. She couldn't allow Horwood to take the blame.

Lord Breckenridge looked at George's painting hanging in the center of the opposite wall. He swung around to stare at her. "*You're* responsible for this?"

Damaris lifted her chin. "I did the painting, yes. It's a gift to you. I thought it would be nice if you had a portrait of your son — your living son — for a change."

"How dare you!" Lady Breckenridge was white with anger.

"You have paintings of George everywhere, but none of Freddy. Yet Freddy is your only son and heir." She turned to Lady Breckenridge. "I put those paints of yours to good use, don't you think? It's not a bad likeness." She glanced at Freddy, who was staring at the painting with a strange look on his face.

"You are not in charge of this house yet, missy."

"And you won't ever be if I have my way," his wife hissed.

Damaris braced herself. "I'm sorry if I've upset you, but don't you think it's time you all faced the truth?"

"What truth?" Lord Breckenridge scoffed.

He really had no idea. She took a deep breath and said gently, "That George is dead."

Lady Breckenridge clapped her hands over her ears. "Stop her, Godfrey. She isn't to say such things."

Damaris shook her head. It was going to take more than gentle words. "You are clinging to the past in the most morbid fashion. It's unhealthy. It's also childish." Oh, God, she'd never been as rude to anyone in her life.

"*Childish?*" Lord Breckenridge sputtered, outraged.

"Yes, childish," Damaris said coolly. Because it had to be said, and if nobody else would say it . . . "All three of you — Freddy included — are acting as if . . . as if, if you held your breath long enough and wished hard enough, you could open your eyes and George would be alive again and you could all go on as before."

There was a short, shocked silence. She darted a glance at Freddy, who'd made no attempt to interfere. He was watching her with a strange look in his eye. Had she offended him too? Well, what did it matter? She'd break off the betrothal soon, and he wouldn't have to see her again. But in the meantime, there were things she wanted to say.

"You can't live like that," she hurried on, frightened she'd lose the courage to speak her piece. "People die. People you love and depend on and need, die." Her voice cracked. "And those left behind must grieve — and then move on. From all I've heard, George was a wonderful, much beloved son, clever and talented and noble and affectionate."

"He was perfect," said George's mother.

"Yes. But, tragically, he died. And in your grief, your *sixteen years* of grief, you've forgotten — both of you — that you have another son who did not die. And he's also wonderful, just as wonderful as George —"

"Pfft!" Lord Breckenridge made a puff of disbelief.

"— but in a different way. He's clever and talented and loyal and responsible and kind, but you're blind to it — *willfully* blind. He's even blind to it himself. He doesn't believe he deserves to be loved."

"He caused his brother's death," said his mother.

"No, he *didn't!* That's a *terrible* thing to say."

"How would you know?"

"All he did was hit a cricket ball. George ran to catch it and fell into the water and drowned. It was a tragic accident, that's all. Nobody is at fault."

His father shrugged. "If Freddy had been the one running to catch, it wouldn't have mattered so much. George would be alive."

The casual cruelty of it stunned her. "How *dare* you say such a *wicked* thing!" She smacked the table with her palm, making them all jump. "You don't deserve such a wonderful son."

"Wonderful?" Lord Breckenridge made a rude noise. "He's an idle, feckless —"

"You have *no* idea of the man Freddy has become," she flared. "You dismiss him as feckless and idle but I ask you — how has Freddy lived all these years?" She glanced at Freddy, but he made no move to explain himself.

"I make him an allowance, of course," his father said.

Damaris shook her head. "I don't know anything about that, but —"

"Haven't touched it since I was eighteen," Freddy said mildly. "Don't you ever check the accounts, Father?"

The old man's brows gnashed together.

Freddy leaned back, as if there was no more to be said on the matter. Damaris wanted to shake him. Why would he not defend himself? Why not explain the way he'd built a fortune?

She leaned forward. "Ask yourself how he has supported himself all these years in the elegant style for which he's so well known."

Lord Breckenridge shrugged. "No doubt his women give him —"

"Don't be insulting!" Damaris flashed. She glanced at Freddy again, wishing he would bite back for once. He gave her a cool, unreadable glance.

"Aunt Adelaide's legacy," Lady Breckenridge said triumphantly.

Only to have her husband snort. "The merest pittance. Wouldn't have kept him much more than a year."

"It did, actually," Freddy said but offered no further explanation. He sat back in his chair, his legs crossed, as if he were watching a play. Pretending it didn't matter what his parents thought of him.

Well, it mattered to her!

"You don't know him at all, do you? My brother-in-law, Lord Davenham, told me Freddy built up a fortune from a tiny nest egg. His friend Mr. Flynn, the founder of a worldwide company — in which your son is a partner — says Freddy has real business acumen."

"Eh?" His father grunted in surprise. "Acumen?"

"Yes, acumen. But you have no idea of your son's talents, or what he's been doing in the last sixteen years, do you? Because you don't care to know. You're mired in the past, stuck, like flies in amber —"

"Flies?" Lady Breckenridge echoed angrily. *"Flies?"*

"Yes, like flies in amber, whining like little children about the unfairness of life."

"I do not *whine*!" Lord Breckenridge snapped.

She ignored him. "Life is unfair. Death is unfair. But while you're brooding on the unfairness of it all, think on this — sixteen years ago, when George fell through the ice and died, you only lost a son —"

"*Only?* How dare you say such a thing?" Lady Breckenridge glared daggers.

"We know what we lost," her husband stated.

Damaris smacked the table again. The sound echoed. "Think, for *once* in your self-ish lives, about *Freddy.* He lost his beloved older brother, the person he loved most in all the world, his best friend and boyhood hero. But he didn't just lose George — he lost *his whole family.*"

There was a short silence. Damaris let that sink in a moment.

"What do you mean?" his mother asked stiffly. "We're here."

Damaris couldn't believe it. Had they *never* reflected on what they'd done? "You two treated him like an assassin, when he was just a little boy who liked to play cricket with his brother. Twelve years old, and you pushed him out of the family —"

"Rubbish!" Lord Breckenridge growled. "We did nothing of the sort."

She turned on him. "You sent him away to school immediately after the funeral and didn't even allow him to come home for Christmas, not two weeks later. A grief-stricken, *innocent* little boy of twelve. It was heartless and wicked and cruel.

"And *then* you had him painted out of the family portrait." She shook her head. "The entire time I've been here all you've done is make cutting remarks about him to me — and I'm *his betrothed.* I've heard nothing but criticism, disparagement and negativity. I cannot credit it. You are his mother and you, his father. He is your *son* — your *only* son." Her eyes prickled with angry, frustrated tears. "What kind of parents *are* you? You lost one son, but *you threw the other away.*"

There was a long silence. Nobody was looking at anyone else.

The silence stretched so long Damaris started to shake. She'd gone too far, said the unforgivable. Never in her life had she been so outspoken, so rude. And to her elders and her hosts.

But she was glad of it. It needed to be said. They needed to know what they had done. For sixteen years.

She'd well and truly burned her bridges now. When she put an end to this sham betrothal, Freddy would get no blame. They'd probably be delighted that he was free of the harpy.

She rose and turned to Freddy, who was regarding her with an expression she could not read. "Now, if you don't mind, I think it's best if I leave."

He frowned and stood abruptly. "Leave? Leave for where?"

"Davenham Hall? You said it was only a few hours' drive from here."

"Four, possibly five hours, depending on the state of the roads."

She nodded. "If you will lend me your coach and a driver, Lord Breckenr—"

"I'll drive you," Freddy said.

"There is no need —"

"I said I'll drive you," he said in a voice that brooked no argument. He glanced at his parents, who hadn't moved or spoken since her outburst. "How soon can you be ready?"

"It will take but a few minutes to pack."

He gave a brusque nod. "Then I'll meet you at the front steps in half an hour." His voice was almost harsh, quite unlike his usual manner. He sat back down at the table.

She could see his resemblance to his father now. And his mother. Neither of them had looked at her; neither now said a word. They sat like rigid statues, in frozen, aristocratic disapproval, waiting for her to leave.

She left the room and hurried upstairs.

■ ■ ■ ■

Freddy poured himself another cup of coffee and waited. He was curious to see how they'd taken it, whether anything had sunk in.

He couldn't remember when anyone had last defended him. Not that he needed it, but, God, she was magnificent, the way she'd ripped into his father, his mother — all of them, himself included.

His parents were showing definite signs of shock. Neither of them had looked at him yet. Or said a word. His mother was tidying the table in front of her with fussy little movements, her mouth tight and pinched with displeasure. His father was staring at nothing, his brow knotted, whether in anger or thought, Freddy couldn't tell.

He glanced at the portrait over the mantel, the catalyst of it all. Was that how she saw him? Quite handsome, but with a vulnerability about the eyes and mouth that he was sure wasn't there. It was a little unsettling to see himself through her eyes.

It was damned good, though. He'd had no idea she was so talented. He'd imagined her work in the pottery to be just a matter of painting patterns — he hadn't given it any thought.

Finally his father broke the silence. "Well, I hope you're happy, upsetting your mother like that. Fine sort of bride you choose to bring home to Breckenridge."

Freddy sipped his coffee. "Extraordinary, isn't she?"

"Extraordinary? More like outrageous. How dare she speak to us — how dare you allow her to speak to us like that."

"I've never met such an ill-mannered, disrespectful, impertinent creature in my life," his mother joined in. "Such insults — I've never heard the like."

"Tell me, Mother, which did you find most insulting, her accusation that you were a heartless and cruel parent or her likening you to an insect?"

There was enough truth in the accusation to bring a flush to her thin cheeks. "How dare you!"

Freddy smiled. "Not much fun when you're on the receiving end, is it, Mother?"

His father slammed a fist on the table. "Don't speak to your mother like that! It's a damned good thing that little bitch is leaving; otherwise I'd have to throw her out on her ear."

"That's enough!" Freddy spoke coldly, but it was like a whiplash. Both his parents stared at him. "I will tolerate no insult of my betrothed, do you hear me? You will speak of Miss Chance with respect."

"Respect?" his father said when he'd recovered from the surprise. "When the chit abused me at my own breakfast table?"

"And did you not deserve it?" Freddy said in a hard voice. "Did we not all deserve it?"

"What she said was utterly offensive," his mother declared.

"But true, nevertheless," Freddy said silkily. They didn't like that. "We *are* stuck in the past. This is the first time in sixteen years we've talked about George's death. And what happened after it. Sixteen *years.*"

"We have the memorial service," his mother said defensively.

"Yes, but we don't talk. Yesterday when we went for a walk, Damaris saw the grave. She asked me about it, about George, as if it were the most natural thing in the world." He swallowed. "It was the first time I've ever talked about him. To anyone. And he was my *brother.*" He clenched his fist, willing away the threat of unmanly tears.

"What is there to talk about?" his mother muttered.

"George," he said simply. "We were the ones who loved him best."

"It's none of that blasted vixen's business

what we talk about," his father said. "Damned impertinence, that's what it is. I won't have her in the family! You will sever this betrothal at once."

"Will I?"

His father thrust his head forward. "What's got into you, boy?"

"I've just had an epiphany," Freddy told him.

"Epiphany? What nonsense!"

"For years I told myself if I could ignore your insults and your indifference, and pretend I didn't care, it wouldn't affect me. But it's wrong, that old rhyme. Sticks and stones can break my bones, but names, repeated often enough from a young age, can indeed hurt me."

There was a short silence.

"Deep down I was still hoping it might one day happen."

"What? Speak up, boy. What might happen?"

"That you'd see me. Accept me. Forgive me." God, he sounded pathetic. But he had to say it. "But Damaris just shattered that illusion. You're never going to change. And there was nothing to forgive."

He stood. "I'm not a boy, Father, I'm a man, and I will no longer tolerate any rudeness to me or any member of my family."

"Your family?" His mother's eyes widened. "Frederick, you can't mean that dreadful girl! You cannot marry her! Not after the way she insulted us."

"Girl's a raging harridan," his father agreed.

"She's a young lioness," said Freddy unable to keep the pride from his voice. "And she's going to make a magnificent mother."

"Mother?" his mother echoed, startled.

Freddy grinned. "Can't you see her defending her cubs?" His cubs. He wasn't sure how he was going to do it — she was as marriage-shy as he had been. But somewhere during that magnificent tirade she'd delivered, the realization had burst upon him that he was going to marry her, had to marry her, that she was the woman he'd been waiting for all his life.

"Damn it, boy, if you dare to marry her against our express wishes, I'll —"

"You'll do what, Father? Cut off the allowance I haven't touched in years? Forbid me from entering the house I only step into one day a year? Disinherit me from an estate that's fully entailed?"

His father muttered a curse.

"Face it, Father, I don't actually need you or Mother for anything. You taught me that from a young age, or weren't you listening to my fiancée?" He turned and gestured to the painting. "About that painting. If you don't want it, give it to Nanny McBride."

His mother blinked. "Don't you care whether we want to keep it or not?"

He gave her a weary smile. "I'm long past caring about what you do, Mother."

"But we're your parents."

"Are you? Excuse me, I need to pack. I don't want to keep my bride waiting." He strode toward the door.

"Freddy?" His mother's voice stopped him in his tracks. She hadn't called him Freddy for sixteen years. Dammit, some part of that pathetic needy boy was still inside him.

He turned, feigning indifference. "Yes?"

"You will be here for the memorial service . . . won't you?"

He hardened his heart. "I'm not sure."

CHAPTER EIGHTEEN

"They parted at last with mutual civility,
and possibly a mutual desire of
never meeting again."
— JANE AUSTEN, *PRIDE AND PREJUDICE*

Damaris took her leave of Lord and Lady Breckenridge, thanking them politely for their hospitality in the most hypocritical fashion. But good manners must prevail.

In turn they stiffly wished her good-bye and a safe journey. They'd probably prefer her to break her neck, so no doubt things were even.

She stepped out onto the steps at the front of Breckenridge House, where Freddy was waiting with the carriage, and halted in surprise. "The curricle?"

"Best thing for a quick journey," he said. "Besides, you get sick in closed carriages, remember?"

"But what about my maid, Polly?"

"She can ride with my groom and tiger. I've sent my man to hire a vehicle. He'll be back soon." Clearly he didn't want to borrow any vehicle from his father. He glanced at the bags her maid and a footman were bringing out. "Leave all that here — bring only what you think you'll need on the trip. The others will follow with the baggage as soon as they can — they won't be more than an hour or two behind us."

She hesitated. "But don't I need a chaperone?" It was absurd for her to be worrying about propriety after what had happened to her on leaving China, but she had to keep up appearances.

Freddy shook his head. "Betrothed woman traveling with her affianced husband in an open carriage for a few hours in plain sight of everyone — nothing for the tabbies to worry about there."

He sounded very confident, and, given the awkwardness of her sudden departure, she didn't feel inclined to argue. "Very well."

They loaded her bag into the small boot of the curricle and, with only a few servants to wave them off, were soon tooling down the drive away from Breckenridge House.

"Quite the little firebrand, aren't you?" he said when they were out on the open road.

"I'm so sorry. I'm afraid I lost my temper

with your parents."

He laughed. "You don't say!"

She darted him a cautious glance. "You're not angry with me?"

He turned his head and gave her a very Freddy look and the tension instantly drained out of her. "I didn't mean to be so rude. And I didn't hang your portrait or remove your brother's — I meant it just to sit on the mantelpiece. But Horwood misunderstood, and then I couldn't let him be blamed."

"Never mind. I doubt anything else would have made my parents sit up and take notice half so well."

"I'm not usually such a virago."

He laughed. "You were hardly that."

"Oh, but I was. Once I started — and your father was so angry, and so dismissive of you — and your mother so righteous! And so wrong! My temper got the better of me."

It had shocked her, to tell the truth. She'd never lost her temper in such a way before. It was as though she'd tapped into a well of deep anger that had surged upward, flowing out of her in a scalding flood. Strangely, she felt remarkably calm now.

"They really didn't seem to understand how unjust they'd been to you."

He chuckled. "They know now."

"I hope so. Do you think it will make any difference?"

"To them? Probably not. To me?" He turned his head and gave her a lazy smile that sent a delicious shiver through her, all the way to her toes. "I'm hoping it will make all the difference in the world to me. There's just one small problem I need to sort out first."

She wanted to ask him what the problem was, to see if there was anything she could do to help, but she'd already poked her nose into his business far too much already. She ought to sever the betrothal soon. The thought made her feel oddly heavy. Not that she wanted to marry him, of course, but it had been fun. And surprisingly companionable. She would miss him when he was gone.

They passed through the village and headed west. A heavy bank of gray cloud had settled sullenly along the distant horizon. "With any luck we'll beat that rain," Freddy commented and snapped the reins. His grays picked up speed.

"Want to take the ribbons for a bit?" he asked after they'd been traveling at top speed for ten minutes or so.

"You'd trust your precious grays to me?" she said in surprise.

"Yes, now that the freshness has been taken off them."

She laughed. He passed her the reins and for the next hour they traveled in silence. Her concentration was almost wholly on the horses, but some part of her was aware of her traveling companion. She'd expected him to be rather blue-deviled after the confrontation with his parents, but he seemed quite lighthearted, even happy.

"What's the matter?" he asked her after he'd caught her several times giving him a surreptitious glance. "Frightened I'll fall out of the curricle or something?"

She laughed. "Of course not. It's just that you're . . ."

"What? Handsome? Charming? Irresistible?" He gave her a rakish leer and she laughed again.

"You seem . . . I don't know . . . happy."

"I am." He leaned back and crossed his booted legs, resting them on the front bar of the curricle. "I usually am when I leave Breckenridge."

"That's sad."

"Why?"

"Because I know you love it."

He gave her a curious look. "How did you work that out?"

"The way you talk of it, the places you

showed me, the stories you told."

"Ah, well, we can't have everything we want," he said and though he said it in a light manner, Damaris recognized a "keep out" sign when she met one. For a light-hearted rattle of a rake, he had rather a lot of those.

But then, so did she.

"How are you feeling?" Freddy enquired as they came to a posting inn a few hours later. "We'll change horses here, but we've made good time — we're about halfway to Davenham Hall, so if you want to rest for a while . . ."

"I wouldn't mind some breakfast."

"Breakfast? But —"

"I was so nervous about the painting I didn't eat a thing," she confessed.

The farther west they went, the wetter the country was. The last few days of dry weather had made the roads passable enough, but the low-lying land remained saturated: Sheets of silvery water lay everywhere.

"Talk of flooding farther on, sorr," an ostler at the next staging point warned Freddy as he led out a fresh pair of horses. "Best be careful. Folks say river's about ready to bust its banks."

"Is the main road flooded at all?"

"Not yet, sorr, not as I know of, but any more rain like we've had the last weeks and there'll be trouble."

Freddy nodded. He wasn't too worried. They'd made good time so far, and the bank of cloud that had loomed threateningly ahead the last few hours hadn't seemed to move. Another two hours and they'd be at Davenham.

They set out again.

Half an hour later they came to a wooden bridge across a fiercely swollen river. Dirty brown water gushed and tumbled, carrying with it all sorts of refuse — mud, branches and bits of broken palings — swirling and eddying, spilling out over the banks in places, taking everything with it. The surface of the bridge was about an inch deep in water.

"Do you think it's safe to cross?" Damaris asked.

"For the moment, which is all we need," Freddy said briskly, and he urged the nervous horses across the bridge.

For the next mile or so the road ran beside the river. "Won't be long before it bursts its banks," Freddy observed, "but the road leaves the riverside soon and the rest of the way is on higher ground."

He spoke too soon. Rounding a bend, they were confronted with an angry brown sea of swirling floodwater, into which the road disappeared.

"Dammit, we'll have to go back." He backed the horses and turned the curricle around. There was no side road, no other way except back to the flooding bridge.

By the time they got back, the wooden bridge was shuddering under the sweeping barrage of water and debris. Under their horrified gaze, a section of the bridge broke and was dragged into the swirling torrent. In minutes the remainder of the bridge was swept away, tossed around on the current like a handfuls of sticks.

They were stranded.

"Well, we won't be going that way," Freddy said lightly. He scanned their surroundings. The floodwaters were already nibbling at the edge of the road. "We'll have to move to higher ground."

"There's a cottage back there." Damaris pointed. "I noticed it as we passed. It's on that hill. From here, you can't see it for the trees, but it's there."

"Right, then." Again Freddy turned the curricle around and they headed back, searching for a way up to the cottage on the hill. They found a gate with a narrow track winding upward. Freddy jumped down, opened the gate, then led the horses through it.

"It's too rough and narrow for the curricle," he said. "We'll have to leave it here. We'll take the horses with us. Let's hope there's some sort of shelter for them at the cottage." He unhitched the horses and, slipping and sliding on the steep and muddy track, they made their way toward the cottage.

Damaris glanced at him at one point. "You're quite enjoying this, aren't you?"

"Sorry." He pulled a guilty face. "I must confess I have a sneaking fondness for the odd small adventure. We're going to be all right, you know. We're more in danger of discomfort and inconvenience than actual danger. The floods won't come up this high."

"I know. I'm not worried." Truth to tell, Damaris didn't mind a small adventure herself. Her upbringing had better prepared her for physical danger and discomfort than for London drawing rooms and the pitfalls of polite society.

He turned to look at her. "You're not, are you? Remarkable. Nine out of ten females of my acquaintance would be loudly castigating me for the ruination of their shoes, not to mention their damp and muddy hems. They'd be complaining about having to walk, and screeching at me to 'do something, Freddy, do something!' "

"But what could you do?" she said, puzzled.

"Carry them, probably." He gave her a hopeful look. "Do you want me to carry you?"

She laughed. "Of course not. You have quite enough to manage with those horses."

"Oh, well," he said with a downcast sigh. "If you must be so distressingly independent."

Damaris couldn't help but smile. Even in the midst of trouble, he could find an opportunity to flirt.

The clouds were thickening by the minute and they were barely halfway up the hill when there was a flash, then a rumble, and the first few fat drops of rain fell. "Uh-oh," Freddy said, glancing at the sky. "Hurry." But within seconds the heavens opened and the rain was pelting down.

By the time they reached the cottage, they were drenched. "You get inside; I'll find somewhere to put the horses," Freddy shouted over the rain.

Damaris knocked, once, twice, but there was no answer. Shivering, she tried the door. It opened. "Is anyone here?" she called as she entered. But there was no answer.

The cottage was small, just one main room, with a kitchen scullery at the rear, a small table in the middle with a couple of wooden chairs, and a bed in the corner covered with a bright patchwork quilt. The floor was made of stone flags, made cozier and more cheerful with some homemade rag rugs. It was clean and neat as a pin.

Whoever the owners were, they hadn't been gone more than a few hours, Damaris thought. The fire was out, but a faint warmth remained in the bricks. A bunch of parsley sat in a jar of water, still fresh. She checked the kitchen and found half of a loaf of bread in the crock, a bowl of eggs, and some vegetables in a bin.

They'd need to dry off.

Feeling uncomfortably like a thief, she looked in the chest at the end of the bed and found several lengths of rough towel and some folded clothes — all for a woman, an old woman, by the look of the clothes. She must live here alone. She took out the towels and used one to towel-dry her hair and soak up as much of the dampness as she could.

There was no sign of Freddy. Presumably

he was getting the horses settled.

The storm was getting worse. Lightning flickered, thunder rumbled and rain hammered at the roof and windows in a deafening tattoo. They'd be here for a while. She should light a fire. It was taking a liberty in a stranger's house, but she was wet through, and Freddy would be even wetter, and they didn't want to catch a chill.

She swept out the ashes of the old fire, found some kindling and began to set a fire.

The door crashed open and she jumped. "Only me," Freddy shouted over the noise. "Here, I'll do that." He came forward, dripping, and shivering with cold.

She shooed him away. "I am well able to light a fire, thank you. You're soaked, so go over there and get out of those wet clothes before you catch your death."

"You're wet too."

"Not as wet as you and you've been outside in it longer. You're practically blue with cold, so don't argue — strip."

His eyes danced and she knew he was about to say something cheeky, so she waved him away. "Not another word. I found you a towel and some clothes — they're there on the bed. I'm afraid there are no men's clothes in the cottage — I think an old woman lives here alone — but there is a red flannel nightgown there you can put on while your clothes are drying. It might be a little tight across the shoulders, but I think it will fit. And be warm."

"A *nightgown*?" He picked up the red flannel nightgown between finger and thumb and regarded it with a dubious expression.

She hid a smile. "Don't look like that; there are no frills. It looks much like the nightshirts my father used to wear. More to the point, it will cover you decently and keep you warm while we dry your clothes by the fire. And don't worry, I'll turn my back while you change."

He gave her a slow smile. "I'm not worried in the least."

She busied herself arranging kindling in the fireplace, but her imagination was only too aware that he was stripping off his clothes, one by one. She recalled how he had looked shirtless, chopping wood, and her mouth dried. Just a peep, she told herself.

But that would be wrong. More, it would be dangerous.

She thrust the image of his naked chest out of her mind and concentrated on getting the fire going. She found the tinderbox, struck a spark and blew gently on the tinder until she coaxed from it first a wisp of smoke, then a small flame. Soon the kindling had caught and the fire was crackling brightly.

"You can look now," he said.

At his words she turned and caught her breath. He was practically naked. The red flannel nightgown lay untouched on the bed. He'd wrapped the strip of towel around his hips, tucking the ends in in a way that looked worryingly insecure. One movement and he'd . . . unwrap.

She swallowed. The cottage suddenly felt a great deal smaller. And warmer.

"Red is not my color," he said, gesturing to the nightgown on the bed. "But I'm perfectly comfortable like this — it won't take long for my shirt and breeches to dry." He tossed the patchwork quilt loosely around his shoulders, but even so, there was still too much naked Freddy visible for her peace of mind — between the folds of the quilt there were glimpses of bare chest, bare stomach and long, muscular legs, naked from midthigh down.

Like living marble, lean and hard and masculine. More beautiful than any statue she'd seen. And wearing a worn strip of toweling instead of a fig leaf.

He might be comfortable with his near-nakedness; she certainly wasn't.

She tried not to notice the fine dusting of dark gold hair sprinkled across his chest. It ran in a line down past his belly button . . . and disappeared under the towel.

That towel didn't even have a pin to secure it. What would happen when he moved?

He gave her a grin, seemingly not at all discomposed by his bareness or her struggle not to stare. "Worried about my towel falling off?"

Her face flushed with heat. "Not at all." With an effort she managed to drag her gaze off his body and fix it firmly to his face, refusing to let it drop below the chin. No matter how much it wanted to.

Why was it that men always seemed so comfortable in their skin, and women were so self-conscious? Well, she wasn't going to spend the rest of the day wondering when that wretchedly inadequate towel was going to slide off those narrow male hips.

She stalked to the chest and searched until she found what she wanted. "I thought this would be too inconvenient before, but I've changed my mind." She thrust a folded cotton sheet at him. "Wear that."

"You don't like my current attire?"

"It's insufficient," she said crisply. "You'll catch a chill."

He smiled, as if he knew very well why her color was so heightened, but took the sheet. "Turn your back, then, Miss Innocence."

Miss Innocence. If only he knew. She swallowed. It was a timely reminder.

Before she realized what he was about, he'd turned away and dropped the towel, giving her a glimpse of firm, well-shaped buttocks. She hurriedly busied herself with the fire, using the poker to stir it up, and swung the black cast-iron kettle across on its hook to heat some water. She was dying for a cup of tea.

"Better?"

She looked around. He'd wrapped the sheet around himself several times and tied it at the shoulder, toga style. "Much."

"It was getting a bit chilly," he admitted, picking up the quilt. "Now, your turn."

She blinked. "What?"

He jerked his head toward the bed. "Your turn to strip."

"I — I'm all right, just a bit damp." She ran her hands over her damp dress. "It'll dry soon, now that the fire's going."

"Nonsense, you're wet enough to catch a chill, so strip, or I'll do it for you." He pointed to the bed in the corner. "Now. Don't worry about modesty; I'll do my very best to be a gentleman."

Operating on the assumption that if she kept her back turned, decorum — of sorts — would be maintained, she began to struggle out of her damp clothes. With limited success. Why, oh, why, did ladies' dresses fasten at the back?

"Would you like me to undo you at the back there?" he asked a moment later.

She whirled around, her arms crossed over her fully clothed front. "You said you wouldn't look."

"I said I'd try to be a gentleman. It's not quite the same thing."

"A gentleman wouldn't look."

"A saint wouldn't look. You seem to have an odd understanding of gentlemen. The delightful thing about us is that we come in many different varieties."

He strolled over, twirled her around and started undoing the back of her dress. "Some of us wear red flannel nightgowns; some of us don't. Some gentlemen are mortified if a lady glimpses their bare legs. I'm not that sort, either."

His fingers brushed her skin as he worked. "I'm a helpful kind of gentleman who will gallantly offer to help a damp lady with her laces."

How did he always manage to make ordinary things sound so wicked? She felt a draft on her skin as her dress opened.

"It's not as easy as it looks, getting ladies out of their dresses," he murmured in her ear as he unfastened the laces of her corset.

He, of course, would know.

"There you go." He ran a slow finger down the length of her spine, sending ripples through her. She jumped and gave a small squeak.

She whirled to face him accusingly, clutching her sagging clothing to her.

"What's the matter?" he purred.

"Your finger," she said with as much composure as she could manage. "It's cold."

"Odd." He gave her a slow smile. "It must be the only part of me that is."

She was rather warm herself, but she'd rather die than admit it. Or admit that this situation was exciting her senses. That way lay danger, and, unlike the flood, once released, she knew it wouldn't recede. And this time it would destroy her.

"Turn your back," she told him sternly. "And keep it turned. Tend the fire or something."

"I like the sound of 'or something.'"

Impossible man. She decided to ignore him. Modesty being the better part of valor, and trust not being part of the equation at all, she pulled the voluminous red flannel nightgown over her head and, safely covered, she then struggled out of her clothes. It took rather longer than she expected but she was finally free of her wet things and respectably covered from neck to midcalf — it was too short to reach to her ankles, alas. Then, dressed in the nightgown and with a thick, homespun woolen shawl draped around her shoulders and knotted securely over her breasts, she turned.

And found him sprawled on a chair, convulsed with silent laughter.

"Beast!" She picked up a pair of lumpy socks and threw them at his head, wishing they were a rock instead. He caught them one-handed, still laughing.

"That," he said, "was better than a play."

"You," she told him severely, "are no gentleman."

"I think we already established that I'm a particular *kind* of gentleman." His eyes ran over her and darkened. "Red is most definitely your color," he said softly. Then, in quite a different tone, he added, "Thanks for these. This stone floor is quite chilly," and bent to pull the socks on.

Nettled, she pulled on a pair of socks herself. The stone floor was very cold.

By the time they'd arranged their wet

things around the fireplace, the kettle was singing. Damaris searched in the kitchen for tea but found only various jars of dried herbs. Luckily she knew her herbs.

"It will have to be herbal tea, I'm afraid."

He pulled a face, but anything hot was better than nothing, and when she poured the tea into two cups, he produced a flask from the pocket of his coat and poured a nip of brandy into each cup. "I never travel without it."

They sat by the fire, sipping their hot drinks. "You realize we'll be spending the night here," he said.

She'd realized. She just didn't want to think about it. "I was hoping someone might come to rescue us before then. Maybe the woman who lives here."

He shook his head. "Her hens were already locked in the henhouse when we got here. I'd say she expected to be gone for the day. She'll be on the other side of that flood."

"I feel a little uncomfortable, making so free with all her possessions."

He shrugged. "We have no choice. I'll leave her some money to make up for it. The question that's worrying me is what we'll have for dinner. I'll kill one of those hens if I have to, but —"

"No, you mustn't! You wouldn't know

which one to kill. What if you killed her favorite hen or her best layer?"

His brows rose. "You seem to have given it some thought. You kept hens in China, I gather, as well as swimming pigs."

She nodded. "You won't need to kill anything. There are plenty of eggs and some bread in the larder. And vegetables. I could make soup, and scrambled eggs on toast."

He gave her an exaggerated look of admiration. "Does this mean you can cook as well? Good heavens. There is no end to your talents, Miss Chance. You breed hens and experimental swimming pigs, you paint, you make dried weeds into a drink that's almost palatable —"

She laughed. "Wait until you've tasted my cooking before you judge, Mr. Monkton-Coombes. I may yet disappoint you."

"Never," he said quietly. But she was already searching the larder and didn't see the expression on his face.

As night fell, the cottage seemed to grow smaller and the bed bigger — although, to Damaris's mind, it was not big enough. Since dinner, she'd been putting the moment off, first with conversation, but she had soon run out of things to chat about. It was difficult to think of interesting conversational topics when a man in a toga — naked under that toga — was watching you rather in the manner of a cat watching a mouse, only with a lurking half smile.

Next she'd tried playing a word game. He turned out to be quite good at that, which was disconcerting. Finally in desperation, she'd tried "I spy" but whenever it was his turn he picked *B* and it always turned out to be *B* for *bed.*

Finally Freddy gave an extravagant yawn and stretched. "Time to turn in — that is, unless you've thought of yet another reason to put off going to bed."

"I don't know what you mean."

"No, of course you don't. And I suppose you expect me to be the kind of gentleman who will give you the bed, while I sleep on that freezing slab of stone that passes for a floor here, but I'm not such a fool."

"I never said —"

"You didn't need to. But here is what we're going to do: I shall remain in this toga-shroud affair and I'll wrap this quilt around me in a cocoon of blast— er, perfect chastity. You shall remain in that fetching red flannel tent, and we shall share the bed and the blankets. That way we shall both be warm and comf— well, warm, at any rate."

She hesitated.

"What is it now?" he asked. "Do you want me to promise not to seduce you? I won't. Come along, Miss Innocence, I won't bite." He gave a slow grin. "Not unless you ask me to." He held out his hand to Damaris.

She didn't take it. She was perfectly well able to rise from a chair on her own and she didn't trust herself to touch him. "I will make my ablutions first," she told him and removed herself to the back of the cottage, where she borrowed a pair of wooden clogs to make use of the outdoor privy. The rain had stopped but the wind was bitter and when she came back in she was freezing. She'd needed cooling down, she told herself.

She washed her face and hands and dried them slowly.

It was just a bed, she told herself. They had to sleep. And though he might be the kind of gentleman who was far too adept at helping a lady out of her clothes, he wasn't the sort of man who would force her. She was sure of that.

As long as she didn't let him see that she desired him, she was safe.

He was already in bed. He patted the bed invitingly. "I'm warming it for you."

She slipped into her side of the bed, blew out the homemade rush candle that sat beside it and pulled the covers up to her ears. "Good night, Freddy."

"Good night, Damaris." If his voice were a novel, the title would be *Invitation to Sin.*

The bed was a lot smaller than it had looked. She didn't want to bump up against him, so she arranged herself as close to the edge as was practical. She closed her eyes.

He wriggled around a bit, and she stiffened. "Just getting comfortable," he murmured. He was very close.

Something bumped the back of her legs. "Sorry, I need to curl up a bit. The bed's a bit shorter than me." A brawny arm slid around her waist and pulled her against him.

"What are y— ?"

"It's a small bed, and you don't want to fall out. Now stop worrying. This way we'll keep warm — ouch! Who put icicles in the bed?"

"If you're referring to my feet —"

"Is that what they are? Good God, they're frozen solid." He hooked a foot around her and drew her freezing feet against his legs. "Think of me as your personal hot brick."

She ought to have resisted, but her feet were cold and he was so wonderfully warm. He snuggled against her, holding her by the middle. "There, isn't that toasty? Now you'll sleep."

"Thank you. Good night," she said. How could she possibly sleep with his long, hard body wrapped around her, pressed against her from shoulder to thigh, his knees touching the backs of her thighs, his groin curved around her backside, his arm holding her close? Thank God for the toga and the quilt. What had he called it? A cocoon of perfect chastity.

It had better be.

She lay there, listening to the wind in the trees and gentle hiss and crackle of the fire. And the quiet breathing of the man in the bed with her. It was her definition of heaven.

Sometimes a woman just needs to be held. She understood now what Mama meant.

There was such comfort in it. But such bittersweetness, knowing it would be her only night with this man. She should savor it as long as she could.

She slept.

Freddy knew the moment Damaris fell asleep. Her breathing deepened and she relaxed back against him. He was as far from sleep as ever he'd been. He was as hard as a rock from the scent of her hair, the feel of her body against him. Patience, he told his eager little soldier. Good things come to those who wait.

But the good thing — the only woman

he'd ever truly wanted — was here in his arms. Trustfully asleep, blast it. And he'd promised to be a gentleman. It was the hardship of the long game.

Fools rush in and all that, and she was as wary a creature as any female he'd met.

She shifted a little in her sleep and he felt it; through a toga and a patchwork blasted quilt he felt it. He shifted uncomfortably. Cocoon of blasted chastity? More like an iron maiden of inconvenience.

Such an irony that he, who'd sworn loud and long that he never wanted to marry, was now certain that the only woman he could stand to wed was a sweet, stubborn girl who herself had vowed not to marry.

It was a mystery to him why a girl like Damaris would be so averse to marriage. He could understand that she might not wish to marry him — though there was a future title and a fortune to sweeten the deal. But not to wish to marry at all, when she didn't even have tuppence to her name . . .

It was all academic now. It didn't matter what either of them wanted. After this night together they were well and truly compromised. Marriage was no longer a choice for either of them; it was an obligation.

He wondered how she'd take it when she

realized.

The quilt was rucked up and uncomfort-able. Carefully he wriggled out of it and kicked it out of the bed. The toga would have to stay, he decided regretfully. After he'd promised not to seduce her, she wouldn't take kindly to waking up in bed with a naked man.

The wind rattled the windows and sighed around the eaves. He held her in his arms and waited for sleep to come.

CHAPTER NINETEEN

"Elinor . . . told herself likewise not
to hope. But it was too late.
Hope had already entered."
— JANE AUSTEN, *SENSE AND SENSIBILITY*

Damaris awoke slowly to a sense of warmth and comfort and . . . rightness. She lay without moving, savoring the sensation, aware of her breathing . . . and his. Abandoned in sleep he claimed her, one heavy arm holding her against the curve of his body, his chest pressed to her back, her bottom cuddled into . . . his groin.

He was hard. She could feel him pressing against her. Her eyes flew open and she tensed a moment, waiting. But the rhythm of his breathing didn't change and she slowly relaxed.

If only it could stay like this between them, peaceful, trusting, with no expectations. But she knew better. Those dreams were long gone.

Carefully she lifted his arm and turned to face him, drinking in the sight of him in a way she usually couldn't. When he was awake, those vivid blue eyes of his danced and dueled and offered endless lighthearted invitations to sin. People said eyes were a window to the soul, but his weren't. They were a barrier, his inner thoughts hidden behind the laughing gaze of the lighthearted rake.

On only a few occasions had she glimpsed another side of him, a more serious, thoughtful side. When he'd talked about his brother. A brief glimpse of something darker and more painful. And again when the lash of his parents' dismissal caught him unawares.

Now that brilliant blue gaze was hidden beneath the twin crescents of his lashes, thick and brown and tipped with gold.

In sleep he looked younger, less . . . guarded. Without his usual expression of faint cynicism. More . . . vulnerable.

His dark gold hair was tousled, and not by the expert attentions of his valet. His jaw was roughened with bristle, darker than his hair but with faint glints of gold. Her fingers itched to rub against his jaw, to feel the delicious abrasion and the hard bone beneath.

His lips were parted slightly. She looked at his mouth, his beautiful, mobile, masculine mouth, and remembered that kiss by his brother's grave.

Her first kiss, though no one, knowing what she'd done before reaching England, would believe that. She had difficulty believing it herself. And having done what she'd done, knowing what she knew, how had that kiss been so . . . sweet? So unexpected?

Tender, yet carnal, and deeply arousing. She ached now with the memory of it, wondering how it might feel to lie with this man. If his kiss — one single kiss — could move her so, how much more might there be if they were to lie together? If she opened herself to him and took inside her that part of him now pressing so insistently against her belly?

She ached to do it, to know . . . to feel again what she had felt that day by the lake. Only more.

She'd believed she knew everything about congress between a man and a woman, but that kiss had shown her how little she understood.

It was a mystery. He was a mystery.

And lying with him like this, gazing on his sleeping face and breathing in the scent of him and feeling what she was feeling, she was a mystery to herself.

She ached for him. But she knew it couldn't be. The cost would be too great.

Freddy knew before he'd even opened his eyes that she was watching him. He could feel her gaze on his face, feel the softness of her breath on his skin. The scent of her was intoxicating, her softness pressed gently, trustfully against him and — Lord help him — he was hard and rampant, pressing against her like a randy dog.

Did she know it? More to the point, did she understand it? She was an innocent, he reminded himself, despite the soft breasts pressed against his arm, hard tipped and begging for attention.

He opened his eyes and found her gazing intently at him, so sweetly earnest, as if he were a source of endless fascination. All his good intentions crumbled. "Morning, beautiful." With his free hand he cupped the nape of her neck and pulled her down to his mouth.

She tasted of sleep and surprised, aroused woman. She accepted him softly, with shy eagerness, her tongue touching, then tangling with his.

Desire, already kindled, sprang to a raging blaze in an instant.

He tried to resist, but a small voice inside him reminded him their fate had been tied the moment they'd been alone together and stranded in the cottage overnight. She was going to be his wife, and, strangely, for once he didn't seem to mind the idea of being married.

He particularly didn't mind it at this minute.

He rolled her over, kissing, tasting, glorying in her. He dragged at the tangled folds of the blasted toga affair he was still wearing, trying to free his body. He abandoned that for more urgent needs and swept the hem of her nightgown up along her long, slender legs, finding the satiny skin of her thighs and seeking the heated, damp place between them.

"No." She clamped her thighs together and pushed his hands away. "We can't."

"We can," he muttered and pulled her mouth back to his, one hand seeking the soft nest of damp curls between her thighs.

"No, we mustn't." Something in her voice alerted him. She pushed him away and sat up, wide-eyed and distressed. A flash of something he thought might be shame crossed her features. It was like a dash of cold water, bringing him to his senses.

Dammit, she was an innocent. And he'd

pounced on her with a complete lack of finesse. Where had his much-vaunted skills as a lover gone? Evaporated in a burst of white heat.

He pulled back, breathing deeply, willing the rampant desire to pass. He felt like a ravening wolf, but he gave her a smile that he hoped was reassuring. "Sorry, I'm not usually such an animal in the morning." He would be, if he woke every morning with her in his bed.

The thought cheered him. "When we're married it will be different." He would make love to her at night, as well as in the morning.

She stiffened. "Married? We're not getting married."

He smiled. "My dear girl, you must realize that spending the night together means we're thoroughly compromised. We have no choice but to marry now."

All the warmth and color drained from her face. "No. I can't. I won't."

"We must, don't you see?"

"No."

"But —"

"I don't want to talk about it. Just leave me, please. I beg you." She turned away and pulled the covers over her head.

"Very well," he said a little stiffly. He knew

she wasn't keen on marriage, but her re-action was stronger than he'd expected. "Give me a moment to dress, and I'll leave you. You need time to get used to the idea."

"I don't need time to get used to anything. We're not getting married." She sounded completely certain. Her refusal even to entertain the thought for a moment an-noyed him.

He would have to make her understand; their fate was sealed. It didn't matter whether she liked it or not — they *had* to get married.

If he could accept it with good grace, so could she.

He slipped from the bed and padded across the icy floor to where his clothes had been left to dry in front of the fire. His linen shirt and drawers were dry, as were his breeches. He pulled them on. His coat was still damp. He glanced outside. It was a clear, dry morning, no sign of rain, for which he was heartily grateful.

The fire had gone out in the night, and he cleared the ashes away and lit a new fire. "I'll see to the horses," he said when it was burning well.

He moved toward the door, then paused. "Should I do anything with the hens?"

"There's a bowl of scraps in the scullery,"

came a muffled voice from the bed. "Give them that and let them out."

"Won't they run away?"

"No, they'll come back when it's getting dark."

He fetched the bowl and left. His calmness in the face of her unreasonable obduracy was, he thought, quite impressive. He would see to the animals and come up with a sober, well-reasoned argument that would convince her that they had no option except marriage.

Below, the floodwaters swirled all around them for miles. It was as if they were on an island in the middle of a muddy sea. The rain had stopped and the clouds had passed away, leaving a washed-out wintry blue sky.

Pity. He could do with forty days and forty nights. It might take that long to convince her. . . .

Damaris shook out her dress. It was crumpled but dry. Keeping one eye on the door, she dressed in front of the fire, slipping into her underclothes first. She laced up her corset from the front, tying it as tight as she could, then twisted it around, hoping it would stay up all right. She would rather die than ask Freddy to tie it for her. His words echoed in her mind.

Spending the night together means we're thoroughly compromised. We have no choice but to marry.

If there was one thing everyone agreed on about Freddy Monkton-Coombes it was that he didn't want to be married.

She sat on the bed to put on her stockings and shoes. She couldn't, *couldn't* bear to let him be trapped into marrying her. It was her fault they'd ended up in this situation.

She'd been rude to his parents; she was the one who'd wanted to leave Breckenridge then and there; and because she got sick in closed carriages, they'd traveled in the curricle, without her maid in attendance. If Polly had been with them, the question would never have arisen.

On every count it was her fault.

He'd been nothing but kind to her, and this was how she would repay him? By entrapping him into marriage? Because society expected it? Because he was held to be a rake and she an innocent?

What a joke that was, bitter as only she knew.

There was no question of marriage.

The rain had stopped in the night. Outside the sky looked clear. Would the floodwaters have receded enough for them to pass?

She swiftly made the bed, pulling the

bedclothes straight, wondering whether they'd sleep there again. Could she trust herself to spend another night in the same bed with him? It had been a close call this morning. She'd almost forgotten herself. If he hadn't had to stop to disentangle himself from the sheet, if she hadn't felt a jolt of sensation at his intimate touch . . . what might have happened?

She wasn't sure whether she was relieved or sorry.

She picked up the patchwork quilt from where he had dumped it on the floor and began to fold it.

The door crashed open. Freddy stood in the doorway, his blue eyes blazing with decision. "God wants us to get married."

She clutched the quilt to her chest and stared at him in amazement. *"What?"*

He stepped inside and closed the door and said calmly, "It's all quite clear to me: God wants us to get married."

She didn't believe a word of it. "You don't even believe in God."

He frowned. "How do you know?"

"You said so, back in London when you told me to live in the moment like a Buddhist."

"Oh. Well, I believe in Him now."

"Why? What has changed?"

"He sent a Flood. So that we would have to get married."

"Pfft. You don't believe that for a moment." It was a ridiculous argument. Endearing, but ridiculous.

"I do," he said with an air of virtue that didn't deceive her in the least. "And since you do believe in God, you need to honor His Flood by marrying me."

"Well, I won't."

"And you a missionary's daughter! I'm shocked."

She finished folding the quilt and placed it on the bed. "I wasn't a missionary; Papa was."

"I could convert you."

"I don't want to be converted. Especially by a heathen, manipulative, devious rake," she added, hoping it would annoy him enough to stop this foolish nonsense.

"You say the sweetest things. So, where would you like us to get married?"

"Nowhere."

He considered that for a moment, then nodded. "Oh, yes, I know where that is. I recollect I found myself in the middle of it once. Very well, it is agreed."

"What is agreed? In the middle of what?"

"The middle of nowhere — it's in Yorkshire. Odd place for a wedding, but if your heart is set on it —"

"It's not. And you are ridiculous."

"But eligible, you must admit. And honorable, which is why we're going to be married. So, will it be St. George's, Hanover Square; or the chapel at Davenham, where your sister and Max were married; or — ?"

"I'm *not* marrying you."

"Don't be silly, of course you are. Now, I'll go and chop some wood while you try to make up your mind where the wedding will be. I must say I'm surprised. Never thought you'd be so indecisive, Damaris."

"I'm not indecisive —" she began, but he was gone and the door shut behind him, leaving her in a turmoil of mixed emotions, half laughing and at the same time on the verge of tears. Of course it was all nonsense but it was very sweet nonsense, pretending it was some kind of divine plan. Letting her off the hook and blaming God.

They both knew better.

How she would love to go along with his banter and let herself to be talked into a lighthearted wedding. She longed for a happily-ever-after as much as any other girl. But too much had happened and she was not the blushing virgin he imagined her to be. And when he learned what she had been, and done . . . well, she didn't want to have to live with that kind of disillusion, let alone be the cause of it.

She just had to stand firm, that was all. It would be better for both of them.

The morning passed busily, with Freddy seeing to the horses and Damaris cleaning the cottage — she wanted to leave it as spick-and-span as it had been when they arrived — and searching through the provisions in the larder to see what she could find to cook.

And trying not to think of how it might be if she married Freddy Monkton-Coombes.

It wasn't to be thought of. He only persisted because he didn't understand why it was impossible. And unnecessary.

And because she was too much of a coward to tell him why.

Around midday, Freddy came in, carrying an armload of wood — he'd never chopped so much wood in his life — and stamping his feet to knock off the mud. Round two, he thought.

"Looking at the level of that water, I'd say we won't be leaving here until tomorrow at the earliest. It's not dropping yet, but it's stopped rising." He squatted down and began to stack the wood in the box next to the hearth.

She nodded and went on busily pinching out little lumps of dough.

He finished stacking the wood and brushed off his hands. "What are you doing?"

"Making dumplings for our dinner."

He pulled out a chair and sat down to watch her. She rolled out the lumps of dough into small circles, placed a dab of creamy green mush in the middle, then folded them in half, sealing the edges with some beaten egg.

"Never seen dumplings like that before."

"They're Chinese."

"Ah." He watched as her hands moved deftly. Flatten, dab, fold, seal. The crescent-shaped dumplings multiplied rapidly. It was quite soothing to watch, but Freddy wasn't in the mood for being soothed. "You know, Damaris, for a girl who's normally quite good about grasping the nettle, you're being remarkably reluctant to face the truth of our situation."

Her mouth flattened. "I'm not going to marry you."

"There's no choice, not for either of us. If we don't, you'll be regarded as a fallen woman, and decent women will shun your society, while I'll be branded as a scoundrel."

"We agreed this arrangement was a temporary thing only. A pretense."

God, but she was stubborn. "Yes, but the flood has changed everything."

She wiped her floury hands on a cloth. "I don't care what people say about me."

"Nor what they say about me, apparently."

That gave her a jolt, he saw. She hadn't considered it from his point of view. She gave him a pleading look. "I could make it clear that you offered for me and I refused."

He tamped down on his anger, telling himself she didn't understand the implications, that she was an innocent and had been raised in another culture. It didn't help. "You would tell the world that you would rather be branded as a scarlet woman than marry me? How very flattering."

She bit her lip. "I'm sorry, I didn't mean . . ." She shook her head, as if she were having a silent argument with herself. She finished the last of the dumplings, covered them with a damp cloth and began to tidy the table. "Surely people will forget after a week or two. You know how society moves from one scandal to the next."

He clenched his fist. Her stubborn refusal to face facts infuriated him. "I don't care.

You and I will marry — no argument. If you cannot bear me to touch you — and I don't believe that for a minute" — she flinched — "then we will have a white marriage. But marry me you will."

"I can't."

At the despair in her voice, a possibility occurred to him for the first time. "Are you — you're not married already, are you?"

"No. But there are reasons why I cannot . . ."

"What reasons?"

She shook her head and started wiping down the table. He snatched the cloth and threw it across the room. "Dammit, Damaris, if I'm to be known as a scoundrel who ruined the reputation of a decent young lady, the very least you owe me is an explanation."

She gave him a long, troubled look, then seemed to crumple. She lowered herself onto the chair and said wearily, "That's just it, I'm not a decent young lady. The very opposite, in fact."

CHAPTER TWENTY

"If I could but know his heart,
everything would become easy."
— JANE AUSTEN, *SENSE AND SENSIBILITY*

"I'll explain, but first I'll make us some tea," she said.

Freddy was about to put out his hand and stop her, but changed his mind. Women sometimes found comfort in such rituals, and tea might bring a little color back to her cheeks. That paleness worried him.

I'm not a decent young lady. The very opposite, in fact.

What the hell could she mean by it? The opposite of decent? That was nonsense, for a start. He'd known a lot of women, of various characters and from all walks of life, and Damaris was one of the finest, most decent people he'd known.

He watched her making the tea — well, not proper tea; it was another collection of dried green bits. God knew what it would taste like, but if she made it, he would drink it. It was her way of delaying the inevitable.

Judging from her expression, it was serious, this reason of hers. At least she thought it was.

What could she possibly have done that would make her ineligible for marriage? Because that, beneath it all, was what she was saying — not that she wouldn't marry him, but that she couldn't.

Finally, just when he was about to put his foot down and insist that she stop messing about with blasted herbs and tell him what the hell this was all about, she brought the teapot and two cups over and sat down again at the table.

"It's a long story," she said.

"I don't mind." He didn't care how long it took, as long as he learned what could have put that bleak look in her eyes. Worse than bleak. Stark despair.

At the prospect of marrying him.

Damaris stirred her tea slowly, wishing, praying there were some way she could avoid telling him this. Wanting to put off the moment when the kindness and concern would fade from his eyes and be replaced by . . .

Pray that when she was finished he would

not look at her the way Papa used to look at Mama. With resentment. And disgust. Papa had no respect for Mama, none at all.

Now, on the brink of opening herself to the same condemnation, she wondered how Mama had borne it all those years. She would have been less lonely living alone, without a soul to talk to, than living with Papa and his righteous contempt.

No decent man could respect a woman who came to her marriage bed tarnished. Impure. And worse, driven still by the lusts of the flesh.

And though Damaris had tried all her life to do the right thing, now she was just as tarnished, just as impure and fallen as Mama — more so, probably.

And she had a horrid suspicion she was also driven by the lusts of the flesh.

She stirred her tea, feeling his gaze on her, but unwilling to meet it, dreading the moment the kind light of concern would fade from his eyes.

She traced the grain of the table with her finger, trying to decide how to start — where to start, because it was complicated. "You know I lived in China."

He nodded. "Yes, with your missionary father."

"I told you Papa died, but what I didn't

say is that he was killed. Murdered."

"Murdered?"

She found a crack in the grain of the timber and ran her fingernail along it, back and forth, concentrating as she spoke, as if the story she told was about someone else, not herself. "Yes. I wasn't there when they came — I was at the market. . . ." She told him how she'd seen Zhang Liang and his soldiers riding out but hadn't realized the significance of it until she'd heard the old lord, his father, was dead.

Her shopping had fallen in the dust, unheeded, as she'd realized where the soldiers must have been going.

She told him how she'd run and run, with a stitch knifing into her side, and how she'd stumbled the last few yards on shaky, exhausted legs, up the crest of the hill that overlooked the valley, and had seen the pall of smoke hanging over the mission.

In a voice that sounded wooden to her ears, she described how she'd found their little church looted and destroyed, the children gone — she knew not where, whether they'd fled or been taken by the soldiers. And how she'd found her father's body sprawled in the mission courtyard — beheaded.

He frowned and reached for her hands at

that point, but she waved him off. She'd never get through her story if he touched her, she knew.

She told him how she'd buried Papa. There was nothing to be done about the children — she was helpless in that too. But on reflection she decided the soldiers would not harm them. If they'd intended harm, surely there would be small bodies in the dust along with Papa's. No, it was only the foreign devils they were after.

She was the only one left. She told him how she'd set out to walk to the coast, hoping to find a European ship to take her home — yes, she still thought of England as home, even though she had no memories of it, and no relatives.

She described how she'd walked for days — no, she didn't know how many, she'd lost track of time — and how, to her joy and relief, she had found an English ship. But that by that time she had nothing left, no food, no money to pay for her passage, only the clothes she stood up in — Chinese peasant clothes — and her mother's locket.

She traced the crack in the wood over and over, wishing she didn't have to tell him this part, but knowing it was the whole point of the story.

It was hard to find the words — no, not

the words; it was the will to speak them she lacked. The words themselves were simple.

She told him how she'd spoken to the captain and explained her situation. "I offered to work my passage, cleaning, cooking, mending the sails or whatever." It was important that he understand that, that she had offered honest work in exchange for her passage. "And the captain agreed."

She still hadn't looked at him. He'd gone very silent. He wasn't stupid; he could see what was coming.

She paused, wishing he would speak and save her the pain of telling it in all its sordid detail. She'd never told anyone this part of her story, had hoped she'd never have to.

But he said not a word to spare her.

She told him how seasick she'd been for the first few days. "It's not only carriages I get sick in," she said ruefully, but really she was putting off the moment.

And, judging from the tension that seemed to fill the cottage, he knew it.

She moistened her lips and forced herself to continue. "After a few days at sea I became accustomed to the movement of the ship. I was able to stand and keep food down. One of the sailors told me to clean myself up, that the captain had sent for me." She swallowed. "I was told to report for duty. He — the captain was . . . he was in his cabin.

"And then . . ." She swallowed, and traced the grain of the table with her finger, pressing her fingernail into the tiny crack as if it could somehow swallow her up. She still couldn't look at him. "And then he told me the . . . the manner by which I was to work my passage. He said I had three choices."

There was a long silence.

"What were the choices?" His voice sounded hoarse.

She swallowed again, with difficulty, and tried to meet his eyes but failed. "He said I could become his — his —"

"I know what he meant. What were the other two choices?"

"If I didn't choose him, he would hand me over to the crew, for the same purpose."

He swore. "And your third choice?"

"To swim for shore."

"After several days at sea?" He swore again.

She nodded and forced herself to spit it out. "And so I made my choice, and though I know it was cowardly and contemptible, in the same circumstances, I would make the same choice again." She braced herself for his reaction, but he said not a word. Had he not understood what she'd done? Did he expect her to say it? To admit every ugly detail?

Papa would have.

So, in a hard little voice, she forced out the words that would complete her confession. "I chose the capt—"

He reached across the table and took her hands in a warm, firm grip. "No, Damaris, you chose *life*. And *no one* could blame you for it. No one, least of all me."

They weren't the words she'd been expecting. Not remotely. She forced herself to look at him then. His eyes were blazing blue with some unknowable emotion. His hands gripped hers tightly, so tightly it almost hurt.

"You did the only thing you could. *No one* would blame you. I certainly wouldn't."

She searched his face, not entirely trusting the truth of what he'd said. "I was always taught 'death before dishonor.' "

"There was no dishonor in what you did," he said softly. His thumbs caressed her hands. "Only desperation. And a desire to live. The dishonor was entirely that swine of a captain's."

She tried to swallow but there was a lump in her throat. She wanted to believe him, but a lifetime's experience had taught her the opposite was true. The woman was always at fault. Always.

"Is that your reason for refusing to get married?"

She nodded. "I realize that virginity is a requirement for marriage, that no decent man could respect a woman who came to her marriage bed tarnished and impure —"

"Who told you that piece of nonsense?"

She blinked. "My father." Repeatedly.

"Well, forgive me, but if that's what he thought, the man was a fool. Granted, some fellows prize virginity in a bride, but that's usually about securing paternity, of the first child, at least. And because some men are clumsy brutes and prefer their brides ignorant. Besides, I'm somewhat of a rake, which means I'm not a virgin, either. Which makes us equal."

She shook her head. "It's different for men, as you very well know. You're not taking me seriously. I would rather live alone than live without respect." As Mama had.

He frowned. "I've already said I don't blame you. No one could possibly blame you for what happened."

She could not quite believe him. She lifted her chin and said half defiantly, "I would do it again if I had to, so though I was shamed by the captain, I am not ashamed of my decision. And I won't be *forgiven* for it." Because the forgiven one was always in the wrong. Forgiven didn't mean forgotten. Papa had forgiven Mama, but he'd never forgotten, not for a minute. She'd had to endure his forgiveness daily.

His eyes warmed. "My dear girl, I wouldn't dare."

There was a short silence. "Are you . . . are you laughing at me?" She couldn't believe it.

He squeezed her hands. "Not precisely laughing. Smiling a little at your fierceness, perhaps. There's no need for it, truly there isn't. You don't have to defend your decision to me. I thoroughly approve it. Where would I be if you'd believed that 'death before dishonor' nonsense, for instance?"

She decided to take him literally. "For a start, you wouldn't be stuck in a cottage, cut off from the world by floodwaters and being compromised into a marriage you never wanted."

"Exactly," he said cheerfully. "I did mention that I enjoy a little adventure from time to time, did I not? I have no regrets at all about this one. And neither should you. Let us make the best of the situation life has presented us with. Speaking of which, are you going to do anything with those alleged dumplings, or are they meant to be served dry and cracked around the edges?"

She glanced at the dumplings and tucked the damp cloth over the few that were exposed to the air. She didn't understand this man at all. He seemed not to take her situation at all seriously. She told him so.

"Oh, make no mistake, my dear, I take what was done to you very seriously. Very seriously indeed." She glimpsed a flash of ice in his eyes, but then they warmed as he said, "But as far as I'm concerned nothing you have told me presents any barrier to our marrying."

It was a sliver of hope but she couldn't count on it. "Then let me tell you the rest," she said. She had hoped not to have to tell him this last part. "When we landed in England, instead of setting me ashore, as he'd promised, the captain told me he had found me a job. And then he laughed."

She still felt ill, remembering the moment she'd realized. Her shock, and momentary disbelief, followed by helpless, bitter fury.

What a fool she'd been to believe that such a man would keep his word to a friendless girl.

"He'd sold me to a brothel."

Freddy made some sort of incoherent noise. She glanced at him, but he shook his head. "Go on." His jaw tightened, as did his grip on her. It crushed her fingers a little, but was oddly comforting. Connection, instead of repudiation.

"Of course I refused. I tried to escape, to get off the ship myself, but he was prepared for that. He had me bound and gagged and carried ashore wrapped in an old blanket." The blanket was moldy and damp and the stench of it made her sick. "My first sight of England was from the inside of a brothel. From a locked room."

He swore. "The bastard!"

She forced out the words that still scalded her with shame. "He told me, as they carried me away, that I was born for it."

"The swine will die for that," he said quietly, and then he fixed his gaze on her. "Of course, you do know there's not the slightest word of truth in what he said."

She ran her tongue over dry lips. "That day at the lake, you said —"

"I know what I said, and it's not the same thing at all. I'll show you what I meant, and it's a world away from whatever that bastard told you. But first, finish your tale. You're almost done now — and you need to tell me, I know, though it will change nothing, I promise you. Now, how did you get out of the brothel?"

She hesitated. This was not only her story to share; others were involved. "Will you give me your word of honor that what I tell you will go no further than this room?"

He gave a curt nod, and then, when she still waited, said, "Of course you have my word. Go on."

"Jane had also been taken to the brothel by force — she'd been drugged and kidnapped. She was an orphan too, but unlike me — and unbeknownst to her kidnappers — she had a sister in London — Abby — and she convinced a maidservant to send word to her. Daisy — she was the maid — helped us escape. She came with us."

"Good God. So that's how you girls met? I had no idea."

"Lady Beatrice knows about the brothel — Abby insisted on telling her everything before we accepted her invitation to live with her. Abby told Max too, before she agreed to marry him." She bit her lip. "But I never told anyone about the captain; not Lady Beatrice, nor Abby and the girls." She'd been too ashamed.

There was a long silence. Then, "How long were you in the brothel?"

"Only a few days. I was never . . . sold. Daisy got us out just a few hours before we were to make our first . . . appearance." She shuddered, remembering how close their escape was. She'd been billed as the Chinese

Whore, painted in a crude imitation of a Chinese girl and dressed in nothing but a flimsy, embroidered red gauze wrapper.

"Were you harmed in any way?"

She bit her lip. "Only beaten a few times."

"Only?"

She shrugged. "Mort — he was the owner — didn't want to mark me. But the beatings were worth it." The first few beatings were because of her recalcitrance, but the last . . . She smiled, remembering. "I made up a herbal tea that made Jane ill on the night of her Virgin Auction. She threw up over some of the clients. It saved her."

Freddy glanced at his tea and pushed it away.

"This brothel, where is it?"

"Closed down now. Max reported it, and Daisy gave evidence. Mort was hanged — Jane wasn't the only innocent girl he'd kidnapped."

"And what was the name of the captain?"

She stared at him. "What could his name possibly matter? He'll be well and truly gone now, probably on the other side of the world."

"Nevertheless, I need to know it."

She shrugged and told him.

"And the ship?"

"The *Liverpool Lass*. But it's probably on

437

the other side of the world as well."

He stood up abruptly. "Right, then, that's your story told. Makes not a jot of difference to our getting married. Now, I need to chop some wood."

"But you already chopped plenty of —"

But he'd taken three strides across the room and was gone, the door closed firmly behind him.

Thoroughly bemused by his reaction, Damaris added more water to the soup left over from the day before. It had thickened overnight and she stirred the pot waiting for it to come to the boil.

Outside she could hear the chunk! chunk! of wood being chopped. There was already a neat pile of firewood stacked beside the fireplace, and more in a box just outside the back door, so it was beyond her why Freddy thought they needed more. At this rate they'd use up the old woman's entire winter store of wood. Though he'd said he'd pay for whatever they used, and she knew he'd be generous.

She thought about his response to what she'd told him. *Generous* wasn't the word.

He'd said, several times, that it would make no difference to him, that he didn't mind that she wasn't a virgin, that her sordid exchange with the captain was no barrier to their marriage as far as he was concerned and even — such a shocking concept — that Papa was a *fool* about such things.

Could he really mean it? Was it because he was a rake, that he viewed things so differently? Could she dare to hope? She'd lived so long with the certainty that marriage wasn't an option for her, not unless she was prepared to live with the kind of constant condemnation that Mama had endured, and she wasn't. She absolutely wasn't.

But Freddy had said she had nothing to be ashamed of.

He'd said he approved of her choice. *Approved.*

He'd even laughed at the idea of forgiveness, as if there were nothing to forgive.

Nothing to forgive. A bubble of hope lodged in her chest.

The pot was simmering. She stirred in the dumplings, one by one.

Chapter Twenty-One

"I did not *then* know what it was to love."
— JANE AUSTEN, *SENSE AND SENSIBILITY*

The bastard! *Thunk! Chunk!* The swine! *Thunk!*

Freddy swung the ax savagely, imagining each log as the neck of a certain sea captain. When Freddy found him — and he would find him, no matter where in the world the bastard was skulking — the man was as good as dead.

After all she'd been through — losing her father in such a brutal manner, that endless walk across China, surviving God knew how — of course she'd thought an English ship, an English sea captain, would be her salvation.

Thunk! Chunk! Wood chips flew. It damned well should have been.

Sea captains were by nature a tough lot — they had to be, to command the ruffians

440

and roughnecks who made up the average ship's crew. But most captains had a streak of decency in them, and a recently orphaned girl, an English girl, and the daughter of a *missionary,* for God's sake! To use such a girl as a *whore*! To use Damaris . . . ! Rage boiled in him and the ax flew.

He split a log viciously, remembering the tender innocence of that kiss by the lake.

Christ, the bastard must have taken her with no tenderness, no consideration for her youth or innocence. She'd been fucked from one side of the world to the other, but never — God damn the bastard forever — been kissed. Sold into a brothel, and never been kissed.

And he'd told her she was born for it.

Thunk! Chunk! The pile of chopped wood grew.

The courage it had taken for her to tell him — Christ, there was honor for you! She'd bared her soul to him, to save him from a marriage she thought he didn't want. He'd told her what had happened to her didn't matter. It damned well did.

He'd told her he didn't mind that she wasn't a virgin. He bloody well did.

But not in the way she thought it.

He wanted to be her first. Not some grubby little sea captain who couldn't be bothered to show her the slightest care. God knew what she thought men and women did together. Between her ass of a father and the swine of a sea captain, it was a miracle she wasn't bitter and hostile toward men, let alone trusting Freddy as far as she had.

For the first time in his life, he understood why men wanted a virgin bride — and it was nothing to do with securing paternity or preferring ignorance. It was something deeper, wilder, more primitive.

Not civilized in the least.

It was an utterly primitive desire to possess her, wholly and completely. To initiate her into a world only they two would share. To be her man, her bridegroom, to witness the dawning awareness in her eyes — to cause it. To introduce her to an intimacy she'd never known, to bring ecstasy to her body. And to share it.

That kiss by the lake, that tremulous, precious, exquisite moment — best kiss of his life, dammit. Shook him to his very bones. It was a reminder of what they could have had, if Damaris had not been violated by a filthy sea capt—

The ax paused in midair.

She'd never been kissed. And she'd never been made love to. She'd been used, well and truly. But *she'd never been made love to.*

Freddy put down the ax.

"Delicious dumplings," Freddy commented later that evening, as he spooned up the last of his soup with dumplings. He'd seen to the horses and locked up the hens — they'd returned to their pen as dusk had fallen, just as she'd said they would. Now supper was over and there was nothing to distract her. Nothing except him. "And the soup was excellent too, thank you. How delightful to be acquiring a wife who can actually cook. So useful, should we ever be stranded again. So, have you developed a distaste for the, er, carnal intimacies between a man and a woman?"

The abruptness of that question caused Damaris to almost choke on her soup. She gave him an indignant look.

"Does that mean yes or no?" he said when she'd recovered her breath. There was no delicate way to ask it, so he'd decided to be bold. Best have it all out in the open.

"I — I don't know."

I don't know. What did that mean? How could she not know? But at least it must mean she didn't have an active horror of it. Indifference, then. He could work with indifference.

"Does it matter?"

"Does it —" He stopped himself in time. "In one sense no, it does not matter. We're still getting married — don't think you're wriggling out of that. We can make this thing work. We've become friends, have we not, in these last weeks?"

She hesitated, then nodded.

"Many married couples don't even have that. But if the very idea of sexual congress appalls you, then I won't touch you, of course." And what a whopper that was. He had every intention of touching her. He could barely keep his hands off her as it was. He wouldn't force her, of course — damn that swine of a captain to hell and back — but he'd known other women who'd been mishandled by clumsy brutes and conceived a distaste for bed sports. Freddy had shown them the pleasures that could be had.

He would show Damaris too. She was currently staring at him with a strange look on her face.

"Now, what does that look mean?"

She shook her head.

Seeing she wasn't going to explain, he continued, "If you find you can't bear to live with me, you'll always have your cottage to retreat to — don't look at me like that. Of course it will still be yours to keep. So, that's the way it will be. There's no need for you to worry. I'm a man of my word. I won't pester you."

She didn't say a word. She just gathered up the dishes and took them to the bench at the back of the room and started washing them.

Freddy made no move to help her. He remained at the table, watching her back view, admiring the elegant line of her spine and the slight jiggling of her rear as she scrubbed away at the dishes.

It was true. He wouldn't pester her.

He would seduce her.

You'll always have your cottage to retreat to. Oh, he was a villain indeed, assuring her of her freedom. He was determined to bind her to him in any way he could, not only because he desired her with an ache so deep and fierce it colored his awareness of everything, but because she'd become . . . necessary to him. Her soft voice, her serenity, her stubbornness, her bravery, her beauty, that laugh of hers . . . her understanding . . .

She seemed to regard him as no one else had ever seen him, as he'd never seen himself. Poor deluded girl, thinking him some kind of hero.

He needed to marry her if only to stop

her from falling under some other scoundrel's sway.

Her seduction, now, that was purely for his own benefit. And hers, of course.

Damaris dumped the bowls and plates in a basin and poured hot water over them. *A distaste for the carnal intimacies between a man and a woman?* What sort of a question was that to throw at her while she was drinking soup?

And why bring it up now? He'd pointed out, indirectly, that they'd be spending another night in the cottage. Together. Alone. With all this talk of carnal intimacies hanging in the air between them, was he suggesting that they . . . ?

Before the wedding? If there were to be a wedding, and she wasn't yet convinced of that.

She rubbed soap onto a wet rag and began to wash the plates. She refused to believe a marriage between them was a foregone conclusion.

It was highly possible that no scandal would result from this event. If nobody realized they'd spent a night — two nights — together unchaperoned, there would surely be no need for a wedding.

She glanced out the small window at the

back of the cottage. A tiny robin hopped onto a bare twig and looked at her, his little head cocked curiously. In the cold gray daylight, he looked so bold and jaunty in his little red waistcoat. He chirruped a couple of times, then flew off.

She didn't want to have trapped Freddy into a marriage, even if he was the one insisting on a wedding. Why, when he was famous for being averse to marriage?

Oh, it was all so confusing.

She didn't understand him at all. It was hard enough working out what she wanted. Everything she'd believed about herself and her eligibility had been turned topsy-turvy.

She cleaned the spoons, rubbing them to a shine. What did she want? Not what she ought to want, or what was possible, or polite, or politic to want — what did she really want, deep down?

There was no hesitation in the answer that came back. Him. She wanted him.

She dried the dishes slowly, reflecting on her choices. There was no point in worrying about the future — that was too dependent on others — what they thought, or thought they knew.

Did she have a distaste for the carnal intimacies between a man and a woman?

She wasn't sure. She feared not.

What sort of a woman wasn't sure? Until today, that lack of certainty had shamed her. A decent woman should have been disgusted by the whole thing — and she had been, for most of the time with the captain. She'd fought him — not physically, because after all she had agreed to it to save her life — but she'd held herself stiff, her eyes closed, trying to block out what was happening as he used her body, refusing to react, or cooperate, refusing to acknowledge in any way what was happening, pretending it was happening to someone else, not her, even though at first it was frightening and painful and deeply humiliating and invasive. She'd loathed his every touch, his smell, the way he pawed at her with his thick-fingered hands.

Afterward she'd scrubbed herself clean of him.

But the trip from China to England had taken months and gradually she had become accustomed to the daily invasion of her body, and once or twice, despite all her efforts to block it out, she had felt . . . something. A slight shudder deep within her.

He'd known, too, the captain, and he'd laughed at her, saying he'd always known she was a whore, that all women were whores deep down.

It was an echo of what Papa had implied more than once.

Now the most decent man she'd ever known sat behind her at the table, saying he was prepared to marry her to save her reputation — and his — and that he wouldn't press her to lie with him as a wife lay with her husband. She could feel his gaze on her.

Nothing ventured, nothing gained.

She would give herself to him tonight, with no reservations, with nothing held back, showing him her true self: Mama's daughter.

Then he'd know the full extent of what he was taking on if he married her.

And if he didn't? a little voice asked. If he was disgusted by her sensual nature, as Papa had been by Mama's?

Then at least she would have had her night with him. She thought of how it had been the previous night, sleeping in his arms. She tried to imagine him doing the things the captain had done to her, and couldn't.

But she knew the smell of him, clean and masculine, and his touch, and the way he looked at her. She knew the taste of him. That kiss by the graveside . . . how often had she relived it?

A flutter of movement caught her eye. The robin was back, along with another little bird. His mate. They chirruped back and forth to each other in a series of fluting calls, hopping from twig to twig.

She would take this chance.

One night in his arms, without shame or fear. Giving him all she was, no holding back.

Honesty. A terrifying prospect.

But she had to know. She refused to live her life as Mama had, judged, condemned and found wanting for what was her nature. Best to know now and make her decision accordingly.

She wiped down the bench, wrung out the rag then wiped it again, putting off the moment when she would turn and offer herself to him, brazenly. Risking all.

The two little robins flew off together. She watched them until they were just dots in the sky.

"Will you lie with me?" she said, the words coming out a little throaty.

There was a long silence, then a chair scraped on the flagstones behind her. She turned, and he was standing there, so close she could feel his body heat. He gazed down at her with an expression she couldn't read, his blue eyes ablaze.

"Will you?"

"You mean make love to you," he corrected her gently.

She nodded, twisting the washing-up rag between anxious fingers. She didn't care what he called it, but now, having said it, she wanted it to be done and over, so she would know. She moved toward the bed.

He put out his arm and stopped her, then cupped her face in his hands, framing it with his thumbs, caressing her. For a long moment he said nothing, just gazed into her eyes. She stared back, breathless, then with aching slowness he lowered his mouth to hers and kissed her, a long, lingering kiss that sent warm shivers through her.

His mouth caressed her, teasing, sending flickers of heat through her. His long, lean body pressed against hers. Her back was pressed against the bench, a line of coldness, but she didn't mind.

He teased her lips apart and stroked her with his tongue, sending hot ripples that made her body want to curl with delight.

"What are you doing?" she managed to say when he finally broke the kiss and started nibbling on her neck. She still had the damp cloth wadded in her hand. It was pressed against his neck. He gently disengaged her fingers from it and tossed it aside.

"Kissing you. Why? Didn't you notice? I must have been doing it wrong," he murmured. "Let me try it again."

"No, I — mmph!" She sagged against him as his mouth took possession of her again. The taste of him, dark, masculine and intoxicating, filled her. His fingers speared gently into her hair, loosening the knot she'd secured with a few pins. She felt it slide down around her shoulders.

"Beautiful hair," he murmured, feathering tiny kisses along her temple as he stroked her hair, combing his fingers through it. "Like the finest silk."

He made no move toward the bed. In the meantime, she was melting under his touch.

"I didn't mean kiss me," she gasped when she had the opportunity. "I meant *lie* with me."

He drew back a little and gave her a long, thoughtful look.

"I meant *couple* with me." She pushed at his shoulders. Why didn't he understand? "On the bed," she added desperately. She wanted to get it over with, to know. These kisses, they were too . . . too *dissolving*. They made her want to float forever on the magic.

But coupling was not like that, she knew; it was hard and fast and sweaty and not the slightest bit dissolving.

And if this were to be the only time she lay with him, she wanted to be aware of every moment, every second of it, losing nothing, storing up every sensation for the long winter of loneliness ahead. And while he kept kissing her, she couldn't concentrate.

"You want us on the bed?" he said. "Very well." And without warning he scooped her up, carried her to the bed, laid her on top of the covers and followed her down in a loose-limbed sprawl beside her. Before she could say anything, he was lying half on top of her, kissing her again.

She pressed her palms against his chest, pushing him back a little. "I didn't ask you to kiss me, I asked you to lie with me, to couple."

There was a short silence. She caught a flicker of some expression in his eyes but couldn't interpret it. "The way I do it, the two go together." He smoothed her hair back from her face. "This is just the preliminary."

"The preliminary?"

"Just trust me," he murmured against the sensitive skin of her throat. The deep timbre of his voice vibrated through her. "Relax. Let yourself go."

Her heart was thudding in her chest. *Let yourself go.* It was exactly what she was afraid of. But she needed to see what would happen. And how he would respond if she did truly let herself go.

"Trust me," he said again. "You have nothing to fear here."

She hoped that was true, but it wasn't him she feared; it was herself. As he bent again to claim her mouth, she closed her eyes, wrapped her arms around him and gave herself up to him.

As his mouth plundered hers and their tongues tangled, she rubbed her palms along his jawline, enjoying the friction of his unshaven skin, his rough to her smooth, her soft to his hard.

And he was hard; she could feel it pressing against her. She was braced for him to drag up her skirts and plunge into her, but still he made no move to take her.

His big hands roamed, stroking and caressing her even though she was still fully clothed. And despite the thickness of her dress and underclothes, she felt her nipples rising into hot, hard little buds. He cupped her breasts, his thumbs teasing at the thrusting buds until they were aching with need. Each movement sent delicious shivers through her.

And always, always he returned to kiss her, as if somehow sensing she could never get enough of it, of him. She ran her fingers through his thick, dark gold hair, cupping his head, as she angled her mouth to deepen the kiss.

"Let's get this off you," he muttered and half rolled her on top of him, so he could get to her laces at the back. In seconds, she felt a draft at her back, and as he pulled the dress off her shoulders, she ran her hands down his arms, over his shirtsleeves, and dropped her hands to his chest.

"No." She pushed him away and sat up abruptly, pulling her dress back up. This wasn't right.

"What is it? What's the matter?" His eyes, blazing blue, searched her face with dark intensity; his hair was rumpled where her fingers had roamed; his unshaven jaw, dark gold and deliciously rough to the touch.

She swallowed. This could very well be her only time with this man, and she wanted to have everything the way she'd dreamed it could be. Everything. She moistened her lips. "Take off your shirt," she said, her voice oddly husky. She wanted to feel him, not just his clothing. And she wanted to look at him, feast her eyes on him.

He stared at her a moment, then the

gleam returned to his eyes as he smiled a slow smile. "Whatever my lady desires."

He rose and shrugged off his coat, then hung it on the back of the chair. Slowly he unbuttoned his waistcoat, one cloth-covered button at a time. Her mouth dried as she watched. They were just buttons and she'd already seen him in his shirtsleeves — and less — but there was something hypnotic about the slow way he was disrobing, and the way his eyes fastened on her so intensely the whole time.

Finally the last button was undone and he let the waistcoat slide down his arms. Without taking his eyes off her, he tossed it carelessly toward the chair with the coat. It hit the chair, then slithered to the floor. Neither of them moved.

He stood a moment in crumpled shirt, breeches and boots. He hadn't bothered with a neck cloth.

She was breathless, waiting for him to take off his shirt. She'd already seen much of his body when they'd been drenched the day before, but somehow, this was more . . . intimate. He was disrobing for her. At her request.

He sat on the bed, then bent and pulled off his boots, then peeled off his woolen stockings and tossed them on top of the boots. "Those boots are ruined now," he commented. "Pity, they were a favorite pair."

How could he make light talk at a moment like this? She made some sort of response. It came out as a kind of husky gurgle. She couldn't drag her eyes off him.

A lazy smile danced in his eyes as he rose to his feet again and faced her. "It was the shirt you wanted off, wasn't it?"

She nodded, but her gaze dropped to the fall of his breeches. There was a distinct bulge under it. She moistened her mouth. She wasn't ready for that yet — she wanted to make the moment last.

Slowly he unbuttoned his breeches, then tugged the shirttails free. In one movement he pulled the shirt off over his head and stood there, in nothing but his breeches, which sat low on his hips. There was a faint dusting of hair on his chest. A trail of darker hair ran down from his belly button and disappeared into his breeches.

It was such a strange feeling, she being almost fully clothed and he almost naked. It gave her a sense of . . . power.

He was one beautiful man. Perfectly proportioned, his skin gleaming like marble, but he was more beautiful than any statue she had seen; he had not an ounce of fat, was all hard-muscled masculine elegance.

He saw her eating him up with her eyes and gave a faint smile. "It's chilly; I'll just build up the fire," he said and turned away to put more wood on the fire. It gave her time to catch her breath.

And to ogle him some more. She admired the breadth of his shoulders, the hard ropy arms, the line of his spine as he bent over the fire, and the very fine, firm male backside revealed by the tight-stretched buckskin breeches. And the way the firelight danced over his skin, gilding him.

He stoked the fire to a blaze, then returned to the side of the bed. In one swift movement he dropped his breeches and stepped out of them. Now all he wore was a pair of fine cotton drawers. Through which she could see he was ready for her. More than ready.

As she was ready for him. He joined her on the bed, and she braced herself for him to pull up her skirt and make a swift entry.

Instead he pulled her hard against him and started kissing her again. Long, hot, drugging, glorious kisses. She returned them eagerly. She could never get enough of being kissed.

She rubbed her fingertips lightly over the smooth, hard curves of his shoulders, smoothing her palms over his chest, learning his texture, his taste, loving the feel of his firm flesh, the powerful muscles. His body was hard, cool skinned yet hot beneath, and she loved the feel of it, the feel of him.

His hands sought her breasts again, and as he teased, she ached and squirmed against him, wanting more. He rolled over a little, taking her with him. His knee edged between her thighs against the part of her that throbbed. She hugged her legs tightly around him, pressing his knee against her core and making tiny involuntary rocking movements against him. She was hungry, aching, needy — for what, she wasn't sure. All she felt was that this was right . . . so right.

He kissed and nibbled his way down her neck, and she felt a draft as he peeled the top of her dress down, freeing her breasts to the cool hair.

"Beautiful," he murmured and caressed them with big warm hands. She arched under his ministrations. She felt the faint brush of his unshaven jaw against the tender skin, scraping lightly over the aching tips in a delicious abrasion. She shivered in helpless bliss as he teased her tender nipples first with his tongue and then very lightly with his teeth, nipping gently, sucking and biting. Her thighs tightened, hugging him to her, her fingers buried in his thick hair, caressing him, clutching him almost frantically as the tension built within her.

His mouth closed around one aching peak. He sucked and she bucked, gasping as a jolt of fiery, sweet-hot lightning arced through her, leaving her breathless and wondering. Before she could gather her wits he'd transferred his attentions to the other breast. Vaguely she felt him pulling up her skirts. She was grateful for the cold air on her thighs; she was hot, so hot.

At the first touch of his hands, her thighs trembled with need, falling apart, as he stroked and caressed, moving ever closer to the part of her that ached most. He cupped her, pressing with the heel of his hand, and she pushed against it in jerky rhythmic movements, shamelessly begging for more.

He moved, and suddenly her breasts were cool and damp, still aching and tender from his ministrations. She groped for him, wanting him to keep going, and then her eyes flew open with a small scream of surprise as his thumbs parted her and his hot, eager, wicked mouth closed over her aching center.

She bucked and shuddered around him, thrashing as wave after wave of sensation

crashed through her, as if she were possessed. She clutched at him with frantic
fingers, wanting him to stop, wanting him
never to stop, wanting . . .

The pressure inside her built and built.
Her world narrowed . . . and blurred.

She heard, as if from a distance, someone
scream . . . as her world splintered and shattered and was no more. . . .

Chapter Twenty-Two

"Our pleasures in this world
are always to be paid for."
— JANE AUSTEN, *NORTHANGER ABBEY*

"*La petite mort,* the French call it," Freddy murmured as her eyes fluttered open. "The little death."

She blinked at him in adorable confusion. "What . . . ?"

Her first orgasm. He tried not to feel smug at the thought, but it was hard not to. She'd come apart so beautifully in his embrace. More than smug, he felt . . . proud, tender, possessive.

Possessive? He took that thought out and examined it cautiously. When had he ever felt possessive of a woman? He tucked it away to consider later. First things first. He still had a raging cock-stand to deal with.

It had taken all his considerable self-control to keep himself in check. But when he entered her for the first time, he wanted her to know it, to be aware, to watch him with those big beautiful brown eyes as he took her.

And he wanted her naked. Skin to skin.

"Shall we get rid of this?" he murmured and began to remove her dress. She lay bonelessly, looking sated and a little like the cat who'd eaten the cream, making no particular attempt to help him as he pulled and tugged, stripping her of first her dress, then her corset and stockings, and then, last of all, her chemise.

She was slender, creamy and completely enticing, all silken curves and velvet shadows. "It's a crime to cover such loveliness with clothes," he murmured and bent to kiss her beautiful mouth, now reddened and a little swollen. It curved under his, smiling as he tasted her, her tongue curling around his in sensual play, her fingers sliding into his hair as she pulled him closer.

His fingers slid between her thighs and her eyes widened as he caressed and aroused her anew. He could feel the deep ripples starting within her again. He pressed his face between her breasts and inhaled deeply, taking in the scent of her, essence of relaxed, aroused female.

Almost relaxed. She pushed his seeking

hand away. "Haven't you forgotten some-thing?" she said in a throaty murmur. She reached out a languid hand and tugged at his drawers. "Off."

Impatiently he kicked them off, aware of the way she watched him, the gleam of female approval. He was hard and aching, trembling with the effort to retain control.

"Now," he said, reaching between her thighs again. She was moist and slick and more than ready for him. He moved over her and positioned himself at her entrance.

She closed her eyes and braced herself. What the devil?

With an effort he held himself back.

"Look at me," he growled.

Her eyes opened. The sleepy, aroused look had gone. She looked . . . determined. Somehow gritted.

"Trust me," he murmured. He entered her slowly and felt her body ripple as she ac-commodated him. The gritted look faded from her eyes and they darkened. He stroked her where they were joined, and she gasped and jerked and started to move against him in a series of demanding little shoves.

That was it. All intentions of making this slow vanished as his control shattered, and he started to move then, thrusting into her, feeling her rise to meet him, again and again, their bodies moving as one in a frenzied rhythmic dance as old as time.

She moaned beneath him, thrashing against him, locking her legs around him, pulling him tighter, harder, embracing him, as he pumped and pumped and the tension rose and rose.

He heard himself shout, and at the same time she gave a thin high scream, as together, they shattered into oblivion.

And slept.

Bright morning sunshine streamed into the cottage. Damaris woke to find herself tucked firmly against a naked sleeping Freddy. She lay there a few moments, warm and sleepy and utterly contented, and watched him softly breathing. In sleep he seemed younger, softer, more vulnerable. The previous night he'd felt like a god. When she'd first met him he'd seemed wholly frivolous. So many masks. Not that it mattered. She loved the man behind them all.

She looked at his beautiful mouth and thought of what it had done and how it had made her feel. Even as she recalled it, tiny shivers passed through her, a faint echo of what had been.

Three times he'd taken her the night

before. Each time different. She hadn't known coupling could be like that, so . . . she didn't know what. Extraordinary. Earthy. Sublime.

Languorous and sated, with a bubble of happiness lodged in her chest, she lay curled against him, her cheek resting on his chest, his arms around her, savoring the relaxed feel of his body against hers, feeling warm and safe and right, as she reflected on what had passed between them.

It bore no relation to anything she'd felt with the captain. Thank God.

Did other women feel like this, when they lay with their husbands?

Had Mama felt like this when she lay with Papa? Had she screamed and thrashed and shuddered? Had she shattered into oblivion, experiencing the little death? And later woken in languorous, sleepy bliss?

Had she been woken in the night and taken so slowly, so tenderly that feelings welled up in her till she could contain them no more? And tears spilled down, and were kissed quietly away? Had Papa ever held Mama the way Freddy held her close, possessive and protective, even in sleep?

Damaris couldn't imagine it. She had no recollection of Mama even sleeping in the same room as Papa. She must have lain with him at least once; otherwise Damaris would never have been born. But she'd never seen them kiss or even touch.

She lay sleepily pondering the past, luxuriating in the feel of Freddy's sleeping embrace, the weight of his arms around her, the scent of his skin, the steady sound of his breathing.

Mama *must* have felt something similar, she was suddenly sure of it. *This* was what Mama had missed when she'd lain in bed silently weeping all those nights; *this* was what she'd meant when she'd told Damaris, *Sometimes a woman just needs to be held.*

So what had gone wrong?

It was so difficult. All she had were a child's memories, but now she examined them with a woman's perspective. A woman who now understood what could pass between a man and a woman.

Her bladder made its needs known, so reluctantly and carefully she untangled herself from Freddy's embrace and slipped quietly out of the bed, trying not to disturb him.

The wintry chill hit her warm body and she shivered as she threw on her chemise, dress and stockings and grabbed the old woman's shawl for extra warmth. She looked down at her sleeping lover — lover; she savored the word — and smoothed his hair gently back from his face. Then she slipped into the wooden clogs at the back door and braced herself to go out into the cold air to visit the privy.

Afterward, she stopped briefly to look out at the floodwaters. They were definitely retreating. She hurried back inside, shivering.

She wasn't sure how she felt about leaving — there had been something magical about their time in this little cottage, a few days out of their normal world, away from the everyday pressures and expectations. She was reluctant to leave and half dreaded facing the world again.

She hoped there wouldn't be any gossip about them, though since she had told him her story, and they had lain together, she felt much more sanguine about his insistence they marry. She would make him a good wife, she was determined on it. She loved him with all her heart.

She'd tried not to fall in love with him, but she'd known almost from the beginning it was a battle she would lose. She'd stop fighting it now.

She loved him.

He might not love her, but they were

friends at least, and the bed-loving had been good. More than good. She still felt the effects.

Three times he'd taken her yesterday. Perhaps they could do it again this morning. With that thought in mind she hurried back to the cottage.

She entered as quietly as she could. Peeling off her hastily thrown-on clothing, she tiptoed to the bed. And froze.

He'd turned over in her absence and the upper part of his bare back was visible.

Horribly visible.

There were scratches on his back and shoulders, fresh scratches.

She glanced down at her hands, at her fingernails, buffed and innocent looking. Shame washed over her. She had scratched him *like an animal.*

Her arms wrapped tightly around herself, she stood by the bed, naked and shivering, staring at his mutilated back, and remembered how she'd screamed in ecstasy. And thrashed her legs and head. And wrapped her legs around his body, trapping him, holding him, squeezing him so tightly.

Horribly unladylike. Completely out of control. Like a vixen.

What would Freddy think when he realized she'd clawed and bitten him like a wild creature?

Shivering with cold and dread, she pulled her clothes back on, lacing her stays tightly, as if she could somehow lace in her rampant desires, cover them up, hide them from the world.

She understood now what had gone wrong between Mama and Papa. Papa had made no secret of the fact that Mama's lustful nature disgusted him.

And Damaris had inherited Mama's lustful nature.

Papa had suspected it. The captain had too, which was why he'd told her, *You were born for it,* as they carried her off to the brothel.

And soon, Freddy Monkton-Coombes would know it. He had the scratches to prove it.

She wanted to run, to flee from the look in his eyes when he woke, but there was no place to go, nowhere to hide.

She busied herself by building up the fire, which had fallen to embers while they'd slept. She looked in the pantry for the last of the vegetables. More soup, heavy on the barley, and maybe some pancakes or fritters, if the hens had laid. It was a good thing they'd be leaving soon, and not just because they were running out of food.

She wanted to get away as fast as she could.

Behind her she could hear him stirring. She wished she could just vanish.

"You're up?" he said sleepily. "Cooking? And I see you've stoked the fire. What an industrious little thing you are."

Slowly she turned around, bracing herself against the look she feared to see.

He sat up, bare chested, rumpled his hair and gave her a sleepy smile. "I don't suppose you want to come back to bed, do you?"

And, oh, God, there was a bite mark just below his shoulder.

She felt sick, just looking at it. Further proof she'd behaved like an animal. She dragged her gaze off the livid mark and turned away. She couldn't bear to meet his eyes.

"I need to make this soup, or else we'll be going hungry," she said, trying to sound brisk and matter-of-fact, but it came out a little shaky. She turned back to the bench and started chopping a shriveled-looking carrot.

"I'm hungry right now," he said in a plaintive voice. She forced herself to turn and found him smiling at her in a familiar, wicked way. He flipped back the bedclothes, patted the bed and gave her a suggestive look.

"Don't," she said in a choked voice.

His brow furrowed. "Damaris? What's the matter?"

She stared at him, at the mark she'd made on his shoulder, and tried to think what to say.

In a flash he was out of bed and in three steps he'd crossed the room, stark naked and unashamed. He reached for her. She tried to step back but there was no room. The cold line of the bench pressed against her back and she was reminded of how this had all started, when he'd kissed her.

"What is it, Damaris? What's the matter?"

She shook her head, unable to look at him, fighting tears.

But he wouldn't let her avoid him. "What's upsetting you? Tell me." He cupped her face in his big, warm hands — another parody of that kiss — and gently forced her to meet his gaze. His eyes were dark and troubled.

She tried to look away and saw a small, dark semicircular mark on his shoulder, half bruise, half bite, and knew it to be her mark. She *had* bitten him. Shame washed through her.

She tried to break away, but he held her fast. He glanced down at himself and

472

frowned. "Is it this that's worrying you?" He touched the bite mark.

She didn't answer.

His grip on her tightened. "Tell me what's upsetting you. Was it too much? Did I shock you? Upset you?" He waited, and when she didn't reply, he said, "You climaxed several times, so it mustn't have been too bad, surely?"

She couldn't bring herself to speak.

"Damaris? Sweetheart?" His voice was deep and he sounded oddly uncertain, which cut her to the quick.

"I scratched you," she whispered. "And I bit you too."

"I know." He sounded almost . . . proud?

Her head lifted and she stared at him. "You don't understand. I behaved like an animal."

He grinned. "We both did. Splendid, wasn't it?"

She stared at him in silence for a long moment, then burst into tears.

"I — I'm sorry," she mumbled, scrubbing at the tears with her fists. "I don't u-usually — I never c-c-cry over . . . over —" Her broken speech ended on a hiccup.

"Hush," he murmured and, pushing her hands away, gently mopped up her tears with a large white handkerchief. Where he'd got it from she had no idea; he wasn't wearing a stitch. She was, she abruptly realized, sitting fully dressed, on the lap of a naked man.

She ought to get off him. But if she did, he would be even more naked. And she knew who'd be more embarrassed in that situation, and it wouldn't be Freddy Monkton-Coombes.

She stayed where she was, letting him hold her like a child — no, not at all like a child. Her emotions were in a turmoil, her position was quite scandalous, but she felt oddly comforted.

"Now, then, what's all this about?" he said after a while, his voice deep and easy. "Do I understand that you're upset because you scratched me a bit? And gave me a little love bite? Is that the problem?"

A love bite? Was that what he called it? Being *kind.*

"Don't," she said in a choked voice.

"Don't what?"

"Don't be *kind* about it. Your back is all scratched. By me."

There was a short silence. Then he said, "Many women — many ladies — react uninhibitedly when in the extremity of, er, lovemaking."

She said nothing.

"Speaking as the man involved, I found it delightful."

"Delightful?" She turned her head to stare at him. "But I scratched and bit you. I screamed, like . . . like one of those vixens we heard that night."

He smiled. "Yes, but you didn't hurt me at all. And when a man and a woman lie together, it's perfectly natural for the animal part of our nature to take over."

She shook her head. "It's never . . . never happened to me before."

"No, but then again, you've never had a man make love to you before."

"What?" She gave him a puzzled look. "But I told you —"

"What happened to you on the ship was not the same thing at all," he said in a hard voice. "That swine used your body for his own selfish satisfaction." His voice deepened as his arms tightened around her and he murmured softly in her ear, "I made love to you, hoping you would find pleasure in the act. You did, didn't you, Damaris? Find pleasure? Just a little?"

She felt a blush warming her face and wriggled a little, turning her face away, not wanting to let him see how much she'd enjoyed it.

"Because if you keep squirming on my lap like that, I will be forced to make another attempt."

She froze, and he laughed softly. "My sweet innocent, has your puritanical missionary father taught you to be ashamed of your sexual nature? Is that it?"

She gave a small, awkward shrug.

His arm tightened around her. "Thought so. But he couldn't be more wrong. The pleasure a man and woman find when they lie together is part of God's plan."

God's plan? She'd never heard anything so outrageous in her life. Her father's God disapproved of pleasure of any sort. It was probably some piece of nonsense Freddy was making up — he had admitted to not being the slightest bit religious — but she had to confess she was curious. Forgetting not to wriggle, she squirmed around to face him. "How do you work that out?"

He groaned and adjusted her position on his lap. "I suppose you believe the story that God created man and woman." She nodded, and he kissed her lightly on the nose. "Excellent, and a very tasty little piece of rib you are. So if you believe that, you must believe everything about you was designed by Him."

Again, though a little more cautiously, she

nodded.

"Then let me demonstrate." He cupped her face in his hands and kissed her. "Pleasure, pain, or nothing?"

She just gave him a look. Of course it was pleasure.

"And when I do this?" He cupped her breasts and stroked her nipples through the fabric of her dress. They rose. "Pleasure, pain, or nothing?"

She gave a shuddery little sigh.

"Pleasure?" he asked and she managed a nod, though his thumbs were still teasing her. "Can you make your nipples rise, according to your will?"

"N-no," she managed. It was a stupid question. They just did. When it was cold or when he did . . . that.

He drew up the skirt of her dress, baring her legs to the cool air, and stroked the delicate skin of her inner thighs. She shivered, but not from the cold.

"Pleasure?"

"Yes," she said on a gasp. Her legs quivered and fell apart as his hand crept higher. He cupped her at her apex and one long finger slipped between her heated folds. "And when I do this?"

She moaned.

"You will notice a certain part of my

anatomy has risen and is hard and demanding your attention," he murmured, rolling them both over on the bed.

She had no idea why he was telling her — it was perfectly obvious to them both. His fingers were busy stroking, circling, rubbing. She was too distracted to answer.

"And here, at your center, you're all moist and slippery and delicious." He demonstrated with his fingers, moving in a slow, rhythmic way that was driving her crazy. Suddenly he stopped. His fingers moved away and she felt a draft against her moist, heated skin. He lightly touched her entrance. "Can you make yourself go wet in this way?"

She moved against his hand in mute appeal.

"Answer the question. Can you choose to make yourself go wet?"

"No." She blinked at him, wondering why he was asking her these stupid questions. "Not like that. It just happens when . . . when you . . . you know."

"Oh, I know. I just wanted to make sure you knew — it's not something you just decide to make happen, is it? It's the result of desire. You need to be pleasured for this moisture to come." His fingers resumed their stroking. "And it comes to make it easier for me to do this." He shifted over her and entered her with one long, slow thrust and she moaned. Her legs, virtually of their own volition, rose and closed around his hips. "That's . . . yes . . ." He groaned and started to move within her. "And . . . so we . . . ahh . . . yesss . . ."

She caught his rhythm and they moved together faster and faster until . . .

The little death. Which was a glorious celebration of life.

Later, when they'd recovered, he slid from her body with a little smile. "See? God's plan for men and women," he said solemnly, in the manner of completing a rather dull lecture.

Still floating on a little cloud of bliss, she frowned and tried to concentrate. "Hmm?"

"Tut, tut, wench, haven't you been paying attention? Must I go over it all again?"

"I wouldn't mind," she murmured and stroked her hand down his stomach.

He picked up her hand and kissed it. "Enough of that, insatiable creature. I'm explaining something to you and it's very important. God's plan."

"Oh. Yes?" she said vaguely.

"Yes. The pleasure men and women receive from lying together. Without the pleasure, it would happen far less frequently, and then where would we be? Would we be so happy about going forth and multiplying, as we're told to do in the Bible?"

She stretched languorously and didn't answer.

He went on. "Stop distracting me and listen. No, we wouldn't. So the pleasure is all part of God's plan and it is your sacred duty to enjoy it to the best of your ability. The future of the human race depends on it."

It was so ridiculous she burst out laughing. "God's plan indeed."

"Are you doubting my word, wench?" He held her down threateningly.

She giggled and managed to say in a prim and virtuous tone, "If that's what you want to believe, sir, who am I to argue?"

"Good, and since I am to be your husband, I insist you believe it too."

In the silence that followed she heard voices. Male voices, coming from outside.

He heard them at the same time. "Damn. I think we're about to be rescued. We'll finish this conversation later."

He seemed more irritated by the inconvenience of being interrupted, but Damaris knew it was the end of their brief idyll.

He saw her expression and misunderstood. "Don't worry, I'll tell them you're my wife."

She pushed herself off the bed and stood up. "Get dressed," she told him. "I'll tidy the cottage."

He stood and stretched as if he had all the time in the world, sublimely, carelessly naked. It was probably disgraceful of her to want to look her fill of him, but she couldn't take her eyes off him; he was so magnificently made.

The voices were coming closer, but she couldn't prevent herself from watching every move he made as he pulled on his shirt, boots, waistcoat and coat, caressing him with her eyes, the elegant, sculpted body, the carelessly graceful moves, the firm backside, the proud masculinity.

Memorizing him.

He finished dressing. "Do I look sufficiently respectable?" he asked. "Good God, listen to me. My friends would never believe I asked a question like that — and was serious about it. But do I?"

She reached up and tidied his hair.

"Very wifely," he said. "Wish me luck." He pressed a quick kiss on her mouth, then let himself out the front door. She heard a shout as he appeared.

I'll tell them you're my wife.

Doubts still lurked in the corners of her

mind, but she refused to think about them. She had tried to do the right thing, had done her best to refuse his offer. She'd explained about the captain, and proved she wasn't a virgin, and he'd still said they needed to marry. He didn't even mind that she'd behaved like a vixen in bed.

So if he still insisted on marrying her, who was she to argue?

Wasn't it everything she'd ever wanted?

Apart from love.

She swiftly cleared the bench and wiped it and the table down, then glanced at the bed. They'd slept two nights in that bed. She couldn't just make it and leave it for the old woman to find that strangers had slept in it. And rutted in it.

She ripped the bedclothes off and found fresh sheets in the chest. From the slight yellowing of the cotton and their stiff, pristine creases, she thought they might have been a long-ago wedding present, but she didn't care.

She swiftly remade the bed then took the used sheets out to the scullery. She hesitated a moment and buried her face in the sheets, breathing in the faint scent deeply. Essence of Freddy. Essence of lovemaking.

Not rutting; lovemaking.

She shoved the sheets in a bucket of cold water.

Outside they seemed to be in a dispute of some kind, a debate rather than a fight, she was relieved to note. Freddy sounded amused rather than intimidated, so she decided not to worry. Yet.

She hurried around the cottage, flicking things into place until it looked almost as tidy as when they'd found it. She seized the old woman's brushwood broom and started to sweep the floor.

"Stranded, were ye?" The cracked old voice came from behind her.

Damaris whirled around. An old woman stood just inside the entrance, her bright dark eyes roaming the interior of the cottage. What she saw seemed to reassure her, for she gave a little nod and came right in, shutting the door behind her.

"We saw the smoke. The lads came wi' me a'cos I were worried that you be gypsies, see?" She gave a toothless smile to Damaris, her face a mass of weathered wrinkles. Her accent was thick, but Damaris could just follow her.

"Your man be gentry-born, anyone can tell — a few words from him and they gurt lummocks out there be eatin' out of his hand and all but tuggin' their forelocks."

She gave a scornful snort. "But I can see you be a lass what knows how to keep house proper." She nodded at the broom. "Never saw a lady sweep before." She sat down at the table. "And you took good care of my girls."

"Your girls?"

"My hens. I counted 'em. Not a one missing — neither by fox nor gypsy nor hungry gentleman," she added with a twinkle.

Damaris smiled. "If the flood had lasted much longer we might have had to resort to that. I'm afraid we've eaten most of your food. And used up a lot of your wood."

"Never you mind, my lovely, your man paid me a proper handsome sum, he did. Keep me livin' high on the hog for a few good years, it will."

"We slept in your bed." Damaris tried not to blush.

"You be right welcome to it."

"I haven't had time to wash the sheets. They're soaking in the bucket."

The old woman cackled. "Newlyweds, are ye?"

Heat rushed into her cheeks. Damaris turned and put the broom away. The door opened again, and Freddy stepped in. Three burly middle-aged men, locals by the look of them, in rough frieze coats and muddy boots, went to follow him.

The old woman jumped up, saying sharply, "Stay out o' here wi' thy gurt, mucky boots, Jem Eales. You too, Billy Payne and Frank Eales." The men stepped back sheepishly. Freddy glanced at his own equally muddy boots, but there was no mention made of him, so he stayed where he was. Dancing blue eyes met Damaris's, silently inviting her to share the humor of it.

"All a'right inside, then, Granny Meg?" the oldest man called in.

" 'Course 'tis, ye young fool; don't insult the lady and gentleman." She shook her head and said to Damaris, "Pack of old wimmen, they be. Panicking about a little bit of smoke from a chimney." There was a gasp of indignation from the other side of the threshold, but before recriminations could start, Freddy said smoothly, "We'll be going now. Thank you for the use of your cottage, Mrs. . . . Er. Gentlemen, if I could prevail on you to assist my wife and me with the curricle and horses, I'd be most grateful." He reached into his pocket and there was a clink or two as money changed hands and the men abruptly departed.

My wife and me. She swallowed.

"Ready to leave, my dear?" Freddy asked

Damaris.

She wasn't, but she nodded and slipped on her coat. She thanked Granny Meg for her inadvertent hospitality, bid her good-bye and took a last long look around the little cottage where so much had happened.

Ten minutes later they were back in the curricle, which was damp but otherwise no worse for wear, and were heading along the road. The horses were fresh, champing impatiently at their bits, but Freddy reined them in firmly, frowning in concentration as they made slow and careful progress. Mud and refuse covered the road, making it slippery and dangerous.

There was no conversation, for which Damaris was grateful. She had too much to think about. In an hour or so they'd reach Davenham Hall, and somewhere close by was the cottage she'd been promised in exchange for a false betrothal. She supposed she wouldn't get it now.

They'd be returning to London soon and she'd be back with her sisters and Lady Beatrice. She'd fled them before, unable to bear the lies she was telling them. Now the betrothal was real and, somehow, she was going to have to explain it all to them and hope they wouldn't be hurt by her decep-tion.

How had something that had started off so simple end up so complicated? But it would all work out. It had to.

CHAPTER TWENTY-THREE

"What is right to be done
cannot be done too soon."
— JANE AUSTEN, *EMMA*

Just after noon they turned in at the big gates that marked the beginning of the oak-lined avenue that led to Davenham Hall.

"It feels a bit strange coming here when Abby and Max are still away on their honeymoon," Damaris said.

They'd made a short stop at a large posting inn on the way, where Freddy had ordered a bath for her and a bath and shave for himself. She felt much better for it, and Freddy, bathed, freshly shaved and with his coat, buckskins and boots cleaned by the inn's valet, looked his usual elegant self again.

It was almost as if they'd come straight from his parents' home. Almost.

"Are you sure it will be all right?"

"Of course," Freddy said. "Abby's your sister, isn't she? I mean, as far as the world is concerned. And I'm Max's oldest friend."

Their arrival must have been observed, because before the curricle came to a complete stop, a groom came running out to meet them, going straight to the horses' heads and taking the halter. Freddy jumped down and by the time he'd helped Damaris to alight, the front door had opened and a man in a plain dark suit, a butler, she supposed, waited at the head of the steps to welcome them.

They had just started up the stairs leading up to the door when Abby appeared in the doorway. "Damaris!" she cried. "I saw you arriving from the window. Oh, Damaris, I'm so happy to see you." She ran down the steps to seize Damaris in an exuberant hug.

Damaris hugged her back, feeling suddenly a little teary. It was so good to see Abby again. She was more to her than a sister.

"And . . . Mr. Monkton-Coombes?" Abby added with faint surprise.

Of course, Damaris thought. Abby would have no idea of the betrothal, fake or otherwise. She'd only known Freddy as Max's friend.

Abby glanced down the driveway, clearly

expecting another carriage at least. She gave Damaris a questioning private glance. "Are the others following? And why are you in a curricle, of all things?"

"I'll explain later," Damaris said in a low voice. "But why are you here? I thought you'd still be away on your bride trip. Is everything all right?"

"Everything's perfect." Abby hugged Damaris again. "Oh, Damaris, marriage is wonderful! We decided — well, *I* decided — to ask everyone to come here for Christmas, and I want it all to be perfect — our first ever Christmas together — and so we came back early to get everything ready."

She turned and held out her hand to Freddy. "Mr. Monkton-Coombes, please forgive my rudeness in greeting you so tardily. I was so happy to see my sister again I forgot my manners. What a delightful surprise. Max will be pleased to have some masculine company for a change."

"Miss — Lady Davenham." Freddy bowed over her hand. "You look lovely. I can see that marriage suits you."

She beamed at him. "Thank you, it does indeed. Now, come in, come in, I don't know why I'm letting you stand around in the wind like this. I'm just so surprised and happy to see you." Linking arms with Damaris, she led her up the steps. "You must be tired. Have you come far? And why in a curricle? Don't you have any luggage? Oh, listen to me, running on like a perfect fool, tossing questions at you and giving you no time to respond." She laughed. "I promise you I will be sensible shortly."

In the hallway she turned to the butler. "Proule, this is Mr. Monkton-Coombes, Lord Davenham's oldest friend, and my sister, Miss Chance." To the others she said, "Proule was sent to us by Featherby, and he's proving an absolute treasure."

"Thank you, m'lady." Proule gave a dignified yet fluid bow. "Welcome to Davenham Hall, Miss Chance, Mr. Monkton-Coombes." His voice, though not loud, seemed to carry to all corners of the house.

Damaris thanked him, but it was Abby she was finding most impressive. She seemed to have grown in confidence and ease, every inch the lady of this grand house. Despite her start in life as an orphan and a governess, she seemed quite comfortable with her new title and having an army of servants at her fingertips. And yet she was still the warmhearted Abby Damaris knew and loved.

It was quite an achievement, Damaris thought. She glanced around the grand entry hall and tried to imagine herself doing the same at Breckenridge House. She couldn't see it.

Abby turned to Proule. "Please conduct Mr. Monkton-Coombes to the blue guest bedroom and allow him to wash and refresh himself. I will take my sister upstairs to do the same in the yellow bedchamber. And then inform his lordship we have guests, but don't say who they are. I'd like to surprise him. We'll all take tea and cakes in the drawing room in — shall we say fifteen minutes?"

"Very good, m'lady."

"Where is Max?" Freddy asked.

"In the library, wading through a mountain of correspondence that came in our absence," Abby told him. "We only arrived last night, so he's only just started on it. We, er, slept in." A faint blush rose to her cheeks. Damaris observed it interestedly.

Abby was blooming, her eyes bright, her skin glowing with health and happiness. Clearly this marriage suited her in more ways than one.

"Why don't I surprise him myself?" Freddy said. "There's something I need to talk to him about."

Damaris gave him a sharp look. What would he need to talk to Max about? Something about her? About their situation?

But Freddy gave her the blandest of smiles, saying, "You go with your sister, my dear. I'm sure you ladies have a lot to catch up on."

Abby laughed. "Very well, go ahead and surprise Max. Proule, my sister and I will take our tea and cakes upstairs in the sitting room adjoining the yellow bedchamber. The gentlemen, I'm sure, will prefer wine or brandy, or coffee, and perhaps something a little more substantial and masculine than cakes. And we shall all meet at dinner."

"Lady Davenham," Freddy said with the kind of charming, playful bow he was famed for, "so new to marriage, yet already the queen of hostesses."

Abby laughed. Damaris observed him thoughtfully. He was playing the frivolous fop again. Why? But Abby was tugging her toward the stairs, eager to catch up on all the news, and Damaris forgot to wonder. It was so lovely to see Abby again.

Freddy pushed open the library door. Max was seated at a large oak desk, frowning over a mound of papers, making notes. "Yes, what is it?" he said, not looking up.

"Strange thing for a man to be doing on his honeymoon," Freddy said.

"Freddy!" Max set down the pen and rose, smiling. "Where the devil did you spring from?" He moved toward Freddy, holding out his hand in greeting, then pulled up short. "Is there a problem? Has something happened to my aunt? Or the girls?"

"No, no, nothing like that. They're all well, as far as I know," Freddy assured him. "Mind you, haven't seen them for a couple of weeks — well, Damaris is with me, but I'm sure Lady Beatrice and Jane and Daisy are well. Featherby keeps a pretty good eye on them."

"But I specifically asked you to —" Max broke off. "Did you say *Damaris* is with you? You brought her here from London?" He frowned. "With her maid, I assume."

"We came from Breckenridge, actually." Freddy decided not to mention the lack of maid. Marriage seemed to have brought out an inconvenient moralistic streak in Max. He supposed being responsible for a pack of unmarried girls would do that to a man. It might even happen to him. But not yet.

"Breckenridge? Your parents' place?"

Freddy nodded. "Yes. Introduced her to them."

"You introduced Damaris to your parents? Why? I thought you never went there if you could help it. I thought you were avoiding your mother. Because of the muffins."

Freddy said airily, "As a matter of fact, Damaris and I are betrothed."

Max's jaw dropped. "*Betrothed?* Good God. I don't believe it." He stared at Freddy for a moment then laughed. "You're serious. Oh, this is too good. The eternal rake, captured at last." He yanked on the bellpull. "We must drink a toast to you both!"

"If you must know, I did the capturing," Freddy said testily. "Very beautiful girl, Damaris, but stubborn. Took me all my powers of address to convince her to accept me."

Max laughed again. "Good for her. You say she came here with you? Where is she, then?"

"Upstairs talking with Abby. Sisters, you know. Girlish confidences and all that."

"You rang, m'lord?" The butler arrived with a tray containing a coffeepot and two cups, a plate of ham sandwiches, a couple of slices of cold pie and half a roast chicken. To Max he said, "M'lady thought you might like some refreshments, m'lord."

"Excellent," Max said. "The very thing. Only I think for this occasion we need" — he glanced at Freddy — "brandy?"

Freddy nodded.

"Brandy, if you please, Proule."

"At once, m'lord." The butler bowed and departed.

Freddy inspected the tray of food and selected a chicken leg. Munching on it, he wandered over to the desk and glanced down at the correspondence. "Business?"

"Yes. Blasted stuff mounted up while I was away." Max cut himself a slice of pie. "Don't know why Bartlett sent it here, though, when Flynn's in London, right under his nose."

"Yes, but Flynn's not really the paperwork type, is he?"

"I suppose not."

"Is that a letter to Bartlett?" Freddy pointed with the stripped chicken bone, then tossed it in the fire.

"Yes. I was just finishing it off. I want to catch the afternoon post."

"Can you pop in a message from me?" Freddy picked up a sandwich, ate it in two gulps and took another one. He was surprisingly hungry.

"About your betrothal? Why not? Bartlett will be thrilled."

"Not about my betrothal. It's about business. Sort of."

Max gave him a quizzical look.

"Tell him to let me know the minute he

gets any word of the *Liverpool Lass.*"

"That's one of our ships. Why do you want to know?"

"It doesn't matter. Just tell him to tell me at once. As a matter of utmost urgency."

"Utmost urgency?" Max frowned. "The *Liverpool Lass* trades mostly in China silk and spices. Is that what you're after? Because we might have something in the ware—"

"I don't care about the cargo," Freddy said in a cold voice. "It's the captain I care about."

"The captain? Why? What do you want with him?"

"I'm going to kill him."

There was a short silence, then somebody coughed. They looked up to see the butler in the doorway holding a brandy decanter and two glasses. He looked a little shaken.

"Ah, the very thing," Max said, giving Freddy a meaning look. "Thank you, Proule, that will be all." Max took the decanter and poured a generous slosh into each glass. He waited until the man had left, then handed Freddy a glass.

They both drank, draining their glasses in one hit.

"You'd better explain," Max said, refilling the glasses. "Why do you want to kill the captain of the *Liverpool Lass*?"

"Long story. Private matter," Freddy told him. He had no intention of sharing Damaris's story with anyone, not even his oldest friend. She hadn't even told her sisters. "Just tell Bartlett to let me know the moment the *Liverpool Lass* docks. Sooner if he hears she's on her way."

Max gave him a thoughtful look, then went to the pile of correspondence. He sifted through it then pulled out a paper, which he checked, then he nodded. "I thought so. According to this, the *Liverpool Lass* docked in London" — he checked the date on the letter — "three days ago."

"Three days ago?" Freddy swore and set down his glass with a snap. "I have to leave. At once. Make my apologies to Abby. Tell Damaris I was called away on urgent business — and for God's sake don't tell her what I told you. She has no idea and I don't want her upset. Look after her for me. I'll be back in a week or two. Can I borrow one of your horses?" Without waiting for an answer he headed for the door.

Max was after him in a flash. He grabbed him by the arm. "Just hold on a moment. You can't just rush off like that, talking about killing a man with no explanation. What the devil's going on?"

Freddy wrenched his arm out of Max's grasp. "No time to explain, even if I were free to. I have to leave now! Just tell Damaris I had to leave on urgent business."

"Tell her yourself," Max said. "I'm coming with you." He yanked on the bellpull.

"This is nothing to do with you!" Freddy was practically dancing with impatience. He needed to leave *now*! Ships only stayed in dock a few days, depending on their cargo and the sailing conditions. The *Liverpool Lass* could sail at any moment and that bastard would get away, free and clear, out of reach for another six months or more, damn him.

"If you're planning to kill one of my captains, it is!" The door opened. "Mr. Monkton-Coombes and I have to go to London on urgent business," he told the butler. "Tell my valet to pack a bag and order my curricle and team from the stables. We leave in half an hour."

"We leave at once," Freddy interrupted. "That swine could sail at any moment. And not the curricle — horses. We'll ride across country. It's quicker."

"Very well, we leave in fifteen minutes. Ten, then," he said, seeing Freddy about to argue. "And Proule," he called as the butler hurried away, "where are the ladies?"

"Upstairs in the yellow sitting room, m'lord."

"We don't have time —" Freddy began.

"If you think I'm leaving without telling my wife the reason — *a* reason, at least" — Max amended — "for our unseemly departure, and without bidding her a proper good-bye, you're very much mistaken. And you damned well owe Damaris an explanation too. Or were you hoping to avoid that? Never took you for a coward, Freddy."

Freddy gritted his teeth. It wasn't so much that he was a coward, but that Damaris was too damned perceptive. Not to mention argumentative. And stubborn. She'd try to wheedle the truth out of him and damned if he was going to give her the opportunity.

"All right, I'll talk to her, but don't for God's sake tell her what we're doing or why we're going. Just say it's urgent business. Urgent *company* business."

Max gave him a hard look. "All right, but I'm going to want an explanation."

Freddy nodded. "All right. But you must swear never to reveal it to a soul."

"A fresh pot of tea, please, Proule," Abby said as she and Damaris returned to the cozy little upstairs sitting room. "This is stone cold." Proule took the tea tray out.

Abby plumped down into an overstuffed armchair in front of the fire. "My, what a whirlwind departure. What do you suppose this urgent business can be? Max didn't seem the slightest bit discomposed when he glanced through the pile of letters last night. It must have been a message that just came in." She passed Damaris a plate of pretty little iced cakes, filled with cream. "Cake?"

Damaris took one absently and placed it on her plate. Something was up. And she felt certain from the way Freddy had alternatively not met her gaze and later pointedly looked at her, as he assured her it might be urgent but it wasn't really all that important, that something was wrong. Urgent but not important? What kind of a ridiculous statement was that?

And yet when she'd asked him he'd been all vague and said it was something to do with Max's business. And that she mustn't worry. He'd be back in a week or two. She must enjoy her time with Abby. They should go and look at her new cottage, see that all was progressing well. Not that she'd be living there now, of course. But it was still hers to do with what she wanted.

And then he'd kissed her — on the hand! — and rushed off.

And had ridden away on horseback.

Horseback! All the way to London.

"I don't know what's going on," she told Abby, "but Freddy was certainly lying through his teeth."

"Max was too," Abby said. "I wasn't going to say anything, but if you noticed it too . . ."

When Proule returned with a fresh pot of tea, Abby asked him, "Did Lord Davenham receive an urgent letter in the last hour or so?"

"No, m'lady."

"Then what caused him to rush off like that?"

Proule assumed a blank expression. "I'm sure I wouldn't know, m'lady."

Abby glanced at Damaris, her brows lifted in a silent question. Damaris nodded. The butler knew more than he was telling.

"I'm sure you would, Proule," Abby said crisply. "So tell us what you know."

The butler shifted uncomfortably and glanced at Damaris. "I apprehend it was Mr. Monkton-Coombes who had the urgent need to go to London, m'lady."

Damaris frowned. "But why? Who would write to him here? I'd swear he wasn't thinking of rushing off to London when we arrived."

She looked at Abby, who shrugged. They

both looked at Proule, who did his best to look ignorant instead of troubled and slightly guilty.

"What else do you know, Proule?" Abby said.

He sighed. "Well, m'lady, I did happen to overhear, just by accident, you understand — I was bringing in the brandy at the time —"

"Yes, of course. Just tell us, please."

"I did happen to hear his lordship say . . ." He swallowed. "Something about Mr. Monkton-Coombes planning to kill someone."

"Who?"

"One of his lordship's sea-captains."

Damaris froze. "Is the *Liverpool Lass* in port?"

Proule nodded. "That was the name I heard, miss. It was on the shipping reports that his lordship had been reading."

"Oh, my God, so that's it!" Damaris jumped up, knocking the little table beside her chair and overturning the cup of tea. It splashed her dress and dripped down on the carpet, unheeded. She started pacing anxiously. "I have to stop him. He'll be killed. The fool, the mad fool!"

"I don't understand," Abby said. "Who is this captain? And why would Freddy want to kill him?"

"He'll be killed," Damaris muttered, wringing her hands frenziedly. "The captain is bigger, stronger and more cunning. And if he isn't killed, if by some miracle he survives, he'll be hanged for murder! I've got to stop him." She looked at Abby. "I have to go after them! I have to stop this."

Abby stood and caught Damaris's restlessly twisting hands. "I haven't the least idea what any of this is about," she said calmly. "But if you're sure we need to follow them, then of course we will. Proule, order our fastest traveling carriage and tell Higgins — he's the coachman" — this to Abby — "it is of the utmost urgency. Tell my maid to pack only what we will need for the journey."

"We won't have time to stop at any inns," Damaris said. "Only to change horses."

Abby nodded. "The bare necessities. And some food and drink. We leave as soon as possible."

"Sooner," Damaris said. "And Proule," she added as the butler hurried toward the door, "please ask the cook if she has any ginger. I'll want all she has, a whole root if that's possible."

"Ginger?" Abby asked. "Whatever for?"

"Later," Damaris said tersely.

■ ■ ■ ■

The carriage swayed and bounced as they crossed Hounslow Heath. London lay a few hours away. They'd impressed on Higgins the urgency of speed and he'd pushed the horses to go as fast as they could. He'd even sent a lad ahead on horseback to arrange for a change of horses to be ready at each stopping point.

They'd made good time. But would it be enough?

Damaris clung to the leather straps hanging from the roof of the carriage and chewed grimly on slices of fresh ginger. It seemed to help; she hadn't thrown up yet.

Over and over her thoughts churned as she fretted. Freddy was doing this for her, because of what she'd told him, because he was ridiculously gallant.

And because they were betrothed, he now felt responsible for defending her honor.

Her honor! What did her honor matter when his life was at stake?

It was all in the past anyway. What good would killing Captain Sloane do? Not that she believed for one moment Freddy would kill him. Captain Sloane was a powerful man and a cunning fighter; he'd fought pirates and won.

Freddy was elegant and funny and charming and he didn't stand a chance. The fool. The mad fool.

"Don't look so worried." Abby leaned forward and put a hand on Damaris's knee. "It will be all right. Have faith. Even if we don't get there in time, my Max is with your Freddy and he won't let anything terrible happen."

Damaris hoped she was right, but she didn't have the faith in Max's infallibility that Abby had. Max was Abby's hero, not Damaris's.

She'd told the whole story to Abby . . . was it yesterday? They'd driven through the night but she hadn't slept a wink and the whole journey was a blur. Abby had listened with compassion, and she hadn't responded with pity or horror or even the faintest hint of reproach for keeping it a secret for so long. Instead she'd taken Damaris's hands in a comforting hold and said simply, "You're a brave girl, Damaris. And it's all going to work out, don't worry. You've survived so much, it's your turn to be happy now."

Life didn't work like that, Damaris knew, but she felt comforted anyway. She was very grateful Abby had come with her.

"Max is a lucky man," Damaris had told her.

Abby had smiled. "I'm the lucky one. Oh, Damaris, I never knew such happiness could exist."

Damaris had tried to smile, but it must have come out a bit bleak, for Abby had said, "Oh, don't look like that, love. You will find such happiness with your Freddy, I'm certain of it."

Abby caught her eye now and smiled. "That ginger seems to be doing the trick."

"It is."

"I must say, Mr. Monkton-Coombes certainly seems to have changed for the better." Abby was trying to lift her spirits. Again.

For her sake, Damaris tried to look more cheerful. Worrying fruitlessly over a situation that was out of her hands helped nobody. "For the better?"

"Well, when I first met him he was a rake with a known aversion to marriage, and here he is now, betrothed to you. That's a sign of maturity, for a start — and he couldn't have made a better choice."

Damaris couldn't help but smile. "You wouldn't be a wee bit biased, by any chance?"

"Nonsense," Abby said, her eyes dancing.

"I'm becoming fonder of him by the minute. I've always thought him handsome and charming and very entertaining, but what you've told me has revealed depths in Mr. Monkton-Coombes I would never have suspected." She sighed. "And riding *ventre à terre* to defend your honor is *very* romantic, you have to admit."

Damaris didn't have to admit anything of the sort. "It isn't romantic. It's insane."

Neither Freddy nor Abby knew what Freddy would be up against if he tried to fight Captain Sloane. She prayed his ship had already sailed.

She didn't care what happened to Captain Sloane. All she cared about was Freddy.

She should never have told him her story, never have agreed to a sham betrothal in the first place. And even having done so — because she could not regret the cottage, even if she ought to — she should never have let him talk her into making their betrothal real.

She should have stuck to her guns. She shouldn't have explained to him why she was an unsuitable wife for him, and she sure as goodness should not have made love with him, no matter that it was the most wonderful experience of her life. She should have just done the honorable thing and told him no. And no. And no. Until he gave up.

But because she was selfish, because she wanted him, because she *loved* him, and because he offered her everything she'd ever dreamed of — except his heart — she'd gone along with his proposal. Greedily. Selfishly.

And now, never mind his heart, he was going to risk his *life* in some mad, gallant quest to restore her lost honor.

If he died, it would be all her fault.

She stared out of the coach window and sent up a prayer, no less intense or heartfelt for being silent. *Just let him be safe,* she prayed. *Spare his life, don't let him be killed or badly wounded — or hanged — and I will do the right thing. I will give him up; I'll go back to Davenham and live in my little cottage and I promise, oh, I promise, I'll never ask for anything again. Just let him be safe.*

She closed her eyes, and an image of Captain Sloane came to her mind: big, tough and devious. Oh, God. Freddy didn't stand a chance.

She clung to the leather strap, chewed doggedly on her gingerroot and prayed. Again.

CHAPTER TWENTY-FOUR

"Her heart did whisper
that he had done it for her."
— JANE AUSTEN, *PRIDE AND PREJUDICE*

Freddy and Max headed straight to the docks. They were dirty, unshaven, hungry and tired, but Freddy refused to waste a moment. They'd ridden through the night, making God only knew how many changes of horse.

They dismounted and he handed the reins to a sharp-faced little wharf rat and tossed him a coin. While Max told the urchin to take care of the horses and give them a drink and there'd be another tanner for him when they returned, Freddy scanned the docks. They teemed with men, stevedores and laborers, carrying all sorts of exotic goods. And above all the hubbub, dozens of masts, gently swaying. So many ships, dammit.

"Whereabouts?" Freddy asked.

Max shook his head. "Could be any-where."

"We'd best split up, then," Freddy told him. "I'll go this way; you go that."

He started off but Max grabbed his arm. "All right, but when you find the ship come and get me. Don't tackle him alone."

"I want the bastard."

Max grabbed his arm again. "I know, but he's a tough bastard. Don't fight him, Freddy, especially on his home territory. We can have him arrested."

Freddy shook off Max's hold. "Arrested? He's going to suffer for what he's done. I want his *blood.*"

"He won't fight like a gentleman," Max warned. "He'll fight hard and dirty."

"Of course. He's complete scum."

They went their separate ways. Freddy ran from ship to ship, until finally he saw it: the *Liverpool Lass.* Its crew, if he recognized the signs, was in the final throes of preparation for departure on the next tide. He headed for the gangplank.

"I have business with Captain Sloane," he said when a seaman stopped him.

The seaman gave Freddy an assessing glance that took in his muddy boots, stained buckskins and unshaven face, but Freddy's accent and air of assurance must have tipped the balance, for he jerked his chin and stepped back to let Freddy pass. "Cap'n's in his cabin," he said and jerked his chin to indicate the direction.

Freddy found the man in a spacious cabin, bending over some papers spread out on a table. He looked up and scowled. "Who the devil are you?"

"My name doesn't matter," Freddy said, stepping into the cabin and closing the door behind him.

The coach pulled over to the side of the road and stopped. "I don't understand," Damaris said. "We must be almost there. We've just come off the turnpike." She pointed. "There's Hyde Park, which means we're now on Oxford Street, so why have we stopped?"

Abby shook her head.

At that moment Higgins swung down from the driver's seat. "Where to, miss?"

"The docks," Damaris said. "We told you that before."

"Yes, miss, but which docks?"

Damaris and Abby looked at each other. "Which docks?" Damaris repeated. "The ones where the ships go."

Higgins gave a weary smile. He'd driven

through the night and swayed slightly on his feet, clearly exhausted. "There are a dozen different docks in London, miss. It's not like a port, where the ships is all in one spot; it's a river. Different ships use different docks."

Damaris stared, appalled. After all this trouble, this long, desperate chase, and now they were in London and they didn't know which docks?

"The ships that come from China," she said desperately. "Isn't there a place for them?"

Higgins shook his head. "Depends, miss. Could be Wapping; could be down past Tower Bridge; could be the Pool of London or any part of the docklands."

Damaris turned to Abby. "Do you know which docks to go to?"

Abby shook her head again.

"Then what will we do?" Damaris bit her lip, ready to burst into tears. Only she couldn't; she had to find Freddy.

"Maybe Featherby would know," Abby suggested. "He knows just about everything."

"Yes, Featherby, of course." Damaris pounced on the idea. To Higgins she said, "Take us to Lady Beatrice's house on Berkeley Square. Down there." She pointed.

"Yes, miss." Higgins climbed back up to the driver's seat, and the traveling coach moved on. In a few minutes they'd pulled up in front of Lady Beatrice's house. Damaris couldn't wait for the carriage steps to be put down; she jumped out of the coach, hurried up the front steps and pulled hard on the bell, setting the bell inside jangling loudly.

After several long, agonizing minutes, the door opened. "Miss Damaris," Featherby exclaimed in surprise. He looked past her and his face was immediately wreathed in smiles. "Lady Davenham." He greeted Abby with delight. "Welcome home, my lady."

Damaris interrupted the joyful reunion. "Featherby, where are the docks?"

He looked down at her. "Which docks, miss?"

"The ones where Freddy would go to if he wanted to see a ship that had come from China."

"I'm sorry, miss, I have no idea." He turned back to Abby. "We didn't expect you back so soon, my lady —"

Damaris grabbed his sleeve. "What about Mr. Flynn? Is he here? He would know."

Featherby shook his head. "I'm sorry, miss, he went out this morning and won't be back before evening, he said."

"Abby!" a voice cried and Jane came flying down the stairs and caught her sister in a hug that spun them around in a circle. "What are you doing here? Where is Max? How was the honeymoon?"

"Abby!" Daisy came running and joined in the excitement.

Damaris stood frozen, taking none of it in. She'd failed him. To come all this way and then, at the last minute, not to know where the ship would dock.

She'd landed on that very dock, no doubt, but she couldn't remember. She'd been carried ashore, tied hand and foot and wrapped in a blanket. She hadn't been able to see a thing.

"Bartlett!" she exclaimed suddenly. "What about Bartlett, their man of affairs? We'll go to his office; he'll know."

"Go to the office of a man of affairs?" Lady Beatrice's voice floated down the stairs. "You will do nothing of the sort, young lady. It is Not Done."

"But I *must*," Damaris said. "It's a matter of life and death!"

"Is it indeed? Then come up here, gel, and tell me what is going on that is so urgent."

Damaris hesitated, torn, but she didn't know where Bartlett's office was, and without Lady Beatrice's cooperation, she wouldn't get any help in finding it, she knew. She hurried up the stairs and helped Lady Beatrice back into her sitting room. The others followed.

"Now, my dear, sit down beside me." Lady Beatrice patted the seat beside her on the sofa. "Featherby, tea and cakes, if you please."

Damaris curbed her impatience and sat. Featherby snapped his fingers to an unseen menial and stood by the doorway. They had no secrets from Featherby. He and his friend, their footman William, had been friends with the girls long before they'd even met Lady Beatrice.

"Now, my dear, tell me what's got you all in a lather. It's not like my lovely cool and calm Damaris." Lady Beatrice's words and the shrewd look that accompanied them helped Damaris to compose herself. Lady Beatrice valued control in a lady.

So, for that matter, did Damaris. She glanced at the clock on the overmantel, folded her hands in her lap and, having calmed herself somewhat, began. "Freddy has gone to kill a man, and it's all my fault, so I have to stop him." In measured words that got faster by the minute, she told her story, stopping every few seconds as Lady Beatrice interrupted her with questions or demanded clarification.

When she finished, there was a long silence. She glanced at the clock and was shocked by how little the hands had moved. Every second wasted had felt like an age, but only seven minutes had passed since she first sat down.

"So now, if you could give me the directions to Bartlett's office, I will go, and from there, I should be able to find Freddy and stop him."

"You're not going anywhere," Lady Beatrice informed her. "I told you before, it's Not Done."

"What? But —"

"Foolish child, you're not thinking. Freddy is doing this for the sake of your reputation. If you turn up on the docks and demonstrate your involvement in this matter" — she glanced at Damaris's hair — "especially looking like you've been up all night and dragged through a bush backward, you *will* cause a scandal. Which is the very thing he's trying to prevent."

"But —"

Lady Beatrice held up her hand. "William will go. You will stay here."

"But —"

The old lady's finely plucked eyebrows arched. "Do you suggest that William is

517

incapable of stopping a fight? After all the years he spent as a pugilist? That he would be less effective than one small, distraught female? No, of course not. Featherby, send William, with all haste. And send the footmen with him."

Featherby bowed, and William, who must have been listening from the corridor, poked his head around the door. "I'll find him, Miss Damaris, don't you worry. I won't let nothing happen to your Mr. Freddy." He ran off.

Damaris sat staring after him. Her mouth wobbled, then she burst into tears.

Lady Beatrice gathered her into her arms, murmuring, "There, there, my dear, have a good cry. It will do you a power of good." Over Damaris's head she silently indicated to the others that they should leave her and Damaris alone. They filed out obediently.

Lady Beatrice let Damaris cry until she was all cried out. Then she handed her a wisp of lawn edged with lace and told her to dry her eyes and tell her everything.

Damaris did. She told her everything: the false betrothal, the cottage, the visit to Breckenridge House and the dreadful things she'd said to Freddy's parents — and added with a sob and a hiccup that they'd deserved every word.

She told her about the flood, and being marooned, and how Freddy had said that, having compromised her, he would marry her. She told the old lady about how she had had to leave China and how Captain Sloane had tricked her and forced her to — to —"

"I understand, child." Lady Beatrice patted her hand. "It's why you never wanted to marry."

Damaris had nodded and confessed that Freddy had learned Captain Sloane's ship was in port, and that Freddy had gone after him for — for . . . revenge. On her behalf.

"Now hush, and no more tears, if you please," Lady Beatrice said with brisk kindness. "We shall not dwell on things we have no control over and there is no point talking about them. What I am interested in discussing, however, is your apparent conviction that you cannot marry the boy."

"Well, of course I can't," Damaris said, scrubbing at a few disobedient tears. She explained all the reasons why she couldn't marry Freddy Monkton-Coombes, why it would be selfish and greedy of her to do so, how marrying her would be bad for him, all the reasons she'd turned over and over in her mind all the way to London.

No lawyer could have presented a case

better. It was very depressing.

When she'd finished there was a short silence. Then, "Pish-tush! All these shoulds and oughts and what-other-people-might-thinks. I have no patience with 'em. The question is, what do *you* want, my gel?"

Damaris bit her lip and said nothing.

"Do you love him, child?"

Damaris's face crumpled. "More than anything."

"Then for goodness' sake, marry the boy."

"But —"

"Pish-tush! You've told me all that. As if any of that will matter to Freddy once he gets you in his bed — oho! I gather from that blush that he already has. Was it horrid?"

"No, wonderful," Damaris said tragically.

"Thought it would be. Rakes usually do make good lovers. Give me a man who knows his way around a woman's body any day." She glanced at Damaris's face and chuckled. "Don't look at me like that, gel — I may be old, but I'm not dead! Such a pretty color you go when you blush. I was always a beetroot as a girl. I haven't blushed in years, thank God. Not that I've had anything to blush about, more's the pity."

By the end of that speech Damaris was almost laughing.

The old lady gave her an approving look. "That's better. Not such a Miserable Maud now, are you?"

"No, but . . ."

Lady Beatrice heaved a gusty sigh. "Out with it, gel. What's the real issue?"

"He doesn't love me."

"Good God, what does that matter?" She eyed Damaris shrewdly. "But I see to you it does." She sniffed. "Well, I can't speak for the boy, but it seems to me that a man who's reached the age of eight-and-twenty and managed to avoid every lure and marriage trap the eligible misses of the *ton* and their mamas can devise wouldn't offer marriage to a gel unless he was willing. And that's a start. Add to that his rushing off to confront this captain of yours —"

"He's not *my* captain," Damaris flashed.

"You know what I mean." The old lady waved an impatient hand. "But men, being creatures of action, will sometimes go off to slay dragons for their ladies and expect us to understand." She paused to let that sink in.

Damaris gave her a troubled look. It was all so confusing.

"Oh, pish-tush, just marry the boy and have done with it. Love can grow in marriage. If you don't marry him, you'll never find out whether he's got it in him to love you. And if he doesn't, well, a gel could do worse than marry a handsome young man who's rich and kind and good in bed. Besides" — she poked Damaris on the arm with a bony claw — "if *you* don't marry the boy, some ambitious female will snap him up for herself. Someone who *doesn't* love him. And where would he be then, eh?"

Damaris blinked. She hadn't thought of that. She thought about the girls in the park who'd all been pursuing him. They would make him positively dreadful wives.

"Have a little more faith in yourself, my dear. You have beauty, spirit and courage, but most of all you must believe in yourself." Lady Beatrice patted her arm. "Now, go off and have a bath. If your Freddy survives his encounter with the captain — oh, don't look like that; he will, I'm certain of it — but when he comes here, would you rather greet him looking like a drowned rat or like a fresh and beautiful young lady?"

Damaris hesitated and the old lady gave her a push. "Get along with you, gel. You can worry about the boy just as well wet or dry."

There was no answer to that. Damaris went off to have her bath.

The hot, fragrant bathwater had a soothing effect. Damaris soaped herself absently, turning Lady Beatrice's words over in her mind.

If you don't marry the boy, some ambitious female will snap him up for herself. Someone who doesn't love him.

He needed to be loved, that man, that kind, honorable, proud man. And the little boy inside him who'd blamed himself so terribly for his brother's accident and who'd been cut off from his family because of it. That little boy hadn't known love since.

Love was the one thing Damaris had plenty of, the one thing she could offer him. Each time he looked at her, smiled at her, gave her that sleepy-eyed wicked come-to-bed look, she felt like she could burst from all the love that swelled inside her. And the longer she knew him, the more her love for him grew.

Lady Beatrice was right. It didn't matter if Freddy Monkton-Coombes didn't love her. He needed to be loved, and that was what mattered.

Believe in yourself. She would try.

"You've got damned cheek, marching into my cabin on my ship," Captain Sloane growled.

"I have a bone to pick with you," Freddy said.

"Spit it out."

"It's about illegal cargo, something you didn't list in the ship's manifest."

Sloane stiffened, and his gaze went to the door as if to check nobody could hear. "I don't know what you mean." The look on his face suggested otherwise.

"Slavery is illegal in England."

The man's brows shot up. *"Slavery?"* He snorted. "I've never kept a slave in my life. You don't know what you're talking about."

"Bringing girls into England and selling them into brothels is slavery," Freddy said silkily.

Sloane's eyes narrowed. "Those girls knew what they were in for."

Those girls? So Damaris wasn't the first.

"I'm talking about an English girl," Freddy said with ice in each word. "A girl who you found stranded in China."

"She made the same bargain as the others," Sloane said dismissively. "Come here to talk about a whore, have you?"

At those words Freddy snapped. He launched himself across the cabin and punched Sloane with all his pent-up rage, a savage blow to the jaw that connected with a loud crack. The man staggered back.

Freddy followed, going for his throat.

Sloane twisted away and shoved him back. He made as if to throw a punch at Freddy, but at the last instant Freddy saw the blade that gleamed in his fist.

He dodged but it was a close call; the blade slashed through the fabric of his shirt.

"Come unarmed, did you, pretty boy? Bad mistake." Grinning nastily, Sloane feinted with the blade.

Snap! Freddy kicked the knife out of Sloane's hand. It went clattering across the cabin and slid under the table. Sloane snarled in wordless anger.

"I don't need to be armed to kill you, Sloane," Freddy said softly. He was more furious than he'd ever been in his life, but he was cold and he was focused.

Sloane sneered. "Think I'm scared of a *gentleman?*"

Freddy came at Sloane again. He hit him once, twice. Sloane returned each blow.

He punched Sloane in the eye. Sloane kicked him on the shin and followed it up with two sharp successive blows to the head.

His ears ringing, Freddy managed a short left hook to the man's head followed by a hard blow to the belly. Sloane, gasping, fell back.

For a few seconds they stood, panting,

eyeing each other, then Sloane rushed him, grabbing him in a headlock and raining punches to the side of his head.

They swayed, locked together. The man's hot, fetid breath made Freddy want to gag. He got a hand free and landed a punch to the throat. At the same time Sloane kneed him savagely in the balls but Freddy was expecting it and, twisting, collected the blow on the hip instead.

They staggered apart. Sloane recovered first, with a heavy punch to the chest, followed by a blow to the face. Blood spurted from Freddy's nose.

Freddy, gasping for breath and with blood streaming down his face, managed a sharp left to the man's chin. His head snapped back and Freddy followed it with a punishing right into the solar plexus.

The man sagged. Freddy punched him hard in the face. Again, they staggered apart, reeling a little. Regrouping. Sloane swore, spat, and a blackened tooth rolled across the floor. His breath was coming in loud gasps. Freddy's too was rasping out of his chest. He could taste his own blood.

"All right, I give up," Sloane wheezed. He held out his hand, as if to shake on it.

Freddy frowned. It wasn't supposed to happen like this. Sloane hadn't been nearly punished enough. But the man was offering truce, blast him.

He hesitated, and in that moment Sloane rushed him, head down like a bull, and butted him hard in the stomach. Freddy went down, all breath knocked from his body.

Sloane started kicking him, going for the gut, the balls, the kidneys. Blows pounded into Freddy.

Twisting, writhing, trying to avoid each kick and gasping fruitlessly for breath, Freddy managed to catch a booted foot in two hands. He heaved and Sloane went crashing backward to the floor.

Freddy's breath came back in a rush and, as Sloane scrambled to his feet, Freddy hit him, a huge, powerful blow that connected so hard, the man went flying backward across the cabin and hit the floor again.

Pain reverberated all down Freddy's arm, but it was satisfying pain. Sloane would be hurting more.

He looked. Sloane, in fact, wasn't moving. Was he dead?

At that moment the door flew open and Max burst in, followed by Flynn.

"You damned fool, you've killed him already!" Max exclaimed.

Flynn bent to examine the captain. "He's

still breathing."

"I can fix that," Freddy said.

"Stop right there!" Max ordered, adding, "If you don't mind, I'd rather my oldest friend wasn't tried for murder. Or have to flee abroad to escape the trial."

Freddy glowered at the unconscious man, unrepentant. He itched to finish the job.

Max added, "And I'm sure Damaris would love life as an exile. Again."

His words acted like a bucket of cold water dashed in Freddy's face. This affair mustn't touch her in the least. Freddy looked down at Sloane. The haze of fury cleared. His breathing slowed. It was finished.

"Bind his hands and feet."

"He's in no fit state to —" Max began.

"Bind them." Freddy wasn't afraid of more dirty tricks. Damaris had left this ship helpless, bound hand and foot. So would the captain.

Flynn found some rope and swiftly tied the man's hands and feet. "What are you going to do with him?"

Freddy gave a careless shrug, ignoring the pain as he did so. "We have several choices, but the best is that he will hang for bringing girls into England and selling them to a brothel against their will."

"Girls?" Max repeated.

Freddy nodded. "Turns out it wasn't the first time he'd played that filthy trick." He turned to Flynn. "I suspect you'll find a dozen other crimes he's committed — certainly his expression when I first confronted him suggested he was expecting quite different accusations. I'm certain he's been cheating you, Flynn. Check the records, talk to the crew — you'll find all the evidence we need to hang him, I'm sure. Pity you can't hang a man more than once."

"We could try," Max growled.

"It might be entertaining," Flynn said with a cold smile.

"It might," Freddy agreed. "But I have it in mind to leave him to the tender mercies of British justice."

Max nodded. "Imprisonment, trial and hanging."

"Exactly."

At that point the door flew open again. Freddy stared. Lady Beatrice's giant footman? What the hell was he doing here? Two slightly smaller but still large footmen in livery followed him in. The cabin was getting decidedly crowded.

Max was the first to speak. "William? What is it?"

William bowed. "Lady Beatrice's compliments, m'lord, but she thought Mr. Monkton-Coombes might need some help."

"She what?" Freddy exclaimed. "How the devil could she possibly know that? She doesn't even know I'm in London."

"Begging your pardon, sir, but Miss Damaris told her."

"Miss *Damaris*? But she's in Devon, at Davenham Hall."

"I'm sorry to contradict you, sir, but her and Miss Abb— I mean, Lady Davenham" — he grinned at Max — "are with Lady Beatrice in Berkeley Square at this very moment."

"Good God, she must have traveled all night," Freddy exclaimed. "She'll be sick as a dog."

William continued, "Miss Damaris was in a devil of a state, sir, fretting about you being killed, but it looks like she needn't have worr—"

But Freddy had gone, closely followed by Max.

William cast a knowledgeable eye over the unconscious Sloane. "Looks like we missed a first-rate mill," he said wistfully. "Shame we arrived too late to help."

"You can help now," Flynn told him. "Take this piece of rubbish to Bow Street with the compliments of Mr. Mon— no, with the compliments of Lord Davenham and myself — and tell them to hold him pending charges. Capital charges."

William grinned. "Very good, sir."

"Wearing a hole in my parquetry floors won't make him get here any sooner," Lady Beatrice grumbled.

"William left here an hour ago," Damaris said, continuing to pace. "Something's gone wrong, I just know it has."

At that moment the front doorbell rang. Damaris flew down the stairs and reached the last step as Freddy stepped inside.

And, oh, the state of him. His face was covered in rising bruises, scrapes and cuts; his nose looked crooked, with dried blood still crusting it; and one eye was purple and so swollen that it was the barest slit.

He took a few limping steps forward, gave her a lopsided grin and opened his arms.

She flew into his embrace. "Oh, Freddy, Freddy, I've been so worried. I'm so sorry, it's all my fault. You shouldn't have gone after him, and, oh, look how he's hurt you. Are you very badly injured? Should we get a doctor?" She examined his injuries worriedly. "Oh, your eye, it looks so painful. What can I do? Oh, you foolish, foolish man, going after him. I tried to find you, to stop you, but I couldn't find the docks. I've been almost out of my mind with worry. I thought he'd kill you! I was certain of it. I thought I'd lost you forever." And she burst into tears.

"Hush, hush, my poor girl, I'm perfectly all right, as you can see." He bent to kiss her then pulled back as his split lip started to bleed again. "Oops, sorry."

"Your poor, poor face." She blotted the blood gently with a handkerchief. "Does it hurt dreadfully?"

"Have I lost my good looks, then?" He tried to grin and winced instead.

"It's nothing to joke about," she told him severely. "You could have been killed." She felt sick just thinking about it.

She wanted to hug him and smother him with kisses. She also wanted to strangle him, standing there with that foolish crooked grin, so battered and so cocky. And so beautiful and dear.

"Freddy Monkton-Coombes, while I'm delighted to see you in one piece — or as near as — if you're going to bleed, you can do it in private and not all over my front hall," Lady Beatrice said dryly. "Featherby, put our battered friend in the green bedchamber; provide my niece with hot water, bandages, unguents and whatever else she requires and then leave them alone to get on with it."

"You could have phrased that better, Aunt Bea," said Max, who had entered more quietly, but to no less of a welcome from Abby. "Get *on* with it?"

"Good day to you, Max. I am glad to see you at least don't look like an escapee from the morgue. As for *getting on with it,*" she added with a mischievous gleam, "I phrase things as I see them. Now, come up here and tell me about your honeymoon. Featherby, bring champagne to the drawing room." She glanced again at Freddy, limping slowly up the stairs with Damaris wedged under his armpit, helping him. "Mr. Monkton-Coombes will have brandy."

"Thank you, Lady Beatrice," Freddy murmured as he passed her on the stairs. He winked at the old lady and she gave him a brisk, approving nod in return.

The bed in the green bedchamber was wide and soft. Damaris helped Freddy to it. He gave a little sigh of relief as he sank onto it. Damaris sat with him. She couldn't seem to stop touching him, to assure herself he was alive. Safe. Battered, but safe.

Featherby supervised as a series of maids brought hot water, bowls, cloths, bandages and every kind of plaster known to man. He poured them each a brandy, leaving the decanter on a tray beside the bed. Freddy sipped it gingerly, wincing slightly as the liquor stung his cut lip.

"Will that be all, miss?"

"Thank you, Featherby," Damaris said, and the butler left, closing the door carefully behind him.

"Thank God," Freddy said, and with a groan he sank sideways on the bed, taking Damaris down with him.

"Are your injuries very bad? Should I fetch a doctor?"

"No, I just need some tender loving care." He slipped a hand behind her neck and very carefully kissed her. "Mmm, you taste of ginger."

She eased back. "Sorry, I chewed rather a lot of it on the way here." She wanted to rain kisses all over him, but she feared hurting him.

"So it's true? You came in Max's traveling carriage?" She nodded and his arm tightened around her. "You foolish girl, whatever possessed you to come all that way in a closed carriage? You must have felt wretched."

"I felt wretched because I was worried sick about *you*," she retorted. "What madness possessed you to go after Sloane, Freddy?"

"He needed to be dealt with."

"Yes, but not by you. Not like this." She fetched the hot water, dipped a cloth in it and very gently started tending his injuries. He lay supine, watching her face as she fussed over him.

"I beat him, you know," he said after a while. "Beat him in a fair fight — as fair as a swine like that could understand. Gave him the thrashing he deserved." He closed his eyes, a faint smile on his face.

"You shouldn't have even tried," she told him, trying to sound severe, but failing, largely because there was a lump in her throat. *Slaying dragons.* Lady Beatrice was right. "What if you'd been killed?"

He gave a slow half smile. "This" — he indicated his face with a vague gesture — "is nothing to what he looks like. He's in prison now. Won't ever bother you again. So now you can marry me."

She took a deep breath. "Are you sure, Freddy?"

One bright blue eye opened. The other tried to open and failed. "What do you mean, am I sure?"

She moistened her lips anxiously. "You don't have to marry me."

He frowned. "Don't I?"

She swallowed. *Have faith, Damaris.* "I made a promise to God, you see, on the way here in the carriage. I promised that if He kept you safe, I would give you up."

He sat up and stared at her a moment, glaring at her out of his one good eye. "Well, what sort of a stupid promise was that? What if I don't *want* to be given up, dammit? Promise to God." He snorted. "No wonder I'm a Buddhist."

"You are not."

"I swear I will be if you keep making stupid promises to God."

She thought of the fight he'd just had, how he must have felt meeting Captain Sloane, knowing what she'd done with him in that very cabin. "Are you certain, Freddy? You could marry anyone you wanted. Any fresh young society girl. Untouched. Pure."

He gripped her by the shoulders. "I don't want a fresh young society girl. I want a wife who is also my friend as well as my lover, a woman who has already been tested by life and is the stronger and more admirable for it, strong and good and pure —"

"Pure?" she choked out.

"Yes, pure. Pure of heart. A girl with a heart that is pure and untouched."

She looked away, blinking back tears.

He captured her hands in his. His voice

deepened. "Or perhaps your heart has been a little touched, dare I hope, by a worthless fellow who knows a gentleman should never press a lady, but who can't help it."

"Can't help what?" she whispered.

"Hoping that you care for me. Praying, actually."

There was a long silence. She met his gaze for just a moment, but though her eyes shimmered with tears he saw something that made him catch his breath.

"Of course I care for you, you foolish, wonderful man. More than care for you. I love you."

His pulse leaped and he caught her to him. "I've been seven different kinds of fool not to tell you sooner, haven't I?"

"Tell me what?" She shouldn't care; she knew he'd gone out to slay dragons for her, that he'd shown it to her in so many ways. But she wanted the words, ached for the words.

He stared at her in surprise, then gave a short laugh. "Ridiculous, isn't it, that I am so skilled in the many ways of making love, and yet when it comes to the real thing — the one, true thing — I am a bumbling fool. I suppose because it matters so much."

"The one, true thing?" she breathed.

He gave her a rueful look. "And here I am

blabbering on, drowning you with hundreds of words when I only need three."

She trembled in his arms as she waited, breathless. *Have faith, Damaris, have faith.*

And then he gave her the words she had so longed to hear. "I love you, Damaris Tait, Damaris Chance, Damaris-by-any-other-name-will-smell-as-sweet. And I want to marry you, and be your husband, your lover, your friend, and the father of your children. And that's the reason — the *only* reason — I want to marry you. Because I love you." He kissed her, and then couldn't help saying it again, because suddenly it was so easy to say — "I love you, Damaris. So marry me and make me the happiest of men."

"Oh, yes, Freddy, yes." And as she kissed him, he rolled her slowly back into the bed, the better to demonstrate his love.

"Well?" Lady Beatrice asked softly.

Featherby nodded. "They're asleep on the bed, m'lady."

"Good, toss a blanket over them and let them sleep. They're both worn out. Apart from all the drama, with all this dashing about the country, neither one of them will have slept in days." The old lady grinned. "And then they'll be thoroughly compromised — under *my* roof — so let them try to wriggle out of that! I've had enough of their foolish shilly-shallying. If ever two people were made for each other . . ." She snorted as she stumped away on her cane.

"Yes, m'lady."

Chapter Twenty-Five

"A man does not recover from such a
devotion of the heart to such a woman!
He ought not; he does not."
— JANE AUSTEN, *PERSUASION*

Freddy paced restlessly about the room,
picking things up and putting them down.
"I suppose it has to come to us all, in the
end — getting married, I mean."

"Mm-hm." Max finished tying his neck
cloth.

"The old ball and chain."

"That's right." Max gave the neck cloth
arrangement a critical look.

"Never thought it would happen to me."
Freddy picked up a ruby tiepin and perused
it.

"But you changed your mind."

"No, fate intervened, in the form of a
flood that stranded us for two nights alone.

After that, of course, I had to marry the girl."

"Naturally, you being the soul of honor in such matters," Max agreed sardonically.

"Well, yes, I —" Freddy broke off, frowning. "Are you saying you don't believe me?"

"That's right." Max carefully inserted a ruby pin in one of the folds of his neck cloth. "You're a fraud, Monkton-Coombes."

"A fraud?" Freddy repeated with as much indignation as he could muster.

"Mm-hm." Max adjusted the pin. "You can't wait to get married."

Freddy tried but failed to keep the smile from his face.

Max saw it and nodded. "Thought so. You fell for her the first time you saw her, that day I tricked you into entering Aunt Bea's drawing room. You stood there staring for fully half a minute, your jaw hanging."

"Can you blame me? There she was, sitting on a chaise longue, looking at me with those big brown eyes." Freddy sighed.

"Who, my aunt?"

"Damaris, you fool. And bang!"

"The *coup de foudre*?"

"The *coup de foudre*," Freddy agreed. "Never believed in it until then. But one glance and I was done for."

"For a long time I thought you were

541

avoiding the girl for all you were worth."

"A man has his dignity," Freddy said obscurely. "Took me the devil's own cunning to reel her in, I should say. You have no idea of the stratagems I had to resort to, the places I had to go. Potteries!"

Max, in the process of donning his coat, slewed around to stare. *"Potteries?"*

"Potteries," Freddy affirmed. "Damaris is the stubbornest little creature."

Max decided not to pursue the pottery question. "But you got her in the end."

"I did," Freddy said with satisfaction. He looked at Max and frowned. "Or I will, as soon as you've finished primping in front of that looking glass. Dammit, Max, I don't want to be late for my own wedding. Can't you dress any faster?"

"Oh, Daisy, it's beautiful." Damaris gazed, misty eyed, into the looking glass. Abby, Jane, Daisy and Lady Beatrice and several maids were gathered in Damaris's bedchamber, helping Damaris dress for her wedding.

Freddy had applied for a special license the day after he'd fought the captain, and had it not been for Lady Beatrice's interference, he would have married Damaris a bare three days later.

Lady Beatrice had pointed out the flaw in that plan with an acid tongue. "By all means, if you *wish* to give the gossipmongers enough fodder to suggest it took a good thrashing to force you into wedlock, go ahead. I'm sure Damaris won't mind being known as the female who finally trapped you."

As a tactic it was masterly. It was too close to the bone not to succeed.

Nettled, Freddy had set the date for ten days hence and had taken himself out of town — he didn't tell Damaris where — to wait impatiently for his injuries — the visible ones, at least — to heal.

And now her wedding day had come.

The dress Daisy had made for her was quite the loveliest dress Damaris had ever worn. Made of heavy cream silk, tied at the high waist with a blue satin ribbon, it flowed around her limbs like warm water, caressing them subtly.

With a square-cut neck framing her face, it suited her, Damaris had to admit. And if it left quite a bit of her chest exposed, well, that was all the rage, and she had every intention of being as fashionable as Freddy.

The trouble was . . .

"Neck looks a bit bare," Lady Beatrice said, frowning. "Dammit, I should have bought you some pearls or something. Or prompted Freddy to buy you pearls for your bride gift."

"But I love what he gave me," Damaris said, picking up the cream silk velvet cloak Freddy had sent her three days earlier and rubbing her cheek against its thick softness. It was warm and elegant and luxuriant and ridiculously impractical, for which she loved it all the more. The hood was edged with soft white fur. *For my lovely winter bride, to keep her warm when I can't,* his note had said.

"Yes, yes, it's very nice, but your neck is so bare."

"You could wear my necklace," Abby said, reaching to undo the diamond and pearl necklace Max had given her for her bride gift.

"No!" said four voices at the same time.

"Your wedding necklace is special and just for you," Damaris said firmly. "I don't think my neck looks too bare at all. I think it shows off Daisy's clever design beautifully."

Just then there was a knock on the door. "Come," Lady Beatrice said.

Featherby entered, carrying an oblong white leather box on a tray. He beamed at Damaris. "From Mr. Freddy."

There was a card attached. She took her

time opening it. She wanted to savor every moment of this day. On the card was written in Freddy's hand: *I'm told this makes an auspicious gift for a very special bride.*

Auspicious? An unusual word to use. She opened the box, pushed back the layer of fine red silk that covered the object within — red, the Chinese color for good luck — and gasped.

"What is it?" The others crowded around to see.

"It's a necklace. White jade," she whispered. "It's very old, I think, and very valuable. And very, very special." A series of delicately carved oblongs, linked with gold, the centerpiece of the necklace was a superbly carved intertwined Chinese dragon and phoenix. Over and above the delicate beauty of the piece was a layer of meaning that touched her to the core. She wondered if he knew what the dragon and the phoenix symbolized. On so many levels, the symbolism worked.

Yin and *yang,* the dragon and phoenix complemented each other and symbolized blissful relations between husband and wife. She gave a little chuckle. And as well as being a symbol of good luck, the dragon also represented power over water and floods. Did Freddy know that? He would claim it, she was sure. *You need to honor His Flood by marrying me.* And lastly, you could say that she was the phoenix, rising from the ashes of her past life.

In every way she could think of, this necklace worked. He couldn't have found anything more perfect.

"Put it on," Jane urged her.

She lifted it to her neck and fastened it. There was a simultaneous sigh from all the watching females. "It's perfect," Abby said.

"Couldn't be more perfect if I'd designed it for the dress meself," Daisy agreed.

Jane examined the necklace curiously. "It's lovely, such intricate carving and so unusual. It's you, Damaris."

Lady Beatrice put up her lorgnette and scrutinized the necklace. "The boy's surprised me. A very subtle, unusual and lovely piece — exactly right for you, Damaris, my dear. Now, are we ready? If that boy has to wait a moment longer, I suspect he'll explode."

The carriage pulled up in front of St. George's in Hanover Square and, seeing the couple waiting for her on the pavement outside the church, a cold hand clutched at Damaris's heart. It couldn't be.

But it was. Lord and Lady Breckenridge,

Freddy's parents. Looking very grim.

She stepped down from the carriage and turned to her sisters and Lady Beatrice.

"Would you mind waiting here a moment? I won't be long." She hoped.

As she approached, she pulled Freddy's velvet cloak around her protectively. Lord and Lady Breckenridge, seeing her, came forward. There was a long moment of silence as they looked at each other, wondering where to start.

"Lord Breckenridge, Lady Breckenridge, how do you do?" Damaris said coolly. Because politeness is the first defense.

"We're not here to spoil your day," Lady Breckenridge said abruptly.

"You're not?" Damaris said warily.

Lord Breckenridge said stiffly, "We're here to wish you well."

"And to apologize," his wife added.

Damaris blinked. "Apologize?"

"Yes, and thank you."

"*Thank* me?"

Lady Breckenridge moistened her lips and glanced at her husband. "You gave us a great deal to think about. We made some . . . errors."

"With your son, not me," Damaris told her.

"I know." Lady Breckenridge laid a tentative arm on Damaris's gloved arm. "Will you allow us to attend your wedding?"

"*Allow?* But of course you can —"

Lord Breckenridge said, "Frederick said we had to ask you, that it was your day."

"He came down for his brother's memorial service," Lady Breckenridge said.

"I'm glad," Damaris said simply. So she hadn't ruined everything. "Did he tell you you had to apologize too?"

Lady Breckenridge shook her head. "No, that was my idea. What you said shocked us, but it also woke us up to the injustice we'd done our son — our living son. We — we'd like to try again."

Damaris considered her words. Freddy's parents were still quite prickly, but underneath the awkwardness, they seemed sincere. She hoped they were, anyway. If they meant it, really meant it, it would be a wonderful thing for Freddy.

And if they didn't? What difference would it make? Besides, it was her wedding day, and she wanted everyone to be happy.

She gave Lady Breckenridge a warm smile. "Of course Freddy and I would love to have you at our wedding. You're his parents, aren't you, and he loves you. I will too, if you give me a chance."

"Oh, thank you, my dear," Lady Breckenridge said, her voice suddenly husky. Lord Breckenridge cleared his throat noisily and gave her a brisk nod.

"All finished?" Lady Beatrice interrupted. "Nice day for a wedding. Wind getting a bit fresh to be standing around, though. And there's a groom inside who'll be getting anxious. Breckenridge, Louisa, coming?"

"Yes, of course." Lord and Lady Breckenridge entered the church with Lady Beatrice. Featherby, William, Damaris, Abby, Jane, and Daisy hurried into the vestibule and fussed for a few moments to ensure Damaris looked perfect. Then Jane and Daisy took their places inside. Damaris was having only one attendant: Abby, her matron of honor, whose husband was the best man.

Then, at a signal from Flynn, the church organist played the opening chords and Damaris stepped out onto the red carpet and began the long, slow walk down the aisle to where Freddy waited.

The happy ending she'd never expected to have, never even dared to dream of. All her dreams were gathered here under this sacred roof today: a family who loved and accepted her, friends to wish her well and, best of all, a man who loved her, who she loved with all her heart, Freddy Monkton-Coombes.

CHAPTER TWENTY-SIX

"It is such a happiness
when good people get together."
— JANE AUSTEN, *EMMA*

"Oh, this was such a good idea. I'm so glad we thought of it." Damaris was having the loveliest honeymoon. Because Abby was planning a special first family Christmas at Davenham Hall, she and Freddy had decided to spend a little time exploring the England Damaris's mother had told her about. Then, after Christmas, he was taking her to Venice for what he called a *proper* honeymoon.

She hadn't believed such happiness was possible, but she was bursting with it now, aglow with it, ending each day weak with lovemaking and with laughter, waking each morning with anticipation of what the day would bring. And with a kiss. And one kiss led to another and then . . . more lovemaking.

She was awash with love and happiness. She leaned against her husband, her arm entwined through his. Life could get no better.

The phaeton — Freddy had given her her own phaeton and pair as a wedding present — came to a crossroads, and Damaris gave a small cry of excitement and clutched his arm. "There it is, Freddy, that's it. Mama's village."

It was the prettiest little village, a cluster of thatched, whitewashed houses set around the village green and with a stream flowing through it under a pretty stone bridge.

She felt a little teary. She'd heard so much about this place, the site of her mother's childhood and girlhood before she'd married Papa. She wondered if she could find the house Mama had grown up in. All she knew was that it was on the outskirts of the village, on a hill overlooking a small lake, a handsome redbrick house that her grandfather had built. His hopes for a large family had come to naught; Mama had been an only child. And all Damaris's relatives were long dead. Would anyone even remember her mother?

"There's the churchyard," she said. "Can

we stop and look? There might be . . . some sign of my family. I would like to see my grandparents' grave."

They got down, tied up the horses and entered the churchyard through a lych-gate smothered in the twisted gray vines of wisteria. It would be magnificent in spring. The graveyard was very pretty, tidily kept, with ancient stones softened by grass.

"What were their names again?" Freddy asked. "We'll split up and search."

"Howard. Charles and Mary Howard. My mother's name was Catherine."

They searched, taking their time, reading the words on the headstones. So many stories, some tragic in their stark simplicity. An elderly lady was tending a grave, replacing dead rosemary with fresh and weeding the surrounds. Damaris slipped quietly past her, glancing at the headstone. Her son, she thought from the dates. Poor lady.

"Damaris," Freddy called.

"Yes?" Damaris and the old lady answered in unison. They turned and looked at each other in surprise.

"Don't tell me you're called Damaris too!" the lady said.

Damaris nodded.

"How delightful," the lady said. "People are always saying what an unusual name it is — they really mean it's odd, of course. And though I do tell them it's from the Bible, they still think it's outlandish." She smiled. "Well, well, I've never met another Damaris."

"Damaris Monkton-Coombes," she said and held out her hand.

The lady shook it. "Damaris, Lady Templeton." She glanced at Freddy, who was threading his way toward them between the headstones. "And that's your handsome husband, I suppose."

"Yes." Damaris couldn't help but smile. "We're on our honeymoon."

"Oh, my dear, how delightful. Congratulations." She gave them a quizzical look. "Is there any reason you're spending some of your honeymoon in a graveyard?"

Damaris laughed. "It does sound odd when you put it like that, but this was my mother's village. She died when I was twelve and this is my first visit. I thought I might be able to find the headstones of some relatives, maybe my grandparents."

"I've lived here all my life. Perhaps I could help you find them. What were their names?"

"Howard. Charles and Mary Howard."

The lady turned a little pale and swayed. Damaris caught her and asked, "Are you all right?" The lady clutched her hand as if fearful of falling.

Freddy came hurrying up. "Is something wrong?"

"Oh, Freddy, this is Lady Templeton and she's just been taken ill."

"No, no, just a bit of a turn," Lady Templeton said. "I'm prone to them, a disadvantage of old age, I'm afraid. I'll be right as rain in a minute." She held out her hand to Freddy. "How do you do, Mr. Monkton-Coombes. Your wife was just telling me her mother was born here."

"Ma'am, are you sure you're all right? You're looking rather pale," Freddy asked. He glanced around but could see no other carriage but their own. "Can I offer you a lift?"

The lady hesitated. "I do feel so foolish, but yes, I think that would be best. I just live a step away, up there, on the hill." She pointed to a graceful Georgian house set in a pretty park. "It's not far. But a carriage would make it easier. Thank you."

Freddy and Damaris helped the lady into the carriage and a few minutes later they pulled up in front of the house. It was as elegant as it had looked from the church-yard, fronted with Corinthian columns and with a sweeping vista to the village and beyond.

"Please come in and take tea with me. No, I insist, you've been so kind. Besides" — she glanced at Damaris again — "I know my husband would wish to meet you."

Damaris nodded. "Thank you, Lady Templeton, it's very kind of you. Are you sure you're well enough?"

"Oh, I'm well enough," Lady Templeton said in a voice that trembled just a little.

They entered the house and Lady Templeton led them to an elegant drawing room with a large bay window. "Tea and refreshments," Lady Templeton told her butler, "and ask Sir John to join us immediately. We have guests he will want to meet."

The color had quite come back to her cheeks and she seemed almost excited. Perhaps they didn't get many visitors, Damaris thought.

A few moments later, a tall, distinguished-looking gray-haired man entered. He took one look at Damaris and blinked. He turned to his wife. "Damaris?"

"Our first name is not all we have in common," Lady Templeton said. "John, she's Catherine Howard's daughter."

Sir John Templeton stared at Damaris. "Oh, my God," he exclaimed in a whisper and sat down abruptly on the nearest chair.

"Catherine's daughter."

Damaris gave Freddy a mystified look. He frowned and rose to his feet. "I think we'd better go."

"No!" Sir John and Lady Templeton exclaimed at once.

"Please don't. I'm sorry to be so mysterious," Lady Templeton said. "It's a little awkward to know quite where to begin. You see, we knew your mother very well, my dear. She was very dear to . . . to us." She glanced at her husband. "Perhaps Martin's portrait?"

He nodded and hurried from the room. Damaris and Freddy waited in silence. Sir John returned in a few minutes, carrying a portrait. He turned it around and held it up in front of Damaris and Freddy.

It was of a good-looking young man with dark hair and eyes and a lovely smile. Damaris smiled politely.

"You don't see it, do you?" Lady Templeton said. She glanced at Freddy. "Ah, but you do."

Damaris looked at her husband. He stared at the painting and then at her, and then he kept looking from the painting to her. "It's uncanny."

"What is?" Damaris asked. Sir John couldn't seem to take his eyes off her. She felt a little uncomfortable.

"The likeness."

Sir John Templeton nodded. "She has his eyes, his smile, his warmth . . ."

Puzzled, Damaris looked at the painting more closely. Yes, there was a strong resemblance between Lady Templeton and her son, but that was not so surprising, surely. "I don't understand."

"My dear." Lady Templeton sat down in the chair closest to her and took her hand. "This may upset you to hear, but we believe you are our granddaughter."

Damaris frowned. "How can that be possible?"

"Your mother, Catherine, was engaged to be married to our son, Martin. They were very much in love. We loved her like a daughter. But just two weeks before they were to be married, Martin . . . Martin . . ."

"He died," Sir John said gruffly. "Came off his horse and crashed into a stone wall. Broke his neck."

"I'm sorry to hear it, but what does —"

"We think they anticipated their vows."

"Your mother became pregnant," Freddy said bluntly.

Lady Templeton nodded. "We weren't sure; there were whispers — this is a village, after all. But your grandparents wouldn't let us see Catherine; in fact, she wasn't seen in the village again after Martin's funeral."

"What, ever?" Damaris said.

"No. The first we heard was that she'd married a minister and moved out of the district. To tell the truth, we were hurt by what we thought was a rather too quick recovery from loving our son, so we made no attempt to contact her. We didn't know, then, that she was increasing."

"If she'd come to us, we would have taken her in, taken care of her and the child," Sir John said.

"Some years later, when your grandfather was dead, your grandmother told me about the child. Her husband had paid the man a handsome sum to marry her —"

"Prided himself on his respectability, Charles Howard," Sir John interjected.

"The minister had apparently known she was pregnant by another man's child, but he didn't care."

He'd cared, Damaris thought. Papa had an austere and unforgiving nature that found fault with human frailty. He'd done his duty by her and her mother, but he hadn't been able to love them. Or truly forgive her mother for her lapse.

So many things she'd always wondered about now started to slip into place. It was such a relief to understand finally.

"And by the time we tracked her down, she and her husband had gone to China. Taking their daughter with them. And so we lost all track of them. Of you."

"I didn't take after either of my parents," Damaris told Freddy, staring at the painting. "But I do look like him." Her father. Her *real* father. The man Mama had loved. And who had loved Mama.

It all made sense now. Papa's coldness, his constant slurs on her mother's lack of morals. And the fact that he'd never really loved Damaris. He couldn't. He would have seen her as a child of sin. *Original sin.* That was what he'd been talking about.

At that realization some of the misery and guilt she'd borne all her life slipped from her shoulders. So what if he didn't love her? He wasn't her father.

This was her father. This smiling young man cut off in his prime. The man her mother, she now understood, had probably never stopped loving. Poor Mama.

"You don't mind knowing?" Lady Templeton asked quietly. "That the man you thought was your father wasn't your real father?"

"It doesn't affect your legitimacy," Sir John said quickly. "You were born in wedlock, and nobody can prove otherwise."

"I don't mind," Damaris said softly. "I am very pleased to discover my real father. And his parents."

"Martin would have loved you," Lady Templeton said, as if reading her thoughts.

"I came to this village looking for my relatives," Damaris said slowly. "Only I thought I'd find them in the churchyard."

"You did," Lady Templeton said with a little laugh. "But not all of us were dead."

"Perhaps you won't want to know us," Sir John said heavily. "We'll understand if that's the case. We're just glad to have met you."

"Oh, I'll want to know you," Damaris said, slipping from the chair and going to plant a kiss on the old man's cheek. She turned and embraced Lady Templeton. "I always wanted grandparents. *Always.*"

"Oh, you sweet girl," Lady Templeton said, hugging her.

"Your Damaris looks just like my Damaris did when I married her," Sir John told Freddy.

"Then it's good to know that my Damaris is only going to become more beautiful with age," Freddy said with a smile.

"Poor Mama, she didn't have a very happy life, did she?"

"She had you, and I'm sure you made her

very happy," Damaris's grandmother said.

Freddy leaned across and pulled Damaris to him. "We'll just have to ensure her daughter has a very happy life, won't we?"

Damaris turned and smiled mistily at him. "I'll do my best."

EPILOGUE

"I must learn to brook
being happier than I deserve."
— JANE AUSTEN, *PERSUASION*

"Your sister is a glutton for punishment," Freddy commented as he helped Damaris over a stile. They were walking back to the cottage from Davenham House. Only a fifteen-minute walk from the main house, it was their own, very private retreat. Damaris adored it.

"Do you mean Abby? Why do you think that? She's having a wonderful time."

He feigned a shudder. "Getting everyone, all the family, under one roof for Christmas? It's madness. Max should have put his foot down."

"Max is enjoying it as much as Abby and I are, and so will the others when they get here." Damaris was loving every single thing about it — the excitement, the decorations, the baking, the rituals — all the things her mother had told her about English Christmases but which she'd never experienced for herself.

"Thank God you wanted a cottage. Think if you'd asked for a diamond necklace that day. How useless would that be? Can't hide out from relatives in a diamond necklace."

She laughed. "You're a fraud, Freddy Monkton-Coombes. You're enjoying it as much as any of us."

"I won't when my parents get here. Why on earth would she invite my parents?"

"Because you're part of the family now, and so, therefore, are they." Damaris had been delighted when Abby had told her Lord and Lady Breckenridge had accepted her invitation to come for Christmas. Little by little the barriers were being whittled away.

Freddy grunted. "It's taking the notion of family to extremes."

He didn't mean it. Damaris knew he was as pleased as she was. He just hid it. He'd been hurt too many times to show his feelings openly. It would take time.

"Abby invited my grandparents too." She gave a little skip. They were almost at the cottage.

In the time Freddy had stayed away from

London while his injuries faded, he hadn't just visited his parents, he'd come here and furnished her cottage for her. Thick rugs lined the floor; there was a large and comfortable bed, a cozy sofa — everything needed to keep them warm and comfortable. He'd stocked it with provisions too: enough food and wine to last them through a blizzard.

He'd even included a shelf of books, just for her, getting Abby to give him a list of anything she thought Damaris might enjoy. He'd also included a box of paints, brushes and an easel. That had touched her most of all.

They walked up a small rise. This was the part of the walk home she liked best, the part where from the top of the rise she could see her lovely little white stone cottage, and beyond it the sweep of the sea. She never tired of the view.

They reached the top and she stopped, frowning. "What's that?" There was a sign over the front door. She couldn't quite read it.

"Come on, let's run," Freddy said and, grabbing her hand, he tugged her down the hill so they arrived at the front gate laughing and breathless.

Damaris stared at the sign. "Roon? You

named our cottage *Roon*?"

"Not me. You can blame that little she-troll from the pottery for that." Freddy's eyes were dancing, bluer than the sea.

Damaris blinked at him in utter bewilderment. "Mrs. *Jenkins*? What has *she* to do with my cottage?"

"She predicted it."

"Predicted what? I don't understand."

"That I'd lead you down the road to Roon." He opened the door then swept her up into his arms. "And here we are." He carried her over the threshold.

Laughing, they fell on the bed.

"Roon Cottage, was there ever such a name?" she said much later. She was sleepy and sated and so happy she could burst. "We're never going to live it down."

"Don't explain, then."

She stroked his chest. "She was right, you know. Mrs. Jenkins."

"In what way?"

"You were a rake and you did have your wicked way with me."

"Ah, but I'm not a rake anymore," he said, kissing her. "But I did seduce you. I probably deserve to be flogged."

"Flogged?" She opened her eyes, shocked. "No one deserves to be flogged. It's a terrible punishment." She'd seen it done on board the ship.

"Oh, I don't know. You could manage it, I'm sure." He darted a look at her from under his lashes. "Perhaps with a silken whip?"

"A silken —"

"You could wear a corset."

"A corset?"

"One of those French ones. Red with black lace. Or white," he said, warming to the theme. "Pure virginal white in that lacy stuff with the holes."

"Broderie anglaise?"

"No, it's French. And you'd let your hair down, streaming over your not-quite-corseted breasts like a black silken waterfall, and you'd stand over me with those long, glorious legs of yours and —"

She laughed. "You're incorrigible."

"Yes, but you knew that when you married me. I need taking in hand."

"Do you, now?" she said, taking him very firmly in hand.

He groaned in appreciation.

"So you think you need to be punished?" she said thoughtfully.

"Just treat me as I deserve," he said humbly.

"I think I know a much more effective

punishment," she purred, squeezing him gently.

"What?" He moaned.

"Nanny McBride," she said with a straight face. His old nanny.

His eyes flew open. *"Nanny McBride?"*

"I'm sure she'd be much better than I am at administering a good whipping. Yes, I can just see Nanny McBride in a red French corset with black lace —"

"Stop!" he roared. He shuddered. "That's an image that's going to stick in my mind forever. Horrible."

She laughed. "You didn't really want me to whip you, did you?"

"No."

"See? I've got your measure, Freddy Monkton-Coombes."

He looked at where her fingers were wrapped around him and grinned. "Is that what they call it in China? By all means, take my measure. Do with it whatever you like. I'm all yours."

And he was.